SWANSONG

VALE AIDA

BOOK TWO OF THE MAGPIE BALLADS

Copyright © 2017, 2018 Vale Aida
Cover design and illustrations © 2018 Jocelin Chan

All rights reserved.

ISBN-13: 978-1724241085
ISBN-10: 1724241087

For Gerry & Evette

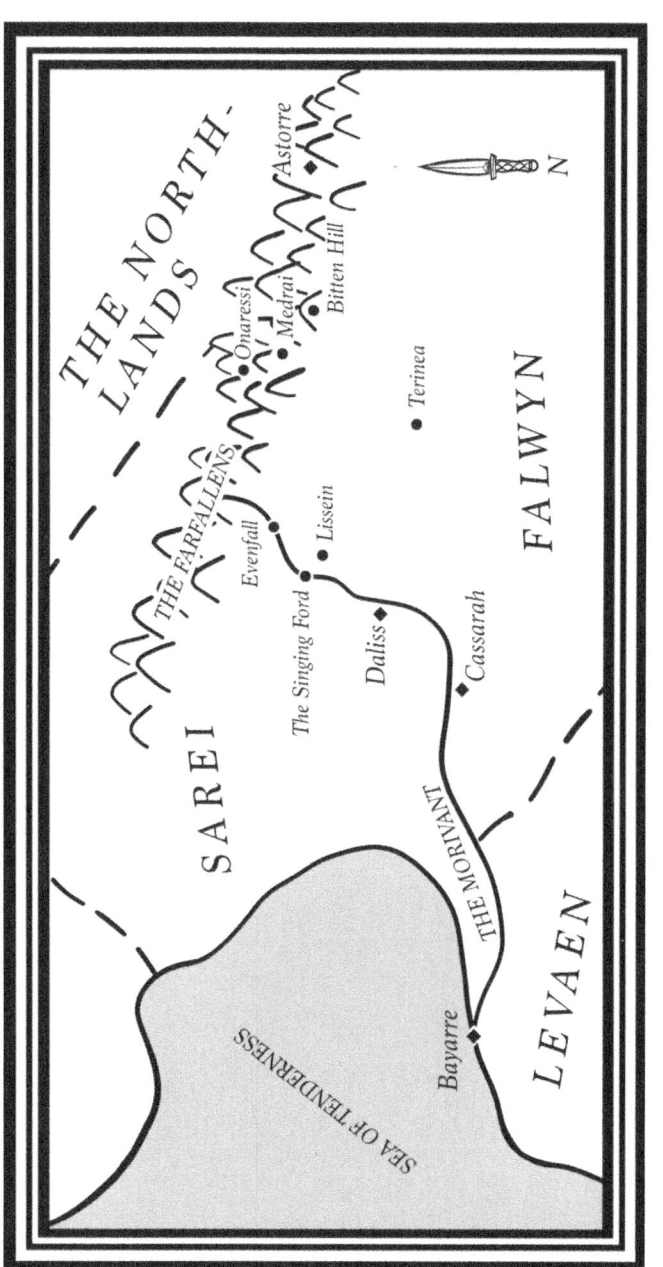

PRINCIPAL CHARACTERS

The Council of Cassarah & Their Households

- WILLON EFREN
    - His middle son BONNER
    - His captain of guards, CAHAL
- YANNICK EFREN, Willon's cousin, the Council's scribe and steward, recuperating in the country
- ORIANE SYDELL
    - Her nephew DARON
- IYONE SAFIN
    - Her father LUCIEN, stationed at Medrai
    - Her mother ARETEL DONNE
    - Her brother HIRAEN
    - Her maid ELYSA
- JOSIT ANSA, half-sister of Queen Marguerit, mistress of the late Governor Kedris Andalle
    - Her captain of guards, ZARIN

The Soldiers of Betronett & Their Families

- SAVONN ANDALLE, "Lord Silvertongue", Captain of Betronett, missing and presumed dead
- HIRAEN SAFIN, the Second Captain
- EMARIS, a patrol leader
    - His sister SHANDEI
    - Their late father RENDELL
    - LOMAS, VION, ROUGEN, KLEMENE, & CORL, members of his patrol
- DAINE, a patrol leader
    - His wife LINN
- ANYAS, a patrol leader

Cassarah's Sometime Allies

- CELISSE, Lady of Astorre
- JEHAN CAYN, Lord of Terinea
    - His daughter DANEI, late wife of Kedris Andalle

The Saraians

- MARGUERIT "the Magnificent", Queen of Sarei
- ISEMAIN DALISSOS, Marshal of Sarei
- NIKAS, assassin of the Sanctuary
- DERVAIN TERAILLE, "the Empath", assassin of the Sanctuary, a prisoner in Cassarah

ACT ONE

LIE IN THE LIGHT

REPRISE: AUTUMN 1530

Savonn Silvertongue, newest and youngest member of Rendell's patrol, was fast growing like mould on the city of Astorre.

Tonight he had an invitation to an underground dance hall of some notoriety, where—if one believed Rendell's warnings—orgies and demon-summonings transpired after dark, and rivers of absinthe wound through the rooms like snowmelt. So far he was unimpressed. There were no orgies, and certainly no demons; the absinthe went for six silvers a cup; and the dancing was not even very good, given that the only music was a honking symphony of crumhorns.

It was a pity the harpsichord was not working. It stood silent in a corner of the hall, looming dark and sullen over the revelries like a disapproving mother. "Oh, she's worn out a couple of strings," said the proprietor, a rosy-cheeked woman called Xante, when he inquired. "I know a man who'll fix her up when he shows, but till then we'll have to live with the crumhorns."

The horns were liable to start plagues and ignite wildfires, or at least give Savonn a headache. He wondered what course of action would be deemed most appropriate. Then he decided it did not matter, since no one here knew him. "I can have a look," he said.

In a minute he was peering under the lid of the harpsichord, feeling his way around the strings; in another he was on the floor, opening the pedal-box. The problem was rapidly identified. "Have you got a spare plectrum?"

"One moment," said Xante.

She did not return alone. Crouched behind the harpsichord, Savonn saw Xante's jewelled sandals approach, moving in step with a pair of high calfskin boots. "Your little pet's under the weather, Red," Xante told the person in the boots, handing the plectrum down to Savonn. She had switched to Saraian. "I've already got someone on the job."

"*Who*?"

A fluid tenor, sharp with alarm, as if interrogating a lover about an affair. But the object of jealousy was not Xante. The boots advanced, and a hand came to rest on the varnished lid of the harpsichord. "Baby, what is ailing you?"

Savonn felt an instant affinity for anyone who would croon at a musical instrument like a lapdog. Without thinking, he responded in the same language. "A broken plectrum. I'm replacing it."

An auburn head appeared above the soundboard. A reeling pause ensued.

Two weeks ago, a lyre-player in a crowded tavern had saved them from being arrested for brawling. The Saraian was as heart-stopping here as in the dim firelight of the Merman—as striking as Hiraen, who was after all the yardstick against whom all men must be measured. One noticed first the warm eyes and fine jawline, the hair braided back into a circlet round the crown of his head; then followed the proud sweep of his shoulders down to the long-fingered hand on the soundboard. Alone among the dancers in the hall, he wore neither kohl nor powder. He did not need any.

"*You*," said Red. Then, almost quick enough to hide his shock—"You know about harpsichords?"

They had met only once. Savonn had a face crafted to be forgettable. The man should by no means have recognised him. And yet, and yet.

Xante had disappeared, abandoning them to the laborious process of cobbling words into sentences. "Yes," said Savonn. "Help me, if you doubt the steadiness of my hands."

Red stared at him. His eyes were a liquid hazel. A Saraian demigod in crimson and gold—*and there you are,* said his father's voice in his ear, *kneeling before him like a dockside whore.*

Savonn pushed the thought away. At last Red appeared to make up his mind, and crouched down next to him. Too late, Savonn realised he had been expected to give way. Because he had not, they were pressed together from shoulder to knee in the tight space under the keyboard, screened behind the instrument from the rest of the hall.

Red went still. He smelled of rain and wind and wild grass, as if he had just come indoors from a day of hard riding. When he bent to look in the pedal-box, his hair slid along Savonn's shirtsleeve and tickled his exposed wrist. "I see how it is."

He was not, Savonn knew, talking about the harpsichord.

Between them it took five minutes to swap out the broken plectrum: the same time it would have taken to plough a cavalry charge down a hill, to much the same thunderous, spine-tingling effect. They sat back to survey their work, and without looking at him Red said, "Is it finished?"

They both knew it was. "You tell me," said Savonn.

Red gave him a fleeting glance through his lashes. They were a light russet-gold, and stood out against the deep amber of his skin in a most distracting way. "I prefer," he said, "to talk about beginnings... Xante is coming. Close the soundboard."

It came back to Savonn that they were in a public place. On his feet once more, with the proprietor coming over to them, he smoothed his face to bland cheerfulness. "It's fixed," he told Xante.

"Of course it is," she said. "That's why I keep you around"—she pointed at Red—"and that's why you"—Savonn—"should come round again. Now, will one of you favour us with a song?"

Savonn dipped his head, making himself look small and diffident. "I know my lord for an excellent musician."

Red narrowed his eyes. It was the cool, assessing look of a connoisseur who knew exactly what he was seeing and liked it. That was a surprise. One wanted to be seen through, sometimes. Xante was smiling, and the crumhorns had fallen silent, and Savonn would scarcely have noticed if the room had taken flame around them.

"Duet?" suggested Red.

"It would be my pleasure," said Savonn.

* * *

Three songs: a duet on the harpsichord, and two dances on the ballroom floor. Then Red made his excuses and vanished, and Savonn recalled that he, too, had to go before Rendell came looking for him. He was a soldier now, with a job to do, and a commander to answer to.

Three songs. Just like that, he had misplaced all his masks.

He did not remember walking back to his lodging. He did not know what he said to his patrol to excuse his absence. In a way, like a moth on a lantern's edge, he was already lost to them.

CHAPTER 1

"Again," said Emaris. "Aim lower. And keep your eyes on the target."

Archery practice with his patrol was a chore if one was participating, a joke if one was spectating, and a tragedy if one was trying, as Emaris was, to make a rabble of uncoordinated boys shoot straight. "I can't," said Lomas plaintively, staring at the stubby grass at the edge of the practice yard where his first two arrows had disappeared. They were at the foot of the Bitten Hill, the home base of the Betronett company, so named for the distinctive shape of its twin peaks. Legend had it that the ice giant Forech had taken a bite out of the hill a hundred thousand years ago, but it tasted so bad he spat it out again, making little bluffs and knolls from the crumbs. "Look at the target. He's grinning at me. Any minute now he'll open his fat cloth mouth and say something smart."

The dummy was sixty yards away—an easy shot as far as Emaris was concerned, though if anyone had asked him, its woollen hair was more vermilion than auburn. "You made that straw man, Lomas, you can damn well live with it."

"He can't, really," said Vion. He was sitting cross-legged on the grass, hugging an armful of arrows they had retrieved from trees, shrubs, and—in one memorable instance—a passing sentry's shield. "His father was a farmer and his father's father before him and his father's father's father before *him*. Can't hammer a ploughshare into a bow."

The other boys made morose noises of agreement. "I'm from the choir," said Klemene, sprawled belly-up beside Vion with his face swaddled in three scarves and a snotty handkerchief. Winter had furred every rock and tree with dirty frost, and the wind kept them up all night, howling like a bagful of mad zephyrs against the little keep on the hill. "I'm a countertenor, not an archer. Eh, Rougen?"

Rougen bobbed his head up and down. He never spoke. No one even knew if he could, but it was common knowledge that if a sparrow so much as beat its wings at the far end of a field, he would hear it. "Well, you're all we've got," said Emaris. "So you could at least try to survive the war."

After Onaressi, that seemed a lot to ask. They just stared at him, huddled close like a dozen wet-nosed pups. "Emaris," said Lomas, with the awkwardness of one trying to carry a larger handful of tact than he could manage. "Wasn't there another dispatch from Medrai yesterday?"

"Yes," said Klemene eagerly. Through his blocked nose, he sounded rather less like a countertenor than a sick parrot. "Did they find Savonn? Or Hiraen?"

Emaris ground his molars together. They had been waiting for a full fortnight. The speculation was unbearable, and every day the temptation to desert his post and join Lord Lucien's search parties grew. "You know they haven't. They're dead or captured or don't want to be found. Savonn's good at disappearing."

"And reappearing," said Vion. "That's why you don't believe he's dead, not really."

Sometimes Emaris forgot that his patrol had been hand-picked by Savonn himself, and only pretended to be obtuse to annoy him. He wished he could confide in them. It was one thing for Savonn to be dead, quite another for him to be in hiding because he had done something horrible—something to do with the Empath, or his late father, or worse, *Emaris's* late father. His mind had become an echo-chamber where Nikas's accusations resounded without cease. *Marguerit's double agent. The Empath's favourite plaything.*

But such thoughts were poison, and best kept to himself.

"Look," he said. "Either they'll turn up or they won't. And if they do, they'll die laughing at the way you shoot. Vion, your turn."

Lomas's shoulders sagged with relief. With all the enthusiasm of a silver miner descending into a shaft, Vion uncurled in a scatter of arrows and took the bow. "Maybe," he said, "we need our patrol leader to demonstrate? How to stand and how to adjust for the wind and all?"

"Oh, yes," said Klemene. Rougen bobbed his head some more, and another boy, Corl, gave a cheer. "Go on, Emaris. You're the best shot in Betronett now that—ow!"

Lomas kicked him in the shin. Emaris ignored them. "Vion first. Three shots. Now."

Vion was the bravest of the lot, and the least unaware of where his limbs were at any given moment. His first arrow struck the dummy square in the chest. Lomas and Klemene whooped. Unfortunately, so did Vion, with the effect that his second shot flew twelve feet wide. "Lower," said Emaris, as Vion sighted again with his tongue between his teeth. "That'll go into the trees."

"I can't find his head for all that hair," said Vion, scowling down the arrow-shaft. "Why don't we leave the shooting to you when the Saraians invade? I'll carry your quiver and Lomas can hand you arrows."

"He'd probably stab me by accident," said Emaris gloomily. "No, that's too low now—for Casteia's sake, you're doing this on purpose—"

"Emaris?" said Lomas.

"What?"

But Lomas was looking at Rougen. The boy had gone still as a deer, gazing past the dummy into the grey daylight. He squinted. Then he dropped flat to the grass and pressed his ear to the ground. Vion lowered the bow. "Should we be running?"

"Quiet," said Emaris. "Let him listen."

Klemene sprang to his feet, scarves flying. "There! There! I see it!"

And so did Emaris. A lone rider was coming up the dirt track that passed for a highway in these parts, connecting the Bitten Hill to the villages in the shadow of the Farfallens. He bore no standard, but the grey stallion trotting beneath him was young and plainly expensive. Possibilities scuttled through Emaris's head, each grimmer than the last. A Saraian herald, with a proclamation of war. Orders from some new commander sent to replace Savonn. News from Medrai, only a day's ride away, that Lucien Safin had found the remains of his son and his protégé. Emaris was just becoming convinced of this last option when the rider adjusted his seat and unslung his bow.

It was like waking from a dream. Emaris yanked his own bow from Vion's hands and snatched up a fistful of arrows. "Move."

The patrol scattered for cover. The grey stallion broke into a gallop, hooves clip-clip-clopping down the track. Freeing his hands from the reins, the rider nocked and sighted. "Emaris," called Vion.

Emaris hated shooting horses, but the stallion was a bigger target than its rider. Going this fast, a fall would kill the man as handily as a shot through the heart. He took aim. "Emaris!" Vion yelled. "Look, damn you!"

Emaris glanced up. Then at last, he realised that the rider was not aiming at them, but the straw redhead. And his bow, golden-wood and ebony, was one they all knew.

He stopped breathing. The rider released his arrow without slowing, his bow tilted to compensate for the wind. There was a streak of brilliant orange. The arrow pierced the target where its heart would have been, if either the dummy or the devil on whom it was modelled had had one. Klemene squawked.

But the rider was not done. He hurtled past the target, turning in the saddle with the sureness of a highbred cavalryman trained from earliest childhood to ride without reins. His arm was a straight line, his back an elegant arc. Another bright whistling flight. The second arrow struck the dummy from behind, quivering a half-inch from the first. Then the man reined up, vaulted from the saddle, landed on his feet, and shot again.

The third arrow sprouted through the target's neck. This was no more than a hand's width across, an impossible shot. The dummy rocked reproachfully on its pole. "Mother Above!" yelled Lomas.

Emaris's eyes watered, though the wind had died down. His own bow was still drawn. He drew a lungful of chilly air, picked a spot for his arrow to land, and loosed.

Vion shouted. So did the rider. The arrow flew into the grass four feet to the man's left. Emaris loosed another, this one lodging point-down an inch from the man's foot. The great stallion startled and tried to bolt. The man dropped his bow and seized its bridle, swearing at the top of his lungs. Emaris shot again. The last arrow flew over the heads of horse and rider both, ruffling mane and hair; and finally Vion yanked the bow out of his hands.

Straining with the horse, Hiraen Safin yelled, "What the hell d'you think you're doing?"

A strange hush fell over the patrol. The boys gathered round, wide-eyed, as Emaris started across the field to the newcomer. His fingers were tingling, his palms clammy. This, at the end of two long weeks. "Teaching archery," he said. "You shoot like a madman."

"So do you," said Hiraen. "You've grown."

He was alive. More than alive—his green eyes were bright, his cheeks flushed, his dark hair tumbled like that of an errant schoolboy just out of bed. The echo-chamber in Emaris's head had fallen silent. "I turned eighteen," he said, "while you were dead."

Last summer, weeping for his father on the threshold of a lamplit room, he had thought death a close acquaintance. What he had not known then was that grief came in many flavours, each as unpalatable as the last. He had shed no tears over Savonn and Hiraen—he was too old to cry, or so he told himself, and his patrol looked up to him as an example—but he *had* nearly fractured a knuckle punching a wall, and several doors in Onaressi were going to hang askew on their hinges for a long time.

He meant to reveal none of this. But an intimation of it must have crossed his face, because Hiraen came closer and flung an arm around him. "I'm sorry," he said. Then, softer—"I'm sorry. I'm sorry. I'm sorry."

Used to Savonn's stand-offishness, Emaris did not see it coming. The embrace was a relief, like a cold drink after a long hot march, one he had not even known he needed. He pressed his face into the collar of Hiraen's shirt and screwed his eyes shut. Even blind, it was impossible to mistake him for Savonn. "You could have sent word."

"I know," said Hiraen. "I'm sorry."

"Where were you?"

"Took a detour. I'll tell you later. Your patrol's coming. Can you keep a secret?"

Emaris scowled. "Depends what it is."

Hiraen lowered his voice to a whisper. "I got Savonn out. He's gone to Cassarah. I couldn't stop him. But he's fine, and you have to remember that, no matter what happens. He said to tell you so."

Emaris's heart stuttered. He wriggled one arm free. "What'd he go there for?"

"The Empath. The Council has him."

"*What?*"

But the others were upon them, and Hiraen's attention was called away. Now that the showboating was over, Emaris saw how ragged and worn he looked. He was smiling, but it did not hide the grim shadows circling his eyes, even as he slapped Klemene's back and reached up the requisite five inches to tousle Lomas's hair. "I swear, Lomas, you're turning into a lightning hazard. Where's Vion? Oh, there you are." A punch on the shoulder, almost natural. "The second-best archer in this little pack, so long as no one makes you laugh. Someone fetch Daine. We're going back to the city."

"Now?" Klemene's handkerchief had fallen off, and his nose was redder than ever. "What about Savonn?"

He might as well have uttered a magic word. The shouting gave way to a sudden, expectant quiet. Vion glanced at Emaris. Emaris did not look back.

"Nothing to be done," said Hiraen. He had stopped trying to smile. "The search is over. The real work's in Cassarah now. You see," he said, jostled shoulder to shoulder against Emaris in the crowd, "Savonn is dead."

CHAPTER 2

It was the day Willon Efren was going to die.

Iyone found the citadel ghost-empty as always, and shrouded in thicker shadow than usual, as if it sensed what she had come to do. She knew it well—a labyrinth of musty rooms and echoing hallways, so vast it could have swallowed a thousand households and all their goods besides. The outer walls were peppered with arrow slits, and a murder hole lurked above every door. Ederen Andalle's architecture left a great deal to be desired, but his defences did not.

Challenged by a guard on every landing, she descended six flights of rough-hewn stairs to the deepest dungeon. At the bottom she had to pause to compose herself. It was too late for doubts now. Josit always had her way.

She was in a narrow aisle between rows of small unlit cells, blocked off by a striation of steel bars. The place smelled like a birthing-room, or a hospice: of sweat and ordure and blood, all that put a man on the same plane as a beast. The cells were empty. Murderers and rapists and slavers tended to go straight to the noose now, per Kedris's orders—the late Governor's approach to justice was nothing if not pragmatic—and petty thieves and thugs served their time in a separate gaol that was, though squalid and wretched, at least above ground. As for traitors, there were none. No one had ever rebelled against Kedris Andalle, except his son.

The aisle ended at a door flanked by four armoured guards. Here was the very heart of the dungeon, a cell for the most dangerous prisoners, where the Council had put Dervain Teraille.

It was a day for stout-heartedness. It was the day Willon Efren was going to die. Iyone allowed herself a fleeting thought for Hiraen and Savonn, her brother in blood and her brother in mischief; for Shandei, stubborn Shandei, back in Cassarah with a blood feud and a quick temper. Then she closed her hand around the envelope in her pocket, and stepped forward.

The guards eyed her. Willon's strident voice drifted through the door, distant and hollow, as though out of another universe. "Gentlemen," said Iyone. "I need to speak to Lord Efren."

The guards glanced at one another, eyes darting behind their visors. She knew what they were thinking. Since his one-man assault on Onaressi and subsequent disappearance, Hiraen had become a tragic hero of near-mythic proportions. He had survived a murderous ambush. He had wrested Onaressi from the Marshal and freed the Betronett garrison, alone, with nothing but his bow and arrows and the stoutness of his own heart. Then he had gone to search for Savonn Silvertongue, and had not been seen again.

It was all anyone could talk about. And nature ruled that where the names of Hiraen and Savonn were invoked, Iyone's would soon follow.

"His lordship is with the prisoner, milady," said one of the guards at last. "A rogue of a man. Safer to wait outside."

She had already had this conversation with three different sentries on the way here. If one believed the gossip, the Empath had felled twelve men with Savonn's silver knives before Cahal finally overcame him. "He is shackled?"

"Yes, ladyship, but—"

"He has endured a full night of torture?"

"Yes, but—"

"Then," said Iyone, "he can hardly injure me. I understand the Council is interrogating him. I am on the Council."

More eye-skittering. Then the guard said, "If milady insists."

They opened the heavy door. It swung back with an aching groan, revealing a foul-breathed tunnel mouth on the other side. This ran for a couple yards, then opened onto the cell itself—little more than a cube hollowed out from bare stone, about eight feet across. Resigning herself to the smell, Iyone stepped through.

A torch guttered in a sconce by the entrance. As her eyes adjusted, she made out a man-shaped figure on a straw mat, chained to the floor at wrist and ankle. Standing over him, but looking at Iyone with their usual alarmed irritation, were Willon Efren and Oriane Sydell.

But the prisoner spoke first. "*Sidrat.*" His voice was a barnacled creak. "*Vi annas?*"

Damn it. Another one? The darkness was an unhelpful shroud, masking what little Iyone could see of his face through his hair. She said, "*Lo, vi annas.*"

Yes, another. The shadow that was the Empath's head rose a couple of inches. The shadow that was his mouth curled up at the ends. He could have been a wizened philosopher-king holding court in his cave, dispensing wisdom on his supplicants. Not that Lord Willon would ever consult a philosopher. Rounding on Iyone, his lordship snapped, "What are you doing here?"

She could warn him. She might still stop it. But she would not be believed. "Filling my father's Council seat, as is my right," she said. Lord Lucien was still away, combing Forech's Pass for any trace of Hiraen or Savonn. "What did the prisoner say?"

Willon laughed. "Wouldn't you love to know?"

Whatever it was, it must have pleased him. Always ruddy, his colour was higher than usual today, his cheeks mottled like raisins; and Iyone did not like the knowing way he looked at her. "He told me most of it before you arrested him," she said. "I assume the fabulous tale concerning Savonn Silvertongue has not changed."

The Empath was still smiling, eyes distant but not vacant. "No need to be so doubtful," said Oriane. "The torturers are... skilled. Everyone breaks sooner or later."

"I can imagine," said Iyone.

In fact she could not. She had seen plenty of executions in Kedris's day, some more creative than others, but of torture she knew only what she had read in books. She had half expected to find the Empath in bloody pieces, strung up on meat hooks like a pig at the butcher's with only the relevant parts left intact so he could talk. But he was whole as far as she could see, his legs folded, his hands relaxed in his lap. The sheer fact of his presence seemed to take up more space than his physical body. If he was broken, so was a shard of glass, raised high to plunge into one's jugular.

Iyone wondered if, somewhere far away, her brothers were enduring the same horrors with the same pride. Better that they were dead.

"If I wanted you here," Willon was saying, "I would have invited you. Where's Josit? Still hiding?"

Next to the Empath, he seemed terribly inconsequential. The envelope crinkled in Iyone's pocket. "Still indisposed," she corrected. "It's not every day a Saraian spy infiltrates your home and serves you tea. You must allow her time to get over the shock."

Willon grinned. It was a sight to curdle blood. "You're loyal to your masters, I'll give you that. But don't worry. Our friend here will testify, you mark my words. And both Josit and the Silvertongue will tell us exactly what manner of dealings they had with him."

"The logistics may be complicated, my lord," said Iyone. "Must we hire a necromancer so Savonn can stand trial? And an exorcist, to get rid of him afterwards?"

The smile lines deepened around the prisoner's mouth. "Oh, for heaven's sake," said Oriane, as Willon took a jerky step towards Iyone. "Can't we talk outside?"

Seventy next spring, her ebony skin webbed with wrinkles, her cloud of curls more silver than black, she was still keen as a kingfisher. Willon—of whom the same could not be said—made an impatient noise and snatched the torch from the wall sconce. They went back up the tunnel and through the door, slamming it behind them for the guards to lock. This, Iyone realised, left the prisoner in pitch darkness. "Don't be so cocky," said Willon. "One could very well ask what *you* were doing with Josit the night the Empath came visiting. For your father's sake, I have given you the benefit of the doubt. Don't make me change my mind."

"Gods forbid," said Iyone. "But has it occurred to you that this fellow may not be the most reliable witness? A servant of Marguerit, confessing under torture, with every reason to sow discord among us?"

"Believe it or not," said Oriane, "you are not the first to think of it. We need corroborating evidence. It's a pity no one can get to Astorre till spring, or we'd be able to ask someone there."

Her stare was pointed. No doubt she believed Iyone to be in on this new devilment of Savonn's, a fair assumption for anyone who had known them growing up. But even he—her closest friend in the world—had confided nothing to her. "I'm afraid I can't help on that front," said Iyone. "The most nefarious thing I can remember Savonn doing is hiding a live earthworm in my shoe. As for Josit, though..."

She pulled the envelope from her pocket. It was time. "This may be of interest."

After an inert moment, Willon took it from her. He peered at the unbroken wax seal, fashioned like a canary with a tulip in its beak. "Josit's sigil. What's this?"

"She gave it to me when I called on her today," said Iyone. "As my lord can see, I haven't opened it." This was true. She had only dictated the note, and stood witness as the envelope was sealed: the price she had set on the secret of Josit's child. Of Savonn.

Willon was already reading. Iyone glimpsed Josit's familiar looping hand, spilling the damning words across the page. *To the Council of Cassarah: Here is the answer you have sought to the riddle of the Rose Killings. They were my doing. They were carried out by those loyal to me, with the purpose of unsettling the Council and preventing Willon Efren from wresting control over the city, thus paving the way for Savonn Andalle to return as ruler of Cassarah.*

Savonn was unaware of these plans. Needless to say, the girl Shandei is also innocent and should be exculpated of all suspicion.

With the rumours of Savonn's death, I have abandoned my plans and am leaving Cassarah for good. Any attempt to pursue me will end only in regret on your part. Keep well.

The last line was not of Iyone's dictating. With her customary wit, Josit had signed the note *Josit Ansa, once of Terinea, later of Cassarah, presently of nowhere in particular.*

Oriane said, "Gods be good."

Willon exhaled noisily. "Well," he said. "Well!"

"Well?" repeated Iyone. "Surely none of this is news to you, since the Empath has been so informative?"

A crack appeared on the surface of Willon's solipsistic triumph. He paused, frowned, and glanced at Oriane, whose dark eyes were still narrowed at the letter. "No," she said. "He knew nothing about the Thorn. And believe me, we asked."

"Oh," said Iyone. "How strange."

"It doesn't matter," snapped Willon. "She confessed." Then his gaze fell on Iyone over the top of the letter, and the urgency of the situation seemed to impress itself on him. "Gods damn you both. When did she give this to you?"

Iyone proffered her sweetest smile, the one Hiraen said made her look like an evil marionette. She was complicit, now. "An hour ago, maybe two. Or three. Dear me, I didn't know it was urgent. You had better go."

He did not need telling twice. He did not even need telling once. He brushed past her and set off for the stairs at a ferocious stride, shouting orders to the sentries. "Summon the city guard. Barricade the Street of Canaries and surround Josit's manor. No one goes in or out. Oriane, aren't you coming?"

A door banged, cutting off his footfalls. Oriane had not moved. She was studying Iyone with a pinched look, like a hungry lioness watching a herd of antelope. "Why on earth did Josit write that letter?"

"I suppose," said Iyone, "someone forced her hand."

"No doubt," said Oriane. "But was it the Empath, or someone else?"

Iyone met her stare. Oriane was sharp, and after tonight she would be Iyone's chief opponent. "You mean, someone like me? It's always possible. But there's no sense asking unless you'll believe what I say."

Oriane's face changed. The lioness had spotted a younger, faster leopard, every bit as hungry. "My lady," said Iyone, "next time Lord Willon levels some accusation against me, remember who it was that pruned the Thorn."

A high-strung pause. On both ends it was half threat, half appraisal, all tension. Oriane looked away first. Without a word, she swept past Iyone, stumping up the stairs after Willon. It was a conversation that would not be forgotten, and one they would have to have again, probably sooner than Oriane expected.

Thus concluded the first gambit. The next would be harder. Josit, her preparations complete, would have left her manor by now—her latest home, and perhaps her last. And Iyone still had her end of the bargain to uphold. It was going to be a long night.

She took a deep breath and set off, chin up, to the day's second labour.

* * *

Night fell early this time of year. A mist had risen from the Morivant, not the gossamer wisps so common in summer, but a thick white blanket that smothered the streets and housetops under its quelling weight. Windows glowed along the roads like beacons, and lanterns winked in and out through the fog. The streets were full of people hurrying home. Mist-ghouls walked abroad on evenings like this, superstitious folk said, spuming through the air to suck the breath from your lungs. Best to stay indoors with the lights on.

Iyone often thought her life would be simpler if she were superstitious.

Halfway to her rendezvous at the Fire Gate, the alarum-bells began to toll. *Bong. Bong. Bong.* The clamour rolled from the rooftops and the watchtowers, slow and dirgelike, so deep it seemed to pierce her chest and resonate between her ribs. It was a warning, a summons. *To arms, to arms.* Josit would depart with a queen's fanfare after all.

Voices rose in speculation all along the street. A few windows came open. Others banged shut, as if to keep out whatever was coming. A small boy shrieked with excitement while his mother tried to hustle him on. As Iyone passed a shophouse, the front door opened a crack, and a woman with her hair in a towel peered out. Her eyes were large and rabbit-bright.

"No need for alarm," said Iyone automatically. "It's not the Saraians, just Lord Willon in a good mood."

Bong. Gong. Her bones shivered. The woman retreated, but not all the way. She was staring. "Milady Iyone?"

Iyone identified the mix of recognition and abashed curiosity that had grown so familiar in the days since Onaressi. "Yes?" she said. Or maybe it was just, "Yes," a tired acknowledgement. Her brother was a hero. Her brother was dead. It felt like one and the same thing.

"Is it true they've caught the Saraian sorcerer?"

Iyone stopped walking. Her irritation fled as quickly as it had come. What was wrong with wanting some good news? She was only a girl, too young to remember a time before peace. This lady, at least ten years her elder, had come to womanhood under the shadow of war. Probably the tinkle of her shop bell was enough to send her back to the fearful days before Kedris's victory at the Morivant, when the great bronze tide tolled every week to warn of some new Saraian incursion. Dead brothers, long-away fathers, blood feuds that would not rest—she must have been acquainted with them all.

Josit had lost because she had forgotten the stakes for which she played. Iyone could not make the same mistake. She wished, desperately, that she were not so young.

"His lordship thinks so," she said at last. "Hence the good mood. It is chilly, madame. Stay warm."

She watched until the woman disappeared inside. Then she went on her way, drawing her cloak more closely around her shoulders.

Ordinarily, Cassarah's gates stood open from dawn to midnight, admitting and disgorging a fitful stream of merchants, artisans, and farmers with wagonloads of wet produce to hawk at market. But the Fire Gate was shut when she arrived. At this hour there was only one party of travellers trying to leave the city: some distinguished person in an elaborate palanquin inlaid with silver and filigreed with twining ivy patterns, borne by six men and guarded by six others in anonymous grey doublets. The leader seemed to be having a civil argument with the gate warden. Iyone came forward. "What's the matter?"

Again, she was recognised at once. Both men dipped their heads to her. "Milady," said the warden. "Lord Willon gave orders. The bells, see. All gates to be barred. These people—"

"My mistress's business is urgent, ladyship," said the other man. "We have a deal to conclude in Bayarre. A matter of thousands of drochii. The ferry departs at midnight."

The palanquin curtain had fallen open, as if for an eye to watch them out of the crack. It was a good disguise—the entourage of a sensible merchant, flaunting just enough wealth to command respect without attracting the wrong sort of attention. "Oh?" Iyone turned to the warden. "Why the curfew?"

The man shifted his weight. "We were not told. In fact, we hoped you might know—you being on the Council and all—"

"So I am," said Iyone. "Unbar the way. I know the mistress. She has a long way to go."

For some time, a rhythmic drumming had been building on the threshold of her hearing, a sound she had initially taken for her own pulse. Now she knew what it was: the brisk tramp of approaching feet. She had minutes to spare. "That will be Lord Willon's men," said the warden. "If milady will wait, we could ask permission—"

"Unbar the way," said Iyone again. "If there are repercussions, I will bear them."

It was the first time she had ever gone against Willon in deed and not just word. Her father was not here to back her up. For better or worse, she held the Council seat in her own name. The warden scratched his chin, looking miserable, even as the distant marching grew louder. He might balk; it was not unthinkable. On such small moments was the history of cities hinged.

"Yes, ladyship," he said at last. "If you must."

He called an order to the winch workers. Wiping her palms on her skirts, Iyone approached the palanquin. Her authority had been tested and confirmed, and no one else tried to stop her. She lifted the curtain and looked inside.

The merchant was an older woman with greying hair. She shifted uneasily in her furs. Pearls gleamed in her hairnet; sapphires dangled from her ears. Under the jewels and powder, it was the wide-eyed face of Elysa, Iyone's former servant, that looked back at her. With her was a smaller figure in a man's shirt and trousers, holding a riding crop. Her hair was piled beneath a black cap that sported a jaunty pigeon-feather, and something roguish glinted in her eyes.

"My horse is waiting outside," said Josit Ansa. "How was the fallout? As amusing as you hoped?"

"Soon," said Iyone, "it will be more amusing than I bargained for." It was impossible to match Josit's cool façade, and she did not try. "Shandei is back. I haven't seen her."

"Trust Zarin," said Josit. "He will take care of it." Leaning across Elysa, she put a gloved hand on Iyone's arm. "Come with me. If Willon lives, he will not pardon you."

Iyone's mouth was dry. The marching men were almost upon them. "This is my city. I fear nothing."

Josit smiled. "Then we won't see each other again. But we are on the same side now, false daughter. Always remember that."

The curtain slipped shut. The gate swung open, and the road stood clear. Iyone stepped back from the palanquin. Pressure was building in the corners of her eyes—the beginnings of a headache, surely; it had been a vexing day, and a worse night was coming. The chief guard shouted, and his men began to march, bearing their mistress through the open gate.

Thus departed the Thorn of Cassarah: once a princess, once a slave, now an unhoused spirit, set loose to wreak havoc where she would.

Out of the fog, a horn blew. A spear crashed on a shield. A whip whistled through the air, and a horse whinnied. Willon's men had come. Nothing for it now but to stand her ground, back to back with Josit for the first time in her life. *This is my city*, she thought. The words resounded through her, gaining vehemence with each iteration. *I belong here. I am the city's blood.*

I am the city.

Speartip-first, the Efren men emerged from the parting mist. She could not see how many there were, only the glitter of their cuirasses and the black iron of their weapons. Those in the front were all mounted. They spread out, filling the street as far as she could see. A hound bayed. There was a creaking noise she usually associated with festive games and the training yard, so it took her longer than it should have to identify it: the winch of a crossbow, trained on her.

She stayed where she was, between the guards and the gate. A tall figure in cream and bronze dismounted and came forward. "Milady," he said, a perfunctory greeting. Then he raised his voice to call to the warden. "Lord Willon ordered the gates to be shut. Why are they open?"

It was Cahal. The warden said, "Her ladyship—"

She had promised to take the consequences, and she would. "Don't bother, sir," she said. "Josit is gone. She won't trouble us again."

Planting her weight on both feet, she absorbed the impact of Cahal's stare. He made an abortive movement towards her, and then to his horse. "You *let her go*?"

She contemplated her options. Placed where she was, he would either have to ride her down or remove her bodily from his path. The former was unthinkable—more than ever now, the Safin name counted for something. The latter, courteously done, would cost him time. Josit was an excellent rider. A few minutes was all the head start she needed. "I thought to save Lord Willon the inconvenience," said Iyone. "Our quarrel is with Marguerit, not Josit. Perhaps you should remind him that."

Cahal's brows formed a deep funnel over the bridge of his nose. He was a good man, as she had cause to know. Not long ago he had rescued her from the Thorn, or thought he had. "It ain't my place to do that," he said. "Beg pardons, ladyship, but it ain't yours either. Step aside."

"I could," said Iyone thoughtfully. "But on principle, I don't retreat, especially before men like Lord Willon. You could say I have an allergy. Shellfish, pollen, and pompous Efrens..."

"Milady, if you please."

She meandered back to the matter at hand. "I don't please. It's sheer stupidity to empty the city in pursuit of one fugitive. If you disagree, you'll have to move me yourself."

His eyes returned to the gate. He knew how much time she was wasting. "You leave me with no choice."

He seized her wrist and dragged her to the side of the road. She did not struggle. He was strong, stronger than she expected, and it was like having her arm jammed in a vice. "Take her away. His lordship will want to see her."

She almost laughed. Willon never wanted to see her. He bore her presence as a necessary ordeal, like having a rotten tooth out. Two guards stepped forward and took her by the arms. Their grip was not cruel, but neither was it gentle. The road thus levelled, Cahal swung back onto his stallion and jabbed his spurs into its flank. "Quick!"

They cantered out through the gate past the gaping warden, first the horsemen, then the footsoldiers, their hunting dogs trotting alongside. Iyone tried to count them as they passed, but soon gave up. There were too many. It did not matter: by now Josit must have leapt from the palanquin and mounted her horse, on her way to whatever new home she might make for herself. No one could stop her now.

Iyone said nothing, and let the guards lead her away.

REPRISE: WINTER 1530

Winter forced a return to the Bitten Hill. Savonn did not want to leave Astorre, but he had no choice: Lord Kedris was visiting to inquire after Captain Merrott's unremitting good health, and his reformed son had to be put on display for his benefit, on his best behaviour, all the circus soldiered out of him.

"Your friend Hiraen is in open rebellion against me," Kedris had said, the last time Savonn had seen him. "I should have that treacherous silverspoon boy whipped through the streets and beheaded. Gods know I will, if he doesn't do anything about Merrott."

Savonn was under no illusions about his position. When Kedris wanted a job done, he knew whom to hurt to make sure of it. And yet—for the first time since he left Cassarah—Savonn was preoccupied with neither Hiraen's life nor Merrott's death. Xante's harpsichord had put other matters on his mind.

"Something's gone out of you," Rendell said on the way down Forech's Pass, and of course he was right. The lowland air was hard to breathe now that Savonn had seen Astorre. He had stopped sleeping, and barely tasted his food. He smiled with the same mechanical regularity with which he breathed and his laughter was off-kilter, off-key. His body had become a house he haunted.

When at last he was sent back in spring with new instructions, it was nothing short of a resuscitation. Celisse's city was home in a way Cassarah had never been. Up here there was music everywhere: buskers, ballroom quartets, fire-dancers who twisted and whirled at nightfall on the mountainside, lullabying the sun to the beat of tabor drums. Savonn was alone this time, without his patrol. The free world was full of colour, and like a desert traveller looking for water, his eyes found treasure where there was none. The auburn of someone's hat, or a scarf at a market stall, or the mountain blazing with alpenglow in the last light of dusk: red, red everywhere.

But he did not find what he wanted. Not till he broke into the Saraian consulate to lay hands on some papers for his father, and the door of the solar clicked open, and in walked the consul himself.

It was the middle of the night. Savonn was sure he had made no sound. But in Astorre—where the cityfolk watched for the red blessing of Lady Fidelity and invoked the name of Amitei only in whispers, for They were real and would hear—anything could happen. It was entirely possible that he had summoned the man out of desire alone.

"Hello," said Savonn, for lack of other recourse. The incriminating papers were still on the desk in front of him, unread: a trade treaty between Marguerit and Celisse, of great interest to Kedris since it involved gunpowder, though Savonn himself could not have cared less. "Fancy seeing you here."

Red's hair was down, his nightshirt half unbuttoned, revealing a triangle of golden skin against which a small emerald pendant hung. He gazed at Savonn with interest, looking neither surprised nor displeased. One might have thought he found burglars in his solar every night. "A soldier, a musician, and now a thief. I see you are a man of many faces."

"So are you," said Savonn.

Since his return, he had been conducting a subtle investigation among the clientele of Xante's ballroom and the Merman. The Saraian was a familiar face at both. No one knew where he lived, or what his business was; only that he showed up now and then, played a few songs, had a drink, and left. He used three or four different names, but people inevitably defaulted to *Red*. Many reported trying to flirt with him, only to be levelled with a hard gaze and stared into silence. It seemed he visited solely for the music.

In all this, no one had mentioned that the man also happened to be the consul of Sarei, servant to none other than Queen Marguerit. It was, as Hiraen would say, the sort of predicament only Savonn could contrive for himself.

"So tell me, thief," said Red. He was barring the way to both door and window, his right hand listing towards the sleeve of his left. The consulate had no shortage of guards. He had only to call. "What happens next?"

"You could throw that knife at me," said Savonn, considering. "Then I'd have to throw mine too."

"And then there would be shouting and running, and possibly blood," said Red. "Tedious."

It was a delicate situation. But Savonn's father already held a monopoly on his fear, and there was none left over for Red. "We could do better," agreed Savonn. "What do you suggest?"

Red looked at the treaty papers, and then at him. "Bribe me."

Savonn hesitated only a split second. He stepped around the desk.

It was a small room. In one step he was inside Red's reach, so close they were almost chest to chest. Red smelled like books, like new lutestrings, like the earth before a thunderstorm. He was half a head taller, and the white voile of his shirt did nothing to conceal shoulders and a chest shaped by what had to be many years of hard training. No doubt he could hold Savonn down with just one hand, pin him against the wall or the desk or the floor, probably snap his neck as well.

It was, Savonn thought, a most excellent state of affairs.

Red did not appear to think so. "Not that sort of bribe," he said. A muscle worked in his throat, near the pendant of his neckchain. "My bed is not a marketplace."

Was Savonn's? He had never had the chance to find out. Red did not touch him. He could not decide if he was relieved or disappointed. "So ask another price. Unless, of course, you desire nothing else."

Red's lashes dipped as he looked away: a minute lapse, but an uncharacteristic one. He was no longer reaching for his knife. "I am not so dull. Your name, then."

"No," said Savonn.

He was flattered, though, and Red knew it, judging by the way his lips curved. "No?"

"You are inept," said Savonn, "at driving bargains. A name is only a word."

"Hm," said Red. "If it is so, tell me who sent you."

He came no closer. Savonn stood light and poised on his feet like a gymnast on the trapeze, ready, though he was not sure what for. "I might be here of my own accord."

"No," said Red. "You are not."

Savonn pondered. One way or another, he needed to read the treaty. If he could also pique Red's interest while he was at it—well, he was nothing if not resourceful.

"I have not read your papers," he said. Red could see this was true: they were still face down where they had lain, untouched. "So as yet I owe you nothing. If you truly wish to know, let me look at them first."

"Or I could throw my knife at you," said Red.

"At best you would miss," said Savonn. "At worst you would kill me, and then you'd never know who sent me."

Red's eyes glimmered, a fox's in the night. They were so close Savonn could see his own reflection mirrored twice in the vast darkness of his pupils. His blood sang. "I see," said Red. "Not just a soldier or a thief, but a little bird playing games. You would play with me?"

Would he, Savonn wondered. "Given the right inducements, I might tell you a thing or two. It might even be true."

Red peered at him, his brow furrowed. They said he hardly gave anyone a second glance; that he never said three words if he could say two and he never said two if he could just glare. Some of Savonn's informants attributed this to shyness, most to disdain. But Red had always given him his fullest attention.

"Very well," said Red at length. "Read the treaty, but touch nothing else. I will collect a suitable payment at a time of my choosing."

"Aren't you afraid I'll disappear first?"

"Thief's honour. Anyway, I know where you are lodging."

Now he did seem shy. He glanced away again, his smile crooked, as though he wanted to stop but didn't know how. "You were gone a long time," he explained. "I kept my eyes open."

Savonn had to work, then, to master his own face. An actor had to belong nowhere. But one liked to be missed from time to time. It provided a comfortable illusion of home.

He leafed through the treaty papers, memorising the gist of the terms, then put them back and went to the window. Red trailed him, but made no move to stop him climbing out. "You will meet me?" he asked. "When I call on you?"

For such a formidable man, he sounded uncertain. Savonn had to laugh. In earnest of his goodwill, he did what he had wanted from the first: reached up, touched the chain of the emerald pendant, coiled a sleek tendril of auburn hair around his finger. Red's expression flickered. They were bold and young and alive, and all things under the sun were theirs.

"If you can catch me," he said.

CHAPTER 3

Awaiting punishment, Iyone had more than enough time to consider all possible outcomes.

Exile would at least be entertaining, if she could get Shandei to come with her. There was no shortage of havoc they could wreak outside the city bounds. Other contingencies were less palatable. She might be executed on the spot. Or—her recent jaunt to the dungeons fuelled her imagination—Willon might throw her in prison, where she would no doubt learn a good deal more about torture than she ever wanted to, up close and first hand.

This was improbable. Her mother would not countenance it. So she was only a little surprised when, in the end, her captors took her to her own house. A dozen Efren men had been set to guard her; these arranged themselves in a circle around the manor as if settling down to a siege. Predictably, Aretel Safin marched out of the house while they were still getting into position, and met Iyone on the portico in a maelstrom of brimstone and dragonbreath. "What," she said, "is the meaning of this?"

The glare was for the Efrens, but the question was for her daughter. Iyone sought valour in discretion, and did not answer. "Please, ma'am," said one of the two men flanking her. They both appeared to have shrunk at least a foot in stature. "She was caught helping the Thorn escape—that is, Josit Ansa—"

"Beg pardons, milady," added the other, as his colleague quailed beneath Aretel's stare. "We're to keep her under guard till his lordship comes to question her."

"*In our own house?*"

"If you prefer," said Iyone, losing patience, "they could put me in the dungeon. Then I could question the Empath myself."

With a mixture of guilt and childish dread, she received her mother's unimpressed gaze. Aretel had been pinched and sallow all summer. Now she had grown waif-thin, her cheeks sunken, her eyes shadowed with bruises. Already the servants were hauling in bales of black cloth to drape the windows in mourning for Hiraen. And now this: a blow from her other child, unfair and unforeseen.

"It's all right, Mother," said Iyone, though this was patently untrue. "It won't be for long."

She headed into the house. Her gaolers trailed her across the front hall, up the stairs and down the hallway to her room, tracking mud and grass all over her father's fine carpets. "Would you like to come inside?" she asked, favouring them with a cold-eyed smile. "Or would that be unseemly?"

They exchanged shifty looks, then withdrew to the landing, where they found themselves confronted with Aretel again. "Believe me," her mother said, "I will have words with Lord Willon about this. I didn't ask for his help disciplining my children, difficult as that might be." A menacing pause, the sort taught in schools of rhetoric. "Well? Am I barred from my own daughter's room, or will you move aside?"

They moved aside. Not even the gods dared stand between Aretel and her children, let alone a couple of Efren hirelings. Aretel shut the door on them and barred it from the inside. Little hen's-feet wrinkles had appeared around her eyes. "All this for a murderer on the run? I don't know if I could be so tender-hearted."

She must have had the news about Josit already. "Mother," said Iyone, exasperated. "When have you ever known me to do anything out of tender-heartedness? Will you trust me for once?"

"Not when it comes to Josit," said Aretel. "Or Savonn."

An airless silence. Iyone's head hurt. She retreated to the window for a breathing space. A few guards had gathered on the lawn beneath, as though they thought she might tie her bedsheets together and climb down the wall like an acrobat. It was almost flattering. "What about Savonn?"

"You know what," said Aretel. "Who is the Empath?"

Iyone conjured up a blithe smile. It was no good trying to quash the rumours, and neither she nor Josit had tried. The Empath had been shouting Savonn's name for the whole street to hear. "Don't listen to Willon. He'd say anything to turn people against Savonn."

Aretel's lips went white. "So explain this."

She drew something from the inner pocket of her robe. It was a narrow jewellery box made of cedarwood, about the length of her wrist, smooth and unadorned save for a small ruby in the centre of the lid. The lock had been smashed. "What's that?"

Aretel did not answer. Foreboding came on slowly, like the first shivers of ague. Iyone took the box and flipped back the lid.

A whiff of jasmine rose to greet her. Inside, nestled on a lining of black velvet, was a thick roll of parchment. She glanced at the topmost leaf: a letter, written in Saraian. Accustomed to reading the language only in Josit's exquisite cursive, it took her a moment to decipher the brisk untidy hand, one she did not recognise. Only then did she realise what she was holding.

Home is not a place, said the letter. *On this we agreed last summer, when we watched that Dalissan play and you asked me if I was ever homesick. Home is not a thing made by hands—not walls of stone or roofs of brick, or a name on any map. And yet we wanderers, we feel the shape of home like an abscess in the soul. It is the hunger of a fast, the deep cold of the desert night. Like you, I have sought long and far for a hearthstone, but never found it.*

Perhaps home is a line in a play delivered unto perfection. Perhaps it is a chord struck by the virtuoso on the lutestrings, which yearn ever after for his touch and despise the sticky fingers of the novices who follow. Perhaps home is a person we meet once, and never again.

Partway down the page, the prose gave way to musical notation. The letter recovered its verbal form on the next leaf: *But home as a person means love, and we are also in agreement how laughable that is. No more than a defiant fanfare of trumpets which, like all music, cannot be made without a knowledge of time and rhythm and all the transience they bring. Love is barren, impermanent: the chord is struck, and the vibrations die away, and the lute is hung up, and the lutenist himself goes into the ground.*

Why, then, do I write to you? Love is a legend. But perhaps I am afflicted by its distant and very corporeal cousin, sentiment. You are so long away. Perhaps you have been found out and killed. Perhaps you have had to flee, and my letters will never reach you. I have kept no copies for myself. I like to picture my words outliving us both, lingering a hundred years like a blight on the earth after an enchantment has passed: the cullings of my mind, addressed to the leavings of your heart.

Love, that most brazen sound.

The other letters read along similar lines. There were dates, but no signatures or salutations; one supposed there was no need. August 1531. September, November; a break for winter, when no couriers crossed the Farfallens; then again in the new year. The last was dated July 1532, the month Savonn had been made Captain of Betronett with Merrott fresh in his grave. That letter had no words at all, only a rough ink sketch of a bird leaving a cage.

Iyone banged the box shut. "You went through his things?"

It came out loud and sharp, much more like her mother's voice than her own. "I had the servants pack his room," said

Aretel. Now she would not look Iyone in the eye. "And Hiraen's. Better sooner than later."

For as long as Iyone could remember, the bedroom down the hall had unofficially belonged to Savonn. They were all used to him flitting in and out of the manor, ghosting through the halls like a benign daemon, or else disrupting the peace with explosions and declaimings and demonstrations of his latest circus trick. Even now, years since he had left for the Bitten Hill, the servants kept the room for him. He was family. No one questioned it. No one needed to.

When Iyone could trust her voice again, she said, "Where was it?"

"Under his old lyre," said Aretel, still looking at the wall-panelling over Iyone's shoulder. "The one Danei smashed."

Iyone knew that lyre. She and Savonn had spent their boisterous childhood squirreling things out of his house and into various caches around the city, of which the Safin manor was only one. Silly little treasures, too precious to be kept within reach of his parents. Sweetmeats. Stones sharpened to dagger-points. Books of plays and poems. Books about the gods, which his father abhorred; and books proclaiming that there were no gods, which Danei threatened to burn. Books with dirty pictures in them. Iyone had been an efficient smuggler: Kedris's steward liked her, or at least did not make her turn out her pockets whenever she visited. There were other hoards she had not known about, but she had not asked. One could not share *everything*.

The trouble, it seemed, was that Savonn had shared nothing at all.

"They're just love letters," said Iyone. She choked out a laugh. "Nothing sordid."

"Sordid enough for Willon," said Aretel. "Perhaps, before you went and got yourself arrested, you should have spared a thought for your traitor friend. What if they'd searched the house?"

Dimly, Iyone remembered that her mother was still angry. "I didn't know," she said. By gods, it had been a trying day; her feet hurt, and her clothes still reeked of the dungeon. "He didn't tell me. Do you think I would have kept this from you? Josit knew, but she's as bad as him, and Hiraen—"

The thought struck her like a blow. Of course Hiraen had known. Hiraen knew everything about Savonn. He had been at Savonn's side all these years, watching over him, keeping his secrets. It all made sense now. The rainy night, the crying blond boy. Hiraen in the portico, soaked through and shivering, begging an inexplicable promise from her—

Shandei had spent months trying to catch her father's killer. But Iyone, already knowing *who*, had given no thought to *why*. Hiraen's garbled thread of thought was easy to follow in hindsight. It had all been for Savonn. She had not seen it before, because she had not liked to think her brothers might keep things from her.

Unpardonable. She had learnt nothing from Josit, after all.

"It doesn't matter," said Iyone. A hot, sick rage was frothing up from the baser parts of her heart. "It doesn't change anything. But thank you, Mother. You keep giving me useful ideas." She rapped her knuckles against the box. It made a sound like a magistrate's gavel, ringing with finality. "First Poire the physician, and now this."

Her mother frowned. "What are you talking about?"

She had reached the eye of the storm. It was the day Willon Efren was going to die. The day her brothers had betrayed her. A day for stout-heartedness, for steady hands and a clear mind. "The letters," said Iyone. "I won't be in trouble for long, I think."

* * *

Willon arrived at cockcrow. He blew through the house like a devil's sneeze, stomped past the guards on the stairs, and presented himself in the parlour, where Iyone had been brought to await him. "She escaped. Are you happy now?"

The parlour was a cosy room, full of plush armchairs around a cherrywood table, where her father had so often hosted his fellow councillors for tea. Sitting in one of the chairs, Iyone looked at Willon over the top of her book (*A Mathematical Treatise on the Higher Infinities*, a head-throbbing read, and therefore an excellent distraction). "You mean Josit wasn't in the palanquin, my lord? Then why am I under arrest?"

Willon's face was shiny with sweat, his breathing stertorous. A blade of grass clung to his right boot. He must have joined the chase himself—an idea as hilarious as it was hard to imagine, until one remembered that Josit had had his son murdered. "She wasn't. But I know you smuggled her out somehow. Will you deny it?"

Iyone laid aside the *Higher Infinities*. "No."

He laughed, sharp and furious. "I didn't think so. You're too arrogant for that. No," he said, as she drew breath on instinct to retaliate. "You're mad, and shameless, and desperate for your betters to take notice of you. I know how you adored that woman. It doesn't matter to you that she schemed and murdered to get her way, does it? That she would have killed you this past summer if my men hadn't been there to stop it? No, anything goes, as long as she tells you how clever you are."

The last words were delivered in an outright shout. She flinched, but only because his spittle had struck her cheek. "That's *enough*," said Aretel.

She had come unnoticed into the room, Oriane behind her. "Set that aside for now. Is the search still on?"

Willon ignored her. It was Oriane who answered, though her eyes were on Iyone. "The city guard's out in force. Cahal's sniffing along the river with his bloodhounds, and my men are on their way to Amarota."

Amarota was the closest of the fords across the Morivant, an hour's ride from the Fire Gate. "For the Mother's sake," said Aretel. "You think she'll go back to Sarei? After what they did to her?"

"And so you've sent every last man and beast tearing after her," said Iyone. With each new development, the urge to laugh grew harder to suppress. She had been awake for over twenty-four hours. "Except, of course, the generous escort you've left here in case I attempt to break out of my own house. Very sensible."

Oriane frowned. Willon said, "I fail to see what you—"

"You fail to see anything," said Iyone. "What if Marguerit marches on us tonight? Who'll defend us? Lady Oriane's grandchildren, with their toy swords? We'd have three for each gate and one left over to sing the paean. I'll dress my maids in mail, they'll look dashing."

Willon reddened, then crimsoned. The flush spread all the way across his face and down his neck. "Hold your tongue."

"Why?" Restraint no longer mattered. This time tomorrow, either he would be finished or she would. "Does it perturb you to be wrong all the time?"

Aretel said, "*Iyone.*"

With fantastic swiftness, Willon lost his colour again. "I know what you want, you vile, scheming spider. You hope to frighten me into withdrawing the search parties. Well, I won't. Not one man will return till Josit is found. And if Marguerit does materialise at our gates overnight, yours will be the first head I sling over the walls."

Aretel stepped between them. "Control yourself, Willon."

Willon blinked at her, as if he had no idea who she was or where she had come from. "Your daughter's put herself in the way of justice, Lady Safin," said Oriane. "Best not to shield her."

"If you press me," said Aretel, "I will."

A nervous pause. Iyone waited, amused in spite of herself. Not having grown up under the hawk-stare of the Safin matriarch,

Oriane and Willon had no immunity, and were both developing a pronounced list towards the door. At last Willon looked back at Iyone. "Before the Ceriyes, I will see you stand trial for this. You and all your traitor friends. That's a promise."

"I suppose you'd better," said Iyone. "You need *someone* to hang, don't you?"

"Shut up, Iyone," said Aretel. "Willon, it's very late. See yourself out."

Gathering himself, Willon whirled and marched from the room without another word. Oriane stayed where she was, her thoughtful gaze lingering on Iyone, until Aretel said, "Good *night*, Oriane," with rather more force than courtesy. Then she, too, retreated. Willon yelled a few brusque orders downstairs. There was a clamour, as the guards scrambled back to their posts. The front door banged. Then silence.

The worst was over. Iyone had seen the last of him, unless they invited her to the funeral.

After a long moment Aretel said, "He was absolutely right about you and Josit."

None of them knew the first thing about Josit. But Aretel knew her daughter. "He was."

Aretel paced to the window. Under the black silk of her blouse, her shoulders trembled. "You want me to die childless, is that it? First your brother, now you. What will I do when they hang you?"

Iyone felt nothing but a killing fatigue. She looked down at her hands, and wondered if they really belonged to her. "I told you to trust me. Everything is going according to plan."

"Plan? What plan? You're in prison!"

"Dear Mother," said Iyone. She could be gentle now, with no one else to hear. "We have nothing to fear. If we're under guard here, by Willon's own men, then we can't be elsewhere."

Aretel looked round sharply. "Such as?"

"Such as," said Iyone, sick with exultation, "the Efren residence."

CHAPTER 4

What with one thing and another, it was daybreak by the time Willon got home.

The first pallid rays of sunlight were creeping through the thinning mist, dragging his spindly shadow before him. Growing season was over: the daisies were withering, the dahlias dead. It was always quiet in the colourless gardens now. His wife hated the city, and his sons had grown up and gone away, as sons usually did; or died, which sons usually did *not* do. It was difficult to believe that his halls had once rung with the clamour of high boyish voices, or the unsteady patter of toddling feet.

The butler was the only one who came out to receive him. He had, in fact, run out, and now stood on the porch windmilling his arms. "Milord! No, milord! Turn back!"

Willon stared at him. He was ten steps from the door. Probably thirty more from the fireplace, fifty from the warm featherbed for which his aching bones had been crying out all night. One might as well have asked a horse to trot backwards. "What did you say?"

"It's bad luck!" cried the butler. "Your shadow coming into the house before you! Go round, milord, and come in the back way!"

One of Willon's retainers chuckled, not politely. The butler, grey of hair and slow of wit, was full of harmless little superstitions. Ordinarily Willon humoured him; it made life easier, like oiling an axle. This morning he was too tired for that. He gave the old man a pointed look, handed him his cloak, and shouldered through the door. "I'm already brimming over with bad luck," he said. "If the gods give me any more, I'll just overflow. Where are all the servants? Is there no one to fetch me a bath?"

"Everyone's gone out," said the butler, trailing him into the house. "To help search for Josit Ansa. On your own orders, sir. It's just me here."

Willon stared. "I am certain, my dear man, that I gave no such order."

The butler's brows came together. "But you sent a note. Saying that every man, woman and child capable of amu—ambu—ambul—"

"Ambulating?"

"—*ambulating* on their own two feet should join the search. Those exact words. Really, sir, you know I never went to school... I have it here."

They were in the sitting room, with its array of sensible armchairs. The low settees had gone when Willon's knee started giving him trouble. The butler began to riffle through a tray of missives on the side table, talking all the while. "And your lady wife sent a letter, lamenting that Lord Yannick is useless on the estate—begging your pardons—and asking that you send Bonner back to her..."

No note, grandiloquent or otherwise, was forthcoming. Willon laughed. "Forget it. I need a long rest. See that no one disturbs me."

It was a relief to be home, surrounded by the civilised comforts he had curated over the years. Delicate black-figure bowls shipped upriver from Bayarre. Glass vases blown in Astorre. Thick woollen footrugs from Pieros, to stave off the winter chill. He had earned his luxuries. He had spent a full and toilsome life in the service of two Governors before him: subtle old Raedon Sydell, who had inexplicably passed him over in favour of that creeping vine Kedris; and Kedris himself, dead before his time in all his charm and caprice, leaving behind only a wastrel son and a double-dealing mistress. It was not an end Willon coveted.

Something had to be done about Iyone Safin. Her meddling had already cost him Josit. A quick trial would be the thing, quiet and discreet—conviction at noon, the noose by nightfall. It would be simple to arrange. She had been friends with the Silvertongue, and no magistrate would conceivably rule in her favour once *his* indelicacies were exposed. Then a convent for the mother, and a permanent post at Onaressi for Lucien. Good thing the brother was dead. The Safins were finished, and the girl only had her own insufferable arrogance to blame.

Going over these plans, he climbed the marble stair to the upper floor and shut himself in his bedchamber. The door-latch gave a pleasing click behind him, sealing him off from the world and its barbarities.

It was dark. The curtains were drawn, the chandelier unlit. He fumbled his way to the window, cursing the maids under his breath. They had even managed to put up the wrong curtains. These were dreadful, stitched from some coarse black fabric that scratched and scraped between his fingers. Where were his silk taffetas? His gauzy chiffons? He peeled back the hanging to open the window. Then, in a shaft of half-hearted dawn light, he saw what he was holding.

His fingers went limp. He let the curtain drop, as if scalded. The room darkened again.

"It's bad luck, opening a mourning drape," said a soft voice behind him. "My lord had better leave it. I have a light."

Willon spun round. He had just enough time to distinguish a lean figure by the fireplace, holding a glowing match. Then something slammed into his right thigh, near knocking him off his feet. Pain exploded up his leg: not the dull background chatter of bad knees and weary bones, but a shrill, concentrated shriek. He looked down. Something was sticking out through the fabric of his trousers. A dagger-hilt.

His wits returned. With them came outrage. "Who the hell are you?"

The figure flung the match onto the hearth. The blaze of firelight illuminated a tall narrow-faced man in a leather jerkin, a second dagger already spinning between his fingers. "No one you have cause to remember," he said. "The drape is on loan from the Safins. Soon, this house will be in mourning as well."

"The—the Safins," gasped Willon. He sank to the rug. Something hot was oozing down his leg, a great deal of it, pooling in his boot and squelching under his foot. Gods be good. The bastard must have hit a vein. Through the descending haze of delirium, he struggled to remember why the man's face was familiar. "You're..."

He had seen the fellow not long ago, in the host Lucien had taken to the Farfallens. "You're Josit's man. The commander she sent."

"Aye," said his assailant. "She bids you farewell."

The second dagger took him in the stomach like a mailed fist. Somehow he was on his back. The crystal globes of the chandelier swam and doubled and quadrupled above him, a remote, unhelpful bystander. He coughed blood. Another blade was protruding from his abdomen. Dear gods, what was it they said about gut wounds? The slowest death, short of being impaled... So much accomplished, and all for nothing. "Josit..."

By the door, one of the shadows moved.

The man glanced over his shoulder. His hesitation was brief. In the next instant he was springing across the room and swinging over the windowsill, dislodging the drape to let in another rush of daylight. When the darkness settled again, the man was gone. And in the space between blinks, another figure had materialised at Willon's side.

He fought for breath. Every thought was a feat of endurance. "You..."

This face was familiar too. Shandei, daughter of Rendell, was standing over him, her eyes brilliant with unshed tears. "I wanted to do it myself."

This made no sense. His stomach was screaming with agony. "You... sent him?"

She shook her head. No, of course not. The man had fled at the sight of her. "He interrupted me last time. Now I've interrupted him." She swallowed. "She beat me to it."

She, too, had a blade in her hand, though this one had an ivory hilt. It occurred to Willon that he ought to be afraid. "This was my father's," she said. "You wouldn't recognise it."

Her father. Who? The late Second Captain of Betronett, the Silvertongue's deputy. Would the poor fellow's ghost never leave him alone? "I didn't. I swear..."

She was trembling, taut as a bowstring. A blonde little thing, young and pretty, but the muscles in her arms were anything but ornamental. "Then who did?"

"Don't know." An avowal of impotence. He did not want those to be his last words. With a final savage effort, he fought to speak. "Useless... stupid to kill me. I can help. Find the killer."

Her face relaxed into a mask of contempt, as if she had just remembered how much she despised him. "You never bothered before. I don't see why you should start now. Anyway, you were only ever a pawn. Already you've been supplanted."

He managed a scoff. "By whom?"

He could no longer see her. His eyes were dimming, and her silhouette had melted and run into the other shadows. "But you know," said her voice, somewhere close at hand. "By Iyone Safin. I must have words with her. In the meantime, I could leave you to suffer, but I won't."

Iyone, he thought; *Iyone*, that walking pestilence, of all bloody goddamned people to succumb to. But then something cold slid between his ribs, and his breath faltered, and he stopped thinking altogether.

REPRISE: SPRING 1531

Savonn was kept waiting a full week. His rounds of the taverns and dance halls proved fruitless, and his spy network of chatty buskers informed him that only servants had entered or left the consulate since his visit. Either Red travelled exclusively by secret passage, or did not leave the house for days on end. Going by what Savonn had seen of him, neither was unlikely.

Then he returned late one night to the room he was renting in a traveller's hostel, and found a single white jonquil on his pillow.

He retraced his steps. The hostel was a shambling one-storey lodge, built around a rose garden with a maze of hedgerows and a stone fountain tinkling in the midst. The other residents—merchants and craftsmen for the most part, some Pierosi, most from the Northlands—must have been asleep by now. But he knew he was not alone. He waited in the doorway, moths and fireflies flitting about his head, until at last the shadows stirred and parted and one of them came to him.

"I expected you sooner," he said.

Red was cloaked and hooded, a lute in one hand, a bouquet of jonquils in the other. A clever guise. If anyone saw him skulking on the grounds, he would have looked nothing more than a moonstruck lover come to play a serenade at his beloved's window. "I was—tidying up," he said. "A lot of things went missing from the consulate after your visit."

Savonn beamed. "Truly? How unfortunate."

Red's mouth twitched. Tonight he smelled of wine and fruit and flowers: good things, sweet things. "Without a doubt," he said, "you are a terror among thieves. Now I will exact payment, with interest. Tell me who you are thieving for."

He went right to business. Savonn liked that. "You know I belong to Betronett. You've seen me with my patrol."

"Harmless men." Red wrinkled up his nose, as if *harmless* was the worst thing a person could be. "They are soldiers, not spies. People like them do not hire thieves."

Behind that masterpiece of a face lay an even more admirable mind. Savonn should not have been pleased, but he was. "I thought you were here to play me a song on that lute."

"I might, if you talk."

"You won't be in the mood for music once I do."

Red continued to eye him. He would not be side-stepped. *Hit fast, hit hard*, thought Savonn. If he was known to be a thief and a sneak, the most devious thing he could do was tell the truth. "Very well," he said. "It seems you have come here looking for a fight, so I shall oblige you. I work for Kedris Andalle."

He could have said Merrott, or Rendell, or the Council. But he did not play for low stakes. The playful spark went out of Red's eyes. "The Governor of Cassarah?"

Of course he recognised the name. In Sarei, the sound of it alone must have been like the crack of a whip. Savonn shrugged. "Do you know any other Andalles?"

Red took a step forward, crowding him against the door-post. "You are lying."

It would be hilarious if, the one time Savonn told the truth, no one believed him. "That is a thing I do on occasion, yes."

"What does he want?"

Red's hood had fallen back, spilling tendrils of bright hair that flamed in the lamplight coming through the open door. Savonn took his time admiring this new spectacle. He had the upper hand now. But whether it was an advantage over Red, or Kedris, he was not sure. "How should I know? What men like him always want, I suppose. The world."

He had meant to sound bored, not bitter. Red was more than subtle enough to know the difference. A look of surprise crossed his face. "He has some hold on you?"

In his voice, Savonn heard an echo of his own bitterness. Perhaps Red knew a thing or two about Kedris; or, more generally, about kings and pawns, check and checkmate. "If you choose to put it that way," said Savonn. "Am I still lying?"

"Perhaps not." Red had dropped all pretense of menace, and now looked more preoccupied than anything else. "But still... Hold these for me. I need a hand free."

He thrust the bouquet of jonquils into Savonn's arms, and in the same movement drew his knife.

Savonn stood still, unalarmed. The blade was cool and gentle on his throat, so light a touch it tickled. The jonquils wafted up a sharp springy fragrance. He did not shiver. "His lordship cannot fault you for divulging secrets if you are robbed at knifepoint, can he?" asked Red. "Show me around."

Savonn had six of his own blades concealed on his person, eight ways he could have twisted out of reach and gotten free. He did not want to get free, and Red knew it. "My jewels or my virtue?"

"If that was all I wanted," said Red, "I would not have to use a knife."

He was smiling one of his crooked smiles. Savonn found himself grinning back. He was prepared for this. "Come in, then."

He led the way into the room. "What's this?" asked Red. "The Lord Governor keeps his thieving magpie in such squalour?"

The rented room was furnished with only the bare essentials, but there was nothing squalid about it. One supposed Red was used to the luxury of the consulate. Still holding the knife to Savonn's throat, he sifted through the papers on the desk. This was a curated display, full of nothing but enticing trivialities. A letter from Iyone, the broken wax seal still recognisable as the Safin sunburst. An old dispatch from Merrott, mentioning a few merchants the Lord Governor wanted Savonn to watch. And of course, Red's own emerald pendant on its fine gold chain, enthroned in a place of honour under the table lamp.

Red's expression was inscrutable. "You did not have to steal my jewellery to make me come to you."

"What can I say? Thieving's a habit."

"I see that." Red picked up Merrott's dispatch, put it down again. "What do I care for an old soldier's letters? This is boring. Surely that rat-scourge in Cassarah speaks to you directly."

A better son would have been angry, and defended his father's honour. But there was no worse son than Savonn, and so he only raised a single brow. "Do not forget," he said, "we are trading secrets only because I need a way to obtain what my—employer—wants. I am not giving you his letters."

"Almighty gods, no," said Red. "I would not go near anything of his with a plague-doctor's mask."

He looked so offended that Savonn laughed. Perhaps that was his first treason. Certainly Red did not see it coming—he bit his lip in thought, and looked down at Savonn with softer eyes. "I will ask another price," he said. "This dispatch from the Bitten Hill is months out of date. There must be newer ones."

The knife was slipping from Savonn's throat. Red was forcing nothing on him but the atrocity of choice. He could not know that all Savonn's choices had already been stripped away: by Kedris, who wanted the world; by Hiraen, who would die if he did not get it. One looked for gentleness from one's father, cruelty from one's foes. There were no instructions for what to do when things were reversed.

Savonn leaned into Red, chasing the blade, testing the bounds of its protection. "There are plenty of dispatches," he said. "But your sloppy knifework will get you nowhere."

Red hesitated. With a barber-surgeon's care, he pressed the knife back to Savonn's carotid. "I shall throw in a bribe of my own. The Marshal's lieutenant is calling at the consulate next week to discuss a number of important issues. If you bring me the dispatches, I will be—shall we say, oblivious to anyone listening on the roof."

No doubt the meeting would be scripted for Savonn's benefit, full of misdirection and lies. Still, he might learn something interesting, worth the small price of Merrott's tedious missives. "Only on the roof?"

Red sighed. "If I invited you inside, sweet bird, my house would be picked bare. But—"

"But?"

The emerald pendant glittered in the lamplight. They stood side by side, like soldiers in a phalanx facing down a common foe. Perhaps that was what they were. Perhaps Red, too, had lost the opportunity for choice long ago. "But," said Red, smiling once more, "I may join you up there for a few drinks after the lieutenant has gone."

If a tree fell with no one to hear, it made no sound. If there was a blade at his throat, he was not a traitor. Savonn inhaled, and counted his heartbeats, and exhaled.

"Very well," he said. "I shall be there."

Red ran a thumb over the knife-hilt, apparently lost in thought, his lashes shadowing his eyes. Then he lowered the blade. *No*, Savonn thought, *put it back*, but before he had time to feel bereft of its loss, Red reached up and touched his fingers to the place on his neck where the knife had been.

It was a long time since anyone had touched Savonn, except in anger. His stone-sharpened senses were starving. He could feel the scrape of dry skin on his throat, count every callus on Red's fingertips. The blade gleamed between them like a sliver of moon. Red's eyes were at once full of declarations and impossible to read, a treatise in a language Savonn had not yet learnt. He wanted to know it; he wanted Red to teach it to him, whatever the cost.

Moths beat at the window. A cricket whirred. The fountain in the garden whispered to itself, oblivious to what was transpiring, as Red leaned down and brushed his lips over Savonn's cheek.

It was a ghost of a kiss, soft and soundless. Red drew away almost at once. His eyes were wide, as if he had surprised himself; as if he had come up against a puzzle he could not solve, and was fascinated.

Savonn pushed aside the mad instinct to seize Red and drag him back in for a proper searing kiss. If he was going to fall, it would be a controlled fall. Red deserved nothing short of cold-blooded premeditation. He said only, "Do I frighten you?"

"You terrify me," said Red.

He sheathed his blade and stepped back from Savonn. Quiet, like a reverence: "Good night, my thief."

Savonn watched him go. His cheek tingled where Red's mouth had been, and his pulse thrummed a bass note deep in his bones. Long after his serenader had vanished, he stayed by the open door, looking out into the garden.

He was still holding the jonquils, but the emerald pendant was gone.

CHAPTER 5

"Murdered," said Oriane. "In his own home."

She was in the Safin manor, which in recent days she had come to think of as a den of snakes. It was not how she had envisioned spending her post-breakfast hour, but there she was, sitting in an armchair in the girl Iyone's room. "They had to break his door down. He said he wasn't to be disturbed, but his household knew he never slept so late. I saw the—the body myself."

The girl and her mother exchanged glances. Aretel was pale except for two spots of high colour over her cheekbones, her hands twisted in her lap. Iyone, on the other hand, looked as if Oriane had ridden across three districts at eight in the morning merely to comment on the weather: tired but tranquil, curled on the window-seat with a thick book open on her knees. "Oh? How?"

"Two throwing daggers, and a blade to the heart," said Oriane. "The killer knew their business. No locks or windows broken, nothing out of place. Then again, the gallant fool sent away his whole household, so…"

She was too old for this. Until Kedris had gone and died, she had been planning to retire that summer, and to hell with it if her son and daughter tore the city apart squabbling over her Council seat. Now she was not so sure. "So no one knows who did it?" Iyone asked.

By all the gods, she really knew nothing. "Everyone knows," said Oriane. "Listen to the talk among your guards, for heaven's sake. There was a signature, same as all the other murders. A garland of black roses stuck under his window."

"Josit came back?" asked Aretel.

Iyone's shoulders rose and fell. There was more tension in them than her face betrayed. Perhaps she was not imperturbable after all, when it came to Josit Ansa. "One of her hirelings, more likely," said Oriane. "No use questioning her servants. She's like an empress to them, they'd never talk."

"That wasn't what you were saying yesterday," said Iyone, "when you were interrogating the Empath."

Looking back, it was funny how Willon had once been so alarmed by Savonn Silvertongue. At his core, the boy was just a colourful nuisance. The girl was much worse. Aretel said, "*Iyone—*"

"No," said Oriane. "Let her speak." She leaned forward, propping her chin on her interlaced fingers. If Iyone Safin thought she knew something they didn't, Oriane wanted to know it too. "That's what I came for. Go on. Tell us all you know about Josit."

If you don't want to hang in her place, she could have added. But Iyone needed no further prompting. She crossed her legs, laying her book aside. "First," she said, "you'd have to forget everything the Empath said. He knows nothing about her. He probably fed you a handful of equivocal insinuations, hints about secret meetings in Josit's parlour, and poor Lord Willon filled in the gaps himself."

Oriane was, like Iyone, a thinking woman, and had already discounted most of what the Empath had said about Josit. "But she did own to the murders. Where is she now?"

"I don't know. All I did was secure leverage against her. The idea was that she would confess and I would help her flee the city." Iyone shrugged. "It seemed only fair. Why should she be executed for her false crimes when she could be exiled for her real ones?"

"And Willon?" said Oriane. Mother Above, she hadn't thought she had it in her to miss him until he was gone. "Did he deserve to die?"

"My lady," said Iyone, "I do not dabble in moral philosophy. I would have come clean about the Thorn long ago if I thought the Council would take me seriously. As it was, I could only deal with her myself. Are you still making the Empath testify against Savonn?"

Oriane paused, wrong-footed by the change of subject. "Of course."

The Empath had been equivocal about Josit, but not Savonn. Everything he'd had to say about the Silvertongue had the ring of truth. "You'll need this, then," said Iyone.

She swung down from the window-seat. As if drawn by magnetite, Oriane found herself turning to keep the girl in her line of sight as she crossed to the chest of drawers and lifted out a narrow cedarwood box. Gingerly, Oriane took it from her. "What's this?"

Aretel had turned her face away, as though the box were too painful to look at. "We found it last night," said Iyone. "Don't worry, it's not poisonous. Not in the usual sense."

Something awful was probably going to leap out at Oriane as soon as she opened the box. Against her better judgement, she did.

There was no howling manifestation. The box contained only papers. Oriane did not know much Saraian, but she did not have to read them to recognise them for what they were. It was evident from the perfume, the sketches and sheet music, the worshipful way in which the papers had been stored. It was decades since anyone had written letters like these to Oriane. "These are from the Empath?"

Iyone nodded. "Any scribe can make a translation, but it doesn't matter what they say. They'll prove that he and Savonn knew each other. That should corroborate whatever he told you."

Oriane frowned. Her suspicions did not abate. If anything, they compounded. "Savonn was your friend."

"So was Josit," said Iyone. "I'm finished with them both. The Council can no longer afford to be divided. I'm sure you take my meaning."

Oriane was incredulous. "*You're* telling me what the Council needs?"

Aretel kneaded her brows. Not for the first time that week, Oriane felt sorry for her. "You haven't heard the half of it, my lady," said Iyone. "I could, for instance, discourse at length on cannon and gunpowder and the Marshal's movements, but there's no use if you don't trust me."

Oriane thumped the box shut. "We'd best get this clear," she said. "Josit was a snake on the Council long before she killed anyone, and you are just like her. I've seen what the two of you are capable of doing, to us and to each other. So what if your counsel is sound? No one would trust you farther than they could bowl you uphill."

"That's wise," said Iyone. "I don't presume on your trust. All I need is your good faith. You hold mine in your hands."

Oriane could still remember when Kedris Andalle had been appointed a councillor, the penniless heir of paupers and criminals, with a surname even a tramp would have been loath to wear. He had gone from street urchin to errand boy to Council scribe and then, when her uncle Raedon had seen the gold inside that reptilian brain and made him one of them, kept on rising. None of them ever had cause to regret it. Maps had been redrawn in Kedris's time, battles won, miles of riverside territory regained.

Still, the man had unsettled Oriane. So did Iyone, for much the same reasons.

But Kedris was gone now. And Oriane had been on the Council long enough to know that when a tree was felled, the ivy on it would have to find another wall or trunk on which to grow, or else die. That was what power came down to when you looked past the smoke and curtains: a matter of survival, plain and simple.

"All right," she said. "I take your meaning. I trust your intentions, if not your methods. I just need time, after—after all this. Give me a day."

Iyone let out a breath. She was untried, still unsure of herself. Perhaps there was hope yet. "And then what?" asked Aretel.

"And then we convene," said Oriane. "We serve justice to the Empath and the Silvertongue. We speak no more of Josit. And we fight this war."

There was so much to do. The search parties had to be recalled. She would probably have to plan Willon's funeral on top of everything else. "They say the Marshal's returned to Daliss, and the Queen's forces are mustering," she added, half to herself. "I'll need to summon Yannick. There must be an Efren on the Council. Better him than one of those wretched boys. Aretel, you'll have to help me. It's absurd me being the only one left."

They would have to elect a new Governor. It would not be Lucien, who'd had the chance to put himself forward after Kedris's death and had not. Josit was gone. Yannick was a joke, if an amiable one, and Oriane—gods knew, if she took the post, she would not see retirement before she was a hundred and ten.

"We'll discuss it tomorrow," said Aretel, squeezing Oriane's arm. "You'd best get some rest, my dear."

Oriane got up. She had the sensation of having fought a long and indecisive battle. The cedarwood box was still in her hands. She gazed at it, and then at Iyone, feeling she would sleep easier that night for having had the last word. "By the way, good faith means not doing anything drastic without consulting me. One sign that you're plotting something behind my back, and you can damned well go back into house arrest. Good-day to you both."

She did not wait to be shown out. Standing on a precipice with the world unfurling below, one did not trouble with niceties. Until a few months ago, she had thought her work done, herself on a final stroll in a peaceful twilight. But it was not so. She had seen too much of the world, and would see more yet.

Oriane Sydell rode home, and went about her affairs, and wished, at the back of her mind, that she were young again.

* * *

Iyone had attained a level of fatigue so profound she might have been sleepwalking. She sat in a stupor for a few minutes, listening to Oriane leaving—leaving, with Savonn's letters in her hands—until Aretel stirred and said, "There was news from the Bitten Hill this morning."

It took a moment for the words to sink in. "Be still," said Aretel, when Iyone looked up sharply. "It's good news. Your brother is alive."

"Which brother?"

Her mother's mouth was a forbidding line. "Do try to remember that you have only the one brother, even if you have as little in common with him as a leopard with a house cat. Hiraen has rejoined his company. What took him so long, no one knows. He's on his way home. I presume your father will soon follow."

Iyone registered a dim relief. Dear, sweet Hiraen. He had truly made a mess of things. The least he could do was be alive. "And Savonn is still dead?"

"So it seems," said Aretel. "Excuse me if I don't mourn."

But the Empath had said Savonn was alive. Iyone had sold a living man's secrets to the Council. And Hiraen, who had killed a friend for those same secrets—Hiraen, too, had survived, and would soon find out what she had done.

Aretel went to the window and threw it open, pressing a handkerchief to her face. She had mastered the skill of weeping soundlessly. Iyone had not, and therefore cried as little as possible. "Mother—"

What could she say? It was done. Willon was dead. Shandei had wanted to kill him, but Josit had spared her that. Josit, who should have been leading the fight against her sister Marguerit, and yet was gone, lost to Iyone forever. She was as alone as she had ever been.

"You know why I had to do it," she said. "Josit had to be stopped. So did Willon. The most efficient way was to have them get rid of each other." She dragged the back of her hand across her eyes. "It was—a terribly circuitous plan. With many casualties. No doubt you could have come up with something better."

To Iyone's surprise, her mother's tear-streaked face held no censure, only astonishment. "Oh, idiot girl," said Aretel. "If you think I wouldn't have done the same, you're as foolish as all of them together."

CHAPTER 6

Shandei came home from killing a man, and tried to do some gardening.

It should have been restful work. The harvest from her herb garden was in, the Council's tithe paid. Now it was time to sow the winter herbs in the indoor pots—chives and chamomile, basil and rosemary, garlic and beans. With the invasion looming, food from private gardens was more important than ever, and to qualify for the annual stipend one had to have at least a few seedlings when the inspector came round. But while the soil was cool and reassuring between her fingers, her heart was not in it, and by noon she had abandoned her pots to drift from tavern to tavern, soaking up the day's news.

It was chaos. Josit was the Thorn. Josit had killed Lord Willon. Josit had fled. Iyone Safin had either driven her out or helped her escape, no one knew which. No, some said, of course she hadn't *helped* her. Iyone herself had been attacked by the Thorn last summer, or had you forgotten? All she had done was urge Willon to moderation, but everyone knew what a temper his lordship had. The Council had tried to lock her up, but seeing as she was half the Council at this point they'd had to let her out again.

From Betronett, also, a mixed bag of good and bad. There was no mention of Emaris. Hiraen was alive, and on his way home—their first proper war hero since Kedris, wasn't it exciting? It almost made up for Savonn Silvertongue getting himself killed at Onaressi. He had it coming, of course. Someone must have lost their patience with him and struck his head off at last. It was too bad: they had all counted on him to liven up the war, which promised to be long and tedious. There was no body. The Saraians burned their dead.

"I wonder who did for him," said the barmaid of the Ice Prince, a tavern popular with theatre folk. She leaned over the counter, sloshing another round of ale into Shandei's glass. "Bet you a drochon it was the Marshal. Stodgy old fellow, just the type to let our Savonn get to him."

Shandei said nothing, her hands furled tight around the stem of her glass. She must have washed them a dozen times this morning. Still she fancied she could smell Willon's blood under her nails, stronger than the garlic she had been planting. She had not murdered him, not really—just sent him on his way, the least she could do—but it would have made no difference to the Efrens if they'd caught her. It was Vesmer all over again, except this time she knew who had beaten her to the kill.

"Maybe," said the girl beside her, a button-nosed brunette with the look of a stagehand. "But I'd lay good money on the Empath. Didn't you hear how he killed all those guards with the Silvertongue's knives? I wonder how he got hold of them, don't you?"

"They're putting Savonn on trial," a young man piped up. "Before the Council, not just a magistrate. They're saying he had dealings with the Empath."

"Of course they had dealings," said the brunette. "Have you *seen* the man? I'd have dealings with him, too."

General laughter. Shandei buried her nose in her glass. She had plenty of gossip of her own to share, if she wanted—she had, after all, met the Empath at Lord Kedris's funeral, and witnessed his arrest first-hand. But he had become a matter of no small chagrin to her. After their first meeting she had sorted him into the large and nebulous group of people she called friends, no different from Linn or Daine or the men in her father's patrol she used to spar with. But then he had turned out to be a Saraian spy, and slaughtered his way through a troop of Efren guards before her eyes. They had tortured him for a full night. *Anything,* he'd said, *for my sweet, lying lover.*

No one liked to be lied to, after all.

From the start, Iyone had been set on preventing her from killing Lord Willon. And for good reason: with his dying breath, he had denied murdering Shandei's father. But how could Iyone have known that? Unless she knew who had really killed him?

Shandei had stopped listening to the chatter. It was hard to care about rumours of spies and treason when there was another betrayal festering closer to home.

She drained her glass, slid the barmaid a few coppers, and got up. She had to speak to Iyone, even if she would not like what she heard. It was much more tempting to order another ale and drink herself into a stupor, but Rendell had raised her to be brave.

She had to know.

* * *

The Safin manor was in a state of disarray. The lawn was muddy and trampled, as if an army had just marched through; and some, though not all, of the broad bay windows were curtained in black. The doorman knew Shandei's name without being told. He informed her that the Lady Iyone was working outside today, and led her down a gold-pillared colonnade between greenhouses and flowerbeds, under delicate balconies and white marble walls, to the back of the property.

She half expected to find Iyone gardening, as she herself had been. Instead, the daughter of the Safins was writing at a wooden table in a shady patio among beds of blooming camellias, overlooking a rocky pool full of flashing blue-green fish. She was not dressed in mourning. Except for the long roll of vellum spread across the table, packed with neat sections of writing, it could have been a scene from an old painting, perfect in its tranquility: the vivid pink flowers, the quiet pool, the proud-chinned woman in the midst.

Shandei almost wished it was so. Perfection was harmless; it lived in picture-frames and could not let you down, or break your heart.

"Iyone," she said.

Iyone looked up. The quill froze on its way to the ink pot. "Oh. It's you."

The look on her face could not be fathomed. Shock, perhaps, and something that made the lines of concentration around her eyes smooth over and vanish. She flipped the sheet of vellum over so it lay face down. "It's good to see you."

It had been a couple months since their last meeting. It felt like longer. Iyone's lips were chapped from the cold air, her eyes unfocused, as if she had just come from a dark room into sudden daylight. She would never be thin, but she had lost weight, the dips and hollows of her face laid out in sharp relief. It made her look pinched and savage. Deadly.

It was just the war, Shandei thought. It didn't have to mean a thing. War did this to everyone.

"I heard the news," she said. Platitudes, polite and painless. Iyone was not a stranger, but she was not a friend, either. She was more than that, and less. "I thought to see how you were doing."

She might have smiled, or not. Thought always came to a shuddering halt when she was confronted with Iyone, and it was hard to be sure what her face was doing, or any of her limbs. "I brought you a gift," she added.

It was a scarf, knitted in the long dull days at the Terinean convent from the finest crimson wool she could afford. The pattern was of entwined roses and vines, which she thought Iyone's odd sense of humour might enjoy. At first Iyone just stared, as if she had never in her life been presented with such a thing. Then her face assembled, from scratch, the rudiments of a smile. "Put it on for me?"

An animal would have had better sense. Even a roach knew to scuttle to safety when one lit the lamps. But Shandei had not been born a prey creature, a hare or a deer; she had no idea what to do with danger except run headlong into it. "If you like."

She had forgotten her gloves. Her hands were clumsy with cold and other things, and her knot did not hold until Iyone helped pin down one end of the scarf. Their fingers were a hair's width from touching, and the top of Iyone's dark head would have fit comfortably against Shandei's chest if she leaned back. *Forget what you came for*, Shandei thought. *Forget Willon and Josit and your father. There is only her.*

So said one moth to the other, as they peered into the lamp.

The thought broke the enchantment. Abruptly, she dropped her hands to her sides and stepped back. "Tell me. How did Willon die?"

Iyone paused. Her hand lingered on the end of the scarf, over the soft swell of her breast. "Old men have accidents," she said. "Old men with enemies have violent accidents. Why don't you sit down."

It was not a question. Shandei did not sit. "Enemies like me?"

"Like Josit and me," said Iyone.

Shandei stared at her for a few moments before she elaborated. "Willon's judgement was compromised. Placed where he was, he could have cost us the war. We didn't kill him for you. His blood is not on your conscience."

She might have meant it. In the gentle winter light, filtered through the ever-present shroud of mist, her irises were a deep grey laced with webbings of lighter brown. A voice to lead armies, a gaze to turn ice to steam. Small wonder Shandei had fallen hard, too early in their acquaintance. Up till now she had regretted nothing.

She said, "Who killed my father?"

Iyone stood up. She was taller than Shandei, a fact that had never seemed important before. Her quill was blotting ink all over the table. "Were you there? When Willon died?"

Shandei did not have to answer. Not when Iyone was looking straight through her, as if she were only a window-pane behind which something more important was happening. "You were, weren't you? His guards were away. You saw your chance. But Josit—"

"Zarin beat me to it," said Shandei. "I know you ordered it, or Josit did. Innocent people keep dying around me. Maybe I should have taken vows and stayed in the goddamn convent." Her voice had risen, loud enough to be overheard. She did not care. "Willon didn't murder my father. So who did?"

Iyone tugged on the ends of the scarf. "If you're asking me, you know."

"Say it."

"No," said Iyone. "Telling you who would betray one of my brothers, and telling you why would betray the other." Her mouth curled like a whip, rueful and sad. "I've done enough of that for the day."

Shandei snatched up the ink-pot and smashed it on the ground. "*Say it!*"

They both stared at the spreading violet puddle. Shandei imagined the ink seeping through the floorboards into the soil beneath, poisoning the grass, blighting the flowers. She remembered Emaris in the Arena of White Sand the morning after their father died, ready to follow Hiraen and the Silvertongue anywhere they led. There had been tears in his eyes.

He must never be told. It would kill him.

"Secrets are dangerous things," said Iyone. "Your father knew many. You can lance a boil or cut out a tumour, but you can't unknow something. It shouldn't be hard to imagine what happened."

Her voice lost its briskness, only briefly. "Hiraen never wanted to hurt you. He made me promise to look after you, to try and keep you out of it. So I did. At first for his sake, and then for yours. I shan't patronise you by pretending it's made a difference. But you have a brother too. You know what it is to—to protect your family."

Some primal impetus drove Shandei back a step. This—whatever it was that ran in the veins of the Safins and their dead friend—this madness was contagious. If she came too close, she might contract it. Perhaps she already had. She thought of the High Priestess shrieking with laughter from the shadows of the altar. Vesmer and Willon, both dead. Her father's dagger, sheathed at her hip even now. Awaiting the real killer.

"If Emaris had done such a thing," she heard herself say, "I would renounce him, brother or not."

"Then you are a better person than I am," said Iyone. "You will simply have to find someone worthier of you. I—"

She lifted her hands to her face, stared at them as if she could not remember what they were for, and put them down again. "I have a letter to finish, and three cannon to inspect, and a gunpowder merchant to swindle, and after that I am probably going to lie down and weep for several hours, and get up to do it all over again. So if we're done here..."

There was nothing more Shandei wanted to know, nothing else she could imagine saying. She had come to ask a question, and she had her answer. "We are. Goodbye."

She turned away, her shoes crunching on the broken ink-pot. "No," said Iyone suddenly. "That's not what I meant."

Shandei did not care what she meant. She stalked off without looking back, out of the patio and back up the colonnade. Her vision swam, so that the gilded pillars swayed and the half-bare trees reshaped themselves into one many-limbed monster, jeering at her through its waggling branches. When the doorman asked if she was all right, she walked straight past him.

It was over. Quite possibly, it had never even started.

REPRISE: SUMMER 1531

The meeting at the consulate went more or less how Savonn had envisioned: he overheard some unrevelatory conversations with the lieutenant, and then had a far more interesting one with Red on the rooftop after. He also took a fancy to some of the lieutenant's papers, which then had to be paid for in kind, so after that they had another rendezvous in the market square. Then another on the city wall, and again in the garden of the Dome of Stars, and before long Savonn was seeing Red every day.

"You meet your factor very often," said the hostel proprietor, who still thought Savonn an aspiring merchant. His eyebrows formed a suggestive arch. "A lot of buying and selling to do, eh?"

Savonn smiled. "If you only knew."

It was still possible to believe that he had not compromised himself. Red did not even have his true name. Savonn was gleaning plenty about Marguerit's interests in Astorre and the Farfallens, which pleased his father and kept him distracted from Hiraen's failings. Kedris did not have to know that Savonn was giving away as much as he received; that he was now a frequent visitor at the consulate, and often returned at night to find Red in the garden, waiting to have secrets whispered in his ear.

They kissed each other, now, without a knife as chaperone. He was walking the edge of disaster, waiting for it to swallow him whole.

"In the consulate," said Red one night, "they say you are a shapeshifter. Like the magpie demon of old. They think that is how you get in and out unseen."

They were in a clearing on the grassy slope of Lady Fidelity, counting meteors. Savonn had nothing to trade that night. He had invited Red there anyway—meteor storms only happened so many times a year—and Red had shown up, no questions asked. "And what do you say?"

"They do you a disservice," said Red. "You are no shapeshifter, only a mortal man who is too good at what he does. You have no need for devilry."

Savonn looked up, tracing the constellations with his eye. The Lion, the Lyre, the Bear. He and Red spent so much time outdoors, on housetops and in gardens, on mountainsides under the stars, as if what they became when they were together was something that could not be cooped up behind walls. He knew he was good. He had never heard it said aloud, not the way Red was saying it.

"I have been wondering," said Red, "about your patron."

Savonn came back to earth, none too gently. They had not spoken about Kedris since the night Red first came to him in the rose garden. "You doubt me still?"

"Only a fool would not doubt you." It was delivered as a compliment, and so Savonn received it as one. "You loathe the Governor. I can tell. And yet you spy for him."

Savonn had known he would not escape this line of questioning for long. But the Lord Governor had no place in a night like this, when the very air was sweet with bracken and wildflowers: a night for mystery, for enchantment, for dangerous games with a dangerous man. It was brutally cold for late summer, but there was a line of fire all along his arm and down his leg where they were touching Red's side. He had not gone to bed with Red yet. It would be soon. Maybe tonight.

A streak of light arced overhead. "Forty-three," Savonn murmured.

The sky was clearer in the mountains—so clear it could strike a lowlander's heart still, the first time he lifted his eyes to a night embroidered with stars. But Red was not looking up. "You are not the first Cassaran I have met," he said. "You are the first, though, who does not worship him."

Silver flame dashed itself across the sky. "In Cassarah," said Savonn, "they call these Aebria's tears."

"Gods do not weep." Red touched his gloved fingers to Savonn's. "Songbird, what would he do to you if he found out you were betraying him?"

The touch was diabolical, at a juncture like this. Savonn wrenched his hand away and sat up. Clumsy—he ought to know better, he who had made a life out of feigning dispassion. Look behind the curtain of the magic show and you would never believe again. "I suppose he would kill me," he said. "I suppose I would die. One tends to follow from the other. Red, you are missing the meteors."

Red sat up too. His eyes were intent, thoughtful: the eyes of a hunter coursing down a hare. "I see it is not a theoretical question."

It was not. A creature like Kedris could not be fed on secrets alone. Merrott was still alive, years since Hiraen had been asked to kill him and Savonn had gone to do it in his stead. Eventually his father would grow tired of waiting. Like Hiraen, he would lose his utility; and like Hiraen, he would be done away with if not kept alive by a complicated system of plea and barter. There would be no trial for him, no public execution, just a quiet disappearance and an unmarked grave. Red might walk over his bones a dozen times and never know.

"Why do you not leave?" asked Red. "What chains does he have on you?"

It took Savonn a moment to recall that Red did not know. One could not run from family. It was a sickness in the blood. "There is nowhere to go."

The night was ablaze with meteors, but they were no longer counting. "I see," said Red. "I was mistaken. You do worship him."

Savonn tasted bile. There was nothing coy or duplicitous about the statement. It was not rhetorical, engineered to hurt, only an honest observation to which there could be no rebuttal. It was truer than the truth. He could wear all the masks he wanted, and still be nothing more than his father's puppet.

"If we speak of chains," said Savonn, "he has many. There is a good man who will die if I do not do his bidding. But I think you have changed the parameters of the game, and I am no longer playing. Good night."

He rose and set off down the mountainside. Far below, the towers of Astorre glowed silver-gold in the starlight. Grass rustled behind him. "*Etruska*," said Red.

He ought to make Red kill him. He ought to make Red hit him. A good punch, a split lip, a bit of blood to wash them clean. Then this thing between them would be over, and he might be saved. But Red, who moved and stood like a man bred to violence, had never been anything less than gentle with him. "*Etruska*," he said again.

Darling, dear one, my love: it all sounded sweeter in Saraian. Savonn had exhausted his stores of art and artifice. "No," he said, and then, "What."

A meteor flared, illuminating for a split second Red's face and the complex melange of emotions on it. "Of course you must stop playing the game if it hurts you. I only wished to know who was doing the hurting. Me, or Kedris."

Hazel eyes, warm eyes, eyes that looked past Savonn's carefully blank expression to what lay beneath. A threshold had been reached. They both knew it. Savonn could turn his back and walk away, and they never had to see each other again. But if he stayed, the board changed forever. They could not go back to being opponents. They would be on the same side, playing against an enemy that could not be beaten, and the game could no longer be won.

Savonn had never cared much for winning, anyway.

"You are not hurting me," he said. So much for premeditation; so much for thievery. "And I will play to the end, as long as it is with you."

They were so close he could almost feel the coiled tension in Red's body, hear the cogs in that quick mind turning and working to absorb this. He wondered, just for a moment, what answer Red had been expecting; what he would have done if Savonn had turned and left him standing there. If he would have cared enough to pursue.

"If I speak no more of this," said Red at last, "if that name does not pass my lips again—will you not stay, and watch the stars with me?"

The sky flashed: fifty, sixty, Savonn no longer knew. It *would* be tonight, then, that he went to bed with the Saraian consul, while Aebria wept and the stars wheeled overhead like a pack of watchful scavengers. "I might be persuaded."

Red smiled, small and bittersweet. Perhaps he was in chains too, though they did not speak of it. Savonn stepped into the shelter of his arms—open-eyed and willing, so afterwards there could be no excuses—and together they went back to their clearing, and lay down to count the falling stars.

CHAPTER 7

For propriety's sake, the Betronett homecoming was not meant to be a joyous affair. Cassarah was in mourning, the soil just settling over Lord Willon's grave, the windows covered in honour of the city's long-serving, long-suffering councillor. Waiting at the citadel drawbridge to receive the new Captain of Betronett, Iyone, Aretel, Oriane and the just-returned Yannick had covered their hair and gowned themselves in dark silk, and even the onlookers thronging the streets stood in respectful silence.

It lasted all of five minutes.

The murmuring began as soon as the lookouts spotted the banners from the ramparts. It swelled to a rumble, which became a buzz. Then Hiraen Safin, liberator and destroyer of Onaressi, cantered through the Gate of Gold on his splendid grey stallion, cavalry riding four abreast behind him, footsoldiers in polished cuirasses marching in the rear. A tentative cheer went up. Hiraen waved. It grew louder. Someone blew a blast on a trumpet, strident and joyous, and then at last the people abandoned their reticence altogether and began to shout.

Iyone could have been five years old again, lifted over the ramparts in her nanny's arms to see Kedris return victorious from the

Morivant. Certainly she had not witnessed such rejoicing since. The gate wardens wound their horns, and the city guard—deployed to keep order on the roads—crashed their spears on their shields. Three separate troupes of street musicians started playing at once, their drums booming out three quite different beats. Children ran ahead of the banners to scatter flowers on the road: sunflowers, lilies, tulips in vivid Safin orange, so many that the air began to smell like a hothouse. There were, Iyone noted, no roses.

The host reached the broad tiled piazza in front of the citadel. With ceremonial gravity, the portcullis rattled up, and the drawbridge creaked down over the spiked moat. "Tell me again," said Oriane, "that we're not making a mistake."

Iyone beheld the approaching figure of her brother, tall and gallant, his horse stepping prettily over the petal-strewn ground. Hiraen: confidant, protector, murderer. At his side, carrying the sunburst banner, was a big blond cavalryman she almost did not recognise as Emaris, Savonn's former squire. Shandei must be somewhere in the crowd, watching her brother as Iyone was, and feeling the same anxious pride.

There was nothing they could do now that was not a mistake. Obligingly, Iyone said, "We're not."

Hiraen dismounted on the sweeping lawn on the near side of the drawbridge. Iyone was the first to reach him. He had been stony-faced, but at the sight of her he broke into a smile like the sun. There were orange petals stuck in his hair. "Iyone!"

His embrace was as forceful and steadying as ever. She had forgotten what it was like not to have to fight alone. She put her mouth to his ear and yelled, "Did you get my letter?"

"Don't ruin the mood, you savage," he yelled back. "I left some men at Lissein to take care of the first matter. Father will be back soon. I thought he'd best stay at Medrai till we resolve that other thing. Where's Savonn?"

Iyone's stomach lurched. "I thought he was with you," she said, and then the others were upon them, and she had to pull away.

Hiraen embraced their mother, and clasped hands with Oriane and Yannick. "I'm sorry about Lord Willon," he said. His voice was grave and formal now, pitched to carry. The trumpeters had the good grace to fall silent. "Shocking news."

This last was said with a pointed look at Iyone. She ignored it. She, too, could keep her own counsel. "Thank you, Captain," said Yannick. His sojourn in the countryside had done wonders for his health: he had sprouted a few new tufts of hair, and looked only mildly terrified. "You will be glad to know we have captured the Empath. We put off his trial till you got back, thinking you would like to be present."

The Betronett men looked at one another. They would have heard all this already, but it was part of the ceremony, staged for the benefit of the onlookers. "Damn right I do," said Hiraen. "Let's have the trial now. I can't wait to hang him."

"Wait," said Aretel. She glanced at Oriane. "There's one more thing."

And there it was, the culmination of hours of frantic planning. "I'm sure you notice how few we are, Lord Safin," said Oriane. "What with Willon dead, and the Council leaderless since Kedris's passing..."

Hiraen looked appropriately grave. "I act as Governor these days," Oriane went on. "But that's not enough. We need a skilled general, a High Commander who will marshal our forces and lead us against the Queen of Sarei."

The crowd rustled. Everyone knew what this meant. A High Commander was elected only in wartime. Kedris had held the title last, but for eighteen years it had only been a nominal honour, the office itself defunct. The need to fill it again was obvious, as was the choice of candidate. Oriane had been rapidly persuaded once Iyone laid out the facts. She was no field commander; none of them were, except maybe Lord Lucien, who was still away. With their luck, one of Willon's surviving sons would end up in command if they did not act fast, and that, Oriane agreed, would be the end of them.

Hiraen said nothing. His gaze, a little accusatory, had come to rest on Iyone again. "On behalf of the Council," said Oriane, "I offer you that baton. Your courage is unsurpassed, and dozens of our best men owe you their lives. No one could ask for a better commander."

Hiraen's mouth twisted in what Iyone took, at first, for a grimace of loathing. It would truly be a joke for the ages if she had outwitted Josit, outlived Willon, and outmanoeuvred Oriane only to be thwarted at this last juncture by her own brother. Then she took in the stiff set of his jaw, and realised he was struggling not to burst out laughing.

"What an honour," he said. He even managed to sound surprised, as she had instructed in her forewarning letter. "An honour I do, in fact, accept."

The cheering went on for a long time. It spread from the front ranks of Hiraen's troops to the back, across the lawn, and from there to the far side of the drawbridge. The ground shook with it, and the trumpets renewed their blaring, almost in time with the drums. Emaris was gazing at Hiraen with raw pride shining in his eyes, so sincere it was painful to see. Iyone could not look at him.

"Of course," said Yannick, when they could all hear one another again, "you need the blessing of the High Priestess. It is a, a tradition, shall we say. We will take you to the Temple later. But first—"

"First, the Empath's trial," said Hiraen, High Commander of Cassarah. He looked round, his gaze sweeping over the sentries on the bridge, the crowd on the citadel battlements. Iyone knew what he was looking for, but could not tell if he found it. "Or the Silvertongue's, I suppose, as there doesn't seem to be a difference... Very well, sir. Lead on."

* * *

It was a public trial. And so, as with plays, executions, and all such productions, there was only one place it could be held. The Arena of White Sand, Cassarah's duelling ring turned theatre.

The Empath had a full house. The whole city had turned up: the noble households filling the prime seats at the bottom, the commoners in the upper circles, where it was standing room only. The Betronett corps, as the High Commander's own men, had the place of highest honour in the first two rows. Oriane presided from a long table at centerstage with Yannick, Hiraen, and Iyone. Aretel had declined any part in the matter.

"It's all," said Hiraen under his breath. "It's all very..."

Iyone knew what he meant. The Arena was an entirely different place when one was looking up instead of down, surrounded by the audience on all sides. And still her gaze kept landing on the pair of blond heads in the first row, one watching them hungrily, the other averted. "Very Savonn?"

"Yes. That."

A horn blew, calling for silence. Movement stirred at the top of the Arena. As everyone turned to look, a double file of guards issued down the steps through the stone bowl of the theatre, their spears and scabbards winking in the sun. They reached the stage, saluted the Council, and fanned out in a half-circle to reveal the man in their midst.

The buzzing voices, which had reluctantly attenuated, reached a sharp crescendo.

One could not be in the same room as the Empath and not stare. Everything about him demanded attention. He was still manacled, but his gaolers had cleaned him up and made him presentable for the Council—his jaw was closely shaven, his clothes changed, his long hair washed and combed to tumble in lazy copper waves against the white linen of his shirt. It drew the eye to the proud line of his neck, the mocking tilt of his head. Kings had worn their crowns with less hauteur than this man his shackles.

"Doesn't look like he's been racked, does he?" Iyone murmured.

"Lots of things don't leave marks," said Hiraen. His face was stony again. "You didn't see him when he was well."

Yannick was whispering at the other end of the table. "I meant to tell you, Oriane, there was a missive from Daliss this morning. The Queen is offering a princely sum for the prisoner's safe return."

They all looked over. Oriane gave a joyless laugh. "Of course she did. How much?"

"We are at war, sir," said Iyone, before Yannick could answer. "I should hope no amount of gold would persuade us to return Marguerit her finest weapon. Shall we begin?"

Yannick coughed, and cleared his throat. "Yes, yes. Of course."

Oriane sighed. She raised her voice to address the Empath. "Identify yourself."

Every word spoken on stage was amplified tenfold. Hungry for sound, the Arena drank it in and flung it back from the high stone walls, so even the rattle of the Empath's chains carried loud and clear. The prisoner surveyed the half of the audience he could see, and then his prosecutors, his gaze more supercilious than insolent. It flicked over Yannick, dismissive; slid more slowly over Oriane; narrowed at Hiraen, whom he must have recognised; and came to rest on Iyone. It was to her that he addressed his response. "If it please you."

His accent sharpened the consonants to stakes. "I am a priest to the Nameless Father of the Sanctuary. Some call me the Empath. Others have used different names. But Dervain Teraille was the name I bore when the god found me, and it is the one I prefer."

He looked into the audience again. All sorts of people had turned out to see what the Saraian spy had to say about their Lord Silvertongue. Fur merchants in their finest winter wools. Rainbow-fingered dyers. Blacksmiths with arms like tree trunks. Even a group of well-dressed people who, judging by the colour and quantity of their facial hair, must have been from the circus. Farther up, the faces shrunk to little dots. Iyone saw no one of interest. Judging by the Empath's bored expression, neither did he.

The trial was proceeding. "You claim to read hearts?" Yannick asked.

The chains rattled, like a tittering laugh. "Oh, no, my lord," said Dervain. "How the word misleads. *Read.* So gentle. So pleasant. As though my gift were merely a way to pass the time..."

"Answer the question," said Oriane.

"Yes, ladyship," he said. "Say rather that hearts make themselves known to me with much noise and violence, whether I wish it or not. It is difficult to understand, I know. Allow me to show you..."

The audience was spellbound. Cold with foreboding, Iyone leaned over to hiss at Oriane. "*Stop him.*"

It was too late. "You are all relieved, are you not," said the Empath, "that this man Willon is dead? One must not be misled by your little mourning curtains. My lord Yannick looks forward to his peaceful retirement. So does Lady Oriane, and yet—"

Oriane gestured. The guards, dazed, jumped to attention and brandished their spears. Dervain bestowed on them an indulgent smile. "And yet," he went on, "she goes around in some envy of Lady Iyone... Why, I wonder? And my lord Hiraen, high and pulchritudinous—dear me, I love the Falwynian language—I cannot tell who it is you loathe more, me or yourself."

Hiraen's stare was a compendium of insults. Unfazed, the Empath continued. "Why so nervous, Lady Iyone? Perhaps you are afraid I will say something incriminating?"

Cold prickles of sweat broke out along Iyone's spine. She spoke quickly, to cut him off. "A clever party trick. No wonder you think so highly of yourself. After all, who is to prove you wrong?"

Dervain inclined his head to her. "It is," he said, "a most tiresome gift."

Oriane did not change the subject so much as wrench it round by the horns. "You were caught visiting the house of Josit Ansa, who—I might add—has confessed to a great deal of murder and treason since the last time we spoke. I will ask you again. Why were you there?"

Dervain looked pained. "You did not believe me the first fourteen times you asked. I was only paying my respects on behalf of a mutual friend."

"You mean Savonn Silvertongue," said Yannick.

"Him."

Murmurs. Looking around the Arena again, Iyone spotted a door at the bottom of the theatre carved with a scowling unicorn head. Gathered there was a group of young people she had not noticed before. Their roughspun shirts were smeared with paint and dirt, as if they had just been called away from some messy menial task. One of them looked familiar: a tiny brunette of a stagehand Iyone used to know, though it took her a while to be sure, having been rather less acquainted with her face than the rest of her. Still no Savonn.

Shandei caught Iyone's eye from the front row. They both looked away at once, a recoil so sharp it could only be called a flinch. Hiraen gave them a curious look.

"Yes, you said you knew the Silvertongue," said Oriane. "Repeatedly. So you must recognise these papers."

Movement in the wings, as a Sydell servant came up bearing a box on a silver tray. Something twinged in the vicinity of Iyone's heart. She felt it the instant Hiraen recognised the box: he went rigid beside her, his breath hitching. "Is that—? Did you?"

It was like witnessing a terrible accident, unable either to help or look away. "I couldn't save him," Iyone whispered. "It was either give him up or go down with him. If he's still anything like the boy we grew up with, it's what he would want."

Hiraen did not speak, but the look on his face was answer enough. The servant opened the cedarwood box and lifted out the letters. "These," said Oriane, for the benefit of the audience, "were discovered among the Silvertongue's personal effects. Did you write them?"

"I did," said Dervain. His complacent half-smile had slipped from his lips. "What am I on trial for? I forget. If it is maudlin sentiment, condemn me now."

"Did you kill him?" yelled someone behind Iyone.

A hushed pause. Oriane said, "You may answer that."

The smile returned, sharper than before. "I am afraid not. I was not even at Onaressi when he disappeared—being, at the time, quite busy retreating from the valiant Lucien Safin. Lord Hiraen can vouch for me. He was there, you see, having taken up residence in a stable."

"In that case," said Iyone, before Hiraen could start an argument, "how is Savonn purported to have died?"

Dervain's eyes gleamed with marmoset mischief. It was plain to Iyone what the Governor's ungovernable son had seen in him. Savonn had never been drawn to frippery—it was strength he admired, both of the body and the mind, and the danger it brought. "I have no idea. I thought the thieving magpie had flown away. Why, *I* let him go."

"But it was your colleague Isemain who captured him," said Yannick. Unlike Oriane, he had not been present for the first interrogations in the dungeon, and so looked genuinely baffled. "Why would you do that?"

Dervain Teraille laughed. "What a question! My lord, surely even a priest must be permitted some few sentiments. Savonn Silvertongue is my lover."

There was a long, stunned silence. Then the deluge broke.

Everybody began to talk at once. Half the Betronett corps leapt to their feet, shouting. "Liar!" someone screamed. "Well *done*," someone else called, and a few parties began to applaud. A burst of giggles erupted from the stagehands by the unicorn door, and was shushed in a flutter of wrists. But Shandei and Emaris were silent and flat-mouthed. So was Aretel.

"Quiet!" Oriane called, banging her fist on the table. "Order!" And then, "Shut the hell up!"

The last one worked. The commotion subsided, though the Arena continued to echo, and the stagehands were still shaking with soundless giggles. Here and there, money seemed to be changing hands. There was the Silvertongue for you. You looked to him for excitement, and he always delivered, even from beyond the grave. You only felt let down if you had expected more from him than a good show.

There, thought Iyone, was where she and Hiraen had erred.

"We were not aware," said Yannick, wheezing, "of such a development. When did you meet?"

Dervain had gone pale, as though the sudden tumult had pained him. He shifted in his irons. "You run into all sorts in Astorre. I represented the Queen's interests there for some years."

"You, a slave?" asked Oriane.

"Me, a slave," said Dervain. "I am, you see—how shall I put it?—good at people. Even pretty boys who burgle your house and steal your jewels."

Yannick rubbed the bridge of his nose. "You must be a terrible priest. What was your, ah, arrangement with him?"

"For our sakes," Oriane added, "please omit any details not of political or military interest."

Someone laughed, and smothered it in a cough. Dervain shifted again, like a boxer bracing himself for another round. "What on earth do you think spies do when they are alone together? You keep invading us, and we wish to invade you, and all that requires intelligence. Savonn was very fond of reading my papers. A nuisance, but luckily he was willing to pay. We... swapped favours."

"What kind of favours?" someone shouted.

Dervain raised a brow. "What dirty little minds you have. Savonn let me read his dispatches in exchange for reading mine. After some months when, shall we say, the tenor of our relationship changed, he began to steal plans and maps for me, and kept me informed of Betronett's dispositions through the Farfallens. *Very* useful, when I was looking for somewhere to put all the Marshal's bandits..."

He was too good a showman to try and make himself heard over the racket. He trailed off, looking solicitous, while the guards thumped the butts of their spears on the floor and Oriane called for order again. The shouting was loudest from the Betronett men. They all remembered their hard campaign in the mountains, driving out Saraian-paid bandits from one holdfast after another. "And in return?" said Yannick, looking nauseated. "Did he ask anything of you?"

Dervain did not answer at once. To Iyone's consternation, he glanced at Hiraen. This could mean nothing but evil.

"Yes," said Hiraen softly. His hands were fisted around the edge of the table. "You may as well tell them what you did for him."

It was the first and only time Dervain had asked permission to speak. "Well," he said, "like a cheap whore, I only have the one skill. There was a fellow he needed dead quite urgently. Gods help me, I always forget his name. My lord Hiraen, will you be so good as to remind me—?"

Like a cat, he played with his food before he ate it. Iyone answered so Hiraen, his jaw clenched, would not have to. "You mean Captain Merrott."

"Yes!" Dervain beamed. "That one."

The guards were thumping their spears again, to no avail. Yannick made the warding sign against evil. The younger Betronett men sat in a stupefied silence, but the veterans who had fought side by side with Merrott were all on their feet and shouting once more. Emaris ducked around Shandei's restraining arm. "Why the hell would he want *Merrott* dead?"

Just then Hiraen drew a short breath. Iyone followed his gaze to the stagehands by the unicorn door, and saw.

At first her eye had slid right over Savonn. He had a slippery face, which met all the conventional expectations of symmetry but went no farther towards attractiveness, and so was utterly forgettable. His curls were tucked beneath a shapeless cap, his crumpled shirt flecked with spots of blue paint. Emaris's shout had drawn him forward—otherwise neither she nor Hiraen would have spotted him. Savonn glanced at the stage, and saw her looking.

I am sorry, she tried to tell him. It was difficult, perhaps because she was also trying to say, *You deserve it.*

He grinned, a chimeric smile she could not decipher, though she had thought herself well-versed in all his subtleties. Then his gaze flitted off again.

"There are many reasons a man might want his commander dead," Dervain was saying. "A hired killer need not ask questions. Others draw up the blueprint, and I lay the bricks without—"

He broke off and stared at Iyone. His pupils had gone wide. She wondered, disconcerted, if he was about to faint. Then she realised what had derailed him: she had given herself away. Dervain was facing the wrong way and could not have seen Savonn, but his sixth sense had picked up her jolt of surprise, along with whatever feeling lay behind Hiraen's magnificent glare. Now he, too, knew that Savonn was here.

This revelation seemed to floor him. Could it be, Iyone thought, could he possibly have gone this far—given himself up for torture, let a foreign nation put him on trial—and yet entertained even the shadow of a doubt that Savonn would be here to see it through with him?

She had the short-lived satisfaction of watching the Empath struggle to recompose himself. Colour returned to his face; his cheeks were vivid with it. "I lay the bricks," he said again. "I do not have to see the building. I only regretted it once."

"Over what?" asked Yannick nervously.

"A personal matter," said Dervain. "A blood feud. Not long after I killed Merrott, I learned that Savonn Silvertongue was Savonn Andalle, son of a man I have cause to loathe like the gates of hell. But no matter. There are no more secrets between us."

He looked to the Council, but Iyone knew he was no longer addressing them. His voice was deeper, softer than before. "I had never trusted anyone before Savonn. I thought he had ill-used that trust. I set out to make good my debts, as any decent man would. Now all is paid. So I will say in court, under torture, before the gods: he was as honourable a foe as he was a lover. If I give up my life for him it will be worth it."

Dead silence. Iyone dared not move, dared not think, for fear of what she would betray this time. "And what, exactly," said Oriane, "did you do with your lover's gifts?"

The spell was broken. Dervain blinked at her, blithe and easy once more. "Oh, that? I was just about to say. I have been hard at work in the Farfallens these past years, with no Betronett patrols to stop me. Arranging some bandits here, contriving a little ambush there, taking myself step by step towards the vengeance I always prayed for..."

There was a strange lightness in Iyone's stomach, as though she were falling. A useless premonition, the last move before checkmate. "Yes," said Dervain, full of quiet triumph. "This name I remember. Kedris Andalle. I killed him."

* * *

After all that, the verdict was an anticlimax. There was nothing to discuss. It was simply a matter of restoring order and preventing the crowd from stoning the Empath to death right there in the Arena, which would have done the world a favour as far as Iyone was concerned. "Did you know he killed Kedris?" she asked.

"We found out on campaign," said Hiraen. "Look at that smug bastard. Anyone would have guessed."

Iyone made a noncommittal noise. "What about the other smug bastard?"

Hiraen's knuckles went white around the armrests of his chair. Fortunately, Oriane had gone out for a breath of fresh air, and the seat on his other side was empty. "Savonn never expected this to happen. He didn't want any of it. If you really knew him, you'd know that."

Whether any of them had really known Savonn was a point of contention. It would almost be a relief if he *had* killed his father. That crime, at least, Iyone could reconcile with the Savonn she remembered. "He hated Kedris."

"No," said Hiraen. "He was terrified of him. If he wasn't, none of this would have happened. Stop talking to me, I think I'm having a stroke."

Oriane returned a minute later. She did not sit down, only rapped her knuckles on the table to call the restless crowd to attention. "Before we sentence the accused," she said, "here is the late Lord Willon's judgement regarding Josit Ansa, which we have decided to uphold."

Oriane had not, in fact, consulted anyone on the matter of Josit, so the ruling was all hers. "For orchestrating the Rose Killings, including the murder of Willon and Vesmer Efren, the Council banishes Josit Ansa from Cassarah under pain of death. To shelter or succour her in any way shall be a crime punishable by thirty strokes of the whip."

There was a faint chorus of *yeas*. Iyone found herself looking at Shandei again. If any part of her plan had gone wrong, it could have been one or both of them receiving that sentence. Shandei's eyes locked on hers, and this time it was a few seconds before they looked away.

"Next," said Oriane, "regarding the Empath."

Dervain seemed quite at ease in his shackles, but a moon-grey pallor was stealing over his face. He was worn out, as they all were. "For murdering the Lord Governor Kedris Andalle, conspiring with the traitor Savonn Silvertongue, and countless other crimes against the city of Cassarah, the Council sentences Dervain Teraille to death by the noose. At sunup seven days from now, he will hang."

Another smattering of cheers. The Empath gave no sign that he had heard. He was staring into the middle distance, his head at a wolfish cant, as if listening for a tell-tale strain of the heart belonging to the man he had just damned. Shandei put her face in her hands.

"Technically," Yannick whispered, "we cannot hang a Saraian subject. Marguerit's ransom—"

"Yes, thank you, Lord Yannick," said Iyone.

"Now," said Oriane, "regarding Savonn Silvertongue."

Dervain looked up. "Dead or alive," said Oriane, "we find him guilty of the most severe charges. He consorted with the enemy, gave away military secrets, and—inadvertently or otherwise—brought about the death of his own father. Earlier this year he incited rebellion against the Council and led away hundreds of men to suffer and die in the mountains. We convict him of treason, sedition, and fraudulence of the highest order. Should he be found alive, he will be put to death, also by the noose."

This time the pronouncement was met with silence. Someone burst into tears, and was led out sobbing. People exchanged uneasy glances. Even the stagehands were quiet. Dervain dipped his head, and let out an audible breath.

One had to admire him, Iyone thought. He had orchestrated the entire farce of a trial like a master puppeteer, playing to his audience with an expert hand. The prospect of execution did not seem to faze him. Perhaps he set a low price on his life, or perhaps it was just that no price was too great when pitted against love. Iyone would not know.

She remembered Shandei's hands around her neck, ungentle but not unkind, and a frisson of inexplicable grief overtook her.

There was a stir in the front row, as someone stood up. "Beg pardons, Lady Oriane."

It was Daine, Linn's officer husband. His bald pate gleamed with perspiration. "Savonn was a man of Betronett," he said. "Traitor or not, he belongs to us. His sentence is for us to decide. It has always been our law."

"Oh, for heaven's sake," said Oriane in a low voice. "Will it never end? Commander?"

Hiraen stared at her, and then at Daine. Iyone saw comprehension seep in. She found his hand under the table and squeezed it hard. "You can't save him. Not this time."

"I have *never* saved him," Hiraen whispered.

He stood up. There was no escape; one way or another he would have to bear the unbearable. All eyes were on him, and no wonder—he lacked the Empath's unsettling beauty, but with his strong clean-cut features he looked wholesome, honest, a commander one could follow to the ends of the earth. "First of all," he said, "I do not believe for a moment that Savonn intended to cause his father's death. He was many things, but not a patricide. I vouch this on my honour."

There were a few dubious looks, but no one interrupted. Hiraen drew a long harsh breath. "That said, I abide by Lady Oriane's decision. As Captain of Betronett, I do sentence Savonn Silvertongue to death."

And so it was over. Emaris whirled on his heel and stormed up the stairs to the top of the Arena, shoving aside anyone who got in his way. Shandei was already gone. Hiraen resumed his seat without looking at anyone. Oriane gave an order, and the guards began to lead the Empath away.

But they had only gone several steps when Dervain stopped, chains clanking, and looked to the unicorn door. He lifted his right hand and touched his fingers to his lips, then his heart—a gesture so small no one would have noticed unless they knew where he was looking, and at whom. One of the guards gave him a shove in the back, and he began to walk again. They started up the stairs, and in another minute the top of his bright head vanished over the rim of the theatre.

They had killed Savonn. It was done.

CHAPTER 8

A carriage was waiting outside to take the councillors to the Temple of the Sisters, so Hiraen could receive his ritual blessing from the gods. Iyone could not help but think the whole thing a bit of a joke, but there was no getting out of it—all Cassarah's High Commanders had to be presented to Aebria and Casteia before they could go off and make war. Apparently it was all right to kill and plunder as long as one had the Sisters' mandate. Not even Kedris had been exempt, and unlike him Hiraen was at least on speaking terms with the gods.

The Temple was as uninviting as ever, its narrow windows peering from ungainly stone walls like so many crusty eyes. An acolyte met them in the courtyard and showed Aretel and the councillors to a parlour, while—at Hiraen's own insistence—Iyone accompanied her brother to see the High Priestess. They were led through gloomy courtyards and up echoing stairwells, and left to wait in an anteroom while Her Holiness made ready to receive them. This was a windowless chamber that put Iyone in mind of the Empath's prison cell, unfurnished except for a single teak bench with no cushions and a few leafless twigs in an alabaster vase. It was a deliberate snub, one she did not fail to mark.

"Well?" she said. "If you are going to detonate, now is the time."

Hiraen was pacing, insofar as there was room to pace. He had been quiet since the trial, only smiling once, when a young woman—the fiancée of one of the Onaressi prisoners—had rushed up to him outside the Arena to kiss his hand. "I don't know where to begin. *High Commander*? You couldn't think of anyone else?"

"Tragically," said Iyone, "no. It was you or Bonner Efren. Have a heart."

"High praise," said Hiraen. "I should have stayed in the mountains and sent Emaris instead. You could've made a lord out of him. Where the hell did Savonn go?"

Iyone shrugged. The ordeal of the trial had left her rattled, and disinclined to be helpful. "I thought you were his keeper."

"My gods." Hiraen stopped in his tracks. "We mustn't misplace him. Do you think he's just going to let us hang his lover? If we don't sit on him, he's going to do something ghastly between now and the execution. Probably there'll be explosions and locust swarms and we'll all die."

She considered this. The frightening thing was how clearly she could picture it. "To save the Empath or kill him himself?"

"I haven't the faintest idea," said Hiraen. "I doubt he does either."

Just then the door slid open without a knock. Iyone was turning to look, a rebuke already on her tongue, when a soft voice spoke. "I never know what I'm doing. But I do it all the same."

They both stared. Hiraen said, "Are you insane? *Here*?"

A manservant had come in. At first glance he looked to be exactly what he seemed, with his smart feathered cap, neat uniform, and polished boots. Then Iyone took in his impish smile, so at odds with the rest of him, and her mind convinced itself of what it was seeing. "Oh, excellent. You may as well come in. Then we'll be accused of harbouring you and we can all hang together."

The man slunk round the bench to the far wall, as if to place them between him and danger. The stagehand costume was gone. His new livery clung to him like a second skin, so natural it seemed unthinkable that he could be anything but a menial servant, tired and loyal, fetching and carrying twelve hours a day. "Surely milord must have someone to attend him. Do I displease, mistress?"

His presence was alarming enough. The fact that he had chosen to manifest here, of all places, was beyond belief. Iyone remembered that she had resolved to cast him off. She wondered how she had ever thought that would be possible. "Hiraen should have let you die."

"I think of it every day," said Hiraen wryly.

"Alas, my death is appointed for another. But milord was *so* dashing at the trial, especially at the end..." The servant slanted a look at Hiraen under his lashes. Iyone imagined picking up the alabaster vase and smashing it over his head. "Do I displease, master? O send me not away!"

In unison, as if they had slipped ten years back in time, Hiraen and Iyone said, "Shut it up and put a rock on it."

"Oh, hell." Savonn grinned. "All right, darlings. I promise to stand still later while you throw things at me. I just thought I should warn you—since you were bickering so very audibly—that someone's coming to collect the mighty Captain of Betronett. Or should I say, our Lord High Commander."

"Don't forget Saviour of Onaressi," said Iyone.

"Defender of the Farfallens," added Savonn.

"*Shut up*," said Hiraen.

Right on cue, there was a knock. The door slid open again, this time to reveal the young acolyte who had brought them there. She looked back and forth between Iyone and Hiraen as though uncertain whom to address, but her gaze passed straight over the manservant, who had fallen back a step and might have been part of the stuccoed wall for all the attention anyone paid him. "Sir, madame," said the acolyte, without looking either of them in the eye. "Her Holiness will see you now. If you will kindly follow me."

As a rule, Iyone neither liked nor trusted people who addressed themselves to her feet. But one had to make concessions. She was a councillor now, no longer a miscreant peddling in minor mischiefs, and Hiraen was hero and supreme commander both. A little nervousness was something they would have to get used to. "Very well."

They followed the girl out of the room and up a short stair. The sanctum was distantly familiar to Iyone from feast-days and ritual cleansings. Coming in, one was first stricken by the bitter smells of sage and frankincense, heavy in the close air; and then the colossal goddess-statues rearing behind the altar, eighteen feet of unpainted marble filling the room from floor to ceiling. The windows were curtained today, the wall sconces empty. The only light came from a trio of tall white candles smouldering on the altar, which was otherwise bare and covered in thick black velvet from end to end, so only its clawed wooden feet showed under the drape.

Hiraen frowned. "Where are the sacrifices?"

The acolyte had vanished. Iyone thought about the shifty way the girl had stared at the floor, and pushed away a twinge of unease. "Probably the Sisters were hungry. They've been busy this week."

Drawn by a volition not quite her own, she raised her head and looked up and up and up. Cassarah's patron goddesses gazed back at her through red carnelian eyes, glossy and inhuman in the reflected candlelight. Aebria wept, her mouth agape in a half-moon of stone-set grief, while her grim sister Casteia hefted a monstrous barbed spear to sling at some unseen foe. Shroud and mail, fist and veil, Sorrow and Strife embodied in marble and gemstone. To be Cassaran was to worship what you feared.

"Well, where's the Priestess?" Hiraen asked. "Is this some kind of test?"

Dread tingled at the base of Iyone's spine. She had missed quite a few Midsummer purifications, including this year's. So had Hiraen. As for Savonn, she was not sure he had ever gone. "I don't know."

"We should call. Something might have happened to her."

It was possible. The High Priestess was a walking fossil, shrivelled and bent double with age. Every time Iyone glimpsed her in the Temple or at festivals, she wondered how on earth the woman was still alive. Perhaps something *had* befallen her, and she was withering away in some secret cloister behind the altar, a mass of maggots and crumbling bones. "Maybe."

A cold draught blew down the hall from the altar. *Ohhhh*, it moaned. The air smelled of dead fish. *Ohhhh. Youuuuu.*

Hiraen's pupils were wide and luminous. "What the hell?"

Iyone turned, searching for the source of the voice. Apart from their manservant, hovering at the back of the hall in what might have been deference or cowardice, they were alone. Goose-hairs prickled on her arms. "She's in one of her moods. We'd better go."

Goooo, said the wind. It was an echo, not a command. *Go, she says!*

The outline of the door was faint and impossibly distant. With a clear, terrible prescience, Iyone knew that if they tried it, it would not open. Hiraen took a step towards the altar. "Hello?"

Lacking the resonance of the whispering wind, he sounded depthless, somehow muted. "My name is Hiraen Safin. I am here for your blessing."

The wind chittered in the eaves. Then a new voice spoke. "You?" It was hoarse and desiccated and toadlike, but unlike the whispers it was undeniably human. "You, of all the accursed race of mortals, desire my blessing?"

Iyone moved forward, closing ranks with Hiraen. This she could deal with. "That's the general procedure, Holiness."

The air shivered with mirth. The High Priestess was alive and well after all. "Look at you," croaked the toad voice. "The lord and lady of the damned, ruling this city by terror and treachery. A *blessing!*"

There was no use looking for her. She was the darkness, puddled in every corner where the candlelight did not reach. She was the fish-breath stirring the altar drape, the dead wind with its unwholesome chill. She was the marble of the goddess-statues, the red gems in their pitiless eyes, the fusty gauze of Aebria's veil and the glittering scales of Casteia's mail. She was the temple, and the temple laughed.

"Keep your blessing," said Iyone. Courage was overrated. "We'll leave."

She grabbed Hiraen's elbow and tried to pull him away. He did not budge. "Your Holiness," he said. "Is it too late to beg forgiveness?"

"You would beg?" the Priestess asked. "You do not deny the blood of a friend on your hands?"

"I do not."

"For heaven's sake," said Iyone. Savonn was still behind them, listening. She had lost Shandei over this. "Shut up."

"You shut up!" screeched the Priestess. The scream rebounded from the walls and ceiling, growing louder with each iteration. It was as if she had a dozen mouths, and those not speaking were laughing at them. "Forgiveness for your unclean hands? Not from me. Eh? Eh?"

Not from us, came the whispers on the air. The voices were deep and genderless, oddly tuneful in the way a gale sometimes was when it howled against the citadel turrets. *We are sorrow. We are strife. Forgiveness is not ours to grant.*

Hiraen's shoulders sagged. "If you say so. Now let us go."

"Not so fast!" cried the Priestess. "What about the blessing you came for, High Commander? Victory, is that what you seek? Victory in your bloody war?"

Iyone answered first, her fingers still clenched around Hiraen's arm. She dared not let him open his mouth again. "What else would a commander want?"

Victory! whispered the wind. *Over our pious daughter Marguerit! Oh, oh!*

The Priestess giggled. It was a terrible sound. "I shall tell you your future, Hiraen Safin. It is writ in the dregs of your soul. I shall tell you all your futures, you and your vicious sister and this low criminal of yours."

The breath froze in Iyone's lungs. "Oh, yes, yes," sang the Priestess. "I see you, Savonn Silvertongue. Did you think to fool the goddesses with a clever disguise? Shall I scream, shall I ring the alarum-bells and cry, *Guards, guards*?"

We are justice, sighed the wind. *We are grief.*

"Come here, little liar," said the Priestess. "Come and let me tell your fortune, like I told your father's before you."

Run, Iyone thought; run, hide, be free. But a soft unhurried step sounded, and Savonn came up at her side, his hat doffed. He looked only straight ahead, and his face told her nothing. *Ahhh*, sighed the wind. *This one. We see him.*

"Tell me my future, since you insist," said Hiraen, cold and clear. "You spoke of victory."

"Oh, yes," said the Priestess. "And you shall have it. You shall be stuffed so full of victory that your mouth hangs open and it bleeds through your eyes and drips out your nose. Victory, yes, but over what?"

Blood and sand, answered the wind. *Blood and sand.*

"And the other matter?" asked Hiraen. "How shall I put it right?"

The Priestess screamed with laughter. The refrain soughed around them once more, not quite gentle, not quite foreboding. *Blood and sand.*

The wind died down. There was a moment of utter quiet. Then it picked up again without warning, puffing down Iyone's neck, swirling round her ankles like a waterspout. She had never been so cold. *This one is beyond us. We cannot touch her.*

The Priestess cackled. "Do not fear the darkness, scorpion-soul. You do not want your fortune told?"

Iyone's hair blew into her face. She imagined clammy fingers probing her scalp, feeling for a way down into her head. Her skin crawled. She had betrayed Savonn. She had kept Hiraen's secret. She had stood by and let Willon die. The Priestess would know it all. "I fear nothing," she said. "As for my fortune, I prefer to make it myself."

"Oh?" A raucous shriek. "Viper in your mother's bosom! Lie and scheme all you want. Never will you be more than what you are."

The wind-voices were silent. They could not touch her, Iyone remembered. So this was no prophecy, only the inane gabbling of a hateful witch. "Nor will I be less."

The wind hurled itself at her in a final tearing onslaught. Her skirts billowed. She shook back her hair and filled her lungs with a loud, defiant breath. The very air seemed to flee from her, and the ghoul-voices screamed. *Proud stone! High wall! We must leave her ere we perish. But see, the magpie is ours. He has a question.*

Iyone braced herself, but only stillness pressed around her, heavy as a shroud. The wind had gone. "I know what his question is," crooned the old woman. "I know, and he knows the answer! Why ask then, fool boy? Did you hope to hear something different?"

Savonn's curls stirred in a breeze Iyone could no longer feel. Under its ministrations he held very still, as if for a dissection. His expression was so bland as to be vacuous. She had only ever seen him like this in Kedris's presence. *Tell us, Holiness. Tell us what he asks.*

"He asks," said the Priestess in a sneering singsong, "oh, he asks if he will ever kill his lover."

Hiraen's boot squeaked on the flagstones. The wind squalled around the altar. *He knows! He knows! We will not answer. Tell him to ask another.*

"Speak, false heart," said the Priestess. "The gods are listening."

Caught in the wind, the flames on the white candles elongated, straining across the altar towards them. An inch, two inches, grotesquely long, longer than the candles and the candlesticks both. But there was no heat, and hardly any light. This was no earthly fire. It was sorcery, and each serpentine flame crackled with ill will. Iyone tried to move, to cry out, to grab the others and stumble back, but her legs were anchored to the floor, and still the flames stretched and undulated and reached for them—

Savonn said, "Does it hurt to die?"

The spell broke. The flames stopped, suspended over the edge of the altar. "Don't," said Hiraen. "Don't ask that."

Tell him, said the voices on the air. *Soul thief! Thief soul! He must know!*

The Priestess giggled again. "Only a little," she said. "Only a little, wicked boy… and much less than the alternative."

One by one, the laughing echoes fell silent. The wind screamed back up the hall to the altar. The candles guttered and died. The darkness was complete, and the High Priestess did not speak again.

The back of Iyone's blouse was soaked through with perspiration. "Move," she said.

She floundered to the door, hauling Hiraen and Savonn with her. It gave without fuss, opening onto wintry air and weak daylight. Trapped with the Priestess, Iyone had forgotten that anything existed beyond the confines of the sanctum, that outside it was only late afternoon, and her mother and the Council were waiting for them downstairs. "Move, move, *move!*"

They began to run. The hallway was strangely deserted: every door was shut, and the acolyte was nowhere to be seen. Their footfalls resonated through the high-vaulted halls, brash and loud, as if announcing their trespasses over and over. They reached the stairway that descended over the main courtyard, and did not stop until they had put two floors between them and the sanctum.

"What was that?" Iyone asked, breathless, when they halted on the landing. Even standing between Josit and the Efren spears, she had not felt like this. "What did she do?"

Hiraen's face was bloodless. So had he looked that night in the rain, under the golden pillars of the colonnade, when he had extracted a promise from her while a man called Rendell lay dead. "It wasn't just her. You heard the voices. Those were spirits. Those were—"

"The Ceriyes," said Savonn. He had replaced his cap, though not his smirk. "Attendants of a wrongful death. How interesting."

He met Hiraen's gaze, and held it like a challenge. Impossibly, in the terror of the last few minutes, Iyone had forgotten about the only thing that mattered. Hiraen, who had sworn her to secrecy, had as good as admitted his guilt aloud. And now Savonn knew. *We are justice. We are grief.*

"Savonn," said Hiraen, "look—"

"Hiraen? Is that you?"

It was Aretel's voice, drifting up from the next landing. They all froze. "Iyone? Are you there?"

Caught out on the stairs, there was nowhere to hide. Savonn dropped to his knees beside Hiraen and ducked his head. A second later Aretel came round the bend in the stair. Her eyes passed over the stooped figure of the manservant to rest on her children, and her brows came together. "What took you so long?"

"Just a minute, Mother," said Hiraen. "My boot-lace came loose."

"The old woman rambled quite a bit," added Iyone. As Savonn untied and redid Hiraen's boot, she came forward to block her mother's view of them. "And she wasn't in the best of moods. I'm ravenous. Can we go?"

Aretel relaxed. "Oriane's been asking me that for the last half-hour," she said. "She may be seventy, but I swear the woman has all the patience of a seven-year-old. We'd better hurry."

It was like re-entering the mortal realm. Well away from the upper sanctum, the courtyard bustled with activity. They passed servants carrying trays of food and armfuls of laundered robes. Acolytes scuttled back and forth on godly errands, and a tiny girl no older than eight or nine nearly ran them over with a cartful of prayer cushions. Every now and then someone stopped to curtsey to Aretel, but no one would look at Iyone or Hiraen.

Aretel led them to the parlour where the councillors were waiting. They had been gone far longer than Iyone realised. The table was littered with biscuit crumbs and empty teacups, and Yannick had fallen asleep on one of the settees. Oriane retrieved him, practically seething with restlessness, while Aretel thanked their hosts and Hiraen and Iyone stood apart, each in a silence of their own.

Iyone was not superstitious. Nor was she devout. But she knew something great and grievous had transpired, and it would take a much bigger fool than she was to deny it.

No matter, she thought. They were together again, she and Hiraen and Savonn, up to their noses in mischief like they had always been. They would go back to the manor and talk things out, safe behind walls they knew. Surely there was no wrong between them that could not be put to rights.

It was only when they reached the temple gate that she looked around, and realised their manservant was no longer with them.

CHAPTER 9

Dervain was lying flat on his back, trying not to breathe.

After the trial, he had been moved from the dungeon to await execution in a tower cell. It had been a trying afternoon. A *headache* was a misnomer for what seemed to be transpiring above his neck—it felt more like his brains had been plastered to the inside of his skull. Previous misadventures suggested he could have endured at least another hour in the miasma of the excited crowd before becoming comatose, but it had been a close shave.

Feet were climbing the stair to his cell. One pair, light-shod. A tray rattled. It must be time for his evening meal. Dervain listened to the guard's approach, though listening, too, was a misnomer. He tasted yellow, heard jasmine and heather. There was an old Bayarric word for it he rather liked, *senossa*, which meant sensing with the whole soul, and not just the eyes or ears or skin. Or something like that. One ought never translate Bayarric on an empty stomach.

The door opened. This gaoler was new and, unlike the others, did not taste of terror. Strange. Dervain closed his eyes to concentrate. Then he saw why.

"There you are," he said. "I was waiting for you."

The tray was set down with a scrape. "Were you?" said Savonn. "I thought you were just waiting to die."

Fear was a useful weapon, which Dervain had taken pains to cultivate in those around him. Among other reasons, his looks attracted the sort of attention a slave was not often at liberty to refuse. If people believed it was a death sentence to lay hands on a servant of the Nameless Father, so much the better for him. And if he had encouraged this superstition with a number of prominent and grisly murders—well, he was only doing what he had to do.

But Savonn had never been afraid of him. He was not fearless: Dervain had sensed him afraid a great many times, of a great many things. It was just that none of these things happened to be Dervain Teraille, the Red Death of Daliss.

It was infuriating.

Dervain opened his eyes and sat up, though it made the whole room split and reform and resonate in B flat. Savonn was standing at the foot of his straw pallet, wearing guardsman's livery. Or perhaps it was more accurate to say that he was wearing the guardsman, as it was hard to tell where the costume began and ended. A black tunic, a boiled leather jerkin, a silver badge at the lapel. His curls were flattened where a helm had sat. His posture was borrowed, too—he stood like a soldier who had done his drills, like a man who had been marching all day in heavy armour. But under the long lashes, the glimmer in the cormorant eyes was all his own.

He held out a thimble-cup. "For your head."

It was poppy tea, mixed well with honey, the way Dervain had always taken it. In Astorre he used to say it was for the migraine. Now it was not only his head that hurt. So did his shoulders, his ribs, the soles of his feet, and the hollows behind his ears. The torturers had been unimaginative, but dedicated.

"You could have run," said Dervain. "I gave you time to run."

Nine days to Cassarah. Nine days to the turn of the moon. "They had you," said Savonn. "My options were limited."

His usual expression of undirected mockery was firmly in place—a mask wrought not of wood or brass or sorcery, but of skill. One learnt to look past it. "You didn't expect me to show up," said Savonn. "I know. I abandoned you before."

The air was humming, words and phrases from all of Dervain's languages jostling each other on his tongue. Abandonment. Yes. Once, Savonn had entrusted a murderous errand to him and vanished without a word, leaving some in Astorre to wonder if the wild bird of Betronett was dead, others to announce—laughing—that no, he had only returned to the Bitten Hill to take up his post as Captain. Their silly magpie, son of a governor, leader of armies. Who would have thought?

If Dervain was honest, he had begun even before then to suspect. Still he bided his time, a month, two months, all summer, waiting to see if Savonn would dare come back now that anonymity was impossible. The stars changed, and the trees browned, and Savonn did not come. One treacherous Andalle was much like another, after all. This one had weighed his father and his lover in his glittering scale, and chosen the former—Kedris, murderer, warmonger, destroyer, against whom Dervain had thought Savonn an ally. So he had put his affairs in order and asked to be recalled to Daliss, where he would lick his wounds until he could return with steel in his hands.

But this time Savonn had not fled. Forewarned, knowing he would be a fugitive, a hunted man, he had set his feet towards Cassarah—towards Dervain—and come to him anyway.

"Red," said Savonn softly. "Drink the poppy."

Left to his own devices, Dervain might have sat unmoving for hours, staring into the colours and the lights until the fog in his head cleared. Instead he swirled the contents of the thimble-cup and downed them in one swallow. Savonn always knew what he needed. He was the only one, besides Nikas, who had ever been able to match Dervain blow for blow. *You only love him because he's the one toy you can't break*, Nikas had said once, and then of course Dervain had to duel him for honour's sake, and neither of them had liked it.

"This was easier," he said, "when I thought there was nothing real about you."

Savonn looked at him from an arm's length away. "Don't be hasty. Nine times out of ten it is only an optical illusion."

His shuttered eyes gave nothing away, but Dervain had an advantage. In his ribcage he could feel the fast, shallow vibrations of a heart that was not his own. "You didn't tell them why I needed Merrott dead," said Savonn.

"That was between you and your friend," said Dervain. "I do not recant my favours."

A long silence. The ghost-lights were dimming, the thunder of his aching body beginning to recede. Savonn said, "Thank you."

His face showed only guarded thoughtfulness. He looked around Dervain's cell, taking in the dirty pallet, the featureless walls, the small barred window near the ceiling. It was a fighter's assessing gaze, and when he spoke again it was in his command voice. "Why haven't you escaped?"

Even ill and in pain, the thought had crossed Dervain's mind. He had escaped from worse places, in worse health. The tower cell was far less secure than the dungeon, and he was no longer shackled. But still—

"Allow me some philosophy," he said. "Which is worse: a quick death in the noose, or a lifetime in slavery?"

Savonn mulled this over. "I suppose it depends on the length of the drop. And the span of one's years."

He sat down on the pallet beside Dervain. The window was purple with twilight, casting a soft glaze over his features that made him look sweet-faced and harmless. Dervain grappled at him with his sixth sense, trying to see, to understand, but he could only tell what Savonn was *not*. He was not afraid. He was not pleased. He was most certainly not harmless.

"You don't want to go back to the Sanctuary," said Savonn. "Is that it?"

At the back of Dervain's mind flared a spark of anger that did not belong to Savonn, and so must be his own. His work was done, now. Kedris was dead, his son ruined, his mistress the false queen in exile. And yet he could never leave the Sanctuary. He was too priceless to ever be freed. If he ran, he would be running for the rest of his life—an endless flight before the spears and whips and hounds, pursued to the grave by those who had once been the closest thing he'd had to family.

"There is nowhere else to go," he said. "I never did find my hearthstone."

"There was Evenfall," said Savonn. "I waited for you."

Dervain had wanted to go, if only to see Savonn one last time. But there was no use fighting him at Evenfall. You could not kill a riddle. It had to be unravelled here, before the courts and the crowds, in the stone heart of the hateful city the Andalles had built. "There is nothing left to do," he said. "I have beaten you. I have won the game. Only the gallows remain to be conquered."

"You would go to the gallows?" asked Savonn. "And what of me?"

What of him? He was unbeatable: fluid as a shadow, impossible to pin down. Years after Dervain had gone to his god, he would still be flying free. "The world is vast for a little bird like you."

Savonn's mask dropped. For an instant they were young again, watching the stars fall in the pastures of the Astorrian mountainside. He flung himself off the pallet, walked to the door, turned sharply, came back. The ghost-lights ignited once more, bright yellow, gushing red. Dervain almost put up a hand to shield his eyes. "Vast, indeed," said Savonn. "Too vast for one to live in it alone. In three years without you I never got the knack of it. Believe me, if I could learn to relinquish you, I would."

Dervain did have to cover his eyes, then, for more reasons than one. He heard Savonn pace to the door again, and stand there breathing slowly. Monkshood, wormwood: the air was acrid with it, a smell with a weight.

When Savonn spoke again, he had recovered his glacial calm. "Don't be prosaic. You have won nothing. All you've done is made a few dramatic moves and backed yourself into a corner, from which your magnanimous foe must now extricate you. I assure you there will be no execution. If you wish to die, you will have to do it at my hand."

He gave no quarter, and asked for none. They were the same, the two of them, twinned from the beginning of the world to the end. "And so," said Dervain slowly, "we are not done fighting?"

"It seems so," said Savonn. "A son cannot disown his father, any more than a priest can disown his god."

His neck and clavicles looked delicate as glass, as if a thought might snap them. Dervain's head throbbed. "Your father had you in chains. I struck them off. He has no more hold on you."

Savonn turned his face to the wall, out of the light. "*Stop.*"

Blood gonged in Dervain's ears. Whose, he did not know. Long ago, standing naked on the auction block as bids were called out for him, he had sworn to kill the man who'd brought him to this. He had done it—drove his spear into Kedris's heart, the way he had rehearsed a hundred times in his dreams. Marguerit had not been ready, but he'd had no choice. Kedris was on his way to Astorre, no doubt to investigate some hunch of his son's treason. Dervain had hated Savonn at the time, but not as much as he hated Kedris.

And yet it seemed the man was still alive and at large, destined to torment them for as long as they lived.

"You are set on death?" asked Savonn. "You see no other option?"

What other option was there? His vengeance was complete. There was nothing left but to lay down his arms the only way the Father would let him, and leave the aegis of the Sanctuary at last.

"Not for me," said Dervain. "But you are free."

Savonn sat down on the pallet once more, and took Dervain's hands. His fingers were ice-cold. "I am free of my father," he said. "But I am not free of what I did. I have—reparations to make. And I will not let you die alone, even if it means we must be enemies a little longer. Do you understand, my dear?"

That was the thing about Savonn. He always surprised, even when you thought you had puzzled him out. Thief's honour: he would belong to his father until he had made good the price of his treason, just as Dervain would belong to his god until he died. As soon as Dervain got free they would be at war again. The game had to be played to the end.

"Yes," he said. "What do you propose?"

Savonn rested his forehead against Dervain's. "There's a poem I like. *You are my tomb and I your sarcophagus. Open me up that you may lie in me...*"

His warm breath smelled of mint and cloves—a real smell, not a phantom one. Dervain breathed him in, wishing he could hold him down and crush him close, wreck him hard and brutal enough that they could forget about everything else for a while. "I know it," he said. "It is very dramatic. Do you want us to be dramatic?"

"Later," said Savonn. "My friends need me. I can't go to you until I've made what amends I can. But after that I will find you, and we can—put an end to this."

The slender curve of his throat seemed to demand a hand around it. His lips were only an inch away. "Together?"

"Together."

"How can I believe you, after all your lies?" Dervain's voice shook. "Show me a sign."

Savonn ran his fingers through the ends of Dervain's hair. He had always liked playing with it. "Come and take it."

This was not to be dared. All the same Dervain reached for him, cupping his chin, skimming his thumb over the fine line of his jaw. He grasped a fistful of those dark curls, not gently, and Savonn leaned into it with a sound that was half exhale, half sigh. His hands came around Dervain's face, bridging the distance between them. Then they were kissing.

In three years they had lost the knack of it. Their noses bumped. Savonn laughed, and caught Dervain's lower lip between his teeth, his half-lidded eyes shining with challenge. *Go on.* It used to be a favourite trick of his, biting and scratching to get a reaction. So Dervain tugged on his hair, mouthing over the vulnerable expanse of bare neck, the soft skin at the swell of his throat; and drew him in, and kissed him again.

He had to pull off when he ran out of breath. But Savonn was still in his arms, warm and pliant as he seldom was, and so Dervain slid his free hand around the column of his neck and kissed along his jugular, feeling the strong pulse beat under his mouth. "I should put you on your back," he said, fingers still tangled in Savonn's hair, "and have you right here."

A rosy flush hued the fine brown skin at Savonn's cheekbones. "Now *that* would bring all the guards," he said, smiling. "You have your sign. I hope you are satisfied."

Dervain's breath came fast and short, as if he had been running. "I am all mouth when it comes to you."

"But you are happy with our agreement?"

He looked at Savonn, the deadliest foe he had ever faced, tucked small and ruffled in his arms. The world was a haze of light. "This is the height of happiness."

"Good," said Savonn. "Then my job here is done."

He drew away. Dervain could feel him reassembling himself one layer at a time, the way one might straighten one's clothes and pat down one's hair. The ghost-lights went out. The air smelled of nothing but prison again. Dervain had to force his muscles into stillness, so as not to reach for Savonn and cling like a child. The window-square was dark and dotted with stars, and in a few minutes the guards would change shifts. Savonn had to go.

No matter, he thought. A little wait, a little war, and soon they would never be parted again.

Savonn was wearing the guardsman's face once more. "The next time you touch me," he said, "it will be to kill."

Dervain's arms felt cold and bereft. For the first time since the massacre of his village, he wondered if he had it in him to take a life. "Is that what you want?"

"Like you," said Savonn, "I do not go in for recantations."

He opened the cell door and let himself out. Dervain watched him melt into the shadows on the landing. As the lock clicked, he smelled lyresong, and tasted firelight, and heard blood, blood, blood.

* * *

Sometime after sundown, a small man in a big cloak slipped out of the prison and away from the citadel. He padded silently, a swift-footed shade, keeping close to walls and trees until he reached the sprawling Sydell manor. He studied the high brick wall around the property. Then he began to climb, moving from handhold to handhold with fastidious care, and disappeared into the manor grounds.

A half-hour later, he reappeared at the top of the wall like a great black bird and hopped back onto the street. He had left no trace of his visit, and took nothing with him except a cedarwood box, stuffed full of letters.

CHAPTER 10

On the whole, Emaris's homecoming left a great deal to be desired.

None of the day's revelations should have astonished him. Hiraen had tried to brace him for what was to come, and even before that he had begun to guess. But nothing on earth could have prepared him to watch Savonn laid bare before all Cassarah while the Empath preened and smiled. And right afterwards Hiraen had been swept off to the Temple with all the important people, so Emaris could not even demand the explanation he had been promised.

His echo-chamber had acquired a new voice. *I do sentence Savonn Silvertongue to death.*

Shandei, too, had been unforthcoming. It felt strange, going back together to the house Emaris had not seen in months, to be surrounded once more by familiar things. The pewter basin by the door, where he used to rinse his feet after a sparring session in the yard. The low wooden table, chipped from being overturned in one too many violent games of make-believe. The mantel on which Shandei had once concussed herself trying to turn a cartwheel. Emaris paused at the door on the way in, waiting to hear their father's cheerful voice or his quick step on the stair. Nothing.

"Did you learn anything?" he asked, the question sticking in his throat. "About—about Father?"

Shandei looked older and paler, and the hug she had given him when they found each other in the press of bodies outside the Arena had lasted much longer than her usual rough, one-armed cuddles. "Not as much as I'd like. Only that the Efrens had nothing to do with it."

Emaris opened his mouth to exclaim. Then he realised that this was not, after all, a surprise, and shut it again.

"I don't want to talk about it," she said. "Tomorrow, maybe, we'll ride out to Father's grave and bring him some winter roses. But not now."

She went out the back door before he could ask her anything else. He stared after her, more alarmed than annoyed. He had always thought his sister untouchable, a force of nature; that nothing fazed her, and if something tried, it would soon find itself black and blue and bleeding from the nose. It was beginning to dawn on him that, for an eighteen-year-old of reasonable intelligence, this was a rather simple way of thinking.

He considered going after her, or marching up to the Safin manor and demanding to speak with the High Commander. But there was really only one person he wanted to see.

It was late when he got back to the Arena. The fog had risen from the river, and the crowds had long since cleared off. Still, the theatre swarmed like an anthill with activity. Carpenters were hammering scaffolds into place where the Empath had stood just hours before, while stagehands tested the crane, raising and lowering bits of scenery over the set. Emaris collided with a girl in a milkmaid costume on his way through the unicorn door, and nearly had his ear taken off by the wooden sabre she was waving. He considered asking her where the local traitor lived, but desisted.

Behind the door was the sprawling warren of underground caverns the theatre folk used for their offstage business. One looked for Savonn in strange tunnels like these, far from the light of day, just as one might find salmon at the wet market or trouble in a back alley. The first few rooms were full of people singing or declaiming, but farther in they grew dark and empty. Emaris passed dusty dressing rooms and storehouses full of ancient props, the air turning warm and stale around him. At last, with perspiration sluicing down his brow, he lost patience and started flinging open doors at random.

It was easy to tell when he had found Savonn. Deep in the catacomb, one of the minor tunnels ended at an unmarked door that opened on a storeroom, only half full. Behind a row of musty crates with labels such as *Wigs (& Lice, Do Not Wear)* and *Tree of Eternity: Boughs Only, We Ate the Fruit*, someone had laid out the rudiments of a sleeping area. There was an old brocade quilt, folded into exacting quarters on a moth-eaten mattress. A brass chest that looked like it might have been pilfered from the hold of some ancient pirate ship, but turned out to contain only a motley assortment of clothes. An oil lamp resting on a well-worn copy of *Poems from the Old Empire*. Most incriminating of all, a battered little lute propped against the wall. This was the bolthole of a creature Emaris knew well.

He lit the lamp, and sat down on the chest to wait.

He was half asleep by the time the door squeaked open. A person-shaped silhouette came round the wall of crates and stopped short at the sight of him. It was wearing an oversized cloak, a broad-brimmed hat, and the reek of stale alcohol. In the fickle lamplight its face was primordial in its lack of recognisable features, like the mould from which Mother Alakyne had cast the race of humankind: ageless and genderless, a face that might have belonged to anybody, and yet was nobody's at all. The mouth made a fractional movement. "Blood and hellfire. It's you, gazelle."

Emaris stood up. There was a strange stirring in his chest, like a flutter of wings. "Yes."

He watched, fascinated against his better nature, as the anonymous figure began to transform. The straw hat was taken off. Then the cloak, revealing a black tunic and trousers of the sort the city guard wore beneath their mail. The eyes were no longer blank, but wary and searching. Savonn's eyes, on him. "What do you want?"

They had last seen each other on the losing side of a skirmish in the Farfallens, getting shot to pieces by the Marshal of Sarei. Emaris was starting to think back on those days with bitter nostalgia. He had not planned what to say—all would be clear once he saw Savonn in the flesh, or so he had thought. Stupid. Savonn never made anything clear. The touch of his shadow probably turned diamonds murky.

He said, "Tell me it isn't true."

"For pity's sake," said Savonn. He had his feet planted, keeping his balance with the exaggerated care one saw only in beached sailors and the very drunk. "Haven't you had enough for one day?"

Emaris stood his ground. He was now a full inch taller than Savonn. "Just say it's not true. Then I'll go."

One word was all he needed. Then this could be put aside, relegated to the benign territory of mishaps and misunderstandings. Merrott's death had been an accident, the Empath nothing but a devious liar, and once he was hanged they could forget everything he had said. "Don't get so worked up," said Savonn. "If it's comedy you want, catch some sleep and come back for opening night." He made a twirling motion in the direction of the stage. "*Cow in Green Grass*. Excellent bit of burlesque about a cattleherder and his wife. You'd love it."

"Tell me," said Emaris again. He knew what it was like with Savonn. If he allowed himself to be driven off the track, he would never find his way back. "So the Empath outplayed you. He put up a good show, and the Council ate it from his hand. People would believe anything about you as long as it was scandalous enough. But it's all lies, isn't it?"

"You ridiculous pastry," said Savonn. He sounded almost tender. "Is that what you think?"

Emaris saw he was holding something: a long wooden box with a ruby in the lid, its padlock smashed. His insides churned, a tectonic upheaval. "How did you get that?"

"Thievery," said Savonn. "I was known for it, back in the day."

He stepped around Emaris and flung himself onto the mattress. The box went on top of the clothes-chest with rather more care. "Your faith is touching. Alas, Dervain is the most truthful person I've ever met, except maybe you on a bad day."

A fine tremor went through Emaris from head to foot. "You want me to believe an enemy's word?"

"Fine. Ask Hiraen, then. The great paragon of virtue." Savonn grinned, or grimaced. "On second thought, don't. He's had a harrowing day. It's probably best if he never has to think about me again."

Emaris drew a shaky breath. "You let us believe you were dead. I'm not going away till you explain yourself."

"Which part?" asked Savonn. He propped himself against the wall with his arms folded behind his head, eyes slackly lidded and thoughtless. "No, never mind. You see, it all goes back to bad blood and rotten seed. All hail Lord Kedris, highest, wisest, benevolentest of rulers, at least until you try to tell him no. Poor Merrott. You remember him?"

He did not wait for a response. "Honest old critter, salt of the earth, right as a square and twice as boring. He was loyal to Kedris in theory, but he had too much good sense to worship him the way most everyone did. Well, you can't outwit a rock, that's what dear Father always said. When you get tired of going around it, you fetch a crowbar and prise it out."

"*Kedris* wanted him dead?"

"Inhumed," said Savonn. "Eliminated. Boxed up and put away. He wanted Betronett, see. A pocket-sized army of his own, separate from the city guard, answerable only to the High Commander. So Merrott had to go."

He tilted his head back. A stray ringlet slipped over his face. "He tried Hiraen first. Smart little bastard, younger than you, with a good eye and a powerful family. Merrott adored him. Squire one moment, patrol leader the next. Just like you."

Emaris felt nauseous, but there was nowhere in the room he could throw up. He remembered being on guard duty when the old captain returned from skirmishing in the Farfallens, wounded in the side by a spear, still laughing and shouting commands at his squires. Three days later, he was unconscious; a week, and he was dead. The doctor said the wound had gone bad. The Lord Governor showed up in person to pay his respects, and overnight they had become the Silvertongue's men. It had all been very exciting.

"Hiraen didn't do it," he said. "He's not like you."

Savonn lacked even the decency to flinch. "Of course not. So Kedris tried to charm him. He was good at that. Merrott was an obstacle in the way of peace, he said, and already ripe for the reaper. He just needed a shove to send him on his way."

He laughed, a loose, dangerous sound. "You should have seen Hiraen as a boy. Brash, brutally honest, head stuffed so full of chivalry it threatened to float off his shoulders. He probably thought Kedris was joking. You think *I'm* joking, don't you?"

Emaris shook his head automatically. Brave, brilliant Kedris. Last summer, all Cassarah had gone weeping to his funeral. "It went on for a few years," said Savonn, "until—well, you've seen Hiraen lose his temper. Smashed a few expensive things, made some observations on Father's soul or lack thereof, and stormed off. You can imagine how much Kedris loved that. He could've found someone else to do the job, but it was a matter of pride by then. Hiraen's handsome head would have been on a pike that very evening if I hadn't gone on my knees and begged for his life, and even that wasn't enough."

Savonn dragged his gaze up to Emaris's face, and smiled at what he saw there. "Yes," he said. "I agreed to do it instead. Goodbye, theatre. Hello, Betronett. I try not to blame Hiraen. He blames himself enough for both of us."

"So you got the Empath to kill Merrott," said Emaris. "Why stop at one? Did you ask him to kill your father too?"

This seemed to amuse Savonn. He propped his elbows on his knees, peering at Emaris between his wrists. "Now we're talking. See, gazelle, you wouldn't look at me like that if you really knew Kedris. But no one did. And to think, I would've liked him a lot better if he'd just beat me himself once in a while."

There was a fiendish light in his eyes. "Maybe I prayed him dead. Prayers are delicate things, after all. You never know which god might hear."

"Or which priest," said Emaris.

"That, too."

Emaris rested his forehead against the cool stone wall. Savonn, the great gilded idol of his youth, against whose shadow everything else had been measured. Up till this morning Emaris would have followed him anywhere. But now—

"No," he said. "Even without you, Marguerit or the Empath would have killed him sooner or later. You didn't do it. You didn't mean to."

"Maybe," said Savonn. "But I betrayed him, and he died. So there is that. Shall I tell you a secret?"

His smile was cutting. Something terrible was on its way. Emaris could sense it, just as an antelope might smell a brewing storm. "I don't want to hear it."

"I didn't kill my father. Probably. Most likely. But—"

"I *said*, I don't want to—"

"But," said Savonn, "I killed yours."

Emaris's heart missed a beat, and restarted.

Silence puddled around them. Every nerve in his body was alive and screaming for action, for movement, for his bow and sword. Not once in his life had he struck with the intent to hurt. To slow and disable, yes, even to kill; never to watch skin mottle red and blue beneath his fists, to beat the smirk off a face, as he now did. This must be what other men meant when they talked about bloodlust. "You're lying."

"Oh, don't be naïve," said Savonn. "Rendell knew about Dervain. He was surprisingly forbearing about the whole thing—I suppose because he, too, once had an ill-advised affair with a foreign minx. Hence you and your sister..."

Emaris looked down at his fists as if they belonged to someone else. At some point, *not* hitting Savonn would be more effort than the alternative.

"He was harder to deal with after Merrott died," said Savonn. "I took you on as squire to keep him happy, but it was only a matter of time before he did something troublesome. Honourable men are so predictable. Men like him. Men like you... Either throw that punch or put your fists away, darling. I can't sit here calculating trajectories forever."

Emaris tucked his hands into his pockets one by one. He would not be provoked. Again, he said, "You're lying."

Savonn got his feet under him and rose. Executed when drunk, it was a careless, powerful swing, more congruent with the Empath than the Savonn Emaris was used to. They must have just seen each other. Mannerisms rubbed off on Savonn the way a lover's perfume might linger on one's collar. "I knew you were stubborn. I didn't think you were stupid."

"I'm not," said Emaris. "You were with me that night. Don't you remember? Did it mean so little to you? We fought off the Council's thugs together, and then Daine came and told us—that my father—"

His cheeks were hot and damp, but to wipe them felt like an admission of weakness. "You ran all the way to see him."

Gone was the wildcat savagery. Gone, too, was Savonn's complacent smile, leaving only hollow bleakness. "Haven't you worked it out? Those were Josit's assassins. It was her idea to frame Willon and discredit him at the assembly. I only found out after, when we got to the Safins'. If I'd had warning, I'd have made sure you weren't with me."

"I don't *care*," said Emaris. When had he started shouting? "You didn't lay a hand on my father. I know what I saw."

Rain pattering on the cobbles. The headlong dash across the city, up and down walls and across roofs. Daine's house, and the door at the end of the hall, opening to spill light and blood and Savonn's rearing shadow—

He blinked, and his vision was as clear as it had ever been. "You're a liar," he said. "And not even a good one. If you wanted to disillusion me, you managed it just fine with your treason and your spying and your godawful lover. You don't have to make up all this nonsense about my father as well. I'm going to find out who really killed him, and when I do, I'll be sure to let you know."

He might have said a lot more. But just then the door creaked open to reveal Hiraen in the tunnel, still in riding leathers, with a fur hood over his head. He glanced between the two of them, taking in Emaris's damp face. "Savonn. I wanted a word."

Emaris could not tell how long he had been there. Where eavesdropping was concerned, he had never been on this side of things. "Oh, come on in," said Savonn. "You might as well. I've already been convicted of high treason, had the gods reveal themselves to me, broken into a prison and a councillor's house, and been ambushed by the world's angriest gazelle on the way to bed. Why not host the High Commander for supper too?"

He looked cornered, half wild, as if seeing Hiraen and Emaris in the same room was the last straw. Emaris moved to the door on instinct, but stopped in the entryway. He was going to be shunted out by Savonn again, like so many times before. It felt like the worst offense of all he had already witnessed. "Was it worth it?" he asked. "All this, just to spite your father?"

"Emaris," said Hiraen. "Go."

Emaris did not go. Savonn picked up the cedarwood box, opened it, and slammed it shut again. "Spite?" he repeated, as if trying to remember what the word meant. "*Spite?*"

Hiraen said, "Savonn—"

"It was never for spite," said Savonn. "I only traded Dervain harmless information at first. When I gave him the patrol routes, it was so he would stay out of our way. I couldn't have fought him."

He looked at Emaris, at Hiraen. The air was thick with the sweet, sad smell of jasmine. "So yes. It was worth it."

Emaris could stand no more. He wrenched the door open and stormed out into the tunnel, leaving Savonn and Hiraen alone with each other. The catacomb was quiet now, the cast and crew long gone. Emaris supposed they had dispersed to their dormitory or inn or wherever they went when they, like normal actors, stopped acting for the night. He should never have come. He had hoped for a shred of truth from Savonn, a glimpse of the face behind the masks, but instead he had seen a version of him he had never wanted to know. It was a trespass he could never take back.

Slamming through the unicorn door, he emerged at the bottom of the Arena, where warriors and slaves had duelled to the death hundreds of years ago. He stared up at the endless rings of stone benches, shivering, and wishing ferociously for someone to fight.

CHAPTER 11

"You said *what* to him?"

Characteristically, the High Commander of Cassarah had announced himself by lobbing a waterskin at Savonn and insisting that he drink, and was now pacing the room with his hands furled into fists. "You're out of your mind. You told him you did it? What the hell do you take him for? Or me, for that matter?"

Savonn had drunk enough to lose his self-preservatory instincts, but not enough to attain oblivion. It was a perilous no man's land. "Maybe," he said, "you should have asked yourself that before you took a knife to Rendell's throat and made martyrs of you both."

His day had passed the threshold of absurdity sometime around his first sight of Dervain in the Arena, cuffed and chained like a common criminal. By this point Hiraen might have been a hallucination for all he knew. "Do you think I wanted to?" asked Hiraen. "Do you think there's been one miserable day since then that I haven't wished I'd just exposed you myself?"

He had stopped pacing. Now he stood over Savonn, frowning like a caryatid. "If not for Josit..."

Savonn's eyes had been slipping shut. It seemed necessary to reopen them. He could not remember the last time he had slept. "Josit?"

"That night," said Hiraen, "I ran into her. She told me Rendell was on his way to Willon's dinner and that he meant to come clean about you, just to stop you making yourself Governor. He didn't know you were planning to leave—well, neither did Josit, I suppose—"

He rubbed his eyes. "I didn't want to believe it, but we both know he always thought there was something odd about Merrott's death. I didn't have time to think, damn you. I owed you too much."

Josit again. Like a dragon at the heart of a labyrinth, she surfaced at the end of every road Savonn took. Two protectors, both vicious enough to kill. Not like Iyone, with her cool macabre strength; Iyone, who had surrendered his letters the way one might amputate a gangrenous limb, to kill the rot and save the rest. He had always trusted her like no other.

"I'm going to tell Emaris," said Hiraen. "I wanted to before, but that would have meant telling him why, and then..." He shrugged. "That's not a problem now."

"What on earth do you expect him to do?" said Savonn. "Strike off your head?"

"He should," said Hiraen bitterly.

Perhaps Savonn *was* hallucinating. Certainly one of them had come unhitched from reality. "Don't be absurd. Put your scruples aside and look—just *look*, damn you—at the consequences. Honour is expensive. Emaris thinks the world of you. You don't mind hurting him? You don't care if the army falls apart and the Council goes back to honking at each other like mad geese?"

He seldom raised his voice like this. Anger was chancy. It gave too much away. But he thought he was allowed to indulge himself a little, when everyone he loved seemed bent on self-destruction. "That's a bloody high horse you've got there, isn't it?" said

Hiraen. "You didn't mind so much when it was you making a scandal in the courts."

"True," said Savonn. "But I'm used to thinking of you as the better man. I forgot that you always disappoint."

He dodged on instinct. But Hiraen's fist went the other way and hit the wall of crates, where it broke one, splintered another, and sent three more crashing to the floor. Savonn eyed the wreckage with distant fascination. "For shame," he said. "It would be *so* embarrassing if you were found buried alive in stage props with a wanted fugitive. At least save yourself for Emaris."

Hiraen studied his bloody knuckles, holding them away from his face as though they were venomous. Now that the rage had passed, he looked deflated. "Like you're saving yourself for the Empath?"

He looked down. In dodging, Savonn had sped up what the combined forces of alcohol and gravity had been trying to do, and achieved a fully horizontal position on the mattress. It was too much trouble to get back up. He lay there, blinking at the fuzzy spot that was Hiraen's face. He should not have flinched. Hiraen was not Kedris.

"I know you," said Hiraen. "You're going to do something ridiculous and get caught, and next week we'll have a double execution. Gods forbid I die for my principles, but it's just fine for you to die for yours."

His tragic expression was unbelievable. People like him should have been stuffed and mounted in a taxidermist's shop window. Savonn longed to be back with Dervain in the seclusion of the tower cell, safe under those gentle, killing hands, with the mirrored image of his soul that understood him perfectly. Or close to perfectly.

He groped for words. "As usual, you're wrong. I have no intention of dying, whatever Dervain thinks, and the only principles involved are yours."

"So you're going to kill him?" said Hiraen. "Or let him kill you? Are we talking about penance, or vengeance?"

There was not much difference. Perhaps he should have been angry with Dervain for exposing him. Perhaps he was. But he had known for some time now that Dervain was a pawn like him; that Kedris's shackles were tight around them both, and it would take much more than a spear to the heart to free them. Hiraen had reason to understand this more than most. "Call it what you want," said Savonn. He was too tired to argue. His eyes had slid shut and refused to open again. "You were there in the Temple. You heard what the—"

"I did," said Hiraen. "I know. You have to settle your blood feud one way or another or you'll go the rest of your life thinking you owe that hellhound Kedris something. *I know.* Don't mention them here."

Kedris would have dismissed the High Priestess as a lunatic, the whole production as a charlatan's trick. But Kedris had strength and arrogance enough to believe in nothing but himself. Savonn was cast from an inferior mould. He was not so sure. "You won't hang Dervain," he said, with effort. "He's not yours to kill. I'll pluck him from the gallows myself if I can't think of a better way."

"For fuck's sake," said Hiraen. "No."

He was always going to be difficult. It was Merrott all over again. "I have to."

"I meant," said Hiraen, "no, you won't do it, because *I* will. This is out of your hands."

Nothing was ever in Savonn's hands unless he seized it by force, with descanting choirs and fireworks. But his mouth felt as soggy as his head, and this was too many words to say. It was possible he was already half asleep. "Smuggle yourself into the war council tomorrow," said Hiraen, "and you'll see what I mean. I owe you. I owe him too."

"You don't," Savonn began, and lost track of the rest of the sentence. A flutter of foreboding settled in his stomach. The last time Hiraen got it in his head that he owed Savonn something, a man had died. "You better not—"

"Don't argue with me," said Hiraen. "You people made me High Commander, you can damn well do what I say."

The silence elapsed. Savonn hoped Hiraen had gone away, and feared he had. Then the mattress dipped, and a weight settled beside him. The backs of his eyelids went dark. Either he was dying, or the lamp had been put out. "Shut up and go to sleep," said Hiraen. "I'll keep watch. Good gods, how much ale did you drink?"

Savonn struggled to get up, but his limbs no longer seemed to be attached to him. "A lot." They didn't make ale here like they did in Astorre. They didn't make anything like they did in Astorre. He couldn't tell if he had said that aloud, or just groaned.

Hiraen sighed. "I know."

Something warm and soft and heavy was flung over him. Savonn gave up at last, and released his grip on consciousness. Just as he was slipping away, the heavy fog of sleep rising to claim him, he thought he heard Hiraen add, "I'd do it all over again if I had to."

CHAPTER 12

"*Release* him?" said Oriane.

Five minutes into the first meeting of the new Council, they were already at a standstill. The fire on the hearth was banking low, and a bone-biting draught gusted through the arrow slits in the wall. Iyone sat back, sipping her lukewarm tea, and luxuriating in the look on her colleagues' faces. For once, this impasse was not of her making. This was her brother's absurd idea, and she wanted none of it.

"As I understand," said Hiraen, "Marguerit sent us another courier this morning, raising her ransom offer. What was it again, Lord Yannick?"

Yannick looked startled. "Oh—yes. I have it here." He shuffled his papers. "Either twenty thousand drochii, or ten thousand and the release of thirty Cassaran-born slaves."

Oriane drew a sharp breath. "So much?"

She and Yannick both looked at Iyone, as if they thought she might have had something to do with this. Iyone forced the laugh back into her lungs, where it belonged. She had resolved to take no part in this madness. "Each of the Sanctuary's trained killers is worth a fortune," said Hiraen. "I'd know, I fought one all summer. Presumably, with his gifts, the Empath is worth even more."

A servant bustled up in a clatter of teacups. It was a young doe-eyed girl sheathed from neck to toe in a grey cotton gown, the depressing matronly sort that turned perfectly good bodies into featureless rectangles. Under her hairnet, her curls were a bronzy orange that could only have been achieved by soaking black hair in bad bleach. Hiraen made a sound that might have been a cough.

"Why all this talk of money?" asked Iyone blithely. "Is the war treasury empty already, Lord Hiraen?"

"No," said Hiraen. "But my men will need to eat, drink, and whore if they're going to be fighting all winter. Unlike Marguerit, I don't lead slaves."

Iyone glanced between him and the maid, deliberating. Hiraen had vanished late last night, after the obligatory family supper. She gathered he had cornered Savonn and talked things out with him. She had not asked, because that would have meant discussing the High Priestess, and that was beyond even her mettle.

"I have had a look at the accounts," Yannick was saying. He might have been worried, or annoyed; it was hard to say, given that his usual expression was somewhere between the two. "Kedris left the treasury overflowing with gold. We ought not face any trouble on that front."

Iyone abandoned her resolve to be silent. Nothing ever seemed to get done unless she took a hand in it. "Yes," she said, "but the High Commander has a costly new strategy to stop the Saraians. Last I heard, it involves fortifying Lissein, and is as sure to stop Marguerit as it is to bankrupt us."

The maid finished pouring the tea. Her bright eyes darted from Hiraen to Iyone, too calculating to be demure. Then she picked up her tray and retreated to the servants' alcove. "The village by the Singing Ford?" said Oriane.

"Surely there are countless other places where an army might cross," said Yannick. "Amarota, Derien, Ilmerat—why Lissein?"

"The Singing Ford," said Hiraen, "is by far the best landing ground for an invading force. The current is slow because the isle of Evenfall acts as a breakwater, and the terrain's hilly on our side, so it'll be hard for us to manoeuvre cannon. Oh, and"—he grinned—"Marguerit's spies won't fail to notice that the defenders stationed there are either twelve years old or eighty-four."

Oriane caught on. "It's to be a lure?"

"Exactly," said Hiraen. "I've taken measures to evacuate the village. Lord Cayn of Terinea will take in the peasants for the winter. In the meantime, our engineers will litter the place with death traps. Collapsing roofs, swinging scythes, falling rocks, things like that. It'll cut Marguerit's van to pieces, and then we can swoop in and rout the rest."

Yannick rolled and unrolled his sleeves, looking fretful. "I see," said Oriane. "A gory circus. The spirit of Savonn Silvertongue lives on, doesn't it?"

A cheerful jangle of crockery rang in the alcove. "It was Iyone's idea," said Hiraen, sounding strained. "But you could say so."

They brooded for a few moments. Shouts and trumpet-calls drifted through the window from the courtyard below, where the city guard was drilling. "It's a good idea," said Yannick, rubbing his chin. "But Lady Iyone is right. It would be costly, very costly indeed. If we bargained with Marguerit, we could transfer the pinch to her purse, so to speak. Say, fifteen thousand drochii *and* a hundred slaves freed..."

"I agree," said Iyone, which was something she had never thought she would say to Yannick Efren.

Oriane set down her cup with a rattle. "Have you all lost your wits? Just yesterday you were saying Marguerit must never have the Empath back."

"That was before we heard him testify," said Hiraen. "Dervain Teraille is a madman who has built his life on the sole idea of ruining the Andalles. Now he's succeeded, I suspect Marguerit will find him less devoted than he was before."

Silence from the alcove. "He murdered Kedris and made a fool of us in front of the whole city," said Oriane moodily. "People will riot if we let him go."

"It's the hanging they want," said Hiraen. "Bloody spectacles are easy to come by. Money less so. And we can't in good conscience refuse to free a hundred slaves."

For a minute they were all silent, and looked at everywhere but each other. If they had been having this conversation only a couple decades ago, they would each have owned a household full of slaves and they knew it. Under her breath, Oriane said, "We should ask for *two* hundred."

"Very wise," said Hiraen. "Yannick, make sure to include that in our response."

Iyone could hardly believe it. It seemed Hiraen was going to pull this off, after all. They were going to free the single greatest threat the city had faced in eighteen years—or the second greatest, depending on one's opinion of Savonn—and turn him loose on the world. She stared out through the window at the leaden sky and thought of freed slaves, of a woman on the run; ghost voices speaking in the dark, and a crying girl and a spreading puddle of violet ink.

They did so much for each other, so much they could never take back.

"But, my lord," said Yannick at last. He had pulled about a full yard of thread from his sleeves. "If we let the Empath walk free, what will he do to us? He, ah, seems like the vengeful sort..."

Oriane laughed, unsmiling. "To say the least."

Hiraen did not have an answer to that. He looked at Iyone. So did Oriane and Yannick. So did the maid, lurking in the alcove with a teapot in her hands. Iyone sighed. As usual, they had managed to leave all the heavy lifting to her.

"About that," she said. "I may have an idea or two."

CHAPTER 13

The day the first frost turned the streets and lawns to filthy silver, Marguerit's carthorses began to arrive, bearing the promised ransom.

The gold and the former slaves came over at the Fords of Amarota, only a half-day's ride from the city. This provoked muttering in certain quarters. The more perspicacious pointed out that the High Commander had stationed his best cavalry at Amarota, so the Saraian dogs were unlikely to try anything; and if anyone had cause to worry it was the poor folk of Lissein, defended only by a crew of greybeards and their prepubescent grandsons. One only hoped Lord Hiraen knew what he was doing.

Other choruses of grumbling broke out elsewhere. People, in particular the Betronett troops, had been looking forward to seeing the Empath hanged. A riot started outside the citadel and was swiftly extinguished by the Commander himself. Then, to everyone's surprise, his lordship invited the rioters inside to watch the gold counted and tallied in terse exchanges between Marguerit's heralds, the Council's book-keepers, and their flustered interpreters. This was an eye-opener, and soon shut them up. Most of them had never seen a real Saraian before, except the red fellow himself, and all agreed he was a poor representative of his kind. Surely not all of them could be so dazzling. Or so glib. It was the law of averages, or something.

The counting done, the Council sent out a proclamation. They had set aside a judicious fraction of the gold to throw a feast in honour of the High Commander and his brave Betronett men. Wagons of roast fowl and sweetmeats and barrels of mulled wine were soon trundling through the streets, accompanied by flautists and jugglers and acrobats. Behold the firstfruits of victory, Lady Iyone announced. The war was only just beginning, and ahead lay trials and privations aplenty, but the present, after all, foretold nine-tenths of the future. This arithmetic was difficult to grasp with a head heavy with food and wine, but few doubted it. Iyone Safin had said so, and that girl knew what she was about.

In all the excitement, a messenger arrived from Lord Lucien, who had reached Terinea with Bonner Efren and Daron Sydell. Their triumphant army had acquired several hundred more volunteers on the way home, and would arrive within the week. This last bit of good news seemed to confirm everything the feast promised. The Safins had come through for them again. With this new force, the High Commander would surely drive off the Saraians in no time, and even the Silvertongue's youthful indiscretion could be forgotten.

The grumbling ceased. The revelries proceeded. All was well, for now.

* * *

The aforesaid youthful indiscretion was, at the moment, being cornered in his cell.

It appeared that Savonn had made good his word. There was to be no execution. This morning a senior priest of the Sanctuary had come to examine Dervain before his release—an unpleasant fellow whose death he and Nikas had plotted countless times.

This second visitor was more interesting. Dervain's five earthly senses showed him the young woman, dark-haired and light-eyed and imposing as a tower, whom he had first met in the house of Josit Ansa. His one unearthly sense flinched away from her. There were too many things simmering in this cauldron, few of them good.

The other councillors feared this woman. Her brother revered her. Dervain could see why.

"You must have heard," said Iyone Safin. "Through some fluke of undeserved mercy, you are to be returned to the Sanctuary in one piece. I am here to discuss the terms of your release."

She carried herself in a way that seemed to take up all the space in the room, and most of the air, too. He was exhausted just looking at her. Savonn insinuated himself around the edges of a situation, a sly, changeable moon; Iyone, however, loomed like the noonday sun, unforgivingly bright. She was alone and unarmed and unafraid, and the bitter tang of disquiet was Dervain's own. "I thought Her Magnificence had paid my ransom," he said. "Must you cut off my thumbs and put out my eyes too?"

"No," said Iyone. "Here in Cassarah, we believe in civility. Look up that word when you get home. What we want is a solemn pledge never to bear arms again on this side of the Morivant for as long as you live, under pain of death."

He pondered this. Like most laws, it was theoretically sound and impossible to enforce. "By which god should I swear, my lady? In my country, there are many you have never heard of. Fair Ysalonde, witch of equivocation? Or Dedos, the little lord of lies?"

"It's all the same to me," said Iyone. "I am not threatening you with the hand of the gods. I am threatening you with my own."

Dervain had been brought up by priests and acolytes. He had studied the sacraments of the Nameless Father and undergone the rituals and, on more occasions than he could count, fed the god his sacrifices. He knew hubris when he saw it. "And what are you proposing to do to me?"

"To *you*?" said Iyone. "Why should I trouble with you? I have your lover. Or your enemy, or whatever you call each other now. All I have to do is hand him over to the Council, and when they finish with him, they'll nail him piece by piece to the city wall for you to collect. And he will know, in his last moments, that he died without you because you were as false and faithless as he was."

Thunder and hot air. Or not. "Would you really? He is dear to you. To your brother too, if my senses do not fail me."

"Yes," said Iyone. A lesser foe would have tried to deny it. "Why else do you think he entrusted his letters to me, Lord Empath? And yet the Council has them, and he stands condemned. After all—what was it you said?—*Love is barren, impermanent: the chord is struck, and the vibrations die away...*"

Dervain's head swam. He had taken a step back without noticing. Marguerit would have to be warned about this new menace. "You hate him? Because he made you release me?"

She laughed. "No one makes me do anything. I mean what I say."

She might be bluffing. Or she might have failsafes already in place, lest pity stay her hand at the last minute. A disharmony of flashing lights danced before his eyes. He longed for Savonn, for the heady musk of his skin, the sudden violence of his kisses. This was their last separation. Soon, Savonn had promised, they would be together for always. But only if they both lived to keep their word.

"Well?" said Iyone. "Will you swear it?"

Dervain collected himself. No matter if he were banished—Savonn would come to him instead. The High Priest would be displeased, but he had Nikas. They understood things like feuds and honour in the Sanctuary, and in any case there were plenty of people who needed killing on their own side of the river. There always were.

"Very well," he said. "I promise not to bear arms on your territory again. I swear this by he who is master of the Sanctuary, and by his consort the Mother Above, and Aebria and Casteia and the Ceriyes, and my dead family as well, though that may be cheating, since I hardly knew them. Let us also include Amitei and Charissos for good measure."

It amused her. He felt her mirth as a light prickle under his fingernails and on the bottoms of his feet, a mocking flagellation. "Who else? Don't leave out anyone."

He had thought to approach her as a Marguerit, a goddess among mortals. Now he saw she was more of a Celisse. "My cat too, in that case. We are very fond of cats in the Sanctuary, in all their nine lives. Every new acolyte is given a kitten when they arrive, did you know?"

"To be disemboweled later with their bare hands, I hear," said Iyone. "It seems like a lot of effort just to instill courage in those who have none."

To her credit, she was not squeamish. "Something like that," he agreed. "But I should tell you that mine lived to the venerable age of nineteen, and the palace gardens at Daliss are still infested with her descendants. On the other hand, a great many of my minders have met with sudden, premature, and painful deaths."

She gave him an appraising look. "Is that a threat?"

"It is an obvious metaphor about you, me, and Savonn," he said. "I am certain you can work out which of you is the minder, and which the cat. Is our discussion over, ladyship?"

She moved to the door. Whatever she felt made itself known to him as a crushing pressure around his lungs, cold and insistent. He had made an impression. "Yes, I think so," she said. "Have a safe journey, Lord Empath. I wish you a long and uneventful life, far from my city and everyone in it."

* * *

The guards came for him an hour later. Blindfolded and chained once more, he was led out of his cell and through the city by long and circuitous means, mostly underground. The cloth over his eyes was so thick as to let in no sense of light whatsoever. Still, there was plenty to take in. The slippery stones under his feet. The rank, fishy air, suggesting they were close to the river. Probably they were going to take him through the Fire Gate; it was the closest to Amarota. The roar of fast-flowing water reached him, and grew louder as they went, underlaid by the rollicking hum of a city at its revels—a strange sound when imposed against the skin-crawling ooze of his guards' tension. Why should a monster go free? They resented him, and by association the Safins, whose idea it had been.

Dervain filed all this away for later use. Iyone was a fool if she thought he could do no harm from the other side of the Morivant.

At the top of an interminable stair—fifty-nine steps—the stuffy warmth receded, and a fresh, chilly breeze beat against his face. They were back above ground. A pair of horses whinnied nearby. Draught-horses, both elderly; their complaisance tasted like wild honey. A carriage creaked. Soft voices murmured in Saraian. His escort: Marguerit's royal guard, come to take him back to a life he no longer cared to lead. His skin was goose-bumped. The fear was theirs.

Then colour blazed against his eyelids, so brilliant he thought they had ripped off his blindfold. The wind turned hot. He could no longer sense the guards. Something stronger and more immediate had displaced them. Deft fingers did away with his chains, and undid the knot of his blindfold. As the cloth was removed, he caught a whiff of rose and hyacinth.

He stood blinking in sudden daylight, recovering his bearings. He was in the middle of a paved square facing the Fire Gate, the red gold and black steel of its struts vivid against the overcast sky. Ahead were the draught-horses and the carriage and the escort of footsoldiers, just as he had pictured. A platoon of spearmen was arrayed around him, as if that would have done any good if he made up his mind to kill someone.

And at his side, the colourful presence.

Looks were deceiving. He saw a young groom with bleached blond curls under a straw hat: a stranger, if Dervain had not recognised him first with the blindfold on. "Milord will allow me to help him into the carriage."

Surprise after surprise, a spectacle that never ceased. Dervain took the proffered arm and let the groom hand him through the door. Inside the carriage smelled of sandalwood, and a lute he recognised lay on the cushioned bench. He touched the strings: perfectly in tune. Of course.

He looked back. Savonn was smiling. His fingers lingered on the inside of Dervain's palm, and his eyes glimmered with secrets. "Fly far, nightingale."

Dervain smiled back. Then Savonn pulled away, and the door swung shut as the carriage began to move. No other words had passed between them. None were needed. In any skin, by any name, they belonged together, and neither god nor man could keep them apart.

By the time the carriage trundled out of the city, Dervain had kicked his shoes off and started up a merry tune on the lute.

* * *

Not three days after the Saraians departed, the alarum-bells began to toll. A lone rider on a half-dead horse galloped through the city, dismounted at the citadel drawbridge, and cried to be taken before Lord and Lady Safin. The Saraians were on the march, he said. The Marshal had at last decamped from outside Daliss and was headed for the river. The far bank was crawling with banners. Marguerit had made her move.

The Cassarans finished the last of the wine, washed the grease from their hands, and awaited the High Commander's orders. War had come knocking. They were ready to answer.

ACT TWO

RIVER PLAY

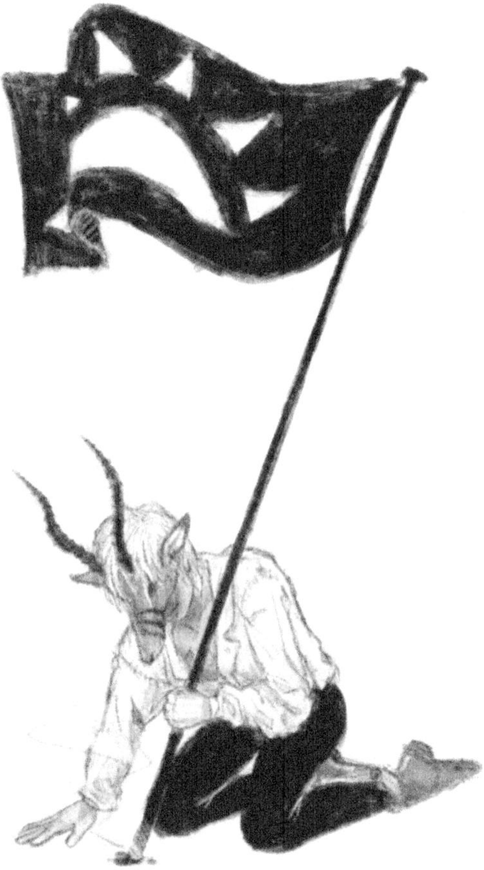

REPRISE: WINTER 1531

It ended with his father, as all things did.

Josit knew the signs, and tried to warn him in her usual cryptic way. "You spend too much time in Astorre," she said one evening, when Rendell's patrol called at Cassarah and Savonn at last found a minute to visit her. "Your father is irritated."

They could speak freely in the house on the Street of Canaries. Not so much Savonn's apartments in the citadel, where servants watched and reported, or the banquet hall where the Governor would feast the patrol tonight. "Didn't he agree with Merrott that I was a useful spy?"

"Yes," said Josit. "But he disagrees with Merrott on many other things. Such as the man's continued existence."

Kedris's phantom voice slid into his head again. Savonn heard less of it with Red in Astorre, but as soon as he was alone it came back in full force. *I should have him whipped through the streets and beheaded.* Hiraen was far away on the Bitten Hill, he reminded himself—safe for the moment, insofar as anyone could be safe from Kedris. The idiot lacked even the good sense to fear for his life. Savonn had to do the fearing for both of them.

Josit regarded him from the settee. A queen in another life, who had never forgotten it, playing champion to Danei Cayn's unloved son. He could never fathom why she did it. "If you are planning to kill the old man at all, I suggest you do it soon," she said. "Your father needs to be distracted. He is beginning to wonder how you get your hands on the information you feed him."

They were speaking Saraian. The tongue of tenderness, as Savonn saw it. Always they had spoken it together, he and Josit and Iyone, a private cypher among friends. Something in him went cold. "I thought he was pleased."

"You should know better," said Josit. "It is only a matter of time before he tries to find out what—or who—is keeping you so busy in the highlands."

They locked eyes. He understood, then. She knew about Red. It was inevitable. Kedris's spies were easy to spot, easy to fool: often Savonn had led them to the door of some unsavoury pleasure-house and climbed out the back window, later to receive with glee his father's acerbic commentary on his proclivities. But Josit was subtle and virulent, and *her* spies might be anywhere. Red's consulate. The Bitten Hill. Even, unthinkable as it seemed, the haven of the Safin manor.

Nothing was safe from her. Nothing was sacred. Even what he had with Red would be dragged through the mud of this filthy city if she so chose.

He put on his blankest face. "If I am to be interrogated on my choice of lover," he said, "I suppose there is no one more suited to the task than you. After all, you chose my father."

He answered in Falwynian, as befitted such profane matters. Josit laughed. Cool as silk, still; nothing ever perturbed her. "So I did. We have such a way of collecting useful people, you and I."

He had never courted Red with the intent to use him. But perhaps it was true. Perhaps he was just like Josit in the end, like Kedris—black-blooded, stone-souled, a merchant of secrets and lies. "Better that I interrogate you than your father," said Josit.

She was no longer smiling. "You are growing sloppy, my cygnet, with your smugglings and your underground dealings. I cannot protect you if you do not protect yourself. Do you *want* him to find out?"

Savonn had a vision of Red stripped, flogged, hanged and drawn and quartered and left to rot on the gibbet while dogs tore the flesh from his bones. Kedris would do to him all the things he had threatened to do to Hiraen, and make Savonn watch. With an autopsist's detachment, he wondered what would happen if he threw up on Josit's fine parquet floor.

"Maybe he ought to," he said. "He could behead us on the same guillotine, and save you both some trouble."

Josit slapped him. An open-handed blow, more sound than anything else. When the shock passed she was still surveying him, straight-backed and high-chinned, an empress in a portrait. "He would do it if he heard you speak like this," she said. "Stand up straight and address me like a man. Your mother did not raise a coward."

Her jewels glittered. She had not struck in anger, and so violence did not diminish her. He refrained from pointing out that Danei used to get out of bed maybe one day a month, and so had raised no one at all. "You were destined for more than this," said Josit. "You will not disgrace me by prostituting yourself to one of Marguerit's dogs. If you have need of a bedwarmer, I can find dozens for you. But you will not give your father reason to doubt you, or you may find me a lot more frightening than he will ever be."

How many miles was it from here to Astorre? He was trapped with Josit in this solar, in this city, and Red was far away. His deadliest secret of all, sharp as the north wind and sweet as summerwine, the only lover it had not degraded him to lie with. The only one who had unfurled the kaleidoscope of Savonn's faces, and loved him for the multitude that he was. And here they spoke of bedwarmers.

Savonn breathed in, and out, till he achieved the dead calm of a mausoleum. "Very well," he said. "I shall go now and murder my commander, as men do. I hope I do not give my lady further cause for embarrassment."

He waited, but she did not dismiss him. She might have been angry, or only thinking. He could never read her. "You don't want to do it."

Of course not. He had hoped that, if he waited long enough, he would not have to. That Kedris would be satisfied with trade treaties and army gossip and demand nothing else. That Merrott would die of his own accord, or sniff out the plot on his life and banish Savonn first. But he was not to say such things to Josit. Coldly: "No, my lady."

There was pity in her eyes. She was, in the end, his only protector. "You will have to live with it," she said. "But we all have to live with something."

* * *

When spring came he slipped past the doormen at the consulate, as he always did; and found Red waiting for him in the upper room, as he always was. But it was different now that Josit knew. Their private world had been breached. It felt purer, rawer, underlaid with bitterness, as if already lost to him.

"There is something I must do," Savonn said. "After that, we might not meet again."

CHAPTER 14

Following custom, the troops assembled that evening in the Arena of White Sand to await orders: the Betronett cavalry and the city guard, augmented by several hundred citizen volunteers. Emaris fetched his excited patrol from the barracks Hiraen had commandeered for them and marched them to the Arena, where the rest of the company had already filled two of the lower rings.

"Look, Emaris," said Vion, brandishing a quiver of arrows. "We've got it all worked out. Lomas will hand these to me, and I'll hand them to you, and you'll shoot them. We'll be unstoppable. Where's Hiraen?"

The Arena was abuzz with the chatter of voices and the chink of mail. Still, with only the army allowed to enter, it was much emptier than on the day of the trial. Emaris spotted Lady Oriane and Lord Yannick just below them, and Lady Aretel across the theatre, each surrounded by the men of their households. But the High Commander was nowhere in evidence. "I've no idea," he said. "Don't move, I'll go look for him."

But he had scarcely taken three steps when a servant in black and orange surfaced at his side. "Lord Hiraen wants to see you backstage. Now, sir."

"Right," said Emaris. "At once."

This was to be his first pitched battle. He had never attended a war council before, but he had the feeling they were not usually held backstage of a theatre. Nor were they so exclusive. Besides Hiraen and Iyone, the only person present was a slight blond fellow Emaris did not know, lurking behind them like a bodyguard. "A thousand foot, according to the scouts," said Hiraen as soon as Emaris came through the unicorn door. "And half again as many horse."

"At the Singing Ford?" asked Emaris, breathless.

"Surprise," said Iyone. "Our plan worked."

Hiraen grinned, without conviction. "Except that the Saraians came early. They'll cross the river by midnight, and my father's troops aren't here yet. Emaris, you'll need to go and relieve our sham army."

He might as well have suggested flying and breathing fire. "*Me?*"

"Show him the blueprint," said Iyone. She had, Emaris thought, a way of speaking that would not have been out of place on a dusty battlefield, in the thickest of the chaos. "You know about the death circus?"

Her bodyguard handed Emaris a vellum scroll. It was a map of a village: an unruly network of roads with buildings demarcated by squares and circles, some filled in with charcoal, others marked off with big red crosses. "Lissein," he said, uneasy.

"A small force will do," said Hiraen. "Take the Betronett troops. We want to lure the Saraian van into the village. If we overwhelm them with numbers, they'll just retreat and come back tomorrow with reinforcements."

Emaris struggled to load this into his mind. He had heard a great deal about the death circus in the past month, but only at second- and third-hand. He had never even set foot in the village himself. "You're not coming?"

Hiraen's brow creased over. "No. I was—counselled otherwise." He scowled. "Apparently, being High Commander involves a lot less fighting and more talking than I thought."

To Emaris's surprise, the blond bodyguard laughed. "I believe our exact words were, 'Think like Marshal Isemain, not a footsoldier in a foxhole.'"

Emaris lost his breath, and caught it again. It was the voice he had not heard in weeks, intimately familiar, dreaded and missed in equal measure. Savonn—last seen swimming in wine and misery at the back of a storeroom—was now impeccable in leather and mail, a sunburst pin on his lapel. This new blond Savonn was overlaid on the old one, two paintings ghosting through each other on reused canvas: one looked at him and saw, discomfitingly, both entities at once. The effect was cumulative.

"He bleached his hair," said Iyone. "Alas, he could not bleach his heart."

"We used four tubs of the stuff," added Hiraen. "It came out orange the first time."

Savonn eyed them sideways. "I'm sure Master Emaris agrees that his great high lordship should stay where his people can see him," he said. "No one doubts his courage. Do you doubt yours, Emaris?"

"No," said Emaris, disconcerted. It had not even occurred to him that Savonn would dare show his face outside the catacomb again.

"The engineers will guide you," said Hiraen. He flicked his thumb in Savonn's direction. "And you can take *him* along."

From his expression, it was clear that this had not been his idea. "He knows the place?" Emaris asked.

Savonn regarded him with a sardonic look. The blond hair made him look younger, his sharp features gentled and rubbed smooth; which was to say, it had about the same effect as weaving daffodils round a crocodile's jaw. "Not well," he said. "But Iyone showed me the blueprint five minutes ago, and I have memorised it, so nothing could possibly go wrong."

Iyone twitched a smile. "One cannot have a circus without a clown."

They exchanged a glance, Savonn's eyes crinkling at the corners. Emaris used to wonder what it would take for Savonn to smile at him like that—small and private, a little joke shared, a friendship acknowledged. He had wanted so terribly to be admitted to that innermost sanctum, before he saw what sort of place it was. Now the very idea stung. He had been so childish, once.

"Oh, ignore them," said Hiraen, seeing the look on his face. "You don't have to listen to anything Savonn says. You'll have sole command on this mission. Daine will help you."

"That's what I said," said Savonn. "You'll give the orders while I hold your standard and look pretty. By the way, where's your sister? I thought to invite her with us. We'd make a gorgeous golden trio."

For some reason, that made both Safins glare at him. "I don't know," said Emaris. He and Shandei had been planting chives in their back garden when the alarum-bells tolled, but he knew better than to think she might stay put while the fighting-men stood to arms. "I never know where she is."

"Oh, well," said Savonn. "The High Commander will watch over her."

"Shut up and study the map," said Hiraen. "Emaris, a word."

He half ushered, half propelled Emaris back through the unicorn door and into the Arena. A cheer rose from the lower stands as the crowd caught sight of their commander, and like clockwork, Hiraen lifted a hand to them. "I'm sorry," he said. "This isn't ideal. I'd much rather go with you and leave him here."

Looking up at the ranks of cheering men, Emaris felt both light- and heavy-headed at once. He wondered if Daine and Vion and the rest ever wished they could have kept Hiraen all to themselves, a selfish Betronett secret. He knew he did. "They're right. People need to see you."

"That's not the point. Look, you have to be careful. As long as the Empath lives, Savonn is in danger. Don't let him slip away."

Emaris stopped walking. "You think he'll try to get to Savonn?"

"No, I think Savonn will try to get to him. I *know* he will. It's only a matter of time. Glue yourself to him if you have to."

"But he—"

"I assure you, Hiraen," said the damnable voice from behind Emaris, "that such extremes will be unnecessary. I won't give you reason to regret what you did."

The bodyguard had emerged from the catacomb. Savonn's voice came out of his mouth, but he did not look much like Savonn at all, a stolid figure with his head lowered in deference. Emaris swallowed the urge to shove him back through the unicorn door and tuck him out of sight. In a rather different tone, Savonn added, "If milord will permit this humble one a suggestion, it might be unwise to dress a wanted man in milord's own livery? And put milord's standard in his hands?"

Hiraen smiled. Devoid of mirth, it looked exactly like what it was, a complex, laborious coordination of skin and sinew. "That," he said, "is exactly why I did it. So—"

The army had begun to chant his name. Hiraen looked from one of them to the other. Of a sudden, one remembered he was barely older than Emaris; that this, too, would be his first pitched battle. "So don't do anything stupid."

* * *

Lissein was a night's hard trot from Cassarah. Emaris led the column with Savonn carrying the Safin banner at his side, while Daine scouted ahead and came back now and then with news. The token force at the Singing Ford had engaged the Saraian vanguard briefly, then melted into the wilderness as planned. The villagers had long since evacuated. They passed a few stragglers going the other way, local farmers fleeing to the city with their harvest. Some saluted Emaris, which made his face grow hot.

Then the tidings turned curious. The invaders had crossed over, but the Marshal was not in evidence. Indeed, the host did not seem anywhere as large as reported. "Two, three hundred horse at most," said Daine, returning for the last time close to dawn. "Either the foot didn't come over, or they never existed."

The column had halted, the men formed up in battle order. The fields and housetops of Lissein had just come into view at the bottom of a gentle hillock, and the eastern sky was lightening, streamers of ruby and marigold drifting among the clouds like blood from some harpooned sea-creature. But to their left, the broad blue ribbon of the Morivant was still in shadow. "A ruse?" Emaris suggested.

"It's an old trick," said Savonn. "Three cookfires for every real soldier, plus a straw man here and there to swell the numbers. The scouts counted them at dusk, when the sun would have been in their eyes. An easy mistake to make."

He had not spoken much during the journey. At first sight, Daine had stared at him in astonishment, then snatched the reins out of his hands and hauled him behind a tree for what appeared to be a concentrated dressing-down. They returned not long after, Daine looking like a thundercloud, Savonn carefully nonchalant. They had not looked at each other since. No one else had recognised Savonn, though Vion and Lomas did glance at the standard-bearer a little too often for comfort. "But why so few?" Emaris asked. "And who's leading, if not the Marshal?"

An awful suspicion came to him. Daine, too, looked grim. "He took a vow. If he's here, he's an oathbreaker."

"So he's not here," said Savonn, in the cool flinty voice he always used when speaking of Dervain Teraille. "Whatever this is, it's not their main attack. They'll try to cross over somewhere else."

Emaris's blood ran cold. Cassarah—with its high walls and stout battlements—had always seemed unassailable, an invasion the punchline to a joke. But now it felt terribly exposed, squatting on the riverbank like a gleaming lure, and all he could think was that Shandei was still there. "Send a messenger back," he told Daine. "We have to warn Hiraen."

"Let's also ask him," said Savonn, "where he left his engineers."

His gut sinking, Emaris rode up to join him at the edge of the hillock. They looked down on Lissein together. Seen from above, the village was ludicrously small, with no walls or other defensive trappings to speak of: just a jumble of buildings, brick and thatch, curled like a hedgehog in one of the Morivant's sweeping meanders. To the west was the river; on the other side, a thicket of leafless sentinel trees sprawled almost all the way to the easternmost houses. Hiraen's engineers should have been waiting for them on the outskirts of the village. But they were alone.

"They must have fled when they saw the Saraians coming," said Daine, after a moment of dismayed silence. "Damn their teeth."

"And their purses," said Savonn cheerfully. "Oh, well. If we're doomed all the same, Lord Gazelle should probably look fearsome and give some orders."

They had no time, Emaris thought. It could just have been an adrenaline-fuelled hallucination, but he thought he saw a few horsed figures already flitting between the trees. This was Marguerit's opening move, the first time the Saraians had crossed the river in force since the Battle of the Morivant. And here he was, meeting them with a tiny host of three hundred light horse, a convicted traitor, and no guides.

"Emaris," said Daine. "I can take point, if you'd rather not."

"No," said Emaris. He had been given his orders by the High Commander himself. He could not let Hiraen down. "I'm all right. It's simple. Look." He drew a shaky breath. "If they're just a distraction, they won't bother with the village. At the most they'll send a looting party in, raze a few houses. That's not enough. We have to make them *all* go into the trap."

Savonn made a noncommittal noise that could have been assent. He had put on his helmet, an ancient grubby thing with a battered black plume and a visor that covered his entire face. "We should get into those trees," said Emaris, mostly to Daine. Savonn's perfect anonymity disturbed him. "Meet them as they come, make it look like a regular ambush. With any luck, they'll try to take cover in the village."

Spoken aloud, the plan sounded abysmally stupid. But Daine nodded, thoughtful. "That might be the best we can do."

"Competently imagined," Savonn agreed. "Lead on, sir."

Emaris was certain, now, that there were riders in the copse. It was difficult to tell how many. When he rose in his stirrups and looked back, the host of his men stretched out behind him like a great armoured centipede, cuirass and harness glinting in the sun. Three hundred faces looked back at him, some sceptical, some nervous, others excited. There was nothing for it.

"Gentlemen," he called, the way Savonn would have done. "We're going to meet them in the wood, try and drive them into the village. Ride hard and shoot on my signal. Remember, they're probably fewer than they look."

A ragged cheer arose. "Be brave," Daine added. "Make the High Commander proud."

The cheering doubled. Emaris resumed his seat and crammed on his own helm before he could lose his nerve. "Now!"

Daine blew a blast on his horn. Then, too soon, too fast, it was happening.

They poured down the hillock in a din of shouts, stringing their bows as they went. One never got used to the cavalry charge.

Emaris still felt it like new every time: the wind in his hair; the pull and give of the horse's muscles between his knees; the moment when the butterflies in his stomach gathered themselves to fly in synchrony, and all his muscles sang. He hoped, absurdly, that he was charging in the right direction. Then the trees swept up to meet him across the field of frost-tipped grass, the darkness between them beckoning, and he ceased to think.

He was the point in the wedge. He was the steel in the arrowhead. He was his father's son. He was not afraid.

He reached the treeline first, with Daine and Savonn on either side of him, his patrol just behind. "Bows nocked," he said.

There was no sound under the sleeping trees. A thick mat of rotting leaves deadened their hoofbeats, and all he could hear was the blood in his own ears. Ahead, between two old trees, movement flickered.

He drew his bow. "Patrol, fire."

His bowstring hissed. So did twelve others. To his astonishment, most of the arrows went the right way. He heard rather than saw them hit their marks—the punch of an arrowhead through mail at close quarters, the sharp release of a breath, the thump of something heavy hitting soft ground. Horses whinnied. Riders screamed. But more were coming up through the trees.

Emaris nocked again. "Fire at will!"

A flock of shining arrows arced over his head. A horseless rider blundered into his path; Lomas hefted his javelin and dispatched the man with a deft underhand throw. Vion pronounced an oath. The Saraians were returning fire now: Emaris ducked as a crossbow bolt zipped past his face, and shot back blindly in the direction from which it had come. Savonn was still at his side, twirling one of his throwing knives. "Your standard's unwieldy. I might have to drop it."

"It's Hiraen's," said Emaris. "You'd better not."

He had lost all sense of time and place. A low-hanging twig whipped across his brow, leaving it stinging. His horse stumbled on something, shrieked, and regained its balance. Scarcely had he nocked again when two crossbowmen on foot launched themselves out from behind a tree, their bolts trained on him. Instinct took over. Emaris released his own arrow, and dropped flat with his nose in his horse's mane.

One man fell. His bolt whistled overhead, lifting Emaris's hair in a brief wind. Emaris straightened in time to see Savonn spin his wrist, and a silver blur took the remaining crossbowman in the throat. "Aiming for the commander," Savonn mused. "Clever."

"Be quiet," said Emaris. At some point he had gotten turned around. Now the river was on his right. A dying man was burbling at his feet, and the bare boughs cast a disorienting spiderweb of shadows over everything. "I can't see. Vion, take two men and ride down to the water, see if they're going into the village. We'll cover you."

"Yes, sir, my lord, sir," said Vion in a rush.

He wheeled his horse and cantered off with Lomas and Rougen. "Emaris!" Daine shouted from somewhere behind. "Watch out. More coming."

A fresh wedgehead of cavalry was advancing on them, about thirty, forty, flowing between the trees with the ease of men used to fighting on rough terrain. Their livery and caparisons were pure sable, and one of the riders bore a plain black standard. "That's not Isemain," said Daine.

"No," Emaris agreed. Visions assaulted his mind, of the Marshal descending in force on Amarota, smashing his way into the city. He saw his father's house in flames, the saplings in the garden shrivelled to crisps, his sister with a spearhead in her chest, her sword still flying with savage glee—

He shook himself. "I think I know who that is," he said. "He won't show his face yet. *Prepare for hand-to-hand!*"

Shooting faster than he had ever known he could, Emaris got off three arrows before the ranks closed and they were down to swords and spears. The Saraian who bore down on him was tall and faceless, a tower of plate and mail; it could have been a man or a woman or a sack of stones for all he knew. He parried several brutal swings at his face, caught a hard blow on his pauldron, then—reeling with the momentum—leaned forward and shouldered his assailant out of the saddle. The hooves closed in. The soldier screamed once, and no more.

Black and orange flurried on the edge of his vision. Savonn swept the standard in a scythelike arc, unseating two riders, and jettisoned it over his shoulder to draw his sword. "Don't tell Hiraen."

"You're a terrible standard-bearer!" Emaris screamed.

He bowled over another foe and took a jarring blow on the side of his helmet. A blade sliced through his mail at the elbow. He felt no pain. The strap of his helm was broken; he ripped the whole thing off and threw it away. His gloves were sodden with blood. "Emaris!" someone shouted. "I mean, Emaris, sir! It worked! The ones farther back are retreating to the village!"

Vion was coming up on foot, trying to nock his bow and run at the same time. A few paces behind, Lomas and Rougen were riding double. "How many?" Emaris asked.

"Not sure, sir! Hard to count when shooting, sir! About as many as us!"

"I meant," said Emaris, "how many are in the village?"

"Oh," said Vion. His face fell. "Maybe ten."

A pair of Saraian riders burst between them. Vion gave up on his bow, snatched a spear from Rougen's saddle-strap, and hurled that instead. At the same time, Rougen drew and shot. Unable to help it, Emaris stopped to watch. They had made the mistake of aiming for the same horseman, but at least they both hit their mark, and the unfortunate rider crashed into the one beside him, taking him down as well. In the breathing room that ensued, Emaris looked around for Savonn and found him practically at hand. "Now what?"

Savonn swept off his helm and plunked it over Emaris's head. The black plume was bent at a crazed angle. "Ever gone fishing?"

Emaris couldn't answer. Another arrow flew past him, and he had to struggle with his rearing horse to keep his balance. "Bait," said Savonn, gathering his reins. There was an odd light in his eyes. "Best hope this works."

"What?"

But Savonn was already galloping off. They were still no farther than a stone's throw from the treeline. As Savonn broke free of the thicket, the wind caught his uncovered hair and whipped it out behind him, bright as a new-minted drochon. Emaris forgot to breathe.

"He's luring them into the village," said Daine flatly. "They know—gods help us—they know you're in command, so he's pretending to be you."

Rougen clutched at Emaris's arm. Vion said, "He's going to get himself killed!"

The Saraians had noticed the blond figure streaking towards the village. Already a few bands had broken off to give chase. Emaris was too tired even for outrage. He said, "I know."

His arm hurt, and his sleeve was red with blood. It was his sword-arm, too. Under the battle-haze his mind was aware of all these things, but it was even more aware of Savonn receding from him, a lone figure on horseback growing smaller with each wasted moment. *Glue yourself to him*, Hiraen had said. Emaris never needed to be told. This was what he did for a living.

He pulled on his reins and started to bring his horse around. Klemene said, resigned, "There he goes."

"Daine," said Emaris, "you're in charge. Pretend to retreat, then circle round to the north and cut them off. Pick off as many as you can. Savonn and I will take care of the rest."

Daine sighed, but did not argue. "Wait!" shouted Lomas. "What about us?"

Emaris looked back at them. His boys, his patrol. "Don't follow."

Then he kicked his horse into a gallop, and plunged out onto open ground.

CHAPTER 15

By the time the late dawn broke, stealing slothful and red-fingered over the horizon, Shandei had made up her mind that waiting was much worse than fighting.

She had spent the long night on the ramparts with her father's bow and her own sword, and her ivory dagger in her belt. No one in the city wanted to be idle on a night like this, and volunteers flooded out to offer help at the guardhouses or the infirmaries, or fetched and carried, or cooked hot meals for those on duty. Lacking any useful skills, Shandei had gone to join the city guard on the walls. She was not the only woman there—there were children too, even freedmen. None of the men complained. If Marguerit could employ not only women but slaves and sorcerers and gods knew what manner of hell-spirits, then Cassarah could not afford to be picky.

There was another reason why Shandei was on the ramparts. The High Commander was here.

Shandei had not seen Iyone since the day Willon Efren died. Neither had she breathed a word to Emaris of what had transpired in his absence. It was likely she would never do either of those things for as long as she lived. Emaris had been in a daze since the Silvertongue's trial, apt to lose track of conversations over dinner, staring into space with his fork in the air until his name was called. She could not be cruel to him. And as for Iyone—

If Shandei did right by her father, she would never see Iyone again. At least, not till she was brought to the gallows for murdering Hiraen Safin.

He was good. She had to admit that. His address to the army— she had caught snatches of it, lurking outside the Arena—had been brief, straightforward, and reassuring in a way that might have reminded her of Iyone, if Iyone could ever be reassuring. After that he had done an inspection of the city walls and the troops stationed at each gate. Cassarah had five: the Fire and Salt Gates to the south, the Bronze and Earth Gates to the north, and the Gate of Gold, last and grandest, to the east. To the west, the Morivant ran directly under the city wall. There was no point of egress there, only stone and water.

Hiraen had satisfied himself of the defences, and gone up to the ramparts. One could easily track him by the explosive gusts of laughter that erupted along the wallwalk wherever he went. At least half the men up here were ten or twenty years his senior, others younger than even Emaris, but Shandei would scarcely have guessed it, watching them slap each other's backs like old friends.

Anyone could command men, her father always said. But it took a special gift to lead them.

Now the laughter was approaching. Hiraen was coming down the northwestern wall, above the Earth Gate, where Shandei had chosen to post herself. It afforded her a good view of both the river and the road to Lissein, where Emaris had gone. She had no wish to jest with the High Commander. For a gut-churning instant, she considered slipping off while she still could. But why should she run from him? He had done her wrong, not the other way round, and she did not have it in her to flee from an enemy.

She stood her ground, watching him approach in the eerie red glow of a nearby brazier. One of their three cannon threw its hard-angled silhouette against the brightening sky behind him. When he came within hailing distance, she said, "Sir."

He stopped. So had Vesmer Efren once, on a bridge of summer roses. "Shandei. Are you well?"

What else had she expected? That he would turn tail and flee from her, with all his men watching? "Fine as daybreak, my lord," she said. "My brother is fighting for his life, and oh, yes, my father is dead, but I suppose these are minor complaints."

He, too, was no coward. That much was plain in his unflinching gaze. He was young, much younger than Rendell had been, and good-looking in the sweet wholesome way of an April afternoon. "We've all seen better days. If it's any consolation, I have complete faith in Emaris."

"And Emaris has complete faith in everyone," said Shandei. "It's not a failing, so long as his friends are trustworthy."

Minute clefts appeared between Hiraen's brows and in his chin. His eyes were green while Iyone's were storm-grey, but they had the same quickness, the same dagger-point intensity. "You'd know if they were," he said. "You've been spending time with my sister, haven't you?"

He might have been honest, but he understood guile. Of course he did. He was a Safin. It was in their blood. "I spend time with lots of people's sisters," said Shandei. "Their brothers, too. But I've never met anyone as black-hearted as you two."

Hiraen's face hardened. She had no idea what he could possibly have to say, nor did she want to hear it. Either he would lie and prove himself treacherous, unworthy of Iyone's protection; or he would admit what he had done, and then there would be no getting out of her duty to the Ceriyes. She was sick, sick to the bones of death.

But before he could speak, a shout shattered the crisp air. "Lord Hiraen! The river!"

Quick as a cat, he was moving. While she was still looking to see who had shouted, he sprinted in the direction of the cry, guardsmen and errand-boys jumping out of his way. Disoriented, Shandei reached for her sword. "What? What's happening?"

The sentry next to her—a girl no older than fourteen—was hopping up and down in a futile attempt to look over the men's heads. "I can't see!"

"I'll go over."

Shandei started after Hiraen. It was an unsoldierly thing to do, deserting her post; but then, she reasoned, she was not really a soldier, and had no commander to tell her off for it. The rampart took her over the Earth Gate, past another cannon, and under the round turret where the wall bent to run parallel to the Morivant. Hiraen was hanging over the balustrade. He did not look round at her approach.

It would have been so easy. One push, and down he would go, past fifty feet of sheer granite to the bottom of the river. They were so high up no one would even hear the plash. It would take a minute for anyone to realise he was gone. Then the guards would converge on her, and—

He was saying something, of which she caught only the last word. "Boats."

She saw them at once. Longboats, narrow and sharp-prowed, coming swift and silent over the black water. The closest were already halfway across. They must have put off from Daliss under cover of night, trusting to the long shadows of Cassarah's own walls to conceal them as the sun came up. Each boat was carrying at least twenty men. And there were so many, dozens, hundreds, their neat lines stretching up- and downstream as far as the eye could see.

Shandei let out a breath. "Gods be good."

At Hiraen's signal, the closest guard blew three sharp blasts on his horn. The warning was taken up by the watchmen on the turret, and repeated all along the walls in a cacophony of bells and shouts, close by at first, then farther off. Sentries hurried to man the riverside wall. Below, more were streaming to the Earth Gate. "Fetch me a light," said Hiraen.

Shandei was halfway to the nearest brazier before she knew it. Like Iyone, he was used to instant obedience, and so always got it. Someone threw her a dry twig, and she stuck it into the coals until it caught. Hiraen had already nocked his bow. "Light the arrow."

There was a little wad of cloth tied near the arrowhead, soaked in something that stank of oil and pitch. He saw her looking, and gave a hard smile. "I had thousands of these made. Better hope they're enough."

She held the smouldering twig to the cloth. It kindled at once. Then his gloved hands moved, the bowstring hummed, and the arrow took flight.

It was so quiet, the whole world might have stopped to watch. The arrow soared like a fiery red comet in a perfect arc over the water, then plunged down into the fleet. For a moment it looked like nothing was going to happen. Then a tongue of fire leapt skywards on one of the boats, and in the deep darkness they glimpsed the colours of the sail: snow-grey striped with white.

"The Marshal," said Hiraen with relish. "Fetch wood and oil. Those with bows, use them. Those without, kindle the arrows. Light those bastards up."

There was no hesitation, not even the slightest flicker of doubt, only shouts of, "Aye!" and, "Yes!" and, "Very good, sir!" Shandei put her smoking twig between her teeth and nocked her own bow with one of Hiraen's fire arrows. Without needing to be asked, the closest guard took the twig and kindled the incendiary for her. She sighted down the shaft, whispered a habitual prayer to Casteia, and loosed.

It was a good shot—not as beautiful as Hiraen's, but a true one nonetheless. Another grey-white sail went up in flames. The other archers were not far behind. Soon, burning arrows were whizzing over the balustrade from all directions, fizzing and plummeting upon the boats. Faint shouts drifted to them across the water. The Saraians rushed to and fro with buckets, dousing the flames, and several burning sails were cut loose and flung off to float away like enormous lilypads. "They're returning fire," Shandei warned.

Several arrows arced towards the walls, fell short of the ramparts, and vanished. They jeered. "The cannon!" Hiraen yelled. "Bring round the cannon!"

Thereafter the world dissolved into chaos. Shandei drew and loosed and drew and loosed, shooting arrow after burning arrow into the fleet. Wheels creaked and cranked. She was aware of a great many heavy objects trundling behind her, but did not look around. People screamed and prayed and cursed. Someone took a shot to the shoulder and was led away to the infirmary, screeching for his friends to avenge him. The hands that held the light to Shandei's arrows first belonged to a guard, then an elderly freedwoman, then a boy of eight or nine. "Ma'am?" he said. "Are we winning?"

She looked down. The fires were put out as quickly as they could be kindled, but even so the boats had been thrown out of their regular lines, some colliding with their neighbours in crashes of wood and canvas, others spinning out of control in the current. That was the good news. The bad was that there were still at least a hundred surviving vessels slipping towards the city, making for the thin strip of bank under the Earth Gate. A few more minutes, and the enemy would be upon them.

Perhaps she would die here after all, and be released from her blood feud.

"Yes," she said firmly, and in the same breath yelled, *"Fire the bank!"*

The sun was high enough now that the Morivant sparkled with silver light, or at least the parts of it that were not choked with dead sailors and debris. Squinting, Shandei leaned over the wall and angled her bow downwards. Hiraen reappeared beside her. They fired together, his arrow a heartbeat behind hers. Smoke began to rise from the grass in thin grey coils. But it was wet with river-mist, and did not burn well. Undeterred, the first Saraian landers leapt out of their boats and advanced on the city.

"Archers to the northwest!" Hiraen shouted. "Protect the gate!"

Someone tugged at Shandei's sleeve. It was the boy with the brand. "Are we winning?"

The muscles of her arms were burning, and a speck of soot was stuck in her right eye. "Yes."

"And you might want to cover your ears," Hiraen added.

The men had brought the cannon round. All three guns stood behind them, their open maws facing the river. "Iyone named them the Rose, the Thorn, and the Dung," said Hiraen in an aside, as they watched the powder being loaded.

"Dung?"

"As in manure. To go with the theme. *Fire!*"

Shandei hauled the boy into her arms and clapped both hands over his ears. There was a flash of blinding light, and her retort was lost in an earth-splitting thunderclap. The flagstones shook. The boy screamed, more from excitement than fear. Beneath, the frontmost ranks of the fleet had become a spinning whirlpool of splintered masts and ripped sails, and the water was red and grey. "Which one was that?"

"Dung," said Hiraen.

The Rose and the Thorn went off in quick succession. Dung was reloading. Shandei's right ear seemed to have stopped working, and both her eyes streamed. She got off two more arrows, shooting blind. "Ma'am!" shrieked the boy. "Look!"

Shandei looked. Her heart went cold. "Hiraen!"

He had seen it too. A dozen more longboats had reached the bank, and soldiers were spilling out of them faster than anyone could shoot them down. Even as they advanced, another boat landed behind them, this one half again as large as the others. The deck was covered fore to aft with a vast sheet of what looked like wet wool to keep out the flames, and through it Shandei glimpsed the outline of something long and narrow and immense.

"Battering ram," said Hiraen, with admirable composure. "Bring boiling oil! Keep the cannon going!"

The Rose went off, or perhaps it was the Thorn, and Shandei lost most of his next sentence. "—have to get down there—to the Gate—hold them off!"

Shandei was ill with the mingled smells of gunpowder and blood. Her father had been braver than this. She wondered how he would have borne it: the screams, the red water, the endless annihilating ranks of men advancing across the smoking bank. "Not forever!" she cried, stuffing her fingers in her ears. "Where's Lord Lucien? Isn't he coming?"

"He'll show up. But—"

Dung, now. Boom. "—have to brace the gate!" Hiraen shouted. "—as long as we can! Go to Iyone—"

Boom. Shandei had lost track of which gun was which. A violent throb had started up behind her eyes. "*Iyone what?*"

"—care of her!" Hiraen yelled. "Till I get back!"

"I can't!" Shandei screamed. "I can't see her again, you don't understand—"

A horn-blast spared her from having to explain. Hiraen called an order she could not make out. A couple dozen men broke off from the group around the cannon and formed up behind him, and without a backwards glance he led the way to the stairs. Shandei's hands felt clammy, her bowstring a dead weight. In her mind's eye she saw the Earth Gate buckling, troops of men pouring down the city streets, driving their spears into anything that moved. The boy was tugging at her sleeve again. "Are we winning?"

She had found the limit of her courage. "For pity's sake—"

The guns went off again, all three together. The boy burst into tears. "Oh, hell," said Shandei, despairing. If Hiraen wanted her to check on his sister, she would. Surely there was nothing to fear from Iyone that was worse than this. "Look—go to the kitchens, help peel onions or something. This is no place for you. I'll take you down, I'm going too."

Boom. On instinct they had both thrown their hands over their ears at the distant call of *Fire!* "You're running away?" asked the boy, with a disdainful sniffle.

"No," said Shandei. Perhaps she was. But it would be cowardice, too, not to go to Iyone. "There's just someone I've got to see."

* * *

Ederen's citadel had always been a desolate place. The Council convened there now and then, but no one lived in it except Lord Kedris when he had been alive—because he had sold his own house for alms, or to make some point about his Andalle heritage, no one knew. His apartments had been shut up by the Silvertongue after his death, and the citadel now lay fallow: the greatest thing man ever built, maze upon maze of locked rooms and empty courtyards, a monument hearkening back to a more savage time.

But today the front hall was thronged like a marketplace. It was a long sweeping room, its vaulted ceiling held up by rows of massive columns. Messengers hurried in and out. Doctors and their assistants stood by at trestle tables, surrounded by trays of scalpels and bandages and pots of foul-smelling ointments. Most had nothing to do yet, but a few men were already being carried in, some with gunpowder burns, others with arrows sticking out of them. The kitchen servants were there too, handing out chunks of bread and bowls of thick mushroom soup to anyone who looked like they needed it.

For all the bustle, the room was eerily quiet. But of course Shandei's ears were still ringing from the cannon-blasts, and she could hear almost nothing.

It was easy to find Iyone. She was directing traffic like a choirmistress in the middle of the hall, one maid carrying her writing-board, another her inkpot. Runners came and reported to her and left again. A host of civilians—mostly women with children—stood around her like attendants, though none of them seemed to have been given any work. They had simply clustered round the source of order in the chaos, the only natural thing to do.

Shandei considered going away. Iyone looked busy, and not in need of any help. But there was some kind of magnetic disturbance in the ground, or perhaps she was just dazed: the tiled floor was moving beneath her shoes, and somehow she was already halfway across the hall, the circle of attendants parting to let her through. "Iyone."

Iyone started. The cool grey eyes widened, and a flicker of a crease appeared and disappeared on her forehead. She was in an unfussy white dress, her sleeves rolled up, her hair twisted back in a knot. There was no trace of arms or armour about her person. She did not need any. If Hiraen was the sword of Cassarah, Shandei thought, then Iyone was the shield: both hard as steel, each as implacable as the other.

Iyone's mouth moved. She heard nothing. "Talk privately," she rasped. Heads turned to stare, and a woman clutched her toddler to her chest. Shandei realised she was still shouting over the boom of a cannon only she could hear. "Inside."

Iyone shrugged, a strangely childlike movement, and beckoned for Shandei to follow. She led the way between the tall marble columns to an archway at the back of the hall, half covered with a tapestry. It gave onto a long corridor, quiet and dim: a servant's entrance. Her mouth moved again. Shandei said, "I can't fucking *hear*."

Iyone leaned closer. Her breath tickled the shell of Shandei's ear. Why, even now, did this raise the fine hairs on the nape of her neck? "Let me guess. Hiraen is dead? The walls are breached? Marguerit is floating across the river on a pleasure barge?"

She might have been joking. With her, it was hard to tell. "You see," she said, when Shandei did not answer, "I can't imagine you'd speak to me under any other circumstances."

Shandei could only keep hold of her patience or her nerve. She opted for the latter. "Don't be ridiculous. They're trying to batter down the Earth Gate. Hiraen's rallying his men there. Where's the Council?"

"Praying," said Iyone. "It can't hurt. Someone might as well do it."

This was absurd. *Take care of her*, Hiraen had said, but one might as well try to keep an awning dry in the rain. The gods had chiselled Iyone out of flint and iron for such a time as this. "If they breach the walls," said Shandei, "what will you do?"

Iyone looked at her. It was a stern look, with no hint of welcome. "The gates will hold."

"Not if the boats keep coming. Marguerit must have emptied all Daliss. Lord Lucien might not get here in time."

"Then," said Iyone, "he will be proud to learn that his children died fighting. You're not going to tell me to flee, are you? You will be, oh, the seventeenth person to suggest that today, and you don't want to hear what I said to the first sixteen."

Shandei almost laughed. Since Willon's demise, she had grown used to thinking of Iyone in much the same terms one might use for rocks and cliffs: smooth and immovable, with an unapologetic bluntness on which bones might be broken. She had forgotten how, in person, Iyone's eyes were always bright with merriment; how expressive her mouth was, with its wry grimaces and ironic smiles. It made everything worse. "Who were the sixteen? Councillors? Admirers?"

"Mostly. And Hiraen, but he was being sarcastic."

"It's one thing to die in battle," said Shandei. "Quite another to be taken alive. I don't think slavery would agree with your constitution."

"Probably not," said Iyone. "I don't see *you* running."

It was a lost cause. Short of demonic possession, nothing could have persuaded Iyone to do anything she did not want to. "I can fight," said Shandei half-heartedly.

"That doesn't signify," said Iyone. "If everyone who couldn't bear arms ran away, this wouldn't be a city, only a battlefield. What would our soldiers fight for?"

To Iyone, nothing ever signified. The matter was perfectly simple when she laid it out like that. Whether the Earth Gate stood or fell was irrelevant. Cassarah was their city, their home; there was nothing Marguerit could do to change that. If the sky collapsed, Iyone and Hiraen would hold it up between them. Where was there to run to?

Shandei scrubbed the back of her hand over her face. When she looked down, her knuckles were grey with soot. "I would have fled with you," she said. "If you weren't so bloody arrogant, we could have gone away together. Someplace far. Someplace safe. Astorre, Bayarre, wherever you wanted—"

In the stories, if you kissed an enchanted stone under the full moon, it turned into a beautiful maiden under your lips. Shandei had never been able to picture it till now. Iyone looked the same as she always did—as if she had been standing on a plinth for a hundred years and meant to stand there a thousand more—but the corners of her eyes grew soft, and her features no longer looked like the work of a glass-cutter. "Don't."

"Don't what? Don't talk? Don't be human?"

"Don't say things like that. Not in the middle of battle. It makes me stop thinking."

"Heaven forfend."

The corners of Iyone's lips made the slightest movement upwards. "I know. I'm being obnoxious. Why are you here? I thought we were through."

"Hiraen sent me," said Shandei.

She would have come anyway, but it was beyond her to admit that. The twinkle of amusement faded from Iyone's eyes. "You're serving under him now?"

"This is war," said Shandei. "I'm not petty. I'll serve under whomever I want."

"And after?"

After, as if she took for granted that they would win, and peacetime would come again. In the mouth of anyone else, it would have sounded naïve. Shandei did not know what to say. She thought of Hiraen at the gate, holding back the Saraian horde; of Iyone with her flock of attendants, the pivot around which the whole city revolved. She had been taught to despise treachery as the lowest evil. But if the pillars fell, so did the roof.

"He knows what he's done," said Iyone. "When all this is over, he'll answer to you. Be fair."

Shandei swallowed. "I don't want to—to *kill* him."

"I know."

On the far side of the tapestry, a baby began to cry. Shandei's hearing was returning. Still they stood with their heads together, close enough to kiss. "I kept your scarf," said Iyone, apropos of nothing.

"Why?"

"I liked it."

Perhaps they were not through after all. If they survived the war, they could survive anything. "I have to get back," said Shandei. "But after this—might we meet?"

Iyone looked away for the briefest of moments. "If you want," she said. "You know where to find me." She took in Shandei's cuirass, the bow and quiver on her back. "But as you said, this is war. What does one say? Back to your post, soldier?"

"Come back with my shield or on it?"

Iyone smiled. It was a proper smile this time, sudden and startling. "Just come back."

Shandei turned and went through the tapestry before she could say anything ill-advised. The hall was exactly as she had left it: the fussing babies, the doctors at their tables, the nervous flurry of activity around them. But something had changed. Iyone was behind her, watching her back—a woman she could love, who would hold up the ceilings and the foundations both. No foe could stand against her. And Shandei was no longer afraid.

On her way back up to the ramparts, she found herself smiling. She had always wanted to fire a cannon.

CHAPTER 16

Up close, Lissein looked less like a ghost town. It was a pretty fishing village of about a hundred gable-roofed buildings, the latticed windows open and inviting, the gardens only a little overgrown. The roar of the Morivant was much louder here than in the city, and the breeze smelled like witch hazel and honeysuckle. It reminded Emaris of Shandei's herb garden, and home.

None of this was any salve to the immediate fact of Savonn's stare, which could have welded steel.

"Turn around," he said. "Now."

They had dismounted behind a woodshed on the outskirts of the village. "No," said Emaris. "I can't let you do this on your own."

Savonn's pupils darkened, or perhaps it was only the lightness of his hair that made it look as if they had. "*Ride back.* This isn't the time for heroics."

"So what are you doing?" Emaris had precious little strength to waste on arguing; the gash in his arm was beginning to throb in earnest. He had bound it up with a strip from his cloak, but already the makeshift bandage was blotched with red and brown. "Anyway, it's too late. Look."

Twenty or thirty riders had peeled out of the thicket behind them, pelting across the open ground to the village. In the other direction, hooves were clattering on the cobbles behind the houses. They were surrounded. Savonn said, "For heaven's sake."

He looked around, then seemed to make up his mind, or at least resign himself to having it made up for him. "Hiraen's going to kill us both. Hurry."

He darted round the shed and started across the road. Emaris followed. They were in a twisty alleyway between rows of tiny cottages, each one hemmed in by hedges and gardens. Savonn led the way past the houses, peering at each in turn. He gave one a wide berth for no reason that Emaris could see, then ducked into the hedges behind the next. "Stay here."

"Wait, *don't*—"

But he was gone, vaulting the low wooden fence around the cottage and flitting into the lane beyond. Emaris took a few steps after him, then gritted his teeth and stayed put. "*El esta!*" shrieked a woman's voice.

Running feet converged on a point behind the house. Emaris tasted his heart, hot and metallic, at the back of his mouth. He still had his sword and bow, but his quiver was empty. And if things came down to close fighting—which they would—his right arm was useless. He could not see Savonn through the bushes, only his shadow, stark and exposed in the middle of the lane. Surely the Saraians had spotted him. Surely they would—

There was a hollow creak, like a cellar door on a rusty hinge, and then a tremendous crash.

Emaris flung himself flat under the hedge, and listened with his nose in the dirt. The woman who had shouted before was swearing now, and a horse was screaming, a high, reedy noise that went on and on without cease. Then both fell silent.

There were distant exclamations from the rest of their pursuers, some horrified, others awestruck. Emaris's imagination supplied the details. A pit opening in the road. A long fall into darkness, ending in quicksand, or a pool of broiling acid. Or spikes, like those they used in ganchings—

Savonn reappeared, skidding on the grass. "That way."

They sprinted past the row of houses. Shouts followed them. Emaris looked back and glimpsed a man silhouetted in the yard between two cottages, sword raised, others streaming to join him. Someone cried out, as if in warning. Then a bang. Emaris tripped on a cobble and flailed to regain his balance. When he looked back, the entire upper wall of one of the cottages was sagging outward before his eyes, showering bricks and stones on their pursuers.

Savonn stopped to let him catch up. "Welcome," he said, "to the circus."

Emaris laughed. He couldn't help it. What was it people were saying these days? Follow the Silvertongue and you were apt to end up in love, in jail, or in a tomb, but at least you would never be bored. They all thought he was dead, the world safe from him at last. But it was harder than that to exorcise a poltergeist.

They had come to a junction. The houses were bigger here, surrounded by fences and walls, the upper windows peering at the road beneath their curtains. More crashes and screams; Emaris thought he smelled sulphur. Savonn paused, and made a left.

They had scarcely gone a dozen paces when three or four Saraians rounded a corner and burst into their path. Savonn reached into his sleeve. A shimmer of steel, and the foremost man fell with a silver blade in his throat not ten feet from them. "In there."

Savonn was pointing at a narrow bronze gate in the brick wall surrounding one of the properties. Emaris flung it open and hurtled through. He registered a tall house with a white porch, a beech tree leaning over a pool clogged with leaves. There were dead fish floating belly-up in the stagnant water. Poison, he thought. There was no time to gawk; Savonn grabbed his elbow and gave him a shove. "Up the back wall."

Emaris tore past the house to the back of the garden. The brick wall there was eight feet high, too smooth for toeholds. He took a running leap and swung himself up by brute willpower alone. "Savonn! Come on!"

Savonn was still by the pool, a stone in his fist. Even as Emaris watched from the top of the wall, their three surviving pursuers barreled through the gate into the yard. His elbow tingled. Two rogue thoughts came to him in quick succession: that Savonn had never voluntarily touched him before, and that they were both about to die.

Savonn hurled his stone. The Saraians ducked, but the missile went nowhere near them. Instead it flew into the branches of the beech, and something big, brown and lumpy fell to the grass.

Emaris swore. So did their pursuers. There was a loud whirring, like the blades of a mill but infinitely worse. He flung his cloak over his head. Under its hem, he glimpsed a nebulous grey shape coalesce over the pool and swarm towards the Saraians. "Hurry up!"

Savonn pelted towards the wall. Emaris reached down blindly and grabbed his outstretched hand, swinging him up and over. They tumbled down the other side, and ran.

But there was nowhere to go. Footfalls were surging down every alley, and someone was shrilling orders, orchestrating an organised hunt by the sounds of it. They turned into a narrow lane just before a group of men came pounding by, and sagged into the shelter of an archway between two houses. Emaris ripped off the black-plumed helmet, gasping for air. "Too many. Can't outrun them all."

His whole sleeve was red; his wound had started to bleed again. His head was curiously light. He supposed he had been prodigious with his blood. "This," said Savonn, breathing hard, "is where I say *I told you so.*"

"Don't."

There was a renewed symphony of crashes from the next street over. A mastiff barked. Savonn gazed down the lane, his curls plastered limply to his face. A red welt was rising on his neck where a hornet had stung him. "Stay here. I'll take care of it."

Emaris threw up his hands. "Spare me."

"Fine," said Savonn. "So tell me what you want. A glorious last stand? A hero's death at the age of eighteen, and a statue in your honour? Best make up your mind now. We're not both making it out of this."

He ran out of breath, and the last words came out in a rush. Emaris had never seen him like this before. Savonn had an iron grip on his temper—even on campaign, when he used to catch Emaris eavesdropping every other day, the worst he had ever done was tease him. Never once had he raised his voice. Emaris had assumed he was above anger.

Regrettably, he had assumed Savonn was above most things.

"Don't patronise me," said Emaris. He could be angry, too. "If I'm being reckless, so are you. Getting yourself killed won't undo all the wrong you did."

Savonn hesitated. That was unexpected. Emaris watched—not without morbid interest—as the killing look on his face was smoothed away like a crease in a bedspread, leaving him looking only bored. "Gods help me, there's two of you now," he said. "And I'm afraid no one is going to kill me, not in *this* rout."

Emaris felt a twinge of apprehension. "I'm still not going away."

"In all these years," said Savonn, "I never worked out how to get rid of you. Well, we'd best hope I didn't read the map upside down."

He pushed himself away from the wall and set off again, this time at a leisurely walk. Emaris remembered, with a distant sense of horror, that he was doing all this from memory. "Where are we going?"

Savonn ignored him. Despite his apparent calm, he was still annoyed. There was a shout, shockingly close; then a blast on a horn. They had been spotted. "*Savonn.*"

"As a rule," said Savonn, "don't run when you're being chased."

They stopped outside one of the houses. This one was much smaller than the others, with no encircling wall or fence. Savonn looked at it for a moment, lips moving silently as though counting. Then he went up to the door and pushed it open. "After you."

The entirety of the cottage consisted of a single room. The windows had been boarded up, and with the door shut behind them it was almost pitch-black inside. At first glance it was obvious that the house had been vacant a long time. The wood in the fireplace was mouldering, and there was no furniture to speak of—no bed or table or stove, not even a footstool to show that someone had once lived here. Only a row of barrels lined up against the back wall, each about waist-high, separated from one another by a scrupulous foot of space.

The air was acrid with a smell Emaris knew. He went closer to look. The orange sunburst of the Safins unfurled on the front of each barrel, a bright warning.

Something crackled behind him, and a flickering glow filled the room. Savonn had lit a fire on the hearth. Emaris sucked in a loud breath. "Are you out of your mind? That's gunpowder."

"Move those barrels away," said Savonn, as if he had not heard. "Leave one."

A horse whickered in the lane. A cuirass chinked, as the rider dismounted. There was no time. Pushing with his good arm, Emaris began to move all but the last barrel across the room, as far from the hearth as they could go. "I'd like some warning if we're blowing ourselves up."

"Shut up and look noble," said Savonn. "We have company."

Right on cue, the door crashed open.

Four men came in. They hesitated in the entryway, peering around for traps, until a fifth pushed past them and sauntered in. Nikas of the Sanctuary looked them up and down, and broke into a face-splitting grin. "Look at you two! Gleaming like a pair of crocuses!"

Blond, bland, and smiling, Savonn said, "Don't draw your swords all at once, my dears, you'll get jammed in the doorway."

The men spread out to surround them. Emaris counted a dozen more reining up in the yard before Nikas kicked the door shut in their faces. "Terrible company," he confided. "The most entertaining thing they do is die." He leaned in to Emaris, as if to whisper a secret. "I rather liked the one with the hornets. Which was your favourite, sunflower?"

"The one where you get drowned in honey and buried in an anthill," said Emaris.

Nikas giggled. "Oh, you're all grown up. Well, you better hand over your weapons, I don't have much time."

Savonn unbuckled his sword-belt and cast it aside with a flourish. "How many knives do you want? I can spare a couple."

Nikas's eyes were wide and inquisitive. "Assist him, gentlemen."

Emaris tried not to wonder what had become of Vion and the others. Before anyone could make him, he gave up his bow and sword, and kicked away his empty quiver for good measure.

"What a hoard you've got here," said Nikas, sniffing the air. If one did not know better, he would have looked like a giant puppy. "What were you planning to do, light yourselves up like fireworks?"

"Oh, you know," said Savonn, as the men searched him. "Blazes of glory and all that."

"Don't be so literal," said Nikas, resting his elbow on the mantel. "Your sweetheart would miss you. Speaking of which! Dervain sends his regards. I invited him along, but he seems to be under some ridiculous pre-nuptial ban."

"It *is* bad luck to see each other before a wedding," said Savonn.

"How old-fashioned!" Nikas beamed at Emaris, wet-eyed. "Poor thing. You should have renounced him."

"I tried," said Emaris. "But I'm stuck with him. It's dreadful."

He smiled sidelong at Savonn. Reckless, defiant, the way sailors on a sinking ship set their rigging on fire, so rescuers would know where to look. To his amazement, Savonn grinned back. It was a private, intimate smile, joining them across the room like a shield-wall. They were going to die together. It was not the worst possible fate.

"Touching," said Nikas. He no longer looked amused. "Shall we get on with the show, then? I have a few questions for you, Lord Silvertongue. Best if you answer them quickly."

"How," said Savonn, "do you presume to make me?"

"Like this."

Nikas seized Emaris's arm, the bad one, with a force that near ripped it from its socket. Emaris stumbled a few paces. Before he could so much as shout, one of the men hit him behind the knees with a spear, and he found himself sprawled on his face in a pile of dried-out rushes. He reared up, a curse already forming on his tongue. Then the man drove a heavy fist into the side of his head, and he fell down again.

Savonn stepped forward. The soldiers grabbed him and flung him back against the wall. "Now we've established that," said Nikas, "where is the gentle Lady Josit?"

It was not what Emaris had expected. "Oh," said Savonn. "Her."

He had always had a virtuoso's control over his voice. Only his eyes betrayed him. They followed Nikas's hands as they reached into the fireplace, and drew something from the hearth. "I thought to ask you. I haven't seen her in months."

It happened too fast to comprehend. The red-hot tip of a poker appeared at the periphery of Emaris's vision like a scarlet eye, and descended. Heat flared against his cheek. He screamed, more from shock than anything else. Then the pain hit him, blistering through skin and muscle, and he screamed again. His mouth filled with something bitter. He choked and spat, and saw it was blood. He must have bitten his tongue.

"Don't lie," said Nikas, remote and peaceful. "Or your sunflower will soon be short a few petals. Where is she?"

Outside the house, something crashed. One of Nikas's men jumped. Emaris laughed, part dazed, part hysterical. The village was still fighting back. "Don't give him anything," he said. "He can't touch you. You're the Empath's. There's nothing he can—"

Savonn's voice cut across his, chilly and precise. "Josit is in Astorre. Go and look her up. You're wasting your time here."

The poker moved again. This time Emaris saw it coming, and managed to turn his scream into a bitten-off grunt. His face was blazing with agony, his eyes pouring. He tried to turn away so Savonn would not see, but Nikas's man had him by the hair. "Oh dear," said Nikas lazily. "One brand for every lie you tell? I don't have all day, and the poor child will run out of skin. He'll bear those marks for the rest of his life, you know. Every time he looks in the mirror, he'll remember how he used to worship a rotten-hearted cheat."

"That's not true," said Emaris. His nostrils were glutted with smoke. Mother Above, he could smell himself cooking. "That's not—"

"Josit is in Bayarre," said Savonn. The words spilled out quickly, each running into the next. "Iyone lent her a sailboat. She went downriver weeks ago."

Mercifully, when the poker descended again, Emaris had run out of strength to scream. He gurgled and spewed a mouthful of blood. It splashed on the boots of the soldier holding him, and the man loosened his grip and jumped back with a curse. Emaris shook him off. Maybe he could—

"Nikas!" someone shouted, pounding on the door. "Lord Nikas! *Els accarra!*"

More crashes. More yelling. The mastiff had begun to howl. Daine must be driving the whole Saraian force headlong into the village. Emaris imagined Vion and Lomas coming to the rescue as they had before, and grinned maniacally with one side of his mouth. "That doesn't sound good."

The big bright shape of Nikas's face loomed above him. "Don't fret. I can handle them. Go on, little liar. Where else is she? Spellsend? Pieros? This time I'll put out an eye."

The poker retreated to the hearth to be heated up for another round. *The fire*, Emaris thought. Nikas hadn't lit it; Savonn had. And once in a great long while, Savonn did know what he was doing.

He lifted his head, tears and snot and all, and met Savonn's gaze. It would be all right, then.

"Josit has gone to Daliss," said Savonn. He had been stalling before, but no longer. "Josit has gone to the Sanctuary with a bag of gold and a mouth of promises and more cunning in her little finger than you have in your whole body. Josit, whom you call mother, is about to buy you from the High Priest, and send you to kill her sister the Queen."

Nikas paused, the poker hanging slack in his hand. In the same moment Savonn curled himself like a cat and lunged for the hearth.

Emaris reeled into motion. He launched himself to his feet and hurled his full weight on Nikas, and they went toppling over together. Emaris landed on top, streaming blood and oaths like a fey pirate-king of old, driving his knees deep beneath Nikas's ribs with a kind of drunken strength. Someone screamed. The poker clattered away. He feinted for it with his left hand, then slammed his right fist into Nikas's nose. Cartilege crunched. Then Nikas's body tensed beneath him, and the next thing he knew, he was careening sideways as if thrown from a horse.

He landed hard on his good arm. The rafters spun in desultory circles above him. He had gotten free. He had broken Nikas's nose. Impossibly, no one had stopped him. He should probably find Nikas and hit him again. Where was everyone? Where was—

A rush of hot air lifted the hair on his head. There was a noise like an earthquake, or what he thought an earthquake might sound like: a hollow boom that emanated from all around him, *inside* him. He flung up his hands to protect his face. Something crashed to the floor an inch from his foot, and he flinched back. "Goddamnit! Savonn!"

The room was filled with smoke and dust. It stung his bleeding face, the cuts on his neck and arms. Fire crackled around him—the floor was on fire, the walls were on fire, the *men* were on fire, screaming and running for the door. Nikas was gone. "Savonn!" Emaris yelled. "Where are you?"

He staggered to his feet, and nearly tripped over someone's head. It was the man who'd held him down. His skull had been caved in by a falling beam, lending his face a buffoonish sneer. Flames were already licking up his legs. Savonn had set one of the barrels alight, but there were more, and when the fire reached them it would all be over. "*Savonn!*"

It took a few agonising moments to find him. Emaris came across one of their captors first, sprawled dead on the floor beside the hearth, and then Savonn's smaller form trapped beneath him. A rafter had fallen lengthwise over them both, pinning them to the floor. Even as Emaris limped over, a glowing spark drifted down from the roof, and the beam took flame. "Wake up!"

No response. Emaris had stopped thinking. Moving of its own accord, his body dropped beside Savonn. His hands grabbed the beam, and his muscles heaved. He felt nothing except a burning numbness in the sockets and joints of all his limbs, as if his whole body had caught fire. He heaved again. At last the beam twitched, wobbled, and rolled off with a crash. Singed and breathless, half blinded by sweat, Emaris put an arm around Savonn's shoulders and the other under his knees and staggered to his feet. The roof creaked, and half the rafters sagged in with a groan, exposing a slice of naked sky.

Wind surged into the house. The flames leapt. Emaris broke into a dead run, and cleared the door.

He flung himself on top of Savonn, coughing up ash. A blast of heat seared the back of his neck. He imagined a great dragon behind him, uncurling, spitting flame. Tiny bits of wood rained down. His eyes were watering again. Every time he thought it was over, another series of crackles and pops went off like cannonshot, and more of the cottage crashed in.

It was going up like a pyre, rafters, roof-tiles, walls and all. A minute slower, and they would both have burned with it.

As the explosions began to die down, Emaris dragged Savonn across the grass and into the lane with the last of his strength, putting distance between them and the fire. "It's over," he said. "Wake up."

Savonn stirred. His face was streaked with soot, the fine arcs of his lashes fluttering against the pooled bruises beneath his eyes. Shaking, Emaris felt for his pulse in the side of his throat, and found it faint but steady.

"My gods." Emaris's voice was ragged from smoke and other things. "I could have forgiven you anything but that."

Savonn murmured something, of which the only distinct syllable sounded like *No*, and flung up a hand as if to ward off a blow. "It's just me," said Emaris. "You blew up everyone else."

Savonn's eyes opened, berry-blue in the morning light. His fingers closed around Emaris's wrist with startling violence. "Gazelle?"

Emaris could find no witty answer. He said, "I'm here."

With a sigh, the roofless cottage settled back on its haunches, still blazing like a bonfire. The rest of the world was coming back into focus. They were alone: Nikas's men had all died or fled. There were a few muffled booms and screams from the far side of the village; then, closer at hand, gleeful laughter and the slap of running feet. "Emaris! Where are you? Come and see! We won!"

It was Vion. "We vanquished them!" added Klemene, sounding happier than Emaris had ever heard him. "They're all vanquished!"

The patrol came into view down the street, all twelve of them, bruised, bloody, and filthy as mountain bandits. "I think the circus did most of the vanquishing," said Lomas doubtfully. "And Daine routed those the houses didn't eat."

"Yes," said Vion, "but we helped, didn't we? Oh, there he is!"

Savonn sat up, and with a look of immense concentration pulled himself to his feet. "Where's Nikas?"

His eyes were glassy. Along the edge of his left vambrace, his skin was mottled with burns, and a bruise was blossoming on his jaw. Someone must have hit him. The thought filled Emaris with impotent rage. "Ran off."

"And Daine?"

This was addressed to Vion, who had dashed up ahead of the others, a sodden bandage tied round his brow like a circlet. "Counting the dead, sir. He sent us to find you, in case you needed counting too." He gave Savonn a pointed look. "Good to see you alive and well, Captain."

Emaris sighed, struggling to his feet. His face was screaming, his arm grumbling, and his back had joined in the general outcry. He must have pulled a muscle lifting the rafter. And now this, on top of everything else. "He's not here. He died at Onaressi. You're not seeing him."

Vion started to retort, then did a double take. "What happened to your face?"

"My—"

The rest of the patrol had arrived, all open-mouthed and staring. "Not that it isn't an improvement," said Vion, "but—"

Savonn cut him off in his command voice. "Did you see where Nikas went?"

"No, sir," said Lomas. He did not seem to know where to look, at Savonn or Emaris. "Probably back to the Ford. His lot's all vanquished, anyway."

Another distant crash, as if to illustrate his point. Then a faint cheer. Little wisps of grey smoke were scudding across the sky. "Not ideal," said Savonn. "But still." He cocked his head at Emaris. "Well, my lord? We await the victory speech."

"What?" Emaris snapped to attention, disoriented. "That wasn't a victory. The Marshal's probably crossed over somewhere else by now."

They were all still gawking at him. He needed to look in a mirror. "Very inspiring," said Vion. "Very encouraging, sir."

"Not bad for a beginner," Savonn added. He was standing very still and straight, his lips tinged with grey. A good wind could probably have blown him over. Klemene offered his arm, and to Emaris's astonishment, Savonn took it. "We'd better move. Give the order, gazelle."

Emaris collected himself. They had to get back to Hiraen, to Shandei. If they hurried, they might just reach the city before Isemain. "Yes," he said. "Go fetch our horses. Tell Daine I'm coming."

Their losses had been substantial: forty men dead in a cairn outside Lissein, and nearly all the rest wounded. Emaris's horse had disappeared. Lomas found him a strawberry roan running loose at the edge of the village, and Corl bandaged his arm for him before they set off. Emaris tried to sluice cold water over the burns on his face, too, but they stung so fiercely he nearly bit through his lip. He had changed his mind about looking in a mirror. He did not want to see.

Daine led the column out of the village, most of them riding double. Emaris handed Savonn the roan's reins and climbed on behind him, too exhausted even for awkwardness. They stayed near the back, trying to be inobstrusive. The silence between them stretched, dilated, and reached disturbing proportions.

"All right?" said Emaris, when he could stand it no more. "If you want, I'll pretend to faint so they'll have to call a halt."

Savonn gave a short pained laugh. "You've done enough today, I think."

Now that the adrenaline had receded, Emaris's vision was fading in and out at the edges, going alternately bright and dim. He was starting to shiver. "Don't let me take all the credit. You saved both our lives."

The silence drew on. "And," he added, feeling it had to be said, "I chose to come with you. I knew the risks and I did it anyway. I'm sorry, I suppose. But I can't promise to do any different next time."

Savonn craned round. His stare was ferocious. "*You're* sorry?"

There was a curious ache in Emaris's heart, one that had little to do with his wounds. Why did things always have to be like this between them? "Nikas was going to be a cruel bastard either way," he said. "You did what you could. By all the gods, no one could have done more."

"Thus says the man who pulled me from a burning building," said Savonn bleakly. "I never asked for your absolution."

"You never do," said Emaris, resigned. "As always, I give it unasked."

* * *

It was evening by the time the towers and ramparts of Cassarah made more than a blot against the southern sky. At first, Emaris thought the sunset was particularly lurid that day, dyeing the Morivant an angry sangria, as if the river had run red with blood. Then he saw that it *was* blood. The water was sluggish with flotsam and jetsam, bits of torn sails and broken hulls floating downriver amid the smaller shapes of dead soldiers. Tiny figures swarmed around the Earth Gate, wheeling a battering ram between them. White and grey banners flew everywhere, on the river, on the bank, under the walls. But on the ramparts, beleaguered, the gallant colours of the Safin sunburst still flew.

Klemene was praying loudly. In a half-whisper, Vion said, "The city is falling."

There was a crash and a great splintering noise. The gate had taken another hit from the ram. One side was already drooping from its hinges. A dark shape toppled from the battlement above, sloshing liquid as it went. Hot oil, Emaris guessed. Then a flare of brilliant white light went off, and he flinched, turning his face away. Three low booms resounded. Their cannon.

"Boats," said Savonn, sounding almost approving. He nudged their horse up to the front of the column. "Isemain's braver than we thought."

Emaris had been so sure the Marshal was crossing at Amarota. That would have been all right. At least he would have time to go to the hospital and get his face mended, and find his sister, and after a good meal and some sleep he would be ready to fight again. But this was more than he could bear.

"I want my *bed*," said Corl in a small, tired voice. "If they take the city I won't have a bed."

"There's nothing for it," said Daine. He was guiding his horse with his knees, his left arm in a sling, his right holding a spear. "Give the order, Emaris. We'll charge."

"And *die*?" yelled Klemene. "Look at that. There must be thousands of them. We're fucked."

The sentiment rippled out through the company. It wasn't *fair*, thought Emaris. Their orders had been to lure the Saraians into Lissein and let the circus do its job. They had done just that, and more besides. None of them were looking for laurels and victory hymns. All they wanted was an open door to come home to. Was that so much to ask?

He thought of Shandei, of Hiraen, and a rush of shame overcame him. Only hours ago he had been ready to die, and now here he was, bellyaching with the rest of them. "*Shut up!*" he shouted.

To his surprise, the muttering ceased. There was a terse silence, broken only by the distant crash of the ram and the boom of the cannon. Savonn handed him the reins and slid out of the saddle, and Emaris found himself alone at the front of the host, with hundreds of eyes on him.

His heart struck a beat out of time, and resumed its rapid patter.

"Men of Betronett," he said. Savonn elbowed him in the shin, and he remembered to pitch his voice to carry. "We won a victory, but the job's not done yet. Our friends still need our help. After all, we're the High Commander's own men. One of us is worth twelve of those poor suckers in the city guard."

Lomas cheered and punched the air. He was the only one.

"We're going to help them," said Emaris. He drew the longsword Corl had found for him in Lissein, and lifted it where the blade would catch the light. "I've got half a face and Daine over there's got one arm, and when I give the signal we're both going to charge into that mob. You can piss off like cowards, if you'd rather not. Or you can come with us and show Hiraen he doesn't stand alone."

The cannon boomed again. The horses snorted, nervous. The men looked at one another, or at the ground. With an air of extreme forbearance, Vion said, "Don't be so melodramatic. Of course we're coming. Right, Klemene?"

Klemene tried to outstare him, and quailed. "Of course."

Rougen nodded fervently. Lomas cheered again. This time the cry was taken up by the rest of the patrol, and slowly, reluctantly, rippled across the company. Emaris let out a shaky breath. This was it, then. "Daine, sound the horn."

But Daine was looking past him, distracted. Savonn, too, had gone a few steps off, gazing eastward, where dusk had already fallen over the rolling plains that spooled away to Terinea. "Wait."

"What's the matter?" snapped Emaris. If they lost their drive now they would never find it again. "That speech wasn't good enough for you?"

Savonn came back, grasping Emaris's bridle for support. Inexplicably, he was smiling. "It was impressive," he said. "But I'm afraid you've been upstaged. Look."

Emaris looked. Shapes moved on the highway. A column of man and horse was approaching, bristling under a forest of spears. Dozens of them, hundreds, a thousand. An iron vice closed around his heart. He squinted in the half-light, trying to make out the device on the banners. There were many. A bronze eagle, open-beaked, swooping across a field of cream. A silver porpoise leaping from an azure sea. And high above the others, the beloved sunburst, orange on black, twin to the one on the ramparts.

The vice loosened. Stricken stock-still into abject dumbness, Emaris listened as the first horns wound, solemn and mournful. Then the trumpets joined in from the city walls, bright and brazen and defiant. *Da, da-da, da-da, da dadada*. Lucien Safin had come.

The attackers at the Earth Gate fell into confusion, caught from behind with their ranks in disarray. The bells started up in the city: the deep bronze tolling Emaris had heard the morning after his father died, and again just yesterday, when they had been summoned to the Arena. But this time it was a joyous, chiming tumult that cried, *We are saved.*

In the west, the sun sank at last into the river, plunging them into an unearthly fire-streaked twilight. The banners on the highway dipped once in salute. The standard on the rampart answered. Then, like a wave starting slow and gathering speed, the ranks of Lord Lucien's host surged forward.

Daine threw his spear in the air, and caught it again one-handed. "What are we waiting for?"

Savonn swung back onto the roan, this time behind Emaris. Everyone was cheering. "Go!" Emaris yelled. And the voices of his men, glad and brave, answered him. *"Cassarah! Cassarah! Cassarah!"*

He kicked the horse into a gallop. Like an arrowhead, they drove headlong towards the city. The Earth Gate flew open before they were halfway there, and out came a stream of cavalrymen in gleaming mail, the sunburst shining on every cloak. The man at the front had a great goldenwood bow. Emaris lifted his fist in greeting, and thought he saw Hiraen do the same. They closed in, from the north and the east and the south; and screaming, the Saraians fled before them.

CHAPTER 17

All things considered, Iyone thought it had been a profitable day.

They had scraped a double victory by the skin of their teeth. Hiraen had held the Earth Gate for almost a full night and day, while the Saraians—under the command of Marshal Isemain himself—surged against the walls and broke and rallied and advanced again, until Lord Lucien arrived and threw them back into the river. The men of Betronett, too, had done well at the death circus. The Marshal and that turncoat assassin Nikas had gotten away, but no one particularly minded. Victory had to be eked out and cherished in little scoops.

In the midst of it all, there had been Shandei and her awful, beautiful face, saying, *I would have fled with you.* They had seen each other only for a few minutes, but it felt significant somehow. Iyone did not understand it. She filed the memory away for another time, a kinder time, when she could puzzle it over at leisure. Their next encounter might not be so gentle.

The family feasted late into the night, back together for the first time since the summer (though not truly: Savonn was missing, and had not even tried to sneak himself into the manor as a serving-girl or something). The next morning Iyone awoke from a long blessed sleep to find a note on her desk, in the exquisite hand she knew so well:

Well done, false daughter. I expected no less from you. Allow yourself a small celebration, then return to your labours. Marguerit will regroup and come again. The Empath is at her side, his counsels full of mischief. Be watchful. May your hands be firm and your heart unyielding, and the works of your life prosper.

Iyone read the note several times, and threw it in the fireplace. She was not sentimental. She would not make Savonn's mistakes.

* * *

The Council and its generals convened later that day. The citadel meeting-chamber had rarely been so crowded: the High Commander at the head of the room, flanked by his father and sister, the Sydells and Efrens filling the rest of the table. Others were not present. Aretel held war in low esteem and so had not come; and Zarin, according to Daron, had turned the command of his troops over to Lucien and disappeared soon after Josit's fall from grace.

Iyone studied each of the servants in turn, but to her disappointment, they were all real.

"Well, that was a nice bit of fighting," said Lord Lucien, when the healths had been drunk. "Iyone's circus went off admirably, and I hear Hiraen crossed swords with the Marshal himself."

He beamed at them, in good spirits. He had reason to be. They had won all three of their engagements with the Saraians so far, and he had fought in two of them. His face had lost some of its roundness in the Farfallens, and his arms were ropy with new muscle. Not even the scandal with the Empath seemed to have dampened his mood. As far as he was concerned, Savonn was dead, and whatever he had done could be put in the ground with him. Lucien had come a long way from the man Willon and Oriane had so easily goaded.

Long live House Safin, Iyone thought, and not entirely in irony.

"I beat Isemain off at the gate," said Hiraen. "He floated back across the river on bits of his own boats as soon as he saw you coming. The man has a talent for retreating."

"And you didn't pursue?" said Bonner Efren. "Your lordship?"

Against her better judgement, Iyone answered. "His lordship was preoccupied at the time, holding the Earth Gate together with his own hands. I'm sure you'll agree that was more important than giving chase."

Bonner looked startled, as if a servant had talked back to him. This one was a new danger, Iyone thought. Cut from the same cloth as his father, but smarter and more of a fighter. She would have to learn his ways, and see where she might get under his skin. Young men did not succumb to accidents as easily as the old.

She regretted the thought. Murder was habit-forming.

"The Marshal can wait," said Daron smoothly. He had all his aunt Oriane's features but none of her temper, with a calm, steadying demeanor and the sort of reasonable voice one could not help but heed. "We'll kill him next time. Hiraen, you said Marguerit sent us a missive?"

A fast courier from Daliss had reached Amarota at sunup that morning with a letter bearing the royal seal. The border guards had conveyed it to Cassarah at once, and put it in Iyone's hands. "Yes," said Hiraen. "Perhaps I'll have my jester read it out for a laugh over dinner. Long in short, the Queen's suing for peace."

That drew a chorus of sneers and chortles. "She is offering ten thousand drochii and a peace treaty," added Yannick, "on the condition that we hand over Josit Ansa."

Bonner spat on the rushes. "Why should we? That bitch murdered my little brother. She's mine to kill. Anyway, we haven't got her."

His hard eyes went to Iyone. Any moment now he was going to remind them all whose fault that had been. "Of course," Hiraen broke in, "we're not going to entertain anything of the sort. Marguerit sued for peace eighteen years ago, and look at her now. We have to sweep her away once and for all. Iyone and I have composed a reply—Lord Yannick, do you have it?"

"Indeed, Commander," said Yannick. He shuffled through his papers, selected one, and cleared his throat. *"To Her Royal Majesty Marguerit the Magnificent, Queen of Sarei. We are in agreement that a cessation of hostilities between our nations is in the best interests of all. However, we reject your terms and propose our own. These are as follows: the sum of one million drochii and the release of every Cassaran-born slave within your borders, to be effected in full in three days.*

"This, we know, is impossible. So is the prospect of peace between Cassarah and Daliss as matters stand. As such, we charge you to gather your forces and meet us at the Singing Ford on the first day of the new year. There we shall make an end of you.

"Health to you and yours, with the regards of Oriane Sydell, Acting Governor of Cassarah; and Hiraen Safin, High Commander, Captain of Betronett, and Defender of the East Bank."

Lord Lucien was nodding in approval. Daron and Oriane looked thoughtful. Iyone watched Bonner's face, counted down the moments till he opened his mouth, and wished, regretfully, that she had invented more titles for Hiraen.

"You might as well style yourself King of Cassarah," said Bonner. "Have we become a monarchy since my lord father's passing? Why were we not consulted?"

The truth was that Iyone and Hiraen had fallen out of the habit of consulting the Council. The obligatory bickering was a nuisance in peacetime, but at war the wasted hours could mean the difference between life and death. "For heaven's sake," said

Lucien. "They haven't sent the answer yet. If you take issue with it, say so now and we can change it."

"That's not the point," said Bonner, his jaw jutting like a ship's prow. "It seems to me that this last autumn has been one great tragicomedy perpetrated by you Safins. Josit's escape. The Silvertongue's disappearance. The release of the Empath, whom my father captured with such pains—"

"Yes," said Oriane dryly. "We are more than acquainted with the failings of House Safin." She slanted Iyone a look that said, *What did I tell you?*

Iyone sighed. Oriane had been snippy with her all day. This morning Bonner and Daron had asked to see the Empath's letters, only to discover that the cedarwood box had vanished from the Sydell manor under the guards' very noses. Iyone had claimed ignorance, and was not believed. "Lord Bonner," she said. "The Empath's ransom paid for our guns and gunpowder and the entire village of Lissein. Would you rather Marguerit had saved all that gold for her own war treasury?"

Bonner looked astonished. "Of course not, but—"

"Then what, precisely, is your objection?"

"Lord Hiraen," Daron cut in. "Perhaps before we break for the day, we should discuss our dispositions for the battle. Surely we ought to reach the Singing Ford well before the agreed date? Marguerit may cheat."

"Right," said Hiraen. "I hope to set out by next week, in fact. I propose to take five thousand foot and a thousand horse. My lord father will stay behind with the remainder to garrison the city."

Lucien looked irritated. "Well, if you're sure you don't want me to come along."

"Daron," Hiraen went on, "I hope you will command the foot. I hear you did a masterful job of it at Onaressi. And Bonner"—he smiled—"it would be an honour if you led my van."

Lucien spluttered. So did Yannick. Iyone dropped the quill she had been holding. Bonner said, "Your *van*?"

"Indeed," said Hiraen, with a warning look at Iyone. "My father has spoken highly of your courage. We could be in no better hands."

Going by the look on Lucien's face, he had said no such thing. Bonner looked just as taken aback. "Well. That. That would be a privilege, Hiraen." His cheeks were going bright red beneath his stubble. "I am pleased to accept."

Oriane looked at Iyone again, a question in her eyes. Iyone shook her head: not her doing. Aretel might have suggested it. But more likely than not, it was all Hiraen, Hiraen and his ten years on the field and his inborn charm oozing through the gaps in people's armour. Bonner's pride might have balked at following a Safin into battle, but this was an honour even he could not refuse.

Daron was smiling, looking relieved. "A wise choice, High Commander."

Iyone glanced at Bonner, who still looked dazed, and swallowed her objections. Her brother had been leading men all his life. She could only hope he knew what he was doing. "Well, now that's settled," said Hiraen, "I vote we all go home and get some sleep before the victory feast tonight. I've got a new jester. You'll love him. Master of the satire, the lampoon, and the innuendo."

"Oh?" said Oriane, as they began to get up in a great scraping of chairs. "Who has he lampooned?"

"The better question is," said Hiraen, his apple-cheeked smile turning grim, "who hasn't he?"

* * *

Hiraen's new jester performed a puppet-farce at the victory feast that night. The subject: the joint trial, as it had come to be known, of the Empath and the Silvertongue.

The banquet was just the sort of thing Emaris would have been excited to attend a year ago, serving and pouring for Savonn at the high table in the citadel's feast hall. Now he himself had a place of honour on the dais, and was expected to comport himself with dignity. Certainly the food was good, though he was in too much pain to chew—there was fried fish and stuffed goose, apple cider and mulled wine, with pumpkin pudding for dessert—and the hall was warm and bright and full of laughter. If not for the farce, he might even have enjoyed himself.

As it was, he was glad for his bandaged face. At least he did not have to pretend to laugh.

For a dinner show, it was a grand production. The jester worked his puppet-strings from behind a white velvet curtain, through which nothing of him could be seen. There were four stern-faced puppets for the presiding councillors, and a red-haired, long-lashed one for the Empath, who delivered his damning testimony in a frighteningly realistic accent. Worst of all was the stuffed magpie, clearly meant to be the spirit of the deceased Savonn, that swooped across the set now and then to interject in a high-pitched simper. "O! love of my life! Soon we shall meet again, and I will pay you back in full. With my sword, and my spear, and my *other* spear..."

The diners roared. Lady Oriane had shrieked with laughter at the first sight of her puppet, and was by now in tears, thumping Iyone on the back. Bonner was in danger of falling off his chair. Even Hiraen had a frozen sort of smile behind his goblet. "How can this be allowed?" Emaris demanded. "Why aren't the Safins stopping it?"

Daine was not laughing, either. "Why should they? I'd wager this was their idea. They need to show the world that their sympathies no longer lie with the Silvertongue."

Emaris found this no comfort. "That jester should be hanged. Who the hell does he think he is?"

"By gods, child," said Daine, who seemed to be in an ominous mood. His left arm was still in a sling; Emaris had been cutting his food for him. "How many people do you know who can speak in six voices and have the guts to do that in front of Iyone Safin?"

Emaris looked at Iyone. Then he looked at the white curtain. "Oh."

He did not know whether that made matters better or worse. At the end of the show, when the jester's assistant approached the dais to present each councillor with their puppet, he stood up with his fried fish half eaten and walked out of the hall.

Night had fallen. A team of labourers was still hard at work in the moat, hammering long rows of iron spikes into place. Some of them glanced up as he crossed the drawbridge, their eyes lingering on his face. This morning, when the doctor came to change his bandages, Shandei had shown Emaris his wounds in a hand mirror. "It looks bad now, but you'll hardly be able to see the scars once they heal—*if* you don't scratch." She slapped his hand away. "Poor boy, at least now you'll find a lover who doesn't just want you for your looks."

He'd scowled at her. Three long burn-marks slashed across his swollen right cheek, blazing an angry red. They would turn brown first, then a distinguished white—"barely visible," the doctor promised, "so long as you use the ointment I gave you." Emaris thought he was probably a quack, but did not say so.

He stopped in the piazza. It was a cloudless night, and the stars seemed to hang lower in the sky than usual, so bright and so close he felt he could have reached up and touched them. A pair of guards paced the perimeter of the square, their lanterns bobbing. A maid trundled a wagon over the drawbridge. Emaris considered going home, or fetching Vion and finding a tavern where they could get rollicking drunk. Neither option appealed to him.

At last he gave up pretending he did not know where he wanted to go, and let his legs carry him there.

The Arena was quiet. The comedy troupe had long packed up and left, and there were no more plays scheduled that winter. The unicorn door squalled at him as he pushed it open. He petted its head in passing, and felt his way down the unlit tunnels of the catacomb until he came to the storeroom he had visited before. A strip of light showed beneath the door. Savonn must have just preceded him there.

He paused for a moment on the threshold, his fingers poised to knock. He dreamt too much about doors and light.

Savonn was lounging on the mattress, a book in his lap. He was in a white chambray shirt, the edge of a bandage showing under one sleeve, the hems of his trousers rolled up over his bare feet. His eyes were kohled, and an onyx fang swung from one ear, half hidden in his blond curls. The redhead puppet and the magpie sat on a stool next to him. In the feast hall, armoured in nonchalance, he would have looked like any other guest: a wolf among sheep, or a sheep among wolves.

"I thought you might be in hospital," said Emaris. "Instead you were out playing with puppets."

Savonn glanced up from his book. He did not look as if he had been reading. His posture might have passed for languid if Emaris had not marked how all his muscles tensed at the creak of the door, gathering themselves to fight or flee. He could not even sit without being deceptive. "If I'd had time," he said, "I would have made one of you. How is your face?"

Everyone asked him that. Emaris had mastered the flippant answer by now. Oh, it was healing well. It was sore, but that would pass. He was lucky, really: he might have lost an eye, or died of infection, or ended up like Anyas, whose face still looked different every other day. He was fine. He was too brave to be anything but fine.

"It fucking hurts," he said. "Daine's angry with you. It's a pity he recognised you. If he still thought you were dead, he'd almost be done mourning now."

Aside from Daine, only Emaris's patrol knew that Savonn was alive. They appeared to have come to a tacit agreement to keep it from the rest of the company. Vion and Lomas had been indignant, but were too loyal to give the secret away. Others, like Klemene, thought the whole thing terribly exciting, and no one knew what Rougen felt except Rougen himself. "I suppose it would be easier," said Savonn, "if I'd really died."

Emaris sat down at the foot of the mattress. "Easier?" he said. "Yes. Better? No."

He wished he were the Empath, and able to read feelings. Savonn's expression was unfathomable, his lips pressed together, his eyes absent. The lamplight played on the lines of his nose and jaw, in the sharp-angled hollows at the base of his throat. He had been Emaris's age when he'd fallen in love with Dervain Teraille. How old was he now? Only five or six years had passed, surely; he was still young. Still a fool, for all that he pretended otherwise.

Emaris's chest was heavy with the familiar soreness he had come to associate with Savonn. He knew what that pain meant, now. It had been growing in him for a long time, perhaps from the very beginning, when he was much too young to understand. Savonn had seen it and, with his usual knifepoint kindness, tried to drive Emaris off before he could do anything inadvisable. Nothing good ever came of a boy's hot-headed love. Savonn knew that better than most.

You should have renounced him, said Nikas's voice in his echo-chamber.

Emaris's head was shockingly clear now, as if his thoughts had been strained through a net woven from diamond. He had not renounced Savonn. He could live with this. He had trekked alone through the mountains to summon an army; had walked knowingly into a death trap and come out again. This was no different. He could grow around the ache in his chest, like a tree enveloping a fence, until one day he might look at Savonn and feel no pain.

He was a soldier, after all. A soldier's brother, a soldier's son.

"When are you going to do it?" he asked. "Fight the Empath?"

Unlike everyone else, Savonn did not stare at Emaris's bandaged face. His icicle gaze went right through skin and bone as though these were no more than garnishes. "When we are ready."

"How will you tell?"

"By ear, as musicians do."

"And after that?" Emaris persisted. "You're still a fugitive. What would you do?"

The kohl made Savonn's eyes look bigger, the blue in his irises more vivid. He tapped a silver-ringed finger on his knee. "The usual question is, *Could you do it?* So far you're the only one who's certain that I could."

Savonn was capable of anything. Emaris had seen that at Lissein. The trouble was that someone had to carry him out of the burning building afterwards, and Emaris was not sure he had the strength to do it again. "I know you."

"Then allow me to pose you a question in turn," said Savonn. "If you found your father's killer—the real one—could *you* do your duty?"

That gave Emaris pause. Up till now, this had been a question of purely academic interest. He had killed plenty of men, but killing was a professional act. It was reserved for faceless foes in skirmishes, not anyone who had wronged him personally, anyone he knew. "It depends who it is."

"It does, doesn't it?" said Savonn. "The priests and the theologians would say that justice shouldn't depend on anything. That it is the principle that matters, and the specifics make no difference. But that is why we are not priests."

"*He* is."

Emaris was looking at the puppet. Softly, Savonn said, "He is."

He must know who had killed Rendell. Emaris was more certain of it than ever. But he could not bear to ask, not now. He had had enough drama for the day.

"I mean to be there when you kill the Empath," he said at last. "Someone has to bear witness."

Savonn stared at the floor-tiles. "It doesn't have to be you."

Proud, prickly Savonn, whom Emaris loved, whose heart was given to another. Who shone so bright that, like the sun, he blinded anyone who looked at him too long. Emaris understood this and, willfully, did not look away. "I'll be there still."

"I know," said Savonn.

CHAPTER 18

On the longest night of the year, the High Commander and his army rode forth to meet Marguerit of Sarei at the Singing Ford, and Shandei rode with them.

Emaris put up a good show of being annoyed that she was coming, but she knew him too well. "Someone has to make sure you don't go rushing off into any more valiant last stands," she said, tousling his hair. He was too old and too tall for that now, so she stood on tip-toes and did it even more. "Besides, I'm sick of cannon."

There were other reasons. Until she made up her mind what to do about Hiraen Safin, she needed to keep him in her sightlines. There was Iyone, too. She had been wearing Shandei's rose scarf when the Council saw them off at the Gate of Gold, with the effect that Shandei forgot where she was and what she was doing, and missed the entirety of Lady Oriane's farewell speech. Near Iyone, she could not think straight. Better to go forth with steel in her hand, and clear her mind in battle.

The journey to the Ford was bleak and cold. Bonner led the van, with Daron's foot marching behind and the Betronett cavalry forming the rearguard. Hiraen was everywhere, conferring with his generals, riding out with the scouting parties, mingling with the rank and file. Shandei stayed near the back of the column on her borrowed mare, out of Emaris's way. He was a grown man with an officer's duties, and ought not suffer the embarrassment of his big sister's presence.

Late in the afternoon, a rider on a black charger approached and drew level with her. "Look," said a voice through a visored helm. "Lissein. The site of your brother's great victory."

Shandei looked. To their left the Morivant unravelled, its bends and bays patrolled by roving phalanges of pikemen. Ahead, a little clutch of cottages nestled against the bank beside a copse of leafless sentinels. She realised this was the village. Quite a few of the houses were roofless, their crumbling walls black with soot. "I've never been there," she said. "Have you?"

"Twice," said the faceless rider.

Shandei gazed, curious, at the slight figure on the horse. She had plenty of friends in the army, and quite a few of the women she had met on the ramparts the other night had joined the host as well, some dressed as men, others—like her—not bothering. But this fellow was unfamiliar. "Who are you?"

"Let me know," said the rider, "if you find out."

He was dressed in a fraying grey cloak and surcoat that bore no device, but the way he sat his horse—chin high, back straight, reins looped loosely around his wrist—had aristocratic training written all over it. She knew only one such person who would conceal himself like this. "Oh." She could not help but laugh, not politely. "Emaris sent you to keep an eye on me?"

"I wouldn't say that," said Savonn Silvertongue. He swung one leg over the horse to sit side-saddle, like a fussy courtesan. "No one sends me anywhere these days. It's one of the advantages of being dead."

She had never been alone with him like this, without the mediating presence of Emaris or their father. "Dead? Or friendless?"

"No difference," said Savonn amiably. "Like you, I am loath to impose my company on the puissant Lord Safin. Or the fledgeling hero Emaris. Did you know our gazelle has dispensation from all relevant parties to assume command of Betronett, should anything befall Hiraen in battle? Or," he added, "out of it."

Shandei refused the bait. "Gods above," she said. "A couple months as patrol leader and he's already had his face burned to the bone. Promote him some more and he might start losing limbs."

"He should be fine as long as I'm not there," said Savonn. "You know me. Chief corrupter and disfigurer of young boys. Poor Hiraen has his work cut out keeping me away from them."

He was determined, it seemed, to keep bringing up the name until it sparked a reaction. Shandei reined up hard, staring at him. "You know, don't you? How does your conscience bear it? Emaris is in love with you."

Savonn halted as well. Aside from the outriders, they were at the very back of the column. "Now, now," he said. "Let's not accuse each other of having *consciences*. Hiraen has one, and look where it got him."

She did not want to dice words with a traitor. "He owes me a blood debt."

He laughed. "He thinks so too. In fact, I'll bet you a drochon he'll come to your sword and beg for death once the war is over. Martyrdom is a hobby of his."

"You and I," said Shandei, "have very different ideas about martyrdom. Where our fathers' killers are concerned, not all of us can be as forgiving as you."

He had no principles to offend, and so did not gratify her by losing his temper. She wondered if he was even capable of anger. "Put me in a duel with the Empath, and you'll see how forgiving I can be." She could almost see his lazy smile through the visor. "I have to go. Try not to murder anyone."

He swung his foot back into the stirrup, resuming his cavalryman's seat. Furious as she was, it was a minute before she realised he was going off-road, headed into the copse of trees outside Lissein. "Where the hell are you going?" She yanked her own mare round and started after him. "Deserting on the eve of battle?"

He ignored her. She hesitated, torn. By now the column was passing Lissein, keeping a wary distance from both the village and the wood. No doubt the outriders would break off and give chase if she called out. But already he was halfway to the treeline, and if she hung back she would lose sight of him altogether.

She spurred her horse into a gallop. "Are you meeting someone? Smuggling more secrets?"

Savonn looked back. "Who are you going to tell, Hiraen?"

The trees rushed up to meet them. Shandei slowed her mare to a walk, and dodged under a low-hanging bough. Scarcely a fortnight had passed since Emaris's battle. The wood still bore traces of it: broken swords and arrowheads glinted underfoot, and here and there the trees were marked with scratches from passing blades. A scrap of bloodstained cloth fluttered from a branch. Shandei wondered about the man who had worn the cloak it had come from, if he was friend or foe, if he had lived or died. If he had been a man at all.

"It's all right," Savonn called. He had taken off his helm. His curls were no longer blond, as Emaris claimed they had been, but back to their pure black. "She's one of ours."

Shandei's hand tightened on her bow. It had been her father's, but since the night on the ramparts she had grown used to thinking of it as her own. If the Empath materialised, she was going to shoot him, friend or not.

But the person who stepped out to meet them was not Dervain Teraille. This man, too, was familiar to her, with his strange pale eyes and narrow, compressed features. Zarin, Josit's servant. Vesmer's murderer, and Willon's. His other murderer, at any rate. His gaze flicked between them, but it was Savonn he addressed. "The Saraians set out earlier than you. They have a sizeable host. Six thousand foot, two or three thousand horse. Even that is not their full strength. The van will cross the Ford soon."

This was no surprise. No doubt Marguerit had hoped to reach the battleground first and sow it full of caltrops and explosives. "The Commander will be informed," said Savonn. He had not dismounted. "Have you seen Nikas?"

"No," said Zarin. "Nor the other one."

A taut silence elapsed. Against all logic, Savonn was even more unreadable without the helm than with it. Zarin added, "Her ladyship exhorts you to stay away from the Empath."

"*Josit?*" said Shandei.

"Her ladyship," said Savonn, "knows how much I heed her exhortations. You have my thanks."

The dismissal was plain. Still, Zarin made no move to leave. "The lady is not without means of her own," he said. "She can go to the High Priest of the Sanctuary and buy this slave at any price asked, if my lord wishes it."

Shandei let out a startled laugh. "Marguerit ransomed him for fifteen thousand drochii. Don't tell me Josit has that kind of money lying around."

Zarin did not take his eyes off Savonn. "Not all currency is coin."

Savonn gazed down from the vantage of his saddle. Shandei saw that she had been wrong. He was in fact capable of anger, the most vast and blinding sort. "Dervain is not a horse or a sword, to be bought and sold at will. Josit has more cause than most to understand this. You may tell her so, in those words."

The threat could not have been plainer if he'd shouted. "You are going to kill him?" asked Zarin. "Her ladyship said you would not."

"I suppose her ladyship knows best," said Savonn. "Give her my love."

He wheeled his horse and cantered back the way they had come. Uncertain, Shandei made to follow, but looked back. She felt in some abtruse way that she owed Zarin something, if only the courtesy of a polite goodbye. "Thank you," she said. "For the news, and—and for getting to Willon before me."

He looked at her, slender and silent as a dryad under the bare boughs. His pale eyes did not so much as flicker. She was nothing to him, she realised, because she was nothing to Josit. It was a chilling thought.

Savonn had cleared the treeline by the time she caught up with him. "Josit's spying for us now?" she asked, as they trotted back to rejoin the column. "Or on us? Where is she? Why would she bother?"

"Don't," said Savonn, "ask me about Josit."

He put his helm back on, but not before Shandei caught a glimpse of his face. It was still pinched and pale with rage. "So what now?"

"If a Saraian died for every question you asked," said Savonn through his visor, "Marguerit would have surrendered last week. Stop talking and get your sword whetted."

* * *

"Good speed today," said Hiraen, as he and Emaris went down the narrow lanes between the tents and firepits of their camp. "And your face looks much better."

They had stopped two miles south of the Singing Ford as night descended. Having got his patrol settled, Emaris fell in with Hiraen on their way to the Sydell tents for the war council. In a show of brotherly equality, the three generals took turns hosting the others in their respective quarters, and it was Lord Daron's turn tonight. "The doctor says the scars should fade some more," said Emaris. "I don't know that I believe him."

At present he looked like he had been clawed by a very large bird. The scabs had flaked off, and the burn marks were arriving at a sort of yellowish-brown on their way—he hoped—to his normal complexion. They no longer hurt, and even the itching had subsided. He'd had the bandages off the day before. Had it not been for the stares, he might have forgotten about the wounds entirely. "Well, it's just a face," said Hiraen. "And still a pretty good one. Where's Shandei?"

They all kept asking him that. "Probably terrorising some poor infantryman with her left hook," said Emaris. "Is it true the Saraians are arriving soon?"

"That's what Savonn said."

Emaris glanced over his shoulder. The helmeted Betronett man he had been glimpsing in the ranks all day was slouching behind them, bouncing a palmful of pebbles between his hands. When he saw Emaris watching him, he tossed them high over his head and caught them again, and disappeared behind a tent. Emaris peeled his attention away.

"We have some breathing room," Hiraen was saying. "Isemain won't cross in the morning, with the sun in his eyes. I had half a mind to launch a surprise attack at dawn, but our colleagues didn't seem enthused... Oh, speak of the devil. Evening, Bonner."

Bonner had appeared on his other side. He nodded at Hiraen and, except for the requisite scar-staring, ignored Emaris completely. That was not surprising. Last they had met, Emaris had called him a moron, and he doubted the man was the sort to accept concussion as an excuse. "This news about the Saraians," said Bonner. "Who brought it?"

They passed a cookfire crackling at the junction of two lanes. Perhaps it was the heat, or the bitter smoke that filled his lungs, but when a Sydell guard jumped up to salute with something in his hand Emaris flinched hard. It was only a chunk of roast hare on a stick, fragrant with grease. Even so, his gorge rose. He turned away so the heat would not beat on his face, and tried not to shake.

Hiraen paused and acknowledged the man with a nod, but he was looking at Emaris. "Our scouts."

"Our scouts haven't come back yet," said Bonner.

"Our other scouts," said Hiraen peaceably. Daron's tent had come into view at the end of the lane, tall and airy, blue silk edged with white. The porpoise banner hung by the entrance. "I'll tell you later. Have you had dinner?"

Bonner was not to be sidetracked. "I thought we agreed you would consult us on everything. I didn't know you'd sent out more scouts. Where are they?"

"Scouting," said Hiraen. "I assure you their news is reliable. Lord Sydell will agree." There was no sentry on duty at the tent flap, so he reached out to open it himself. "Right, Daron?"

He stopped short on the threshold. Both Bonner and Emaris ran into him from behind. He said again, in a very different voice, "*Daron.*"

"What?" said Bonner. "What is it?"

Emaris could see nothing through the narrow opening. He hung back, still queasy. But then Hiraen took a step inside, and he saw.

Always conscientious, Daron had had the tent made ready for the meeting. A low wooden table had been set up near the entrance next to a neat pile of camp stools. Maps and diagrams lay on it, and a brazier was burning sweet incense. Daron himself was sitting across from the tent flap, his folded hands rigid on the table. Behind him, holding a long curved dagger to his throat, was Nikas.

"Who the hell are you?" Bonner demanded.

But Nikas was gazing at Emaris, his usual madcap grin in place. "O gazelle!" he crowed. "What a sight!"

Emaris's burns twinged. His hand jumped uselessly to his empty scabbard. They did not go armed to each other's tents. "*Release him*," said Hiraen.

"I'm afraid I can't," said Nikas. "He's to be an example, or something like that. The common fate of all Efrens and Sydells, you poor things."

The dagger flashed.

Bonner shouted. They all lunged forward. It was too late. A second mouth, gaping red, opened across Daron's throat with a hiss of breath. He slumped face first onto his clasped hands, like a man overcome by sleep at his desk. Even as Hiraen reached for a bow that wasn't there, Nikas spun on his heel and slashed open the back of the tent to make a run for it.

"Move," said a voice behind Emaris. A silver knife whistled over his shoulder.

It struck Nikas across the face, slicing his cheek open. Emaris saw his chance. He swung onto the table and vaulted across, feet flying. His boots slammed into Nikas's ribs with all his weight behind them. Nikas lost his balance. Then Hiraen caught up one of the stools and smashed it over his head in a vicious swing, and he staggered, stumbled, and crumpled to the ground, motionless as Daron.

"Guards!" Bonner yelled. *"Guards! Guards!"* He stared around the tent, mouth agape. "How did this happen? How did he get in?"

Hiraen was kneeling beside Daron, feeling for a pulse, so it was Emaris who had to answer. "I don't know. He was trained in the Sanctuary. They can do all sorts of—"

Bonner had ceased to listen, or perhaps had never started. His eyes retraced the trajectory of the throwing knife, and widened. "It's you!"

Helpless, Emaris looked to the entrance. The slouchy Betronett man was standing there, arms folded. He must have followed them after all. If only Emaris had paid more attention—if he had brought a knife of his own, acted before Savonn had needed to—

But already the tent flap was flying open, and a stream of guards poured in, swords bared. They wavered, uncertain. "Lord Bonner," Emaris began.

"No, don't bother," said Savonn. He grimaced at Emaris, pulling off his helmet and throwing it to the floor. "I should have aimed for the heart."

A collective gasp rippled through the men, as one by one they recognised him. Emaris found his voice. "Nikas. He's not dead. Kill him now."

"Why?" shouted Bonner. "To destroy the evidence?" He stabbed a thick finger into Savonn's chest. "I should have known you weren't dead. Who smuggled you in?"

The touch seemed to break a spell. Emaris's eye was practised enough that he could see the precise moment Savonn's mask snapped into place. "I'm not a piece of contraband," said Savonn, surveying the newcomers with a look of utter disdain. "No one smuggled me anywhere. You could at least give me the credit due my reputation."

Bonner stared at him. His cheeks had flushed a deep purple. "Arrest him."

The guards closed in. Without thinking, Emaris grabbed the dagger out of Nikas's limp hand and swung back across the table to interpose himself between Savonn and Bonner. "Step back. He had nothing to do with this."

"Emaris," said Savonn.

"I said *step back*, soldiers."

The guards retreated a few paces. Hiraen stood up, his hands red to the wrists with Daron's blood. "Don't do this now, Bonner."

Bonner rounded on him. "Daron's been killed. There is an assassin in our camp. The traitor you claimed was dead has just turned up alive. Do you not see how this looks?"

"I see perfectly," said Hiraen. "I'm not sure you do. Call off your guards."

Bonner gave a short hard laugh, all tension and hot air. "You're shielding him. You've been hiding him all this while. Of course you did. Probably laughed about it behind our backs, didn't you? Made bets on how long it would take us to notice?"

Hiraen had lost all his colour. "Save it for later."

"Oh, don't be condescending," said Bonner. "How stupid do you think we were, Daron and I? My father was a bit of a fool, but I'm not. You loathe us, you and your sister both. You suffer us on your Council only to pretend you two haven't taken over Cassarah while we weren't looking. Isn't it strange how we keep dying? First my brother, then my father, and now Daron. How long more? How long till it's my turn?"

"For fuck's sake," said Hiraen. "Your father and brother have nothing to do with it. This fellow Nikas double-crossed us all the way to Astorre and back. What would he kill Daron for—Daron of all people, wouldn't hurt a fly, hasn't got an enemy in the world? Can't you see what he's doing? Marguerit's trying to drive a rift between us, and by gods, it's working."

Savonn said, "*Hiraen.*"

"You revolting hypocrite," said Bonner. He took a step towards Hiraen. Any closer and they would have been nose to nose, two bulls locking horns. "You presided at the trial and sentenced Savonn Silvertongue to death, and you dare stand here—here, over Daron's dead body—and defend him to my face?"

"Damn," said Hiraen. There was a dangerous, erratic light in his eyes Emaris had never seen before. He was holding Savonn's silver knife, his knuckles blanched white on the hilt. "I always knew I'd regret that."

Savonn said, "Arrest me."

"No!" Emaris cried.

"Or," said Savonn, "execute me. Pick one and do it now. You two, shut your imbecile mouths and get out of the way."

Neither of them moved. "See," said Bonner. "I'm right. The great Lord Safin protects his little lackeys, traitors and turncoat murderers and all. Just as long as they do his dirty work, am I right?"

"Hiraen," said Savonn again. "Will you not do even one thing for me?"

It was the same tone of voice he had used to say to Emaris, *I should have aimed for the heart.* A soft, private voice, as though he and Hiraen were the only ones in the tent, as though Bonner and the guards were no more than furniture. Hiraen stared at him, the look on his face less anger than anguish. "You always ask the impossible."

Savonn said nothing, but his eyes spoke volumes. The air went out of Hiraen. He looked down at the knife in his hand, as if he had no idea where it had come from. "Emaris," he said. "Lower that blade."

"But—"

"Now."

Emaris looked at Bonner, and for the briefest moment imagined hurling the dagger in his face. Not *at* him. Just half an inch or so from his stupid boat jaw, close enough to put the fear of Nikas's god into him. Then Hiraen said, "Emaris," and he sighed, and lowered the blade.

Bonner let out a breath. Beads of perspiration had broken out on his forehead. "Take him away."

Two of the guards laid hands on Savonn and pinned his arms behind him. Savonn did not resist, but all the same they were unduly rough, as if afraid he might otherwise turn into a puff of smoke and vanish. Emaris pictured setting the lot of them on fire. "What are you going to do with him?"

"Why," said Bonner, "I am taking him to Cassarah to be executed. Along with that wretch, of course."

He waved at Nikas, whose inert form the guards were already hauling from the tent. A weeping young woman came in and helped the men load Daron on a stretcher. Hiraen said, *"Now?"*

"What else can I do? Leave them here so you can help them escape? Wait till you slit my throat in my sleep?"

Hiraen was blanched with fury. "You've lost us the battle. Quite possibly the war."

"No," said Bonner. "You have."

The guards tied Savonn's wrists with a length of rope, and manhandled him from the tent. After him went Daron's stretcher. Bonner hung back so the weeping woman could pass, and Emaris shoved forward desperately. "My lord. May I speak?"

Bonner looked at him in much the same way Willon had once done, as if he were inspecting some crushed insect on the sole of his shoe. "Believe me," he said, "if anyone could think of a way to shut you up, they'd have done it by now. *What?*"

"The man Nikas is dangerous." Emaris pointed at his face. "He did this to me. He's given us the slip twice already, and he'll do it again if you let him. If you're going to execute him, you might as well do it now."

"So he can't incriminate your precious Savonn?" suggested Bonner, his furry brows creeping up his forehead. "That ship came into port a long time ago, you insolent child. Maybe he'll tell us something interesting about Lord Safin next."

He strode out. In a moment they heard his voice calling orders, snapping for his horse and sword. Emaris looked to Hiraen, waiting for him to stop it, but he only stood unmoving with the silver knife clutched in his hand, eyes fixed on nothing. Wind gusted through the slashed opening at the back of the tent, sending papers skittering to the floor. They were spotted with blood.

Sick with impotent rage, Emaris went outside to watch. The Efrens were already saddling up. Bonner was taking only his personal guard—about eighty men, all light horse—and a couple dozen Sydell retainers who were forming up like an honour guard around Daron's improvised bier. Emaris recognised one of them, Neander, as Daron's deputy. He touched the man on the elbow. "Sir," he said. "Will you not reconsider?"

Neander glanced at Bonner, a large square-shouldered figure at the head of the host. Hiraen had come out of the tent behind Emaris, and was watching too. "Perhaps after I get his lordship to safety."

"It will be too late then."

"It is too late now," said Neander, and swung up into the saddle without a backward glance.

In a few minutes Bonner was moving off with his host, leaving his tents, his baggage train, and his heavy horse to follow as best they could. The remaining Sydell officers watched them go from a tight huddle around their cookfire, looking confused and angry. Others, Betronett men and Safin retainers, were gathering around Hiraen in terse silence. Shandei caught Emaris's eye in the crowd and went over to stand by him. Vion and Rougen were with her, and Lomas too, dragging Klemene by the shirtsleeves. They looked stunned. It had all happened so quickly.

Daine came up to them. Hiraen glanced at him, and then away. "It's my fault."

"No," said Emaris. "It was Nikas."

"Not now," said Daine. "Both of you, come."

He led them to the edge of the camp. Night had well and truly fallen, and the sky was bright with cold, distant stars. He pointed northeast towards the Singing Ford. None of them spoke. There was no need to. Emaris tried to count the banners, and lost track at twenty. They were grey and white, clustered thick like a canopy of clouds, and they said, *We come.* He remembered that their scouts had never returned.

If he broke, so would his patrol. And his sister was here, watching. He had to be steadfast. "Come on," he said. "Let's arm."

Hiraen smiled. It was glossy and gruesome and brave, the kind of smile people made when they wanted to cry. "Poor Emaris," he said. "Why does this keep happening to you?—Yes, let's arm. You'd better find your sword. Savonn will laugh at you."

CHAPTER 19

By the time Nikas stirred, smoke was spiring from the place where their encampment had been, drifting across the sky with its bright networks of stars.

"Well played," remarked Savonn. They were bound hand and foot, jolting up the river road in a cramped wagon near the middle of Bonner Efren's host, and words were the only weapons he had to hand. "Making them fight each other on the eve of battle. They hardly took any prompting, did they?"

Nikas sat up. The knife wound on his cheek was a furious crimson, and an impressive purple bump was rising from his hairline. "But of course," Savonn continued, "this wasn't your idea."

Nikas favoured him with a fuzzy smile, like a triumphant if concussed wrestler. "You don't think so?"

"It's too clever for you," said Savonn. There being nothing else he could do, he was determined to avenge Hiraen and Emaris by inflicting his own personality on Nikas at close quarters, for as long as anyone let him. "From start to finish you have shown yourself unremarkable in every way—oh, except for your obsession with Josit Ansa. It's not really a mother you want, is it? Or you would have latched onto the first woman you met with a decent heart and a few crumbs of love to spare."

A nearby horseman, press-ganged into serving as prison guard, came up to the wagon and drove his fist into the side of Savonn's head. "Shut it, you filthy traitor whore."

Savonn registered the blow without feeling it. He seemed to have departed his body to float above his head, so everything appeared remote and in poor relief. He resumed his discourse as soon as the guard turned away, this time in Saraian. "You picked Josit, though. Did you hope she would overthrow Marguerit and start looking around for an heir? Or did you just see a kindred spirit in her? Enslaved and dispossessed, the queen of should-haves and would-haves—"

Nikas shifted his weight. There was a sharp impact against Savonn's shinbone. The bastard had kicked him. From his rarefied vantage point this was hilarious. "Anyway," Savonn went on, "it's obvious whose idea this really was. No, don't say the name, sweetheart. I got my hands free twenty minutes ago and I'm not afraid to use them."

In fact, he had only managed to wriggle his left hand partway from its bindings. The other small consolation was that his captors, in their haste, had left him most of his knives. But the damage was done. The Ford was lost, and Bonner, glimpsing the smoke behind them, had given orders to make full speed for Cassarah.

Daron would have turned back for Hiraen's sake. But that was why he'd had to die.

"Don't you start," said Nikas. "He's been unbearable these few weeks. Mooning around with his lute, throwing men out of windows for daring to breathe your name... He told me to make sure you weren't there when I killed Lord Sydell, but I'm glad you didn't miss the fun."

"Did he," said Savonn. If he ever returned to his body, he would have strong feelings about this.

"He's not going to kill you," said Nikas. "He thinks he will, but he won't. I've no idea what you plan to do with him. But it can't be worse than anything he's done to himself, so why not?"

"I'm not sure about that."

Nikas laughed. "Really? You expect me to believe that you're going to murder him over a silly blood feud? You weren't *that* fond of your father."

Starlight glinted in the darks of his pupils. They roved across Savonn's face, merciless. "Oh," said Nikas, delighted. "Maybe you were. Kedris got inside your head, didn't he? Maybe—dare I say it?—inside other places too."

In lieu of responding, Savonn gazed at the purple sky and its sequined constellations. His skull was full of fog. It was impossible that he was still conscious, and burdened with the anatomy of ears.

Nikas was giggling again. "Cheer up. My friends should intercept us shortly. I'm sure you'll contrive to get away in the excitement. Anyway, your Lady Iyone won't let anyone hang you, will she? Cassarah will just be a good deal emptier of Efrens in a few days."

Savonn hoped Iyone got her hands on Nikas. There would be little left of him when she was done. He must have said this aloud, because Nikas tittered. "Oh, I'd love to meet her. I hear Marguerit's fascinated with the girl."

The guard was coming up again, glowering. This time he seized them both by the hair and banged their heads against the side of the wagon, so hard that Savonn's field of vision turned first white and then black. "I said shut up, or his lordship will have your tongues out!"

The starlit fields were fading in and out. This boded well for a few minutes of oblivion, at least. "Will he?" asked Savonn encouragingly. "Then how on earth will I confess my misdeeds?"

He might have been hit again. It was better not to know. The guard's meaty face and Nikas's half-shredded one loomed above him, orbiting strangely against a backdrop of woolly clouds. Hiraen would yell at him if he died. And he would miss his rendezvous with Red. Dervain. He and Savonn were spitted like two boars on opposite ends of a hunting spear, pushing it deeper into their hearts with every lunge towards each other. In another life—

He came back to himself after a minute, or five, or twenty. The guard was gone, and he was lying across the bottom of the wagon with Nikas grinning over him. "Don't worry, he's run off. I think it's starting. Come and see."

Savonn could feel all his limbs again, none of which were telling him anything good. Swords were scraping from their scabbards all around them. It was this noise that had awoken him. Unwillingly, he picked himself up and looked around.

About a bowshot's length ahead, the road descended into a narrow gully between rocky overhangs, both sides green with moss and climbing vines. Over the steady rattle-clack of the wagon wheels and the distant thunder of the Morivant, Bonner was rallying the horsemen. It seemed he was not a complete idiot. He knew the danger, but laden as they were with the bier and wagon, they could not go off-road. They were going to ride through the ravine as fast as they could, with shields raised and swords drawn, and hope for the best. People like Bonner did not understand that the best was only the long teeter before the fall.

Irritably, Savonn wrenched his left hand free of its bindings. No one took any notice.

"Poor soul," said Nikas, watching Bonner and his bodyguards lead the way into the gully. "Where now is his heavy horse? Where now the valiant Sydell foot? Oh, yes, still quarrelling with Lord Hiraen, or else strung out along the road behind us, too far off to help. He really doesn't think anyone's going to ambush him."

"Not unreasonable," said Savonn, unravelling the rope from his tingling wrists. He hoped the guard would materialise and knock him back into blessed delirium, but the man was busy waving his sword with all the others. "The Marshal's forces couldn't have overtaken us without him noticing."

"Ah, but not all of them fled after the first battle," said Nikas. "And with so many farms deserted, it wasn't difficult to find a place to hide." He yawned, wide and toothy. "It was great fun. I've never had a house to call my own before."

The shadows closed in. A frond of ivy whisked past Savonn's face. If he had not been so distracted in the last few weeks, he might have thought of this. Dervain wore his life as lightly as a cotton shirt, but Nikas always had an escape plan. "I see," he said. "Since it appears you are not about to die, will you take a message for me?"

A bowstring hissed. It was a sound that always reminded him of Hiraen. But the arrow that struck the road was fletched with black, not orange, and in any case Hiraen never missed. Nikas groaned. "I'm a busy man, little bird. I didn't train twenty years in the Sanctuary to pass lovesick nothings between a pair of idiots..."

The wagon jerked to a halt. Bonner was shouting. Dark figures had appeared on the clifftops above them, prowling down the overhangs to the road. There was an unsettling panther-like fluidity in the way they moved between the rocks, scarcely making a sound. Their guard screamed, throwing up his shield to catch another arrow. It was useless. In a few minutes the ambush would be over as quickly as it had started.

It had a pretty symmetry. Bonner had left Hiraen to die. What right did he have to live?

"Tell Dervain," said Savonn crisply, "that he has made his move, and it is now my turn. I am going to Evenfall to fulfill my promise to him in—oh, about a day or two, depending on whether Hiraen is still alive to hinder me. Tell him I expect him to be there this time. Tell him to wear the red and black cloak. It brings out his hair."

Nikas sighed. "Oh, all right. I'll tell him. He is something like a friend, after all—and as for you, why, there's a chance you might be my half-brother. Do you think Kedris would have liked me better?"

A javelin flew over their heads. Savonn unwound the rope from his ankles and kicked it away. Their guard now had a spear in his throat, and was not at leisure to prevent him. "Don't ill-wish yourself. Dispossessed royalty on one side is bad enough."

"True," said Nikas. "Look at me. Son of a queen and a governor, playing middleman for you and Dervain out of the goodness of my heart. You'd better fly away before the Efrens stop you."

Another of Bonner's men fell shrieking over the top of the wagon with a sword in his chest. Nikas elbowed him back out. Placidly, he added, "It shouldn't be very hard."

Nothing in the world could have sounded less appealing. But Savonn did not have the luxury, just yet, of sitting around and waiting to die. He swung himself out of the wagon and hit the ground on numb feet, stumbling a little. An acute sense of vertigo came and left. The column had dissolved into chaos: the black-clad figures were swarming over the mossy rocks in all directions with swords and spears and bows, and the crags threw back the noise of battle, amplifying it tenfold like the walls of a theatre. Not far ahead, Bonner was fighting off three assailants at once, his longsword in one hand, the staff of his eagle banner in the other.

Hiraen would have run to help him. But Savonn was not Hiraen.

A Sydell man pitched into his path, pursued by a woman with a mace. Savonn dodged them both, dropped to the ground to avoid a descending sword, and slipped across the road to the overhang. He had a man to meet, and many miles to go.

When he looked back, Nikas was reclining full-length in the wagon as if on a supper-couch, laughing and examining his nails.

CHAPTER 20

The news reached Cassarah in the third hour of the morning. So did the bodies.

Lord Lucien rushed to the ramparts, while Iyone pulled clothes from her wardrobe at random, got dressed, and rode pell-mell to the citadel. Two biers were lying in the front hall when she got there, one covered by a porpoise banner, the other with an eagle. By the time she got to the meeting-chamber, Oriane and Yannick were questioning the soldier who had brought word. She started to greet him, and realised with sleep-dulled surprise that it was Zarin.

"We didn't know you were with the Commander," Yannick quavered. He was in his nightgown, his sparse tufts of snowy hair flopping about uncombed. "We thought you'd fled with—with—"

He could not bring himself to say Josit's name. "That's not important," said Iyone. A servant pulled out a chair for her, but she waved it aside. "Tell me. Where is my brother?"

"Of Lord Hiraen," said Zarin, stressing the name as if she could have meant anyone else, "I have little news. We—"

"How can that be?" asked Oriane. "You were with him."

"Not exactly, ladyship." Zarin's voice was soft and even, his manners faultless. "I was scouting ahead of the main host. As my lord Yannick says, many knew me as servant to Lady Josit, so I thought it best to remain hidden. My presence was known only to the High Commander and some of his associates."

Another day, Iyone would have marvelled at his audacity. "Where," she said again, not troubling to phrase it as a question, "is my brother."

"His whereabouts are unknown," said Zarin. "It was chaos. The Marshal descended on us with ten thousand men. The Efren heavy horse went after Lord Bonner, but the Sydell foot stayed with Hiraen. His lordship abandoned camp and split his force into small roving bands. Last I heard, they were taking it in turns to harass the Marshal's rear."

It made sense. With his troops in disarray, Hiraen could not meet Isemain head on. He knew better than to waste lives. "There was a girl named Shandei with him," said Iyone. Why, why was she saying this? "You have cause to remember her. Where is she?"

Whatever Zarin thought of this, he was too polite to show it. "I saw her briefly in Lord Hiraen's host. I imagine she is still there, if she lives."

If she lives. For a horrible moment Iyone thought she felt the fish-breath of the High Priestess on her skin. Then she realised it was only a draught from the window, cracked open to the night air. "I cannot understand it," said Yannick. "I cannot understand it. Bonner was a hothead, not a coward. What made him desert?"

Zarin spread his hands in a gesture of ignorance. "All we know is that he rode straight into an ambush. When I found him, the bodies were already burning. It was only by luck that I recovered his and Daron's remains intact."

There was no such thing as luck. Iyone had not failed to mark that in all this, there had been no mention of Savonn. She looked up, and found Zarin watching her.

Oriane put her face in her hands. "I suppose there'll be a siege, if the Marshal's on his way here."

"A siege!" cried Yannick. "In winter!"

"If Marguerit commanded it, the army would obey," said Zarin. "It is the Saraian way."

"They'll be here in hours," said Iyone. "We need to prepare." Strategies and ideas spun through her mind, half-formed and hopeless. She needed more time. She needed more men. She needed to know what had become of her brothers. "Zarin, a word outside, if you please."

They left the chamber. As a precaution, Iyone led him all the way to the end of the hall, well out of earshot. With his indifferent courtesy, Zarin said, "Lady?"

She collected herself. Whatever she said and did would be reported back to Josit. "Bonner must have had an escort. Were there no survivors? Not even one lucky soul who got away from the ambush?"

Zarin's pale eyes gave nothing away. "Not even one, ladyship."

"So no one will ever know why Bonner fell out with Hiraen," said Iyone. "Some might call that fortunate."

A pause. Then Zarin dipped his chin, a silent acknowledgement. "I saw the battle from afar. My men and I shot down those who tried to flee. I will be the first to admit it was dishonourable work."

Iyone considered this at arm's length, the closest she could bear to examine it. Josit chose her battles with a connoisseur's discrimination. There was only one reason she would have fought this one. "Were there prisoners in the host?"

"There was a wagon," said Zarin, "with bindings for two. The occupants were gone by the time we arrived."

She could summon no astonishment. It was all Savonn's fault, as usual. She wondered who the other prisoner had been. If it was the Empath, she would gut them both. "So Savonn got away. From you, it seems, as well as Bonner. I can't imagine Josit is pleased about that."

"Perhaps not," Zarin allowed. "Your ladyship should be warned that not everyone was silenced. Lord Bonner's heavy horse will arrive by dawn, with strange tales of treason and murder and apparitions of dead men. No one will credit these rumours. Quash them with laughter."

"Thank you," said Iyone. Her stomach felt unsettled. "Tell Josit that I prosper, and do try to remember that we are all on the same side."

She stood still for a moment after he was gone, listening to the alarum-bells toll the bad news through the city. She could still see the frightened eyes of the shopkeeper with her hair in a towel, peering out her front door into the fog. So it had come to this again. Fell tidings and terror, and bells in the dark.

The others were arguing when she got back to the meeting-chamber. "Hiraen's still out there," Oriane was saying. "The Marshal can't sit down to a siege if his supply lines are threatened."

"His lordship cannot stay in the field much longer," said Yannick dubiously. "He has no more food or shelter than the Marshal does. And—"

"And the Earth Gate can't take another battering," said Iyone. "Isemain won't take long to breach the outer walls."

Her father still had a thousand men on the ramparts, and the Efren heavy horse would make three hundred more. If they armed every single man, woman and child to the teeth, they might hold off the Marshal for a while. But to what end? Isemain would get in, sooner rather than later. Hiraen would come back, if he ever did, to a city of dust and bones.

She looked around her, at the chilly interior of the meeting-chamber, and understood what they had to do.

"Face it," she said. "The city is indefensible."

She spoke right over the bickering. The argument came to a sudden halt. Yannick said, "Surely—"

"We could hold out for a day or two," said Iyone. "But only at the cost of hundreds of lives. It's not worth it."

"Are you suggesting," said Oriane, her voice cracking, "that we surrender?'"

"I am presenting our options," said Iyone. "Either we fight, lose, and wind up dead or enslaved; or we fall back. Here, to the citadel."

She gestured around them. The room, with its blocky walls and narrow windows, was its own argument. There was even a tiny murder hole above the door, a fact that had always seemed little more than a morbid joke till now. "Look at this place. It was built for such a time as this. Isemain could never get in here. If we retreat, we can outlast him."

She was used to all her suggestions being met with shocked silence. This time she thought Oriane might actually throw her out. "Have you gone and hit your head on something? Retreat? Tell our people to abandon their homes and businesses to be looted by the enemy?"

"We are more than our homes, my lady," said Iyone. "Some of us are passing fond of our lives."

Yannick rubbed his chin, looking vexed. "There is room enough, of course. But there is so little time, and so many *people*. Nothing of the sort has ever been attempted."

"We'll be living on top of each other," said Oriane incredulously. "There'll be plagues. People will be killing each other for elbow space by the end of the week."

"But we could feed them," said Iyone.

That gave Yannick pause. "True," he said. "The harvest from the herb gardens is in. The granary is full. If we are careful, our food and munitions could last us a year."

"We don't need a year." Iyone knew she was right. Still she longed for Josit's guiding hand, Josit's bored voice to back her up. "We just need to buy time for Hiraen to regroup and cut the Marshal off. It won't take long."

Oriane gazed at them in disgust. "Am I the only one on this Council with a spine? Did Daron and Bonner die for this?"

"A siege lacks the panache of a pitched battle, to be sure," said Iyone, "but at least we won't be risking our people's lives for a few gratuitous heroics. I don't see anything dishonourable in that."

"*You* wouldn't," said Oriane.

"But," Yannick began. He looked imploringly at Oriane, rolling the hem of one sleeve between his fingers as he always did when he was nervous. "Can you think of a better way?"

Oriane gave him a look of utter betrayal. "Are you taking her part now?"

Yannick coughed. Yes, Iyone thought, please, *please* let him take a stand for once in his life. She did not know who she was praying to. Last she heard, the gods had turned their backs on her. "If the Marshal is going to get in either way," said Yannick, "well—we cannot let people *die*, Oriane."

Oriane put her face back into her hands. Iyone looked on, helpless. Precious minutes were ticking away. There was so much to do, preparations to make, thousands of families to evacuate. Iyone could have given the order herself if she had to—gods knew she had been high-handed before. Her father had command of the city guard. They could organise the whole thing with no interference from the Council, and use force if Oriane tried to stop them. But no. Their disunity had already cost Hiraen the Singing Ford. They had to do this together, or not at all.

At last Oriane got up. She went to the window and rested her forehead on the glass, her fingers curled on the sill. "I will address the people. Someone with a soul ought to do it."

Iyone let out a breath. Unbelievably, she had begun to tremble. She sat down and tucked her hands under her thighs, so no one would see. "Thank you." She tried to say something else, but found herself repeating, "*Thank you.*"

"Only because there are so many lives at stake," said Oriane. "Only because of that."

"I know."

Iyone exchanged a look with Yannick, bound in a moment of strange solidarity. Her hands were steady again. "Yannick," she said. "If you would kindly summon the servants and chamberlains and get the citadel ready."

"Very good, my lady." He gave her a watery smile. "It shouldn't be a problem. Room enough for every living soul in Cassarah and more... Did you know, the basements reach eight floors deep in some places? Ederen must have been a sorcerer. Eight floors, in ancient days..."

He huffed a laugh, or maybe a sob, and bustled out of the chamber shaking his head.

She was alone with Oriane. The bells were still tolling. From far off, there was the slap of feet and the slam of doors, as people came out into the streets to see what was happening. The news would spread fast. Soon there would be weeping.

"I used to think I'd never hear those goddamn bells again," said Oriane in a low voice. "After the Battle of the Morivant, I thought it was over. Can you imagine it, Iyone? To be so naïve, at my age?"

Iyone swallowed. Hope was something you never outgrew.

"You don't remember what it was like," said Oriane. "I do. Two of my sons died in the last war. My sister died in the one before that, before Marguerit, in the old king's time. I remember that one too." She sighed, and came away from the window. "The bells rang for weeks on end. The guard ate and slept in armour."

Iyone pressed her knuckles to her face. They came away damp. "Do you think," she said, "it will ever stop?"

Oriane gave a short laugh. "I can't believe I ever thought you were like Kedris," she said. "If it does, I won't live to see it. That's on you, child. But I shouldn't get my hopes up if I were you."

CHAPTER 21

It was mid-afternoon, sixteen hours since the disaster, and to her own amazement Shandei was still alive.

They had gotten out of the way just before the Marshal's van swept through the camp. Without giving them time to despair, Hiraen split them into little bands and set them work to do. Shandei had been put in charge of some of Emaris's men—mere boys, really—and sent to harry the Saraian baggage train. This was easy. She shot three guards and an outrider from the shelter of the sentinel thicket, and the boys made off with a wagonload of grain and a cask of ale besides.

She began to understand. It was the deep of winter. They were cut off from Cassarah, and nearly all their supplies had been lost with their camp. This was to be a battle of stomachs.

Past noon, after she had caught a few hours' sleep up a tree, a strapping youth called Lomas arrived with a message from Emaris. They were to assemble at Lissein. Yes, the death circus. Yes, the Commander was sure. The Saraians were avoiding it like a plague city, so it was the safest place to be. His lordship had even gone ahead in person to clear booby traps from the houses left standing after the great gunpowder explosion. Everyone else was already on their way.

So they crept out of the wood and down to the village by the water. Most of the southern quarter had been reduced to burned-out husks, but many buildings still stood. Errand-boys were going from street to street, scratching big 'X's on the doors of certain houses. These, Shandei was given to understand, were those with traps Hiraen's men had not been able to diffuse. The biggest houses had been turned into makeshift barracks, full of exhausted men who had cast themselves on the floor or the grass and fallen asleep where they lay. One of these served as a makeshift hospital; people were hurrying in and out with needle and thread and bowls of red water. She wondered how many wounded there were, and how many more there would be before this was over.

"Emaris is safe, ma'am," Lomas told her when she found him again, on his way to fetch water from the river. The wells were mined, and not to be approached. "He's in that big barn beside the hospital, parcelling out the food we stole."

"What's that house?" asked Shandei, pointing.

A couple of scouts were heading into one of the little cottages, and another was just leaving. "Oh," said Lomas, "that's Hiraen's office. You should probably go make your report to him. What's the matter, ma'am?"

"Nothing," said Shandei. "Yes, I think I will."

When the scouts had left the cottage, she knocked on the door and went in. Inside was a single room, with a pallet at one end and a hearth at the other, and a firepit for cooking in the backyard. The High Commander was alone, pacing. He had shed his cuirass and jerkin; his bare arms were nicked with scrapes and bruises, and there was a livid gash across his brow. Shandei shut the door, and waited till he turned around.

"Report," she said. "We stole a lot of food. Nobody's dead."

"All right."

He started pacing again. Evidently he had no more to say to her. Shandei took a step towards the door, but drew back. She could not bear to be dismissed by him like a common servant. "They're headed for Cassarah. What will happen to Iyone?"

"Isemain may not breach the walls," said Hiraen, without conviction. "The city guard will hold them off."

In motion on the field, her mind had been clear. Now the bone-aching exhaustion caught up with her, and with it, the weight of every thought she had had to shelve in order to stay on her feet. As far as the men knew, Bonner Efren had simply lost his nerve after Daron's assassination and deserted. But Emaris had been there, and told Shandei in confidence what he had seen. Bonner had made Hiraen choose, and with thousands of lives in the balance, Hiraen had chosen Savonn.

"So," she said, "we aren't going to do anything for them?"

"I'll think of something," he said. "I'll exchange my life for Iyone's, if it comes to that. You aren't the only one who loves her. Now go."

She ought to have gone. But her legs did not obey her, and instead of reaching for the door, she fumbled for the ivory dagger on her belt. "Look at this."

He was looking. He had turned his flank to her at the first sight of the blade, all his muscles tensed to fight. But he had no weapon: his sword and bow lay on the floor four feet away. She knew he was good. She wondered if she was better.

"Yes." He looked possessed, his gaze riveted to the dagger. "I killed him. Is that what you want to hear? I put a knife in his throat and I've seen his dying eyes in my dreams every night since. If you've come to do your duty, do it."

She had known what he was going to say. Still, the shock of it drove her back a step, as if he had struck her. "It was for Savonn, wasn't it? Is there any low you wouldn't stoop to for him?"

"Judging by recent events," said Hiraen, "no."

What if she drove the dagger through his windpipe, the way he had slit her father's throat? Would Emaris ever speak to her again? Would Iyone? "Tell me," she said. "Tell me how it happened."

Hooves clattered on the cobbled lane. Another party had returned. The world beyond the cottage seemed far removed, last night's catastrophe a story from ancient history. This alone mattered: the foe before her, the dagger in her fingers. She had told Iyone she did not want to kill Hiraen. But viewed in this light, he did not look so much like a man as a collection of veins and arteries and organs, a map of vulnerable places that beckoned for her blade. "That was in his hand," he said. "But he put it down when he saw me."

"Then?"

"Then I tried to stop him from going to the Efrens'."

He sounded tired and flat. She could not believe that this was the same man who had held the Earth Gate all night and the next day after, who had stood at her side on the rampart and matched her arrow for arrow. "I thought he was going to tell Willon about Savonn's treason. I had been—misinformed. He wouldn't back down. I grew desperate. I drew my own knife, to show him I meant business."

Shandei laughed again. There were hot, scornful tears pouring down her cheeks. "Why would he tell? He never liked serving under Savonn, but he knew what loyalty meant. He was a better friend than either of you deserved."

In the daylight slanting through the glassless window, Hiraen's eyes had taken on a fierce shimmer. "You think he would have kept quiet about it, like I did? I credited him with more honour than that. If he went to the dinner..."

The sinews in his neck worked. "I had to stop him. The dagger was in my hand. I saw no other way. As soon as I did it, I regretted it."

"Then you went to get help," said Shandei. "You let Linn and Daine believe you'd found him on the street, struck down by some Efren hireling. After all, it was a nice stunt for the assembly, wasn't it? Whose idea was it? Iyone?"

He rounded on her, a swift sharp movement. Her dagger hand flew up on instinct. He was a full head taller, and fast. "She wanted none of it. And Savonn knew nothing. Leave them out of this."

"Too late," said a silken voice at the door. "The prospect of murder and mayhem always summons me, didn't you know?"

Savonn Silvertongue was leaning in the entryway. At first she thought it was an apparition. Regarding them through heavy-lidded eyes, his shirtsleeves and doublet only a little rumpled, he might have just arrived from a refreshing cruise down the river. Shandei followed his gaze to the dagger in her hand. It had been so close to Hiraen's throat. Another inch higher, and—

She dropped her hand. Hiraen scarcely seemed to notice. He was staring at the figure in the doorway, thunderstruck. "Behold," said Savonn. "I am quite capable of getting myself out of trouble once in a while. Skip the histrionics next time."

Any other pair of friends would have embraced. But perhaps snakes had other ways of showing their affection, just as spiders ate one another after they copulated. "You see." Hiraen's voice shook. "The gods lie. That woman promised me victory."

"Dear me," said Savonn. "If our heroes are frauds, and our gods too, what is left for us? Are you done with your farce, or shall I summon an audience?"

The door was wide open, his curls stirring in the breeze. Any passer-by could have seen what was transpiring. Hiraen said, "Don't be stupid. Shut the door."

"You had only to ask," said Savonn, and did so. "Now, before you let her kill you, might we apply our cerebra to a few little details? One, you are the only thing preventing this joke of an army from falling apart. Two, Shandei would never get away unseen, given that, three, Emaris is presently on sentry duty about thirty yards from here."

Shandei clenched her jaw. "Don't you dare use Emaris against me."

"Four," said Savonn. He turned to her, cold-eyed. "I myself will stand between you and Hiraen. I swear to every entity you care to invoke that you will have to mow me down and cut off all my limbs before you lay so much as a finger on him. And five—"

"I'm not—"

"*Five*, there is no shortage of Saraians who will gladly kill us all if presented an opportunity. Does it not strike you as slightly idiotic to do it for them?"

There was a dragging pause. Hiraen said, "Calm down, Savonn."

Despite the airy figure Savonn cut, there was nothing relaxed about the ramrod line of his back, and he was enunciating every syllable with the force of a cannon-shot. "I don't tend to be calm when people are killing my friends."

Hiraen recoiled bodily. "I wasn't going to kill him," said Shandei. It came out too fast and too loud, like a child's lie. "Why should I? The Marshal will take care of it."

"Now you're talking sense," said Savonn.

He looked at Hiraen. The air felt thick and charged, as if before a storm. "I have a plan. But don't get your hopes up. The odds are one in a thousand. Most likely we'll all die."

"So the usual," said Hiraen.

"If I told you what it was, you'd never let me do it," said Savonn. "I'm going away for a while. I have other business to settle first. If I don't come back in a day or two, go to the Marshal and ask to parley."

"And say what?" Shandei demanded.

If possible, Hiraen had gone even paler. "You're going to meet the Empath? Now?"

"I could have gone straight there," said Savonn. "I didn't have to come here and nag you into staying alive."

"I can't let you do it." Hiraen's voice was low and rough. "I *can't*."

"I wouldn't worry. My will to live is rivalled only by yours to die."

A few seconds crept by. Then Hiraen stalked across the room and flung himself onto the pallet. "Then go. And don't come back."

Something altered in Savonn's expression, though Shandei could not tell what. He stood still for a long moment, as if searching for words; then gave up and turned away, pulling his hood over his head. "Come with me," he said to Shandei. "I'll need your help."

"*You* need help?"

Wordlessly, he opened the door and held it for her. The gesture was so absurd it propelled her into motion. With a last look at Hiraen's averted face, she put the dagger back on her belt and followed Savonn out into the garden. He led her down the lane and stopped behind a shed a few houses away. "Handkerchief?"

"No, thank you," she said coldly. "What do you need me for?"

"A small matter," said Savonn. "Only if you want. It may help us, or it may not. It will help you, for sure, by putting Hiraen out of your reach before you do anything you'll regret. I'm taking Emaris and his patrol too."

She wiped her face on her sleeve. "Why? You're going to kill your lover."

"I," said Savonn, "am going to execute a delicate procedure involving my lover and his freedom. There are some practicalities I will not be in a position to attend to. Will you help or not?"

As vile as he was, Shandei had no choice if he was taking Emaris. She did not want to stay here with Hiraen. And for some childish reason, she wanted to witness this meeting between

Dervain Teraille, whom she had rather liked, and Savonn Silvertongue, whom she most certainly did not.

"Fine," she said. "Tell me what to do."

He glanced around for eavesdroppers, lowered his voice, and began to speak. Just as he promised, the plan was an outrage. And her part in it was not a small matter at all. She had no idea why she agreed.

REPRISE: SUMMER 1532

"I wish," said Savonn, "you would ask a price."

It was the fourth hour of the morning: the disquieting time, the hour of cold hearths and farewells. Red was sitting on the floor at the foot of the bed, oiling his cuirass-straps. His sword and spear stood against the wall, and his knives were arrayed on the desk under Merrott's patrol map, whetted and ready. "Death has no price, *etruska*," he said. "I have given you things for free before."

He had. But it was different this time. They were not talking about merchant disputes and bandit skirmishes, but a man of flesh and blood. Savonn's commander, who would have to die like a sacrificial goat to appease Kedris and Josit. This was not the Saraian consul slipping his Falwynian contact a little something. This was Red doing Savonn a favour, unasked, unpaid; and his pride was difficult to swallow.

Savonn said, "Everything costs something."

Red put the cuirass aside and got up. Lying back on the blankets, Savonn saw his head framed perfectly between the gold silk hangings of the bed. "It is too early in the morning for philosophy," said Red. "Would you prefer to kill the fellow yourself? I cannot prevent you, but it would be harder for you to get away. If you were caught, I would have no one to tell me useful things, or get rid of crowds when I am having the migraine, or accompany me on the lute while I recite from Iskellian, and I would be very sad."

Red could always make him smile. Perhaps that was treason too. "It was a terrible recital," said Savonn.

"That did not cost you anything, either."

Up till now, none of it had. Red had kept Savonn sane through his long masquerade as a soldier, exiled from the plays and books and music he had loved as a child. But it was two summers since their first dance in Xante's ballroom, and they were no longer naïve enough to think themselves immortal. All night Savonn had been drinking in every detail of the room—the embroidery on the satin cushions, the spices of the scented candles—in case he never came this way again. Josit's warning had changed everything.

"Ask a price," he said. "And do not ask anything I would give freely."

A minute passed, or more. Time had no meaning in the upper room of the consulate. Only when they were apart did Savonn understand things like seasons, and months, and distance. At length Red came and sat on the bed beside him, leaving a handspan of space between them as he always did, a border he would not cross unless Savonn touched him first. "If you insist," he said, "if you see fit—"

He was never less than confident in public, where strangers could see, but here it was different. His fingers traced the stitching on the blanket like a lifeline. "After the job is done, perhaps you might give me your true name. I will give you mine, too. And perhaps—perhaps you might let me take you to a safe place in Daliss, a house where you will live like a prince, and we can be together."

His hair had fallen across his eyes. Savonn started to tuck it away for him, but drew back at the last moment. In the strange confessional of their bedroom it would have felt too much like an unmasking. "Your home?"

"No," said Red. "But it will be, if you are there."

There was Red; and there was the room around him, brilliant with firelight; and there was the world beyond, that had once been theirs and might be again. It was the worst price he could have asked. Savonn wanted, and feared, and wanted. "*Etruska—*"

"Hush." Red traced Savonn's mouth with the tips of his knuckles. "Don't tell me now. Not till it is done. Or I would think of nothing else."

The pain was too great to bear alone, and so Savonn reached for Red, curling his arms around his neck, pulling him down for a kiss. Perhaps it was not so impossible. In a few days Merrott would be dead, a new and more tractable captain appointed in his place. Savonn would be absolved of his burden. On the other side of the river, there might yet be a home for two.

He was still young, if no longer the youngest of his patrol. Young enough to believe.

"Later," he agreed, "we will speak of it."

A draught blew in through the window. The candles guttered out, plunging them into twilight. Neither of them got up to kindle the wicks again. Savonn took Red's hands in his own. They were warm and strong and callused: a lover's hands, a killer's hands. "Come here," he said. "We still have an hour before dawn."

* * *

On the warmest week of summer the men of Betronett received their new captain, and Lord Kedris himself came to grieve with them on the Bitten Hill. He was sad and solemn, all his ebullience tucked away for his private audiences. "This is a new beginning for us, is it not?" he asked, flinging a wine-heavy arm around Savonn's neck as they came up together from supper in the keep's little feast-hall. "When the time comes we shall overrun the river and sack Daliss together, you and I, and who shall stand against us?"

Savonn could think of a few individuals. He knew better than to argue. "I had hoped to return to Astorre in the fall," he said. "There are affairs I have to tie up."

They stopped in the hallway outside their rooms. Across the yard the windows of the mess hall glowed with candlelight, as Hiraen and his veterans sat drinking in memory of their commander. "Old business," said Kedris. "You are Captain of Betronett now, higher than anyone ever thought you would rise, I daresay. Your troops need you here."

The command was a poisoned gift, one Savonn should have seen coming—the new chain by which Kedris would keep him in line. No more one-man espionage outings. No more evenings alone in a city far away, where he might disappear into a dance hall and become another person for an hour or two. His father was putting a face on him that he would have to wear every day for the rest of his life.

"Sir." He spoke recklessly, desperately, and so had already lost. "Hiraen should be Captain."

The weight of Kedris's arm was no longer careless. His fingers curled around the back of Savonn's neck, a grip some might have called hearty, others lethal. "Hiraen Safin's every breath is an insult to me, an insult I suffer only for love of you. He is lucky just to be alive. You will hold the command I give you. Or will you always be Merrott's puppy?"

Holding still in the powerful grip, Savonn thought of snapped spines and frayed sinews; of Josit, and Hiraen, and a man waiting in a candlelit room a million miles away. He knew, now, that he would never see the house in Daliss. Nor would he set foot in Astorre again, if he did not want to bring Kedris's wrath down on

Red. He was his father's loyal soldier and would always be, just as Josit had decreed.

"No," he said. "I understand."

"So you do," said Kedris. "Look at you. You've come a long way. A son to make any man proud, aren't you?"

Savonn arranged his features into doll-like amiability. He could play this part, if he had to. "If you say so."

Kedris laughed, joyous once more, and embraced his son, and went off humming to bed.

CHAPTER 22

Emaris was just coming off sentry duty when a sinuous shadow sidled out from behind a shed and interposed itself at his elbow. "Don't shout, my dear."

He clamped his mouth shut in time. They were not alone. Farther down the lane, men were spilling out of the large barn they had converted into a mess hall, and a group of women sat dicing over their swords in the yard of the next house. Emaris stared at Savonn, last seen being led away to prison by eighty angry Efrens. "How the hell did you—no, never mind, don't tell me. I bet it's a long story."

"Actually," said Savonn, "it's short, bloody, and boring."

He was in a studded brigandine, with vambraces and matching shinguards, a shortsword belted at his hip. With his curls tucked under a hood, he looked like any other anonymous rank-and-filer. Emaris knew by now to ignore the disguise. Instead he noted the dull fatigue in Savonn's eyes, which were pewter today; the terse line of his shoulders, and the unusual softness of his voice. "What's the matter?"

"It's time," said Savonn. "You said you wanted to be there."

Emaris sighed. He wished he had gotten more sleep, but everything in Lissein still reeked of burning, and he kept thinking he saw Nikas's beaming face pop up around walls and over hedges. "All right. But you don't look fit to fight Klemene, let alone the Empath."

Savonn's smile grew a fraction more genuine. "I will be. It's been a long day... Give me a moment, gazelle." And, incredibly, he leaned in and tipped his head forward to rest on Emaris's shoulder.

Emaris froze. It could not have felt more portentous if the clouds had turned crimson, the moon fallen from the sky. With anyone else it would have been natural to reach forward, to hold and comfort, but one did not do such things with Savonn. He could only stand as if a butterfly had alighted on his hand: breathless, not daring to move, lest he scare it off.

The men from the mess hall drew near and parted to flow around them. They were speaking of Bonner Efren, and the Marshal, and what Hiraen was going to do now. No one looked twice at them, not even to glance at Emaris's scars. No one seemed to realise what was happening.

Savonn pulled away once they were gone, flicking a curl out of his face with a toss of his chin. He looked a little less haggard now. "Thank you," he said. "Get your patrol. Shandei's coming too."

Emaris wandered off as if in a dream. He walked into a tree, and fell over a low wall. He reached the cottage where his patrol had bedded down for a few precious hours' rest, found himself at a loss for words, and said only, "Get up. It's for Savonn."

He did not have the presence of mind to invent a cover story. He did not have to. Some of them, like Lomas, were on their feet at once. A few seconds of drowsy muttering elapsed. Then Klemene said, "My gods, he's going to fight that red demon," as if the thought had just occurred to him, and in a heartbeat they were all awake and arming.

It promised to be a spectacle, of course. But since the gunpowder cottage it had become evident to Emaris that they would follow him to the ends of the earth if he asked; and if he thought Savonn worth fighting for, so did they. It was something to think about at length, later.

No one stopped them on their way out of Lissein. The sun was sinking, a waxing crescent moon on the rise. They took care to stay out of sight of the river and the Ford. Lomas and Rougen, who were scouting ahead, came back once or twice with word of a Saraian patrol passing through—"*Saraians*, in our fields," said Lomas with great indignation—but there was no use picking a fight, so they slunk past in silence, bits of cloth tied round their harnesses to muffle the chink of metal.

Through it all, Savonn was uncommunicative, a remote figure brooding at the head of the party. Emaris decided against bothering him, and urged his horse to the back of the column to join Shandei instead. "Why are we going to Evenfall? It's a haunted ruin, isn't it?"

Hiraen had been unforthcoming about his excursion to the ancient palace of Ederen Andalle. Emaris had come away from his interrogations with only the vague sense that Evenfall was a haunt of ghouls, a wasteland where terrible things lay in wait to drive you mad. "It's the only place he can challenge the Empath," said Shandei. "The Council made Dervain vow not to bear arms on our side of the river. Evenfall isn't on any side."

Her eyes were red and downcast. "Are you all right?" Emaris asked.

"I'm fine." Shandei smiled, not happily. "Baby boy? Keep this safe for me."

The thing was in his hand before he saw what it was: a dagger, with an ivory hilt he recognised. His heart plummeted. So often he had watched his father whetting that blade by the fire after dinner, at home or out on patrol around the Bitten Hill. He never thought he would see it again. "Don't you want it?"

"To quote a fellow we know," said Shandei, "if a Saraian died for every question you asked, we'd have won the war ages ago. Be quiet and let me think."

Emaris hardly saw how he could stop asking questions when no one ever answered any of them. Stewing in this injustice, he left her alone and fell in with Vion and Klemene instead. But as he soon discovered, they were busy speculating if Shandei liked boys—a discussion that involved a great deal of blushing and smacking headlong into branches—and were therefore quite unsympathetic to his concerns.

It was full dark by the time they reached the place where the Morivant forked to flow around the Isle of Evenfall, and cypresses rose dark and whispering from the river mist. Here the landscape undulated in a ridge of foothills that climbed to meet the Farfallens, each rise higher and steeper than the last. They had encountered no Saraian outriders for the last hour: the ruin's morbid reputation was its own deterrent. Savonn stopped beside a sandy embankment where the current was slower, the channel less deep. "Gather round."

They flocked to him. "I will sugarcoat nothing," said Savonn. "You are about to cross into a foreign and unpropitious place, about which—I regret to say—all the stories you have heard are true. The air on the isle is full of strange gases that, when inhaled, play tricks on the mind. You may see visions and hallucinations. It helps to think of these as fever dreams."

They exchanged looks. This was, without a doubt, the strangest pre-battle speech any of them had ever heard. Emaris gazed across the water, half expecting to see the golden spires and turrets of Ederen's palace rising among the cypresses. But they were long gone, and what lay between the trees now, he could only guess.

"I brought you here this evening not to fight, but to bear witness," said Savonn. "All the same, be prepared for anything. You are all people of reasonable courage. I will not insult you by offering you a chance to turn back."

He paused. His eyes moved from face to face. "Shandei," he said. "Emaris."

They came forward. He addressed Shandei first, in a voice that barely carried. "Promise me again."

Shandei's forehead creased with impatience. "I promise. I swear by my father and mother and all the gods you don't believe in. I'll do my best."

Emaris said, "What?"

"And you," said Savonn, as if he had not heard. "If anything untoward happens, lead the patrol back to Lissein. Do not, under any circumstances, interfere with what Shandei has to do."

There was an uncharacteristic pause. Shandei had moved back to give them privacy. Emaris remembered the gentle weight of Savonn's head on his shoulder, and his skin tingled. "I don't enjoy melodrama for its own sake," said Savonn. "But in case exigencies arise that make further conversation impossible: I am sorry, for everything I did and did not do. Tell Hiraen I said so. On the whole, I think you will be a better man than either of us."

Emaris drew a painful breath. "Such a man could not exist."

"Truly?" Savonn arched a brow. "I would have to ask you to present your proofs."

"My feelings," said Emaris thickly, "are not up for debate. Your hands are shaking."

"It's cold," said Savonn. Without another word, he turned and led the way down to the river.

They splashed across in single file, their horses belly-deep in freezing water. Emaris scanned the far shore. There was no sign of a lookout, but he stayed watchful, full of misgivings. Last summer he had learnt to his detriment that the Empath did not need to see or hear someone to know they were there. The trees soon began to thin, and not long after, they came to a clearing by a sheltered cove. There was a small skiff rocking at anchor, and on board, the shape of a single sentry.

They halted, shivering in their wet clothes. The pinprick stars threw their glimmering reflections on the water. There was no birdsong to be heard, not even the snuffle of a night creature. Shandei whispered, "I will need the boat."

Savonn reached into his sleeve. There was a flash of steel, and the sentry toppled backwards and hit the water with a thunderous plash. Emaris swore under his breath.

"Don't worry," said Savonn. "As soon as we crossed the river, our presence was marked." And he rode out from under the sighing cypresses, beads of river water gleaming in the inky coils of his hair.

Emaris kicked his horse to follow. As he rode into the clearing, he had the hazy impression of an ancient colonnade, fluted marble columns running along the treeline and down to the cove. Most had fallen. Nothing grew around them, not even moss or lichen. There were dark shapes in the fog that could have been the remains of a crumbling wall, or just more trees. That was all: the purgatorial remains of Evenfall, seat of the ancient Andalles.

He had little time to take it in. Among the ruins of the colonnade, figures were stirring.

Like Savonn, the Empath had brought witnesses. A dozen men and women sat around a smoking cookfire, armed with swords and spears. There were too many to fit in the boat—some of them must have come on foot, fording the river like the patrol had done. Emaris spared them only a glance before his attention was drawn, like a needle in a compass, to their leader.

Dervain Teraille was in a vest of boiled leather, his auburn hair pulled into a braid. Emaris recognised his splendid cloak from Astorre, sable on the outside, scarlet on the reverse. His restless gaze drifted over the patrol, lingered for a moment on Shandei and Emaris, then came at last to rest on Savonn.

No one moved. Savonn sat his horse like a living statue, his gloved hands clasped hard on the reins. "If there was any other way," he said, "I would take it."

The Empath got up. The knife-edged moon had risen above the treetops, touching them both with grey funereal light. "It is not too late to change your mind."

"I promised you we would make an end together."

"You are certain, then?" asked Dervain, as Savonn dismounted and sent his horse trotting away with a slap. "That this is what you want?"

"I am not here to talk," said Savonn. "Pick up your spear."

He drew his sword and cast away the scabbard. After a fraught hesitation the Empath held out his hand, and one of his companions tossed him a cornelwood spear, eight feet tall, its barbed tip glinting in the shivering firelight. They began to circle each other on the broken ground between the fallen pillars, the way they had once danced at Celisse's masquerade.

It was the first of two duels that Emaris would remember blow for blow to the end of his life. The spear and the sword touched and withdrew, light as a kiss. The Saraians stamped out their fire and retreated under the trees, and Emaris and his patrol urged their horses to the edge of the cove to give the fighters a wide berth. They were evenly matched, with the same birdlike quickness, the dancer's poise, the showmanship that revealed itself in a flourish here, a lightning-quick parry there. But there was the spear, which gave the Empath the advantage in reach.

Savonn had recognised this too. He drove left at Dervain's flank, then at the last moment switched his stance, his sword flashing right instead. The Empath had anticipated it, and his spear was there to meet the blow. Savonn grinned. With a malicious glitter, his blade cleaved sideways through the spear-shaft, slicing it in two.

Dervain laughed. He retreated a step to avoid the backswing, one half of the spear in either hand. "Where did a circus boy learn to fight like that?"

"In the circus," said Savonn.

The circling resumed. And Emaris saw that, up till then, Dervain had only been playing. Now he was a blaze of movement, thrusting and parrying with both hands, while Savonn flitted in and out of reach like an evil sprite, every step a feint. But Dervain was quick enough, or knew him well enough, to counter each one. Emaris's chest felt too tight for his lungs. Shandei, too, was stock still at his side, only her lips moving in silent prayer.

Dervain said, "You are not certain, after all."

They had backed up for a moment's respite. A thin streak of blood was trickling down Savonn's hairline, and his brow shone with sweat. "You think I will not hurt you?"

"You betray yourself."

Dervain swung out with the spearhead. The sword flashed, clipped the cornelwood shaft, and withdrew. With a lurch, Emaris saw what he meant. For an instant he had left his right flank unguarded from shoulder to thigh, but Savonn had not taken the offering. Even now he danced back, on the defensive once more, as Dervain thrust at him again and again. "Oh, gods," said Klemene faintly. "He can't do it. He won't do it. He's going to throw the fight."

Emaris's insides were a tight, painful knot. He tried to call out, to plead with Savonn, but the succession of his thoughts was growing slack as in the moments before sleep, and his tongue was heavy and immobile. Somewhere bells were tolling. Lights moved between the cypresses, ghosting on the surface of the cove. Emaris turned his head to follow them, and all at once he was no longer in the clearing, but standing in a hallway in a house he knew, as a door creaked open to spill forth light and shadow.

That was not right. He had left this place long ago. But he was not in Daine's back room—there was nothing on the other side of the door but a gaping blackness, out of which another bright doorway led. And beyond that another, and still another, and blood was stealing across the tiles, soaking into his boots, hot between his toes—

Klemene gasped. Emaris wrenched himself back to his senses in time to see what had happened. Making as if to hurl the spearhead like a javelin, Dervain had dropped into a crouch instead, catching Savonn off balance as he sprang out of the way. Savonn hooked his leg around Dervain's ankle, and they went to the frosty ground together.

The sword and the spear skidded off into the grass. Savonn reached into his sleeve. A knife flew past Dervain's head. Another slashed his arm, cutting deep above his elbow. Dervain did not so much as flinch. He rolled, threw his full weight on Savonn, and closed both hands around his throat.

Flat on his back, Savonn kicked up to free his legs. It was no good. Blood was streaming from Dervain's arm, but pain seemed to have no effect on him; his fingers were white on Savonn's neck. Emaris started counting knives. There had been the two just thrown, and the one Savonn had used to fell the sentry on the boat. He probably had at least one more. But it would be in his boot, out of reach.

Dervain's braid was unravelling, spilling hair around his face. "Change your mind," he panted. "There is still time."

Choking, sucking in air through his mouth, Savonn groped in the grass for his sword. Dervain leaned out to knock it away. And in that moment of distraction Savonn flung out his other hand, quick as an eel, and closed his fingers around the spearhead.

He brought it up: not in a stab at Dervain's eyes, which would have ended the fight, but a glancing blow off the back of his head. Dervain reared back. Savonn flung off the suffocating grip and wrested his legs free, and closed his teeth around the flesh above Dervain's collarbone. Dervain swore at him, and tried to throw him off in a wrestler's grip. But Savonn only rolled with the momentum, and they tumbled empty-handed between the pillars towards the cove, scattering the remains of the fire.

Bells, bells, Emaris thought. Someone was weeping.

Dervain regained his feet at the very edge of the water, and they staggered upright again. Savonn caught hold of a low-hanging branch for support. His mouth was red with Dervain's blood, his own streaming freely from the nicks and gashes where the spear had caught him. "Curtain call, my turtledove."

Dervain was bleeding, too. His cloak hung askew from his shoulders; he ripped it off and let it fall. "You need not do this," he said. "I release you from our pact. I release you. I release you. *I release you.*"

His cheeks glistened, not with perspiration. In the Arena, or on the dance floor, or in Celisse's garden under the red glow of dusk, the Empath had always seemed an invincible puppet-master, swanlike in his smugness. But this was a different animal altogether. "I am not afraid to die," said Savonn.

He reached up and thumbed the moisture away from Dervain's face, one drop at a time. "You don't want to do this," said Dervain. "I know you don't."

"*Etruska*," said Savonn gently, "all I do is want."

They were half holding each other up, the moon-silvered cove lapping at their feet. The Saraians, wan and drawn, drew close together under the trees. So did the patrol. No one spoke.

Dervain said, "All right, then."

He slid an arm around Savonn's waist, as if to embrace him. But the distance between them did not close, and his hand came away with something bright. Savonn's last knife, not in his boot after all, but tucked in the small of his back.

Emaris screamed a warning. At the same time, Savonn sprang.

He could not tell which happened first: the shimmer of the knife as it slammed hilt-deep into Savonn's shoulder, or the impact of Savonn's body against Dervain's, knocking him backwards. They teetered for a moment, and hit the water.

Emaris dismounted and ran to the cove. Shandei was at his side, shouting something. Ripples ran out over the water, ribboned with blood. The skiff rocked back and forth. They were still holding each other, Dervain's hand on the knife, Savonn rigid with pain. In an instant of excruciating clarity, Emaris saw how the fight would end. Wounded as they were, neither of them had the strength to fight free of the other's hold. Dervain would draw the blade out and stab again, and Savonn, clinging like a limpet, would drag his opponent under with him. Stalemate.

Dervain said, "Go down with me, songbird."

Savonn's voice was brittle, his eyes fever-bright. "It would be my pleasure."

Dervain smiled. He drew out the knife and released it in the reddening water, and the two figures submerged.

The skiff rocked again. Bells gonged in Emaris's arteries, filling his head with noise. A door squealed on a hinge. Gold hair on a pillow, the sour stench of wine and blood. He was pulling off his cloak, ripping at the laces of his boots. He had to go in, he must, he must, or he would die himself. A red eye glowing in a hearth, the sizzle of burning meat. He was ready, he was on the edge of the cove, he was—

The water heaved. An indistinct shape broke the surface. Light as a veil, the mist traced the outline of a pair of dripping heads. The one that had risen first was black as oil, and the other, pillowed on the swimmer's shoulder, was deep auburn.

With a cry, Emaris flung himself into the water. The splash was echoed by another. Shandei had dived in beside him. The cove was deep, but they were both strong swimmers. "Savonn!" he called. "Hold on!"

He reached Savonn's side at the same time Shandei reached Dervain. In the first shock, it was difficult to untangle them. Savonn, barely conscious and spewing water, still had both arms locked around his enemy, and Emaris had to prise them off one by one. Savonn cried out in what might have been Saraian, and tried to fight him off. "It's just me," said Emaris. Shouts were erupting on the shore. He did not look back. "It's only me, I'm here, I've got you."

Without a word, Shandei put her arm under the dead weight of the man who had once been the Empath, pride of the Sanctuary, servant to a queen and a god, and began to swim away. Emaris followed more slowly, towing his charge after him. Hands reached down to pull him to dry ground. Lomas thumped hard on Savonn's back; he coughed up one final spurt of water and subsided, still and silent.

They laid him on the ground at the foot of a cypress. Swiftly, Emaris bound up the deep puncture in his shoulder with a strip of torn cloak someone handed him. "I'm here," he said again. "It's over. It's all right now."

"Emaris," said Vion. "*Emaris.*"

He looked up. The Empath's companions had come out of the trees, swords drawn, spears couched, and every man of the patrol had his bow trained on them in turn. He saw why. Shandei had hauled the Empath's body aboard the skiff. She bent over him briefly, only the top of her fair head visible over the side of the boat. Then she straightened and cut the rope that tethered it to shore, an oar in one hand, a knife in the other. "What are you doing?" Emaris asked.

Her voice drifted to them over the water. "Cover me. Don't follow. And take his cloak with you."

She began to row, putting her back into every stroke. Emaris stared at her. It was Klemene who fetched Dervain's cloak from where it had fallen, and draped it over Savonn's soaking form. "We're not supposed to fight," said Emaris. "Give them the body. It's theirs by right."

One of the Saraians came forward. She lay down her sword, lifting empty hands in parley. "Gentlemen," she said in broken Falwynian. "You win the duel. Now give us our friend to bury."

Silence. No one knew what to say. "He is Sanctuary property, like all of us," added the woman. "Return him to his god."

"We're not gentlemen," said Shandei. Already the fog was swallowing her, muffling the slosh of her oars. "And he's not property."

Emaris shook himself. Savonn had given him clear orders. If ever there was anyone who knew what they were doing, it was Shandei. She had her work, and he had his. Go back to Lissein. Don't interfere. Tell Hiraen—

Tell Hiraen what had happened.

He considered the odds. The numbers were square. But soldiers on foot, however skilled, were seldom a match for mounted archers. At least, he thought, biting back a wave of hysteria, the Saraians did not know that half the patrol could not shoot straight to save their lives. "We're sorry," he said. "We can't give him back. But we'll see that he has all the necessary rites. Our commander loved him."

The Saraians murmured. Emaris could no longer hear the skiff. Where Shandei meant to go from here, he had no idea. Cassarah must be under siege by now, both sides of the river crawling with the Marshal's men. She would be alone, with only her wits to protect her, and a valuable cargo at the bottom of her boat.

The Saraian picked up her blade. Emaris did not know where his own sword had gone. He hunched his body over Savonn, making a shield around him, and prayed.

But there was no charge. The woman eyed them with disgust, her hand clenched on the sword. She must have weighed her chances, as Emaris had, and found them wanting. "Listen, you godless heathens," she said. "You lose your war. When Her Magnificence comes, she crush you all to dust."

She sheathed her sword and marched away, disappearing into the trees on the far side of the clearing. One by one, her companions followed her, some casting venomous looks at the patrol as they went. Soon they were gone. So was Shandei.

"Well, she's not wrong," said Vion, lowering his bow. He snapped his fingers, and Emaris's horse came nosing over. "We better go before they decide to come back."

With Lomas's help, they lifted Savonn onto the horse. Emaris climbed on behind him, sopping wet and shivering, and Klemene threw a saddle-blanket over his shoulders. "Is he going to make it?"

Emaris gathered the reins in his frozen fingers. "Yes." He said it because there was no other answer he could countenance; because the bells were still tolling, an ill omen, and he was afraid to say anything else. "Mount up. Let's go back to the circus."

ACT THREE

CURTAIN CALL

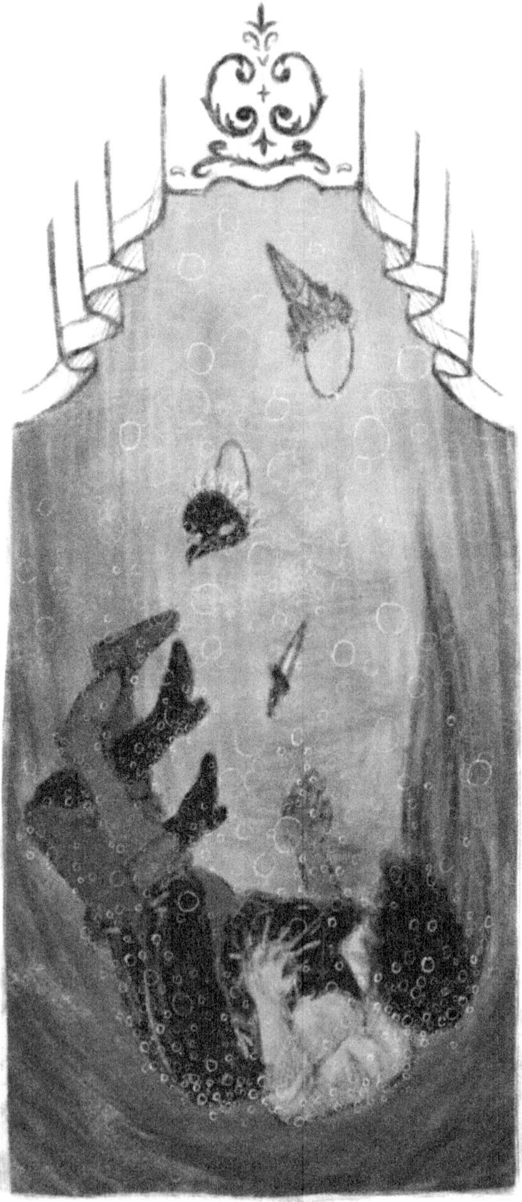

CHAPTER 23

In the early hours of the morning, the Council and the city guard began the enormous task of shepherding the people of Cassarah into the citadel.

They all knew what it was, but no one called it a retreat, much less a flight. "It is an evacuation, nothing more," said Iyone. "Make sure you use that word." Under her orders the guards visited each household in turn, from the grandest manor to the lowest beggar's hovel, to rouse the occupants and hurry them out the door. They were to pack only the essentials. It was just an evacuation, after all. It was temporary.

They came in a steady stream all day, crossing the drawbridge into the safety of Ederen's walls. Many carried shrieking babies in their arms, an elderly grandmother on their back. One family tried to bring an entire wagon with them and was stopped at the piazza, but the guards relented when they saw it was full of grain. "Should we be letting them take their *pets*, milady?" asked one lieutenant, as a child came in clutching a small yapping dog.

"Yes," said Iyone. Lest they think her soft-hearted, she added, "We might need to eat them."

The families assembled in the banquet hall, waiting for Yannick's understewards to take their names and assign them a room. It was messy, but there would be time to sort things out later. Then—almost as soon as the last stragglers had trickled in, the drawbridge raised, the portcullis lowered—the alarum-bells began to toll once more, and the Council gazed from the battlements to see the Marshal's grey and white banners fill the horizon.

They had done it. An evacuation of a city, done in a single day. If they lived through this, the story would be handed down for generations.

The Saraians came all night, marching in their hundreds and thousands. Torches glimmered in their ranks, so that from the citadel, they looked like a field of fallen stars stretching away northward on the river's flank. Cahal led a small force to the outer walls to offer some token resistance. Arrows flew back and forth. The Rose, the Thorn, and the Dung fired a gallant round from the citadel battlements, where they had been moved. Then, sometime after midnight, there was a muffled roar and the ground shook beneath their feet, and the crowded halls erupted into screams.

Iyone had been going over inventories in the armoury. Her maidservant ran out to see what had happened, and came back in tears. Under heavy fire from above, the Marshal's men had simply lit a fuse under the Earth Gate—or what remained of it—and run. A large section of the northwestern wall had been blown to smithereens, and now the van was pouring in through the breach. Cahal had just managed to fall back in time. They were in.

"And what's more," said the maid, "those Saraian hounds are erecting a pavilion in their camp. A mighty thing, twelve feet high and fit for a queen... Why is milady laughing?"

"Because," said Iyone, "there is nothing else for milady to do. I wonder what Marguerit is like, don't you?"

* * *

The siege began at dawn.

A herald approached the portcullis, and called for the citadel to surrender. The defenders jeered him away. Dung shooed him off with a deafening crack. In response, the Marshal crashed his battering ram into the portcullis twice, to no effect; and began to construct assault towers in the piazza, tearing into the neighbouring buildings for brick and stone. Soon his own guns would arrive, with sappers and bombers and trebuchets, and the real work of the siege would commence.

Iyone had to admit a grudging admiration for the invaders' discipline. The camp outside the city was so neat it might have been laid out with ruler and plumbline, and even the looting was orderly. The Saraians being scrupulously religious, they passed over the Temple and the homes of the common folk, and went straight on to raid the rich manors. Everything of value was carried off with care. There was no burning, no wanton destruction. Nothing was wasted.

Iyone had thought herself prepared for this. Houses could be rebuilt, fortunes remade. Her people were safe. But the fact remained that in the thousand years since Ederen had laid the foundations of Cassarah, no invading army had passed its gates, no foreign queen walked its streets. Marguerit would be remembered for this, just as she, Iyone, would be remembered as the one who let her in.

Since the only alternative was to sit and simmer in misery, she went up on the battlements in search of her father. Lord Lucien had been on his feet for close to thirty hours, supervising the evacuation. Now, saddled with the defence of an entire city with nothing but three oddly named cannon and a thousand restive men, he was peering through a looking-glass into the piazza, exhausted and grim. "You shouldn't be up here. Where's your mother?"

Iyone had never seen the battlements so crowded. There was an archer with a longbow at every crenellation, and a boy was pushing a wheelbarrow up and down the wallwalk, handing out fresh quivers and skins of water. She backed out of his way. "In the granary with Oriane, working out how to feed everyone," she said. Neither of them had seemed to want to speak to her. "Any news?"

Dung fired. The flagstones shook. "They're rowing a barge across the river," her father yelled, stuffing his fingers in his ears. "With the royal standard. Black crown on white. The Queen's coming."

It was a good thing Josit was long gone, and did not have to witness this. Iyone leaned against the rampart, looking down at the destruction Isemain had made of the piazza. "I think," she said, "I shall go and parley with Marguerit."

A stray arrow whistled over the rampart. Lucien caught up his shield and flung it over their heads. "What the hell are you going to say?"

"I'm not sure," said Iyone. "I just want to take her measure. I'm the only one on the Council who speaks Saraian, so it might as well be me."

And, she thought, she was the entire reason Marguerit was here. This was on her. "Gods above," said Lucien. "Orchestrating the biggest evacuation in history wasn't enough for you? You want to go meddle with the Queen of Sarei as well?"

Something exploded. Another barrage of arrows flew up from the trenches in the piazza. Swearing, he threw open the stairwell door and shoved Iyone through. "All right! All right! I'll send out a herald. If anyone can scare her off, it's you. Get below, goddamnit!"

She started down the stairs. "Be careful!"

It was a long wait. Marguerit took her time alighting from the barge. Then she made a round of the city on horseback, accompanied by Isemain and a cohort of guards. Iyone imagined the Queen riding over Josit's bridges, past the house on the Street of

Canaries, through the gardens where Iyone had played as a child; and decided these were thoughts best left uncontemplated.

The Saraian herald came back late in the afternoon. This time they did not drive him off. The Queen of Queens was willing to parley, he said. Did her ladyship of Cassarah require a translator?

"No, she does not," said Iyone, and went to dress.

She was nervous, she supposed. The fact that she had gone without sleep for the better part of two days betrayed itself in the lines around her eyes and the cadaverous pallor of her face. Her gowns and jewels were at home, likely carried off by now. In the end she went out as she was, in a white blouse over her trousers and riding boots, her hair plaited out of the way. Shandei's rose scarf sat knotted round her neck like a protective talisman.

Foolish, to take comfort in such things. She might never even see Shandei again.

She trotted out to the drawbridge on a great black stallion, the best the stables could offer. The guns had fallen silent. So had the hammering from the siege towers, by now almost half as high as the citadel walls. Across the moat, the herald was announcing her foe with all her titles. Marguerit the Magnificent, Queen of Queens. Trueborn Daughter of Yocasta the Third and Romett the Fourth, the Blessed Lioness, Chosen of the Gods, Sword of Sarei, Mailed Fist of the Morivant. It went on for a long time. Iyone bit back the inane urge to giggle.

Then: "The Lady Iyone Safin, Councillor of Cassarah." And she spurred her stallion onto the drawbridge over the moat, under the rising portcullis, and out into the open.

The Queen of Sarei met her under the proud colours of the royal banner. She looked nothing like her half-sister. Clad in burnished mail, she was squat and broad and tanned as a chestnut, her thick black hair shorn to a squarish bob above her chin. Her shoulders were bullish, her jaw jutting, and her nose looked like a remote cousin of the Marshal's battering ram. Her sword-belt was empty, as decorum demanded, but her hands were gauntleted, and a helmet with a red plume lay in the crook of her arm.

She had spent her life in battle, putting down one rival claimant to the throne after another. It showed. *I was here before you*, her face proclaimed. *I will still be here after you have gone, and songs will be sung of me when the echo of your name has died.*

They drew rein side by side, within bowshot of the siege towers and the battlements. Iyone counted fourteen arrows on her. She knew without looking back that her father and his men were watching from the walls, their own bows trained on the Queen. She was safe, as safe as a losing general could ever be.

Marguerit spoke first, as befitted her seniority. "My lady of Cassarah. Is the Council so short of warriors that they send a schoolgirl to treat with me?"

There was a violent fluttering in Iyone's chest. "Look up, Magnificence," she said. "The warriors are where they should be, guarding the walls."

"Your commanders are dead, your army scattered," said the Queen. Her eyes were small and black, like prayer beads, and her brown arms were seamed with scar and muscle. "No one will come to relieve you. If you surrender now I may be moved to pity."

"Why surrender?" asked Iyone. "When we have solid walls to guard us and stores to last for years, and the dead cold of winter itself fighting for us?" She smiled at Marguerit. "Alas for you, Queen of Queens! Cut off in a strange land with ten thousand mouths to feed, and the High Commander still at large, harassing your supply lines with his swift horsemen. How long can you stay afloat, O Right Hand of Aebria, Chosen One of Casteia?"

It was like pricking a stone wall with a dinner knife. "A long time," said Marguerit, impassive. "I know where your brother is hiding. My men will bring him to me, and I shall cut off his limbs in your sight and send them to you one by one in my catapult. Do you think we lack for food? For guns? We hold the river. Everything we need, we can ship from Daliss."

"Then you will be here to the end of your days, O Bright Spear," said Iyone. "And your children after you, and your children's children, growing old and dying in the shadow of our walls. Our citadel was built to outlast the earth itself."

"Hubris," said Marguerit briskly. "You are young, and know nothing. You turned down my last bargain. I offer you a new one. Hand over yourself and the woman who goes by the name Josit Ansa, and I will be lenient."

"Me?" said Iyone. "Why?"

But she knew. She had made Josit a promise once, standing in the wreckage of ornaments and window-glass on the floor of her solar. It came flooding back to her in a rush. She knew, then, what to say; where the gap in Marguerit's armour lay.

"O Lioness, it is too late for that," she said. "Josit left a long time ago. And me! To think that the Mighty Sword of Sarei would take such an interest in, as you say, a mere schoolgirl."

The Queen frowned, but said nothing. "Of course, I understand," said Iyone. "If your sister ever turns up again, she might well take away everything you have and hand it to her own heirs. Of which she seems to have plenty. I wonder, are there many in Daliss still loyal to the Queen who should have been?"

Marguerit's hands convulsed on her reins. Her horse fidgeted. "Speak plainly."

"Very well." Iyone was no longer smiling. "You have spent your life trying to stamp out Josit's line. The Terinean orphan, you enslaved and used for your own cause. The frivolous actor, you seduced and destroyed. But there is one more, is there not, O Trueborn Daughter? One more putative child you have never been able to reach?"

Marguerit's jaw worked. "I will have you, Iyone Safin," she said, "whoever you are."

"You will certainly try," said Iyone. "And on my part I shall hold the citadel against all comers, even were I to face the hordes of Sarei alone. I shall outlast you, and I shall outlive you. And after that, who knows? Perhaps I may take a little excursion to Daliss and acquaint myself with Josit's old friends." She drew out the silence, savouring it. "After all, if even Your Magnificence believes that I may be your niece, why not your courtiers? Your allies? Your children?

"Perhaps," finished Iyone, with gentle, devastating precision, "my lady Marguerit, chieftain among women, goddess among men: perhaps anyone can be a queen."

* * *

Her father and mother—the real ones—met her in the front hall of the citadel with Oriane and Yannick. The defenders were cheering. They could not have understood more than a few words of the exchange, but everyone had seen how the Queen blanched as if struck a blow, how she turned and cantered back to the safety of her siege towers without another word. "What happened?" Aretel asked. "What did she say?"

Iyone felt like a berserker fresh to the battle lines, brimming over with adrenaline. All she wanted was to hear the crack of her guns. "In short," she said, "we fight. Victory is near."

CHAPTER 24

Emaris called a halt in a sparse stand of beeches on the east shoulder of the Morivant. They posted lookouts and got a fire going, despite the danger, and he dug needle and thread from his saddlebags and began to tend Savonn's wound.

It was the worst thing he had ever had to do. At first Savonn lay like a wax figurine on the Empath's cloak, so still that Emaris kept leaning in to check if he was breathing. Then—roused by the fire, perhaps, or the prick of the needle—he woke to a sort of fevered delirium, struggling and trying to throw off Emaris's hands. "Stop that," said Emaris. "You'll rip your stitches."

In a heartbeat Savonn went from thrashing to tense, as if anticipating a blow. Emaris regained the presence of mind to dismiss Vion and Lomas, loitering close by with an air of helpfulness. "It's only me."

Savonn's chest rose and fell. His eyes came open. "Gazelle?"

"That's right. You're safe."

"Did I let go?" asked Savonn. "Did I let go?"

Emaris's throat was swelling. It hurt to speak. "No. You brought him up. We put him on a boat."

"I promised him," said Savonn. "But I never keep my promises."

It was unfathomable. Everything Emaris had witnessed felt wrong. Savonn never fought anyone if he could just annoy them instead. But this time he had been true to his word—breached even the last and innermost sanctum of his heart, and made the promised penance. He had spared neither the Empath nor himself. He had been honourable, for once.

And yet Emaris felt sick to his marrow, as if he had witnessed something unbelievably foul.

With difficulty, he said, "You did what you had to do."

"No," said Savonn. His pupils were a bleak grey, wide and unseeing. "He said, *Go down with me*. And I brought him back up."

* * *

Savonn fell asleep not long after, or else lapsed back into unconsciousness. The fading stars wheeled, and the sky brightened to a sullen indigo. The guard changed: Klemene and Lomas stood sentry at the edge of the grove, while Vion and Rougen hunted for food and the other boys slept.

Emaris did not join them. He was afraid to dream.

Savonn woke again when it was fully bright. This time he was lucid, looking around their campsite with his usual guarded calculation. "Don't get up," said Emaris. "You swallowed half the Morivant. I don't know how you're still alive."

Savonn gazed at him, as serene as he had ever been. "Well, I have the most valiant of squires. First fire and now water. I am keeping score."

His head was pillowed on the Empath's cloak. Emaris wondered why they had brought it with them, how Savonn could even stand to touch it now. "You said I wasn't your squire anymore."

"I keep forgetting," said Savonn. "Why do you look so outraged? I thought I gave you a thorough itinerary for last night."

It was an effort to keep calm. *How could you how could you how could you,* went the voices in his echo-chamber. "You left out the part about Shandei."

Predictably, Savonn failed to elaborate. "I will be ready to move on in a moment," he said. "But for now I would like to be alone. Do you mind moving your splendid crocus head and your unbearably brave boys to the other side of those trees for, say, an hour?"

Emaris minded. He minded everything that separated him from Savonn—air, and age, and honour, and dead lovers. But he would never say so. "Will you be all right?"

Savonn's mouth twisted in a lurid grin. "I am bursting with life."

It was painful to look at him, painful to go away. Emaris went.

He spent the better part of the hour pacing back and forth between the bedrolls of his exhausted patrol, until at last Corl groaned at him to take his feet elsewhere, and Emaris went to join the sentries instead. They were sitting at the foot of an old beech, talking over a handkerchief of nuts they had managed to scrounge. "That was sorcery," Klemene was saying, when Emaris sat down next to him. "Pure sorcery, back on Evenfall. I saw—"

He faltered, and shook his head. "I *saw.*"

Lomas patted his shoulder. "Me too."

Klemene sighed. He crammed a handful of nuts into his mouth, and passed some to Emaris. "What the hell do we do now?"

"I don't know," said Emaris. He could not find it in himself to strike a note of false cheer. "Hiraen will think of something."

Lomas looked sceptical. "Like what?"

"Marguerit will love it," said Klemene morosely, "when she finds out we stole the Empath's body. She'll set the whole Sanctuary on us. As if Nikas wasn't bad enough."

Emaris's cheek twinged. All morning he had been trying to ignore the heat of their campfire and the crackle of its kindling, to little avail. "We'll figure something out," said Lomas, with a repressive look at Klemene. "Look, that's Vion and Rougen coming back. They've shot something. Looks like a dove."

"It's bad luck to shoot doves," said Klemene. "I'm not eating it."

"More for me, then. It's been an hour. We better go see if Savonn's hungry."

"Are you joking? I'd sooner take a shit on an anthill than go talk to him now."

But he got up and followed Lomas all the same. Emaris went after them, dragging his feet. Shandei would have told him to set a good example—to take heart, and bring them back to Lissein, and make them believe Hiraen could save them. But Shandei had always been the strong one.

He was looking down, his face turned from the fire, and so did not notice that the others had stopped till he ran into Lomas from behind. His breath wheezed out of him; Lomas was tall as a pillar, and just as solid. "What's the matter?"

"Look," said Klemene.

In hindsight, it was so inevitable it was hilarious. Savonn was gone. The saddle-blanket lay where he had been, folded into quarters without a single crease. "He took his mare," said Lomas, walking over to the horse lines. "But nothing else. No food, no weapons—"

"The Empath's cloak," said Klemene. His eyes bulged. "He took that too."

Emaris had lost his breath again. "I don't believe it," he said. In fact he could believe anything of Savonn; it was his own stupidity that staggered him. He swung a savage kick at a tree. *"I don't believe it!"*

His shout roused the rest of the patrol. They gathered at the edge of the grove, peering for a glimpse of a sole rider, but the winter fields were as empty and desolate as before. Savonn must have set out as soon as their backs were turned. Klemene threw up his hands. "Why is he always like this? Why couldn't he just tell us where he was going?"

"Emaris," said Vion, who had come up with the dead dove. "I think Rougen saw something."

Emaris was almost out of his skin with rage. He had to force himself to look. Rougen made a scrunchy vinegar face, pointed at the ground, and mimed riding a horse.

They saw at once what he meant. Still fresh, the hoofprints made a clear trail away from the horse lines and out of the grove, following the lazy curve of the Morivant southwards. "He must've gone back to Lissein," said Corl, though he sounded unconvinced.

"By himself?" Emaris did not mean to shout; it just came out that way. "What the fuck for?"

An uneasy silence. He knew they were all thinking the same thing. If Savonn was not going to Lissein, he must be headed for Cassarah. The south road did not lead anywhere else. "He's too ill to travel," said Emaris. "He'll die, or get captured, or—"

"I'm sure he has a plan," said Lomas. "He always does. He's probably going to the city to—"

He hesitated, at a loss. "To slip behind the siege lines?"

"To assassinate the Marshal?" said Corl.

"Or the Council," muttered Klemene.

"He won't even get there," said Vion. "The Saraians are everywhere. They'd shoot him on sight. They—*Emaris*! Don't!"

Emaris had broken into a run. Before anyone could stop him, he reached the horse lines and cut free his own gelding. "I'm going after him."

"You can't!"

"I have to." Savonn was a good rider, and on tired horses his lighter weight would tell. And he'd had an hour's head start. Emaris would have to gallop flat out for the slimmest hope of catching up. "You don't understand. He's not himself."

"He's got a death wish!" shouted Lomas. "Don't be stupid! We can't lose you too!"

"He needs me," said Emaris. He shook Rougen off and shoved past Vion, only for Klemene to sprout like a weed between him and his stirrup. "Get out of the way. If I go now I might still catch him."

"And die with him?" demanded Klemene.

"You've got a duty to us, you walnut," said Vion. "To Hiraen, to your sister—"

"And to Savonn," said Emaris. The shock had transmuted into a furious resolve. He felt he could have lifted a house. "I said get out of my way. I'll fight all twelve of you if I have to."

He could take them. He knew he could. Lomas would wrestle him to the ground and try to pin him with sheer weight and momentum. Klemene, if angry enough, might go for his eyes. Vion—

But even as he got his fists up, Vion said, "Oh, what the hell. Let him be. I don't want to be laid out cold by my own patrol leader."

"But he's going to—"

"We can't do anything about it," said Vion flatly. He tugged Klemene aside, and Emaris found the way to his saddle clear. "Go on, you idiot."

In relief, Emaris shouldered past them. "We've wasted enough time," he said. "Go back and tell Hiraen where we went. If you're fast about it—"

There was a blinding crack. He thought the grove had been struck by lightning, though the sky was clear. His scalp was on fire. He found himself first on his knees, then his face. Shouts broke out behind him, Vion's voice chief among them. "I'm sorry! I'm sorry!"

Emaris knew he should have expected this. But he had made a habit of feeling superior—he, son of a commander, squire to another, the only decent soldier in a mob of half-trained boys. It was a mistake neither Savonn nor Hiraen would ever have made.

He had just enough time to feel a stab of annoyance, and then the world grew grey and dim, and slid from him altogether.

* * *

He woke to a babble of confused voices and a splitting pain in his skull. The ground was cold and hard, and a shaft of excruciating daylight bore down on his face, turning the backs of his eyelids a nasty maroon. He groaned and tried to sit up, and a restraining weight made itself felt on his shoulder.

His hand flew to his sword-belt. It seized the first thing it touched, and slashed wildly. The voices exclaimed. None of the words made sense. Then he remembered to open his eyes, and two faces swam into view above him: Hiraen, looking disturbed, and Vion, looking guilty.

Emaris dropped the weapon. "You hit me!"

"I had to!" Vion yelled. "You might have been killed!"

His head pounded. They were back in Lissein, in the Commander's cottage by the looks of it. An ewer of water sat by his bedroll, and his bow and quiver were leaning against the wall next to Hiraen's. "Where's Savonn? Didn't anyone follow him?"

"Ah." Vion shifted his weight. "Well—"

Emaris swore. Long, loud, and fulsome, with all the words he knew and others he made up on the spot. Vion looked impressed. "We need to send someone after him. Right now. There's no telling what he'll do. Hiraen, he—"

Hiraen was not listening. He was looking down, his attention transfixed to something on the floor. Emaris sat up, and saw what it was.

The weapon he had let fall was his father's ivory dagger, the one Shandei had given him for safekeeping. A tendril of cold fog curled around him. An incomplete thought surfaced in his mind, then dissipated again before he could catch hold of it. The hairs on his arms stood.

Hiraen pulled himself together. "Vion, leave us."

Vion gave him a mutinous stare, thought better of arguing, and flounced from the room. Emaris tried to focus. "Savonn killed the Empath," he said. It still felt surreal. "You must've heard."

"Where's the body?" asked Hiraen.

This seemed an odd question. "Shandei took it down the river by boat." By now she must be miles away, paddling her little skiff between Isemain's patrols and the Saraian border guard. And here Emaris sat, unable to help. "Look, Savonn was hurt. We have to find him."

"It's too late. If he's gone south, the Marshal's scouts will have him by now, unless he's found a way to evade them. And if he has, it's not terribly likely he'll let us find him." Hiraen hesitated. "Daine says the city wall is breached. Marguerit's crossed over by barge."

"*Gods.*"

"I know." Hiraen rubbed his eyes. "Listen. Savonn loves a good show, but this isn't his style of theatrics. He doesn't do things for no reason. He knows what he's about."

"Not this time," said Emaris. "You weren't there. You didn't see him."

Already his memories of the previous night were congealing into a writhing mass of exposed nerves, tender to the touch. He knew how slippery Savonn could be. He should have been more careful. "Last night—I think he wanted to die with the Empath. He said he'd made him a promise, but he'd broken it. I think— he's gone to make an end."

His father's dagger still lay between them like a barrier through which no words of consolation could pass. But Hiraen had always treated him as a grown man, and did not try to comfort him. "Tell me," he said. "Did you see the Empath die?"

"No," said Emaris impatiently. "I thought they told you. It was in the river. They went under for, I think it must've been a full minute. He was dead when they came back up."

Hiraen looked thoughtful, but said nothing. He went to the ewer and splashed some water on his face. The sun was past its zenith now, and the evening fog was starting to come up from the river. "Before you set out yesterday," he said, "Savonn told me to go to Cassarah and ask to parley if he didn't come back."

"What've we got to bargain with?"

"Nothing," said Hiraen. "I'll have to think on it. Here, this is yours."

He was holding the dagger out hilt-first. Emaris started to take it. Then the thought he had lost earlier came back to him, coalescing out of a storm of disparate images.

Daine's garden. The back room. The mingling odours of strong wine and blood, a smell peculiar to places of death. Savonn's shadow leaping on the wall. Old memories, made fresh again by the strange visions of Evenfall. He remembered Hiraen facing down Bonner Efren, his hands red with Daron's blood. He'd had the same look in his eyes in Daine's house, at Rendell's deathbed.

He had been the first on the scene, that night. He had found the body. Or so they said.

Hiraen said, "Emaris—"

Emaris stood, went to the window, and threw up. He had eaten almost nothing all day, so most of it was water. A foot scuffed the floor: Hiraen came closer, but did not touch him. "Emaris."

He had been betrayed once already this morning. There was nothing left to feel. "I don't want to hear it."

"Don't you?"

Emaris did not answer. His mouth was sour with bile. The tread receded, then came back. Hiraen set a cup of water on the windowsill beside him. "Drink. You're exhausted."

Emaris knocked the cup away. He found he did, in fact, want an explanation. "Why?"

In this, as in everything else, Hiraen did not indulge him. "I will make no excuses," he said. "Only that when we were younger, Savonn gave up everything to protect me from a wicked man no one else knew was wicked. I felt someone ought to protect him this time."

It sounded like a rehearsed defence. It probably was. Hiraen had had time to prepare, after all. Months of lies and secrecy, during which Emaris had never once suspected. He had doubted Savonn at times, loathed him, despised him, but not Hiraen. In his mind Hiraen had occupied the same space as his father and sister—shining and golden, and above suspicion.

Over and over, he kept making the same mistake.

"You're a fool, then," he said. "Savonn's never needed protection. He's a vicious demon of a villain who'll look his lover in the eye and kill him with his own two hands."

"If you really thought so," said Hiraen, "you wouldn't have just tried to follow him to death."

Emaris stared through the window at the unkempt garden of the Commander's cottage, at the back of the next house across the cobbled lane. It all seemed tiny and quaint and picturesque, an artist's clay model of a village. Hiraen was right. It was Emaris who was the fool, who kept blinding himself with hate or love so he would not have to look too hard at what lay in between: the fact that his idols were men just like him, fragile, fallible, hurting. Small wonder people kept trying to shield him from the truth.

He had been a child long enough. "Give me my dagger," he said.

There was a pause. He held out his hand without looking round, and presently Hiraen gave it to him. Shandei had not said what he ought to do with it. But she must have known. She had had this confrontation with Hiraen already.

"Like I told your sister," said Hiraen, "you may exact payment whenever you please."

The worst thing was not that he was offering up his life. It was how he looked the same as he always did, handsome and good-natured, as if he had not just put a sharp blade into the hand of a man who had reason to kill him. *Could you do it?* Savonn had asked. Savonn, who had paid and paid and paid to settle his own blood debt to his father. *Could you do your duty?*

Hiraen was still waiting. He was not afraid to die. It was only Emaris who was loath to kill.

"I won't do it," said Emaris. His sinuses throbbed. "I don't want payment. It wouldn't bring my father back."

"I don't think it's a choice."

"You've no right to tell me that."

"I know," said Hiraen. "But I—I need to make it right. The Ceriyes—they spoke to me."

To hell with the Ceriyes, Emaris thought. Savonn had killed the Empath, but he was not Savonn. He was better, or worse, whatever that meant. "You don't get out of this so easily," he said. "Dying won't help anyone. If you want to put things right, do something."

Hiraen frowned. "I'm not asking for mercy."

"This isn't mercy," said Emaris. "I mean it. You're the High Commander. If Savonn said to go parley, you better damn well go."

He opened his hand. The dagger slipped through his fingers, hitting the floor with a rattle. That made it final. "You want to pay? This is the price I ask. Fix this. Make it so I don't have to kill you."

He had thought Hiraen would be relieved. Instead he looked like a man who thought he had reached the summit of a mountain, only to find there was farther to go. Perhaps death would have been kinder. But Emaris did not mean to be kind. Atonement was hard work, and there was more to it than dying. If he had learnt anything from Savonn at all, it was that.

"I see," said Hiraen. Then again, more firmly, "I see. If that's what you want, I promise you will have it by any means necessary."

Emaris stayed by the window, not looking at him. As if from a great distance, he heard Hiraen move around the room, buckling on his cuirass, picking up his bow. "Daine," he called, going out into the garden. "Daine, I'm going to Cassarah with Emaris. You'll have command of this rout till I get back.—No, I have no idea.—Yes, I'm afraid so. I'm afraid we're out of options."

Slowly, Emaris gathered up his own things and began to follow. In the garden he ran into Vion, looking pale and dishevelled. No doubt he had been listening in the bushes, but Emaris could not bring himself to care. "You forgot something."

The ivory dagger was still on the floor. Emaris shook his head. "Keep it," he said. "Or throw it away. I don't want it."

CHAPTER 25

"Magnificence," said Isemain. "The walls hold."

The walls held. Marguerit could see that for herself. Their siege-towers had been blown up by the defenders six times in one night, and now sat abandoned in the piazza in sad piles of debris. Two of their cannon had made it across the river, but the gunpowder barge had been sunk by a Betronett patrol that morning, so they still had no artillery. Marguerit had been forced to go about her assault the old-fashioned way, with sappers and pickaxes and explosives.

Her Marshal was getting anxious. An inauspicious sign.

"No food's come in from Daliss," he said. He was almost shouting—the citadel guns had been firing all day, and that appalling schoolgirl had conjured up a band of drummers and trumpeters to add to the general racket. "We lost another flotilla of boats to Safin's patrols today. We've picked the city clean of anything edible, but at this rate we'll have to send half the men home before they starve."

"No one is starving yet," said Marguerit with asperity. It was true they had not accounted for Ederen's godforsaken citadel, or the Cassarans somehow managing to agree with one another long enough to barricade themselves into it. But that was only a minor setback. "We have only just arrived. And Hiraen Safin has to eat like any of us."

In the breathing space between cannon rounds, the defenders started up a raucous battle-hymn. Even without knowing much of their coarse tongue she could tell they were changing the lyrics, singing bawdy and blasphemous things. She turned her back, got on her horse, and cantered away from the wreckage of the piazza, down the empty thoroughfares that led back to the Earth Gate. The Cassarans were unforgivably cheerful. The same could not be said of her own army.

"Marguerit," said Isemain, when he caught up to her. They were just outside the gate, under the great walls no other conqueror in history had breached. No one could claim to share her fame: not her drunkard hero of a father, or her viper half-sister. She had outdone them all. "Marguerit," said Isemain again. "May I be frank?"

He was her favourite consort, and the only one permitted to address her by name. The others had long been relegated to remote estates in the backwaters of her kingdom, lest they grow importunate. She sighed. "When are you anything but?"

"Lord Safin's army knows the land," said Isemain. "And they move fast. They attack in small bands to steal our food, and disappear before we can strike back. Morale is low. We can't go on like this."

"I am waiting," said Marguerit, "for you to suggest a solution."

She was no stranger to long sieges. She had been born *in* a siege—had been pulled out of the womb by the midwife while her uncle rolled his guns up to the walls of Daliss, and grown to girlhood by the time he surrendered. She remembered watching from the ramparts as his siege-towers collapsed in a hail of soot and sparks, and the banners of the pretender king went up in flames. "Look, we're winning," Josit had crowed. Josit, a year older and always a step ahead, beautiful and brilliant as a sunbeam. "Look, Margie, they're running away!"

Of course, a few years later it had been Josit's army running away, but that was the nature of things. That was queenship. Sieges were a matter of patience and bloody-mindedness, and both had been etched in her bones since birth. Cassarah's little citadel was nothing. She would flatten it, as she had so many others.

"There has to be a quicker way," said Isemain. "The Cassarans are notorious for their infighting. If we sent someone to infiltrate the citadel and stir up trouble—say, the Empath, or Nikas—"

"Nikas," said Marguerit, "has been entrusted with the single most vital task in the realm, and will not come back until he has seen it done. And Dervain, bless his soul, is under oath not to set foot here again."

She allowed those damnable slaves too much leeway. This, too, was queenship. One found people whose agendas aligned with one's own, and promoted them, and turned them loose on the world. She could only wonder if the risks were worth the gain.

"We're wasting time," said Isemain. "If the Empath could be persuaded to break his oath, he might steal into the citadel in disguise—"

"Unlikely," said Marguerit. "And unwise. Dervain has shown himself a feckless romantic who does not care if he lives or dies, so long as he brings the Andalles down with him. He will discharge his blood feud and take his own life within the week, you mark my words."

There was a curious pause. "But, Magnificence," said Isemain. "He is here."

She looked up. At the edge of the camp, a sole rider had arrived at a gallop. Servants and grooms scrambled to receive his horse, but he ploughed straight through them and into the tent-lanes, making for the tall white spire of the royal pavilion. His hood was up, covering his hair and shadowing his face, but his brilliant red-and-black cloak streamed from his shoulders like a standard. Even at a distance he was unmistakeable.

The Red Death, they called him. Or—when he was not in earshot, which was rare—the Slave-King.

Dervain Teraille dismounted at the cross-junction of two lanes and, in an explosion of barked orders, sent the attendants scattering. There seemed to be something wrong with his shoulder. "What's he gone and done this time?" said Isemain irritably.

"Murdered his lover, I suppose," said Marguerit.

In spite of herself, she was relieved. Nobody *enjoyed* having the Empath around—it was like sitting on a barrel of wildfire—but one had to admit he was worth a dozen of Isemain's doughtiest soldiers. "You may go. I'm going to receive him before he kills someone."

Her squires took her horse and helmet and escorted her through the encampment to her pavilion. Inside, the tapestries and the thick canvas muffled the guns a little. She did not go in for luxury, and her tent boasted only simple furnishings: a low camp bed screened off by silk hangings, and a carved ebony chair that functioned as her throne when she was on campaign, which was all the time. Forty years wearing the crown, and pretenders still cropped up like toadstools at the least bit of encouragement.

She was studying the rack of spears, javelins and swords by the throne, pondering the merits of Isemain's suggestion, when the tent flap rustled and her servant stepped into her presence. "Report," she said.

A brief lapse. Then a strange voice answered her. "He is dead, Magnificence."

She spun round while he was still speaking, a spear poised to throw. The intruder was a slight young man she had never seen before, wearing Dervain's cloak, standing with Dervain's cavalier grace, looking at her through Dervain's eyes. But no. The Empath had hazel eyes, and this man's were blue. Or green. Or grey. It was hard to say.

Her spear-tip came to rest between the studs of his brigandine, over his heart. "Who are you?"

The man pushed back his hood and slid the cloak from his shoulders. "I am called Savonn Silvertongue."

So this was the Cassaran traitor who had been so useful to her, the son of that vile scourge Kedris Andalle. She would never have guessed. Kedris had been tall, and muscled like an ox. This fellow was more shadow than person, all sleek lines and slippery grace; the lightness of his stance suggested that his earliest training had been in dance, or gymnastics. His left shoulder was a ruin of bloody bandages, and his throat was ringed with bruises. She had never seen anyone so disreputable.

"At the count of three," said Marguerit, "I am going to push this spear into your heart, unless you give me a reason not to. One—"

"I have come," said the Silvertongue, "to give Cassarah into your hands."

* * *

When the Saraian herald arrived with a second invitation to parley, Iyone knew something was amiss.

This time it was more than a drawbridge chat. Marguerit had asked her to the royal pavilion. Iyone took two bodyguards—her father insisted—and concealed a sharp dagger in her skirts, though she did not know how to wield it; and rode once more out of the citadel, into the dominion of the Queen.

She scarcely recognised her own city. The registrars' houses opposite the piazza had been levelled to rubble, mostly by their own cannon. Others farther off had been demolished for Isemain's siege-towers. The herb gardens had been picked clean, and the flowerbeds on Josit's bridges were wilting for want of anybody to tend them. Outside the Earth Gate, the latrine stench of the enemy camp rose to greet her, and soldiers came out of their tents in the dozens to watch her pass.

She waited for the inevitable leers and catcalls. None came. She was, it appeared, an honoured guest.

"This way, ladyship," said the herald, bowing her towards the Queen's pavilion. It was twice as tall as she was, and the guards—a pair of towering women with spears—seemed to have been picked to match. "Milady will kindly leave her servants outside."

The twin giantesses held the tent flap for her. Iyone stepped through, into the presence of the Queen. Then she stopped dead.

There was a writing table in the middle of the tent, on which an ink-pot and two sheets of vellum had been laid out. To the left sat Marguerit in an ebony throne, the Marshal Isemain at her side. On the right, reclining on a pile of silk cushions like a decadent wine-god, was Savonn.

Iyone recoiled. The guards were at her back, blocking the exit. *"What are you doing here?"*

"Ah, there you are," said Savonn. A half-empty plate of figs lay beside him, and a long-stemmed goblet swung between his fingers. "I got bored waiting for Hiraen to lose the war, so I came to broker peace. Come play with us."

She must be overtired, and hallucinating malevolent clowns. He was in a deep green doublet with a high gold-lined collar, and his curls were freshly washed and brushed. An elaborate onyx choker circled his neck, so fine it must have been a gift from the Queen. It seemed he was not a prisoner. "You've escaped your funhouse," said Iyone. "Where's Hiraen?"

No one answered her. "You may be seated, Lady Safin," said Marguerit. "The terms of our agreement are laid out before you."

Iyone looked at the documents, incredulous. One was in Saraian, the other Falwynian. But both had been penned in Savonn's fastidious angular hand, and their meaning was identical. She got as far as the third line before she could read no more. *"Single combat?"*

"The oldest and simplest way to resolve a dispute," said Marguerit, with a satisfied half-smile. For the first time, Iyone saw a little of Josit in the angles of her chin and jaw, and the keen glimmer in her eyes. "Lord Silvertongue agrees with me that this siege is a waste of lives. We have decided to expedite matters. Do finish reading."

Iyone did. The terms were preposterous. The Queen of Sarei and the Council of Cassarah would both elect a champion, to face each other at sunup the next day in a duel to the death. If the Queen's champion was victorious, the Cassarans were to surrender at once. The defenders would hand over the citadel, and those in the field with the High Commander would lay down their arms. Combatants would be put to death. Noncombatants, in the Queen's far-reaching mercy, would be allowed to go free. All but two: Josit Ansa and Iyone Safin.

The rest of the agreement read like an afterthought. If the Cassaran champion won, the Saraians were to withdraw beyond the Morivant, and a hundred-year truce would be signed between Queen and Council. Whichever way things fell out, the Empath's remains would be returned to the Sanctuary as a sign of good faith.

That was a shock. She had not thought Savonn capable of killing his lover. "The Empath is dead?"

She addressed the question to the Queen, but it was Savonn she watched, and Savonn who answered. "I murdered him, Iyone dear," he said. He gestured with a flourish, and she noticed a bloodstained cloak, red and black, crumpled on the floor beside the throne. "I drowned him in the Morivant and then I fished him back out. You should have seen it. Your angry little thundercloud Shandei took the body off for safekeeping."

She could not keep from flinching at the name. Savonn popped a fig into his mouth and, still holding her gaze, began to chew.

With an effort, she composed herself. His artful sprawl was not as languid as it looked. There was a stiff set to his shoulders, and the lazy droop to his kohled lids suggested he was either hazy with poppy or on the brink of collapse. Or both. The high-collared doublet and choker might have hidden any number of injuries. As for the rest—it was never a good idea to believe anything that came out of Savonn's mouth.

"Magnificence," she said at last. "The Council did not authorise this man to treat on our behalf. These terms are void."

"Are they not to your liking?" asked Marguerit. "I thought you young people loved nothing so much as danger and glory. A duel will decide matters just as well as a siege. The Marshal Isemain will be my champion—"

"*So* fearsome," Savonn put in. Isemain shot him a look of pure disgust.

"—and I suppose you may take your pick of the musicians, cooks, and washer-women hiding behind your walls, since no one else is likely to get here by dawn to succour you. Your brother, I understand, is still cowering in his death circus."

Iyone lifted her chin. "My brother does not cower." Josit would not have been afraid of Marguerit, so neither would she. "Perhaps, O Queen of Queens, you worry he might come up in your rear and sweep you all away? Is that why you are abandoning your careful siege on a gamble? You will be disappointed. The Council will never ratify this agreement."

"Oh, dear," said Savonn. "You used to be more sporting. Must we do this the hard way?" He sighed. "As we speak, Shandei is travelling through enemy territory all alone, bearing the body of Her Magnificence's prize cockfighter. What would become of her if the Sanctuary got wind of her whereabouts? Have you looked at Emaris's face lately?"

This time she managed not to react. But they had never been able to fool each other. Savonn had thought of everything. "I think," he said, with a lavish smile, "the Council will find you very persuasive."

Sentiment, Josit once said, *makes you slow and stupid.* Anyone could feel. Iyone had to think. Savonn had lied to her before, but he had never forced her hand like this. His nature was founded on little mischiefs and illusions, not outright cruelty. "We were family," she said. "Why would you do this to us?"

"Why?" Savonn parroted. "*Why*? Sister dear, did I ask you why when you gave Dervain's letters to the Council? When you took the only thing in my life that was true and good and beautiful and paraded it in court like a crime?"

Iyone's blood ran cold. She had known this confrontation was coming, but she had not expected to have it in front of the Queen of Sarei. "You know why I did it. I had to—"

"To save yourself, yes," said Savonn. "So you understand me. Poor Hiraen won't, but you always do."

Did she? Under the kohl and jewels, his face was guileless as a cherub's, and twice as sinister. He was a consummate showman, so good you did not even know you were watching a show till you felt the knife twist in your back. She'd thought she knew him, but that was before the Empath. If it was true, what he said he'd done—

Marguerit seemed to have put her trust in him. But it was likely the Queen had no idea what she was unleashing.

"Yes," said Iyone coldly. "I do understand."

She turned to the Queen. All she could do was hope that the boy who had been the bosom friend of her childhood was still there, lurking under all Savonn's masks; that he was playing Marguerit just as he was playing her, and all this was to a purpose. "I must congratulate you, Magnificence. What reward did you promise him? A mansion by the sea? A harem of homicidal redheads? It doesn't matter. It will never be his."

She smiled an angelic smile of her own. "The Council will, of course, have to talk this over. But just between you and me, I have already chosen our champion. If no one else steps forward, Lord Silvertongue himself shall fight for us."

Savonn's face slid into perfect blankness. Isemain looked startled. Marguerit laughed. "Truly! An interesting choice."

"So," said Iyone, "do try not to kill him, though I guarantee you will want to at some point. I will leave my bodyguards here with him."

It was the least she could do for him. In any case, their prospects were bleak. Isemain was a bloodcurdling sight—easily six foot three, his arms ropy with muscle—and she could think of no champion of her own. If her father volunteered, her mother would knock him out and tie him to a chair. "I shall bring these terms to the Council," she said. "Our herald will give you our decision shortly. I suggest you refrain from shooting at us in the meantime."

It was moot. The councillors would bicker and wring their hands and curse her, and give in. Oriane did not have the temperament for a long siege. Lucien might, but his men were already stretched too thin, and he was feeling the strain. And Hiraen could not stay in the field much longer. If Marguerit's position was untenable, theirs was hopeless.

Savonn popped another fig in his mouth, watching her with large, insolent eyes as she turned to go. "Goodbye, sister," he said. "I wonder if we shall meet again."

She wondered, too. But they would not know till their gambit had been played to the fullest. Between the two of them, they had either doomed the city or saved it. Only the duel would tell.

CHAPTER 26

Daine's scouts had warned Hiraen that the Saraians now occupied most of Cassarah. Still, nothing could have prepared him for the sight.

They saw the enemy camp first: tents and fires and latrines and horse lines as far as the eye could see, sprawling like a second city under the walls. The Earth Gate was in shambles, the Queen's black and white standard flying triumphant from the ramparts and the watchtowers. "They're *inside*," said Emaris in a tight, choked voice.

Hiraen cast about for something reassuring to say, and came up empty-handed. "Run up the banner."

Under cover of night, with just the two of them, it had been easy to travel unseen. But now they stopped in full view of the enemy camp, and Emaris hoisted the sunburst banner and let it run out in the wind. Already two sentries were approaching, one with an axe, the other winding a crossbow. Hiraen hailed them. "Tell your Queen the High Commander of Cassarah has come to parley."

The sentries caught the spirit of the proclamation, if not the letter. It seemed to unsettle them, as if he were a guest that had come too early, while the host was still asleep and the house in disarray. The guard with the axe muttered something to her companion and went back into the camp. The crossbowman stayed where he was, eyeing them as if they had the plague. Minutes slipped by. Then the woman returned, this time with the Marshal and his interpreter.

Hiraen dismounted. Thrice, now, he had crossed swords with Isemain Dalissos, and twice seen his banners in battle. As these things went, they were practically old friends. The Marshal seemed surprised, but not on the whole displeased. "Milord Isemain bids you welcome," said the interpreter, an elderly man. "He says he has failed to kill you twice, but the third time pays for all. You are here to champion the Council in the duel?"

"What duel?" asked Emaris.

The interpreter explained. The Queen and the Council had just signed an agreement to end the war once and for all. Single combat, with the fate of the city riding on the outcome. It made sense: with no great army coming to relieve one side or the other, the siege would draw on interminably. Everyone would suffer. Better to settle the matter in a duel to the death, commander to commander, man to man.

It had a kind of roguish logic to it. All Savonn's schemes did. Hiraen only wondered if the Council knew whose idea this had been.

"Yes," he said. He ignored the interpreter, and addressed Isemain directly. "I'll kill you tomorrow, Lord Marshal. Now, unless you're afraid of me, you'll give us something decent to eat and a place to sleep, and take me to the Silvertongue. I know he's here."

He hoped this might anger the Marshal. But Isemain was smiling, and the grin only broadened as the interpreter finished translating. He cursed approvingly. Then he snapped an order to the crowd of sentries and minor officers who had gathered to watch, slapped a hand to his broad chest in what could have been threat or salute, and stalked back into the camp. Emaris was slack-mouthed.

"Milord says he cannot wait to crush your skull in," said the interpreter, looking pained, "and that his men will take you to the Silvertongue presently, if you will follow them."

Under his breath, Emaris said, "What if it's a trap?"

Hiraen considered this. He had arrived at a state of mind so far beyond fear that all was lucent and tranquil again, as if he had died and attained godhood. "It's not."

They were made to hand over their weapons. Then half a dozen guards marched them along the edge of the encampment and through the breached wall into the city itself. It was quiet, eerily so. All the houses were empty, the stalls of the night bazaar deserted, and the only people they saw on the streets were Saraians. "Where is everyone?" asked Emaris in a strained whisper. "Are they *dead*?"

"I don't know," said Hiraen. *Iyone*, he thought. *What have you done?*

The first buildings they passed were intact, though uninhabited. Then they neared the piazza, and saw at last the true extent of the destruction. Whole neighbourhoods had been levelled, the houses burned to shells, or reduced altogether to piles of rubble. Even the lawns were scarred with trenches. If Hiraen had not walked through the gate on his own legs, he would have thought himself asleep, transported in the throes of a horrible fever dream.

"There they are," said Emaris.

Somewhere, a crowd had begun to shout. Hiraen looked up. They were under the citadel battlements now, and the wallwalks were swarming with people—not just the city guard, but civilians as well, man and woman, young and old, jostling one another for a glimpse of them. The porpoise, the eagle, and the sunburst fluttered overhead. Someone called, "Hiraen!"

There was a triple flash of white light and an earth-shattering boom. The Rose, the Thorn, and the Dung had fired a round in salute. The defenders cheered. Somehow Iyone must have gathered the whole city behind the citadel walls, and brought the guns with her. Out of habit Hiraen lifted his hand to the watchers, and instantly the cheering swelled, as if they thought he had come to lift the siege all by himself.

"Where are you taking us?" Emaris asked, as they drew away from the citadel and the noise grew muffled behind them.

The Saraians did not know their street names. "You want to see the Silvertongue, yes?" said one of them. She pointed ahead, past the Temple of the Sisters and the rubble of the registrars' offices. "Big stage for little clown. Tomorrow you die there."

Hiraen realised what they meant. "The Arena," he said, tickled despite himself. "Of course."

* * *

For the first time in generations, the Arena of White Sand lived up to its name.

It was like stepping into an old painting, the centuries crumbling and slipping away beneath Hiraen's feet. The stage had been dismantled. Where struts and scaffolding once stood, there was now only a flat expanse of empty space at the bottom of the bowl: a broad duelling ring strewn with pure white sand, so clean and crisp it seemed to glow in the dark. So had it been in the savage years of Cassarah's youth, when men and women vied for the privilege of duelling to the death before Ederen and the first Council, and the sands of the Arena drunk deep of their blood.

Hiraen surveyed the scene. He had to admit a certain amusement at the thought of Isemain dredging up sediments from the riverbed just for the occasion. Two awnings had been set up over the stands on opposite sides of the ring, one bearing Marguerit's standard, the other the triple banners of the Council. Under the latter sat a solitary figure, small and hunched in the moonlight.

"Let me speak to him alone," said Hiraen.

For once, Emaris did not protest. Hiraen left him with the guards and went down the stairs, his shadow flowing long and monstrous before him, towards the brilliant circle of the duelling ring. Savonn looked up and saw him coming, but did not speak. "All right," said Hiraen. "What's broken?"

There were no visible signs of maltreatment, but he knew from the finnicky way Savonn held himself that he was wounded. "Our luck," said Savonn. A pause. "And my shoulder."

"Let me see."

He made no objection, so Hiraen unfastened the laces of his doublet and peeled off the choker. Underneath, his neck was bruised with purple finger-marks, and his left shoulder was swathed in clean bandages. A knife wound, deep, by the looks of it.

Hiraen suppressed his first instinctive remarks. He was not here to quarrel. "Am I to believe he came off worse?"

"Emaris must have told you so."

"Emaris," said Hiraen, "thinks you drowned him."

"There were witnesses," said Savonn. Under Hiraen's hands he was very still, almost unbreathing. "So it must be true."

"No, that's mass hysteria." Hiraen refastened the doublet and moved away. "Don't philosophize. I'll believe it when I see the body."

"But the Saraians burn their dead," said Savonn. "So there is no body. You don't have to sit so far away. I won't philosophize."

Hiraen came back. They sat without speaking, listening to the distant buzz of voices from the piazza, the singing on the battlements. The ring of sand was as good a place as any for a duel, he thought. Level, about sixty yards across, plenty of room to manoeuvre. High walls to keep out the sun. Sound would be strange, which might confuse his opponent. Isemain was bigger and stronger, but past his prime. Hiraen was at the peak of his own. A pity this was to be a duel with swords. Put a bow in his hands, and Isemain would be dead before the Queen could so much as blink.

How shall I put it right? he had asked, the day they took him to the innermost sanctum to stand before the gods. And the answer of the Ceriyes had come gusting to him out of the dark. *Blood and sand. Blood and sand.*

His gut tingled. One way or another, Emaris's price would be paid.

"Behold my genius," said Savonn at length. "I have engineered for you the martyrdom you always wanted. Glory. Honour. Redemption. And as a bonus, neither Shandei nor Emaris will have to kill you now. There's one problem solved."

Hiraen looked at him carefully. The moonlight turned the planes of his face to pearl and frost. "Is that what this is about?"

"Yes," said Savonn. "Here I am, pragmatic to the last. If you must self-destruct, I would rather you do it on top of Isemain in a heroic duel to the death, so we'll be done with the war and my poor gazelle won't have to live with the guilt of murdering you—or *not* murdering you—to the end of his days. Is it not clever?"

The silence spun itself out. Hiraen waited. At last Savonn exhaled and said, "Oh, ignore me." His eyes were foggy with pain and whatever drug Marguerit's physicians had given him. "Truth is, it was the only way to even the odds after the mess you and Bonner made. I told you it was a terrible plan."

Hiraen's heart was a knotted snarl of muscle, tight and sore. "No," he said. "You're right. It's better this way. I can take him."

Savonn laughed. "Now you just have to kill a man for me. Isn't it funny how things always come down to that?"

This might be the last time they ever spoke in the world of the living. Hiraen took a deep breath, and resolved to say nothing wounding. "Promise me something."

"No," said Savonn. "I always break my promises."

"*Promise me*," said Hiraen, "that whatever happens tomorrow, you'll find a way to get out. If Marguerit doesn't kill you, someone from our side will, and I—"

He tried not to shy away from the thought. He might lose. It was a possibility that had to be faced, sooner rather than later. "I may not be there to stop it. Go to Astorre or somewhere and start over. You were never happy here."

Savonn passed a hand over his face. "What about you?"

Below, the ring gleamed like a bright mirage. Emaris had made him come here, and Hiraen was glad for it. This was what he had been born for, the steel and blood of a good clean fight. Not the endless bickerings of the Council, or the vast webs of deception Kedris and Josit had spun around them all. He trusted Savonn. He trusted the edge of his own sword. He even trusted Isemain to see this through to the end, the way he had never been able to trust Bonner and Daron.

"I told Emaris I would make things right," he said. "So I will."

Savonn peered at him. The dim light illuminated the dark bags under his eyes, the etchings of worry and exhaustion. "Is this what he wanted?"

"Yes," said Hiraen. "But I would have come anyway. It was the only thing to do."

He searched for a smile for Savonn, and found one more easily than he expected. It was simple now. All he had to do was fight. "I'll kill Isemain Dalissos tomorrow, with my teeth and nails if I have to."

CHAPTER 27

Sleepless, Emaris lay in the tent the Marshal's guards had given him, listening as the two armies passed the long night in their disparate ways.

Marguerit had a pyre built outside her pavilion, sacrificed her prize stallion to Casteia, and anointed Isemain with its blood. Even as the Saraians chanted and prayed over their champion, the noise from the citadel swelled, sending its long tendrils through the enemy camp: the voices of the Cassaran defenders raised in song, accompanied by the shout of trumpets and the crash of sword on shield. It went on all night, hour upon dark hour; until at last day broke and the horns began to call, summoning both besieger and besieged to the Arena.

Emaris went with them. The Marshal's men had forgotten all about their guest, and no one tried to stop him.

He had thought it would be odd to see Saraians in their theatre. In truth Marguerit's soldiers looked just like their own, and without the unfamiliar crests and sigils he would have been hard-pressed to tell the difference. Their own half of the Arena was empty: Lady Iyone had forbidden the defenders to leave the citadel, so besides the Council and their guards, Emaris was the only one present. He cast a long scrolling look over the stands on the Saraian side, hopeful; but without knowing what disguise Savonn was wearing, it was impossible to pick him out.

Then a bell tolled, and the two champions stepped out onto the sand.

Hiraen and Isemain were lightly armoured in leather and mail, with vambraces and gauntlets and greaves. Neither wore a helm. Emaris supposed the people wanted to see who they were cheering for. The Saraians roared at the sight of their champion; less overwhelmingly, so too did the Council's guards.

"We were going to send Cahal," Yannick muttered, from his seat next to Emaris. "But how can we make our servants die for us?"

How, indeed. With a lump in his throat, Emaris caught Hiraen's eye, and nodded in what he hoped was an encouraging way.

Iyone said, "Why is *she* here?"

Emaris followed the direction of her gaze, and had to wonder, momentarily, if he was dreaming. A three-legged scarecrow was tottering out from the stands towards the champions. Its drapery billowed, laden with tassels and ruffles of rotting lace, and a rope of pearls swung from its neck. Then Emaris's tired eyes focused, and he made sense of what he was seeing: a tiny old woman in a dress much too big for her, hobbling across the sand on a cane. Her hair was almost all white, her legs shrivelled to twigs. "Who is she?"

"That," said Yannick, "is the High Priestess. The duel is consecrated to Aebria and Casteia, so she is presiding." He smiled weakly at Emaris's astonished look, and added, as if reading his mind, "She is a hundred and eighteen years old."

Two girls in white dresses, no older than eight or nine, came up bearing identical longswords. They presented them to Hiraen and Isemain, and scuttled away again. Then, in a screechy rasp, the High Priestess began to declaim.

The rules of the duel were simple, though it took an eternity for the old woman to get through them. No spectator was to set foot on the sand for the duration of the fight. The champions would conduct themselves like gentlemen, and use no weapon save the longswords. These had been supplied from the Temple's own armoury, purified and dedicated to the goddesses by the High Priestess herself. Once commenced, the duel could not be stopped for any reason. Hiraen Safin and Isemain of Daliss would fight until one of them was dead.

"And thus shall the war end," announced the High Priestess. "You are all charged in the sight of gods and men to uphold the terms of the treaty, or Sorrow and Strife will pursue you through this life and into the next. By Aebria and Casteia, let it be done."

She began to limp away. "Why did Marguerit let her preside?" asked Emaris. "She's one of ours."

Lord Yannick gazed at him severely, but did not look annoyed. Like so many learned men, he seemed to find the dispensation of knowledge soothing. "She belongs to no one but the Sisters," he said. "There is—ah—much ill that could be said of Marguerit, but she is a godly woman. To her there could be no higher authority on earth."

At some signal Emaris missed, the Saraians quieted. The cheering reverberated against the Arena's amplifying walls for a moment longer, then died away. In the ensuing silence, they could hear faint snatches of singing from the citadel. The Marshal swept the Queen a low bow. Hiraen saluted the Council.

"It is about to begin," said Yannick, tangling and untangling his fingers together. "Oh, dear gods, it is about to begin..."

The bell tolled again, and Emaris stopped listening.

The fight he had witnessed between Savonn and the Empath was dirty, brutal and lawless. This was something else entirely. The champions circled each other, stately and straight-backed, the sand pristine at their feet, the early sun gleaming off their blades. It was ancient, archetypal, like the duels between the primeval gods that had partitioned the young earth into land and sea and sky. The swords met with a ring, retreated, and met again, formal as a handclasp. Then the duel began in earnest.

Emaris had grown up watching Hiraen fight, on horseback and on foot, in the practice yard and the heat of battle. His bow seemed so much an extension of his body that one often forgot he could use a sword, too. If Shandei fought like a bar brawler and Savonn a back-alley thief, then Hiraen was a desert lynx, all speed and nimbleness. Opposite him the Marshal looked old and ponderous by comparison. But Isemain was stronger: his biceps were gourds, his neck an anvil, and even from the stands Emaris could see the jarring force behind every stroke.

"What does he think he's doing?" said Lucien. "He'll tire himself out."

Hiraen was giving ground, dodging blows rather than parrying. The elder Lady Safin murmured something in a reassuring undertone. Yannick continued to wring his hands, rocking back and forth, and Oriane got up to pace. Emaris wished, desperately, for just a glimpse of Savonn.

Isemain had scored the first hit. Hiraen, side-stepping a swing at his flank, had misjudged the distance by a hair. The blade clipped him just above his greave, and a trickle of crimson gleamed through the gash in his hose. The Saraians shouted in approval. Still Hiraen was on the defensive, taking care to stay out of reach of Isemain's sword.

Emaris frowned. It was what Savonn would have done, no doubt. But Savonn fought with tricks and lies and little knives. He had never known Hiraen to shy away from a direct hit with good steel in his hand. And yet...

Isemain fell back, looking troubled. His lips moved. The words were lost in the shouts and the singing, but his meaning was apparent at least to Hiraen. The High Commander tossed his head and laughed. Then they closed in again. Emaris's stomach was tight with foreboding. "Something's wrong."

Hiraen ducked beneath another swing. The toe of his boot arced across the sand, sending a flurry of fine white grains into Isemain's unprotected face. The Marshal flinched. Quick as a whip, Hiraen's sword flashed out and slashed across his chest. "*Yes!*" cried Emaris. The guards cheered, and even the councillors, who had been silent so far, began to clap.

And then there was silence. Abject silence from both sides of the Arena, as they all saw what was wrong. The rings of Isemain's mail gleamed untarnished where he had been struck, and Hiraen's sword was clean. Yannick quivered. "Isn't there—isn't there supposed to be—"

Emaris launched himself to his feet. "Where's the blood? *Where's the blood?*"

Iyone's shout cut the air like a knife. "They gave him a blunt sword! A ceremonial sword!"

The Arena blurred and spun on its side. They were all shouting. "Stop the duel!" Oriane yelled across the ring at Marguerit, who had gone white. "You cheated us! Stop the duel, you despicable tramp!"

Hiraen's sword cut another ineffectual line along the Marshal's leg. When Isemain swung back, the tip of his blade tore through the sleeve of Hiraen's leather jerkin, gashing it open from shoulder to wrist. It was a deep cut this time, and the Saraians roared, though not as loud as before. Hiraen staggered back a few steps. His arm was limp at his side, speckling the scuffed sand with crimson.

Sabotage, Emaris thought. Isemain was hanging back, making no move to press his advantage. By the looks of it, he had taken no hand in the matter. Neither had Marguerit. So who?

His eye landed on the small bent figure of the High Priestess, watching with her girls from a bench between the two awnings. A terrible thought came to him.

He burst forward. So did Iyone. Side by side, they sprinted along the edge of the ring. Emaris had the advantage of longer legs, and got to the old woman first. "Your Holiness! Stop the fight! It's a blunt sword!"

The Priestess did not look at him. Her narrow eyes, milky with age, were fixed on the fighters in the ring. "Did you not hear me, child? The duel cannot be stopped. It is sacred to the Sisters."

"But there's a mistake! With the sword!"

"This was no mistake," said Iyone. She had come up behind Emaris, tall and forbidding. "You did this on purpose. Stop the fight before you kill him."

The old woman laughed. The pearls on her necklace clicked. "Did I not tell you? I am justice. I am grief." She lifted her wizened head at last, and it was Emaris she addressed. "Fool child! The Ceriyes curse you. Would you plead for the life of your father's killer?"

Hot spittle sprayed across his face. He reared back. The crone smiled, or bared her teeth, and then he was no longer in the Arena. A long hallway, an endless succession of doors and light and doors and light. Wind whispered in his ears like an echo of the Priestess's voice, *killer, killer, killer.* If Hiraen died, it would be Emaris's fault, Emaris who had sent him to his death. And always, the bells—

A firm hand took his elbow and moved him aside. Someone said, "You have murdered my son, you witch."

"Mother!" cried Iyone. "Do something!"

Aretel Safin seized the Priestess's necklace in both hands and twisted it around the reedy throat like a noose. The young acolytes screamed, scrambling over the bench in their haste to get away. "Call it off," said Lady Aretel. Her knuckles were bloodless. "I said *call it off!*"

Emaris could not breathe. The swords scraped and crashed and rang behind him, one useless, one lethal. The cheering had stopped. The singing from the citadel had not. The High Priestess gurgled, her lips turning puce, her eyes bugging out of their sockets. "If I—if they stop—the treaty—voided—"

"Then let it be!" shouted Aretel. "Call it off!"

Iyone screamed. "*Hiraen!*"

Emaris spun back to the ring. The sand was blinding white where it was not splotched with red, and everything seemed at once jewel-clear and far away. Hiraen, bleeding freely, was barely staying on his feet, and Isemain seemed to have made up his mind to put an end to the farce. As Emaris watched, he blocked a thrust to his own face and, putting his full weight in it, drove hard at Hiraen.

The blow could not be dodged. Hiraen threw up his sword to parry. The false blade met Isemain's downswing with a terrible clang, and snapped clean in half.

The sound resonated through the Arena like a thunderclap. What noise Hiraen might have made as Isemain's blade sheared through his leathers and caught below his collarbone, Emaris never knew. Both men stopped as if shocked. Blood dripped into the sand at their feet, one red bead at a time. Still clutching the crone's necklace, Aretel began to sob.

"End the fight, old woman," said a new voice in heavily accented Falwynian. Marguerit had come up to them, her hand on Aretel's shoulder. She gave the Priestess a levelling stare. "You dishonour me."

Iyone shouted, "*Wait!*"

Aretel released the Priestess. Sputtering, the woman subsided to the ground in a heap of lace and embroidery. No one looked at her. Hiraen was on his knees, one hand braced on the red sand to keep himself upright, the tip of Isemain's blade still stuck in his chest. He looked at the Marshal, his hair falling in sweaty locks across his brow. His eyes shone. "Draw it."

There was pin-drop silence in the stands. Isemain hesitated. Emaris knew just enough Saraian to catch the gist of his answer. *The fight is over.*

Impossibly, a sunny smile spread across Hiraen's face. His own sword was in his hand, the ragged edge gleaming where the steel had snapped. "Draw it."

Isemain reached for the hilt. Because Hiraen was listing back, he had to lean a long way down. With sudden understanding, Aretel said, "*Oh.*"

Behind them, the Queen of Queens screamed a warning.

At the last moment Hiraen threw himself sideways. The sword in his chest slipped out of the Marshal's reach. The broken blade in his hand flashed between them like a meteor, up, up, until it plunged into the socket of Isemain's left eye.

Somewhere far away, ten thousand Saraians flew shouting to their feet.

Isemain seemed to stay frozen for a long time. His other eye was fixed on Hiraen, wide with shock and something that might have been admiration. Blood trickled down his cheek. Then he folded at the knees, not ungracefully, and crumpled to the sand.

All coherent thought had left Emaris. Pushing past Marguerit, he began to run.

But someone else got there first. A slender figure burst from the stands, sprinting down to the ring and across the sand. Savonn dropped beside Hiraen, putting his arms around him, holding him up. "Too dramatic even for you," Emaris heard him say. "Don't move."

His hands moved briskly, checking Hiraen's pulse, pressing his cloak over the deep gash along his arm. The chest wound, still stopped up by Isemain's blade, was not bleeding much. "I promised," said Hiraen. "I promised."

Emaris skidded to a halt. The world liquefied. The Arena was a shining haze of grey stone and blue sky, dotted with moving figures. "Yes," said Savonn. "You did. Now do try not to die. I would—"

His voice cracked. He was kneeling in open sight of the councillors, wearing no disguise. "—I would be very annoyed."

Emaris unfroze. The fog cleared from his vision, spilling down his face. "The champion lives!" he shouted. "Bring a doctor! A stretcher!"

Iyone was already giving commands. The councillors ran to them across the ring, Aretel and Lucien in the lead. One of the Safin retainers seized the sunburst banner from the awning and waved it high in the air, a shocking splash of colour between sky and sand. The guards took up Emaris's cry. "He lives! He lives!"

Bells were tolling again, this time not just in Emaris's head. *Victory*, they cried. Against all hope, their champion had triumphed. Hiraen had kept his word and made good his debt. Their High Commander had saved them once more. *Victory, victory to Cassarah.*

It was over. They had won.

CHAPTER 28

Rumours had been trickling into Terinea for days, each worse than the last. The disaster at the Singing Ford. The assassination of Daron Sydell. The siege of Cassarah. The town slept uneasily, under heavy guard, and even for Nikas of the Sanctuary infiltration was no easy matter. He had to smuggle himself through the gate in a farmer's wagon, lying still among bales of hay—a dangerous, undignified ride, to say nothing of the fleas.

But he did not begrudge the Terineans the time spent. He was, after all, returning to his motherland.

So far, he had had no luck in his search for the Queen's sister. It had taken him a long time to understand why. He had been operating on the assumption that Josit did not want to be found—that she was a fugitive on the run, hiding from him and the Council both. But she was no coward. Like Savonn Silvertongue, she was a performer of the highest order; and like Savonn, she wanted to be seen.

Now Nikas switched tactics. He went to the most obvious place he could have looked, the convent in Terinea where she had gone to have her baby—wretched whelp that it was, unwanted and unacknowledged, slave child of a slave mother. There was a run-down cottage at the edge of the premises, screened from the main convent building by a thick shawl of weeping willows. Lanterns bobbed in the garden, and faint voices rose in song: the midnight hymn to Mother Alakyne, calling for her protection and the warmth of her embrace.

Nikas approached the cottage slowly. The willow fronds hung heavy and white, desiccated with frost. They whisked over his head and shoulders as he went, like a benediction, like a good omen. The Father was here. The Father was everywhere. He was the darkness between the stars, the pauses for breath in the song Alakyne had sung to spin a world from nothing. Even now Nikas heard him echo through the distant hymns, though the words did not invoke him. The lord of the Sanctuary did not need words. Every silence was a descant, each shadow a paean.

Nikas touched his fingers to the long scar Savonn's knife had left on his cheek, and sent a prayer of thanks to the Ceriyes. Tonight was the night he would kill his mother.

A lamp was burning in the back window. The Mother Above had her priests and acolytes, but the mother below was attended only by a single maid who screamed like a crow and backed away from him. They had been here for some time—books were scattered over the couch and rug, and a lyre lay on the floor by the hearth. Unhurried, Nikas followed the shrieking maid down the hallway where she had fled, and stepped through the door into the inner room.

"You may go, Elysa," said Josit Ansa. "I told you I was expecting a guest."

Then they were alone. The room held a narrow bed, and two armchairs facing each other across a small round table. Josit was sitting in one of these, sloshing wine into a shallow loving-cup. He had never seen her up close before. She was a slender, fine-boned woman in her fifties, still beautiful as Marguerit had never been, with smooth pale skin and thick black curls pinned back in a bun. Her lashes were heavy with kohl, her eyelids powdered smoke-grey. She was smiling.

He sketched an ironic bow. "Mother."

"Nikas," she said. "How nice to meet you at last. Sit down and have a drink."

He sat in the other armchair, ignoring the bowl of wine. His mouth was dry, his chest full of whirring wings. He had to be better than this. He was not like Dervain. He had killed his kitten and strangled his playmate and endured the rigours of his initiation. Twenty-three years of violent servitude, all the while Josit lived in luxury and never once sought him out. "No guards?"

"I sent them away," said Josit. "Try not to do anything drastic. Governess Persis is very kind to harbour me on her premises, though she could be scourged for it."

"I imagine," said Nikas, "she found you more intimidating than the whip."

There was no reason to be afraid. There was no reason to feel anything at all. He had killed princes and priests and babies asleep in their cradles. She was nothing. "Anyway, you know why I'm here. Your sister the Queen wants you. Alive if possible, dead if inconvenient."

"Don't be boorish," said Josit. "If you must call me Mother, at least learn some manners. I insist on the wine. One should conduct affairs like these with style."

He was careful to a fault. He let her drink first, watching as she brought the silver bowl to her lips. The flawless skin of her throat moved as she swallowed. Only then did he receive the loving-cup and drink from it himself. The wine was irritatingly strong, and burned all the way down his gullet.

"Poor Margie," said Josit, folding her hands in her lap. "It would've saved her a world of trouble if she'd had the guts to kill me while she could. But she was only thirteen when she took the throne, a dull little girl, superstitious and terrified of retribution..."

"And now she holds your city," said Nikas. "Things change, don't they? The girl Iyone is beleaguered, and your precious Savonn is lost to the Empath. There's nothing left for you. You may as well surrender."

"Is there not?" asked Josit. "There is you, after all. Sorry child, a slave-boy masquerading as a lost prince. Who do you imagine your father was? Kedris?"

It took some effort not to overturn the table. The cruel bitch knew she was cornered, and so was out to wound. "What does it matter? Kedris was nobody."

"He was not an excellent father, it is true," said Josit. "You were probably better off with the god of the Sanctuary." She took another sip from the loving-cup and pushed it back into his hands. Her lips were red with wine. "I, on the other hand, have always been attentive to my children."

The white willows whispered at the window. Nikas drained the cup, since it seemed the only way to be rid of it, and slammed it down. "*Children.*" The room had grown dim and drained of colour. All he could see was Josit, Josit and her red mouth and her half-lidded, unfeeling eyes. "There is only one."

"I take a broad definition of the word," she said. "There is the son of my womb, and the daughter of my soul. And you, orphan changeling. You who are nothing, but will accompany me on my last pilgrimage... You are unwell?"

Dark spots were dancing before his eyes. His lungs were porous, incapable of holding air. "Son of your womb," he repeated. "Who do you mean? Savonn?"

If forced to it, he could see the resemblance. Something was clawing out of his windpipe, a laugh or a sob; at their heart the two sensations were the same, and he could not tell which it was. He should have killed Savonn; *would* have killed him, if he had not been so afraid of Dervain. "Savonn," Josit agreed. "My silly wastrel boy, full of love and whimsy. I was fond of him despite his failings. Of Iyone too, who is everything a mother could want in a daughter, or a queen in her heir."

Her eyes were slipping shut. "In another world…"

Nikas tried to get up, to unsheath the dagger at his belt, but his limbs were uncooperative. He fell back into the chair, knocking over the loving-cup to shatter on the floor in a devastation of porcelain shards. They chinked under his feet, spotted with dark drops of wine. Comprehension dawned.

"Mother." His throat was closing. It was hard to get the syllables out. "What have you done?"

His vision was leaving him, shrinking down to a single bright spot in which her face hung, full of gentle triumph. She sat where she would die, immaculate as a spellbinder's doll. "I am enfolding my young back to my body," she said. "I have saved my children from you. I have freed you from your slavery. Do you wish to hear me call you son? It is your final chance."

With a last spurt of strength, Nikas pulled himself up and lunged for her. The floor hit his knees. He tried to shout, but only a thin whistle of air came out. His head thudded against the leg of her chair. He could not get up. He could not move. He could not—he could *not*.

"Before us is a long journey," said Josit, distant and dreamy above him. "The road winds, past the fall of night, and on into daybreak… Come, false son. It is good to have company."

CHAPTER 29

Emaris cast off his overcoat, soaked through with sleet, and shut the front door behind him. "They think he'll survive."

He was back in his father's house, a place that felt stranger than ever now that even Shandei was gone. After the duel, the Council had closed ranks to bear Hiraen's stretcher through the sea of shouting Saraians and up to the citadel, and Emaris had slipped off with Savonn before anyone could think to arrest him. Not long after, Marguerit withdrew to the camp outside the walls, and Cassarah had been theirs again.

Not much had been looted from his house, except what little there had been in the pantry. And yet it felt irrevocably changed after the events of the last year: less a home than a waystation, a liminal place where shades went to await their fates.

Savonn was sitting on the hearth-rug. It was another strangeness, seeing him against the backdrop of Emaris's childhood home. "How bad was it?"

"He bled a lot when they drew out the sword," said Emaris. He knew this because he had spent much of the last week at the citadel, loitering outside strategic doorways under the pretext of queueing for his food ration. "But it missed his heart and lungs, and he's been awake more often than not. The doctors say that's a good sign."

"Did you see him?" asked Savonn.

His hands were folded in his lap, his composure deliberate. Emaris realised he had been prepared to hear something much worse. "Just for a few minutes," he said. "He called you a lousy bastard and asked you to come see him. Preferably with wine and sweetmeats."

This drew a faint smile. "He *is* better, then," said Savonn. "What about you?"

Emaris hesitated. By now he had learnt, when talking to Savonn, to listen to the unspoken conversation as well as the spoken one. He knew what Savonn was asking. They were past the stage of glib answers—Savonn was living in his house, in his *room*. "You know I never could have killed him."

Earlier, Lady Aretel had caught him lurking outside the sickroom and said he could come in for a moment, if he wanted. He had nearly lost his nerve and run off. But Hiraen had been a friend, once, and so Emaris went in and sat down by the bed. For a moment they looked at each other without speaking, and then Hiraen said, "Does this count as putting it right?"

Emaris's throat swelled. The smells in the sickroom were the same ones he could never forget: wine and blood, poppy and poultices, the stern cleanliness of fresh linens. Hiraen had killed his father, an innocent man. He had also saved all their lives. You could not see one thing without the other.

"It's a start," said Emaris.

Perhaps he would be damned for letting his father's killer live. The High Priestess had certainly seemed to think so. But *she* was dead too. She had died in her sleep the night after the duel—it seemed the excitement had been too much for her heart—so evidently the Sisters had forsaken her. Or perhaps she had only ever been a raving old woman, no closer to the gods than any of them.

"I didn't think vengeance was likely to move you," said Savonn presently. "You're sensible. It's one of my favourite things about you."

Emaris didn't know if he was. He watched Savonn trace the weave of the rug with an idle forefinger, his head bent. "What are you going to do now?"

"That depends. There is someone at the door."

Emaris reached for his sword. The city guard had not yet shown up to take Savonn away, and he did not mean to let them. But it did not sound like the city guard. There was only one set of footfalls, and it was a tread he knew.

The knot of fear in his stomach loosened as quickly as it had formed. In its place, something that had been furled up for a long time blossomed, breathless and hopeful. He bounced to his feet and flung the door open. "Shandei!"

She must have come a long way. There was a leather satchel slung over her shoulder, through which the outline of something bulky showed. Her hair was slipping out of its braid, falling around her face in limp tendrils, and her clothes were filthy and wet with sleet. But her whole face lit up at the sight of him, and she ran to him and yanked him into her arms. "Baby boy! Look at you! I can hardly even see your scars!"

"That's because you're short," said Emaris. The top of her head now fit neatly under his chin. That would take some time getting used to. "Where the hell were you?"

They retreated into the house, shutting the door on the blustering wind. "I'm sorry," said Shandei, reaching up to ruffle his hair. She knew he hated that. "I was running an errand for the Silvertongue. We thought it best no one knew where I'd gone, not even—oh."

Savonn got up. His face revealed nothing, though only a moment ago he and Emaris had been speaking with something close to candour. "It's you."

"Me," said Shandei, stuffing her wet cloak into Emaris's arms, "and a lot of ditch mud and river water, and several more pounds of fish than I ever wanted to eat in my life. Oh, and let's not forget the bedbugs in those terrible firetrap inns." She reached into her satchel. "I took care of your small matter."

The thing she produced was shaped like a vase, tall and black and glossy as marble. It took Emaris a moment to realise what it was. He started forward in horror. "Put it away! How can you spring it on him like that?"

"No," said Savonn. "It's all right."

After a brief and perilous hesitation he went over and took the urn in his hands. "It went fine, then?"

"Mostly," said Shandei. "I nearly capsized twice, and then I had to set a bandit's boat on fire, and all my life I never even knew there was such a thing as river bandits."

"The Saraian border guard? Did they see you?"

Shandei shrugged. "They chased me in a skiff for a while. Then I sank it. They never saw what I was carrying." She dug through the satchel, and emerged with a crumpled scrap of vellum. "There's the address."

"What address?" demanded Emaris.

For a moment he fancied he might get an answer. But Savonn only glanced at the note, then tossed it in the fire. "I would offer you anything I had as payment," he said, "but I know it would only insult you."

Shandei scowled. "I didn't do it for you."

"Who, then?"

"I don't know," she said. "But it wasn't for you."

Savonn smiled, and started towards the door. Some of the tension had gone out of his shoulders, and for the first time since Evenfall he looked truly present in his own skin. "Gazelle," he said, "I am going to pay Hiraen a visit. I will come back after, if no one captures, maims, or murders me in the interim."

"What address?" said Emaris again. "What on earth is everybody talking ab—"

The door closed behind Savonn. Emaris stared after him. Then, outraged, he ran to the hearth and scattered the logs of kindling with a kick, scrabbling around for the note. "Oh," said Shandei, looking on with interest. "Fire doesn't bother you anymore?"

It did. But by the time the heat started to bite at him in earnest, he already had the curling bit of vellum in his hands, so charred he could make out only one word of the address. "Bayarre," he read. "You went to Bayarre? What for?"

"A holiday," said Shandei. "Do you remember when Father took us there, back when he was looking for Mother? Probably not, you were tiny. I left something for Lord Silvertongue there. But that's for him to tell you."

He glared, but she only cast herself on the hearth-rug and lay down flat, her wet hair fanning out beneath her head. "I've got someone to see, too," she said. "I must look a fright. Will you draw me a bath, baby boy? You'd best stop scowling before your face gets stuck that way."

* * *

Since the duel, Iyone had been up to the ears in work. She met with teams of surveyors, cataloguing the damage to the city walls, and planning repairs. She held long, mollifying talks with merchants whose cargo had been looted. She dined with Marguerit, making pointed suggestions about border arrangements and the homeward march of the Saraian army, and did her best to persuade the Queen of Queens that she did not, in fact, have any dynastic pretensions. She convened the Council, quarrelled with Oriane, and plied Yannick with soothing herbal teas.

In between, she always seemed to end up in Hiraen's sickroom.

He had turned up to champion them, unheralded and unlooked-for, with the perfect timing only Savonn's sorcery could have contrived. Even so, she had not permitted herself hope. She had gone to the Arena with no expectations except to watch her brother slaughtered before her eyes. It had taken the sight of his battered body on the stretcher to drive home what had transpired: he was alive. Isemain was dead. They had won.

He was sleeping now, in the citadel's warmest, least forbidding room. They would bring him home as soon as he could be moved. Marguerit had offered, unasked, the return of the loot from their manor—"out of respect for the High Commander," she explained. "Isemain would have wanted it." Iyone left it to her mother to negotiate the return of Oriane and Yannick's goods as well, in case it became a point of contention later. Marguerit liked Aretel, perhaps because she found the existence of Iyone's real, full-blooded Cassaran mother reassuring.

There was a soft scratch at the door. It was probably her secretary, coming to bring her more news, more work, more injured parties to appease. She did not turn around till the door closed and the lock scraped into place, and an unexpected voice said, "How is he?"

Savonn was in servant's livery once more, a knitted woollen cap over his curls. It was beyond her to contemplate the number of guards he must have passed on the way here, all of whom now knew he was alive, and would have seized him on sight. "Don't worry," he said. "I won't stay long. I just wanted..."

He looked at Hiraen's sleeping form. Her brother looked like most bedridden patients did, wan and small, somehow diminished by the heaps of blankets and bandages and phials of unguents. The surgeons must have stitched up a thousand wounded men like him. The sight was disturbing only to those who knew him best—who were used to seeing him in motion, a quick smile on his lips, a deadly bowstring under his fingers.

Blood and sand, thought Iyone. And so they had paid the promised price.

"He's better," she said. "He asks for you every time he wakes."

"I'll wait till he does," said Savonn. "Are you well?"

Was she? It seemed an irrelevant question. For months now she had been working at a feverish pace, only sustainable if she did not stop to think about it. "I am in perfect health, as ever. The only thing that ails me is a surfeit of noxious colleagues."

There was also the news from Terinea. She would not have believed it from any mouth but Zarin's. Josit could not be dead. She was perennial, indestructible; like an earth-spirit of the harvest she returned to the soil only to rise again with the new crop. But it was true. There was a body; there were two. If anyone could have felled a priest of the Sanctuary, it was her.

And Savonn, it appeared.

He pulled out an armchair and pushed her into it. "Like I said, I did what I did for the same reason you gave Oriane my letters. Damage control."

"I never wanted—"

He shushed her. "No. I know. I couldn't possibly hold it against you. Better that one person should suffer than many." He glanced at the bed. "If I could have made it so the one person was not Hiraen, I would have."

"How did you know he would win?"

"Because he was Hiraen." He smiled ruefully. "I wish I had a better reason. I take his protection for granted, after all these years. Do you think the Saraians will uphold the treaty?"

"For a while," said Iyone. "As long as Marguerit lives, maybe. The full hundred years is probably too much to ask. But we'll be prepared next time."

"Good."

Savonn sat down on the window-seat opposite her. He was cradling some odd-shaped object in his hands, a vase maybe, or a pot. "Shandei is back, and safe. She brought me this. I want you to give it to Marguerit."

Her heart leaped before her mind registered the name. Her vision went grey. It occurred to her that she had not eaten or slept for a long while—how long, she did not know—and that this was a stupid overreaction. Then she felt the solid weight of the thing she was holding, and realised with a second swoop of her stomach what it was. "No," she said. "*No.* I can't take him from you. Bury him somewhere nice, somewhere only you know."

"Don't be absurd," he said. "No one can take him from me. Anyway, I promised the Queen."

He smiled. It was one of his better smiles, sly and knowing. She felt the inane urge to hold the urn to her ear and shake it. "What's inside?"

"Ashes."

It had stopped sleeting. The sun shone through the window at his back, shrouding his face in equivocal shadow. They had been walking in step all their lives, perhaps not always side by side, but in the same direction. He had put his faith in her, and she in him, and between them they had done the impossible.

"All right." She set the urn down. It felt lighter in her hands now, like a stage prop. "There's something else I should tell you. I had word from Terinea."

There was no way to soften the blow, so she gave it to him straight, the way his brittle courage demanded. "Josit is dead. So is the man Nikas. It seems she tricked him into taking poison by drinking from the same cup. She did not suffer."

No movement from the window-seat. She had done all her mourning in private, behind the locked door and drawn curtains of her office. Like her, he would save his grief for when he was alone. "She had too much pride to stay a fugitive," said Iyone. "She died as she lived, on her own terms."

"Will there be a funeral?"

"A quiet one. We can't bury her in Cassarah, but she wouldn't want that anyway. We'll scatter her ashes in the Morivant so she can be free." With satisfaction, she added, "I've invited Marguerit."

It was only half a joke. With her bastard sister dead, the Queen would have one less reason to break the treaty and go back to war. "Josit would find that amusing," said Savonn. Whatever he felt showed only in the dip of his head and the measured calm of his voice. "And Nikas—one can't say he didn't deserve it. But I always felt sorry for him."

Hiraen was stirring. Iyone got up, wanting to give them privacy. "You know you can't stay here. What are you going to do?"

Savonn grinned. "I have an appointment to keep. I don't think I'll come back after. But as you know, I am a prolific letter-writer. Will you be all right?"

"I think so," she said.

She tucked the urn under her arm and went to the door. There was no telling when she would see him again. He was a wild creature, coming and going at will; like Josit, he could not stay hidden in catacombs and dressing-rooms for the rest of his life. She sought for a word of parting, a blessing of some sort, and found none. Between them there was no need for platitudes.

She left the room, heading for her own chambers down the hall. Only when the door had shut between them did it strike her that she had not once mentioned the identity of Josit's child, and that perhaps, this was for the best.

She had taken two steps into the dark harbour of her own room when a small shape stirred in one of the chairs, and the voice she knew mostly from her dreams said, "Hello, Iyone."

* * *

The hearth was cold, and none of the lamps were lit. Shandei's hair was wet and curling at the ends. She had pulled the quilt from

Iyone's bed and wrapped it around herself, her knees drawn to her chin. "Shandei—"

"Don't say anything." Shandei looked very young, curled up like a house cat in the chair. "I had to come and see you. But if you talk, I'll get confused again."

Nobody had briefed Iyone for this. Her secretary had made no notes. "Are you leaving too? Like Savonn?"

"What?" Shandei frowned, disconcerted. "I only just got back. I came as soon as I could, when the thing I set out to do was done. I had to see you. I wasn't sure how to break in, if you were still under siege. I meant to steal a grappling hook and a lot of rope, but..."

Iyone had no doubt Shandei would have scaled the wall in full sight of the Saraian army, under volleys of arrows and cannon-shot, if she got it in her head that she had to. "But then I heard what happened," said Shandei. "With the duel, and everything. So I stole a horse instead and galloped here as fast as I could. I had to see you."

It was the third time she had said it. She fidgeted with the corner of the quilt, tangling it between her fingers. "For a while, I thought—I hoped Hiraen would die. So I wouldn't have to—to do it. But I'm glad he survived. If only for your sake."

"You don't have to be so generous."

"I said don't talk," said Shandei sharply. "I always have so much to say to you, but every time I see you I lose track of myself."

Her brow was creased in concentration. Iyone, who had never known patience in her life, held her tongue and waited. "Even after we held the wall together," said Shandei, "I half thought I'd kill him at Lissein. Even when I realised he'd only done it for Savonn. My father and brother, they're all I ever had."

Iyone started to answer, then shut her mouth. "I saw Savonn fight the Empath," said Shandei. "You weren't there. You don't know what it was like. It was the worst thing I ever saw.

Afterwards, in the boat, I decided it wasn't worth it. Killing in cold blood like that, just for revenge. I didn't have it in me."

Her gaze alighted on the urn, still in Iyone's hands. "Savonn didn't, either."

Iyone recalled all the fleeting meetings she'd had with Shandei. A temple at Midsummer, a frantic night in a city under fire. Hands on her throat in a dark street under a bridge. Moments that would not even have added up to a full day, and yet had taken on so much significance in dream, in memory. It was as if each meeting was a mosaic stone, and Iyone was only now piecing them together to understand the picture they made. They had gone through hell and still Shandei had come back, wanting to see her.

Shandei said, "You can talk now, if you like."

Iyone set the urn aside. One step at a time, she crossed the room and sank to the floor next to Shandei. The other chairs all seemed too far away. She had worn Shandei's rose scarf to her first parley with Marguerit: a declaration as proud as any, if she had only known at the time what she was declaring.

"If I promise," said Iyone, "if I swear never to hide anything from you again—do you think we could start over?"

"You mean," said Shandei, "with all of the roses, and none of the thorns?"

She was smiling, just a little. Iyone smiled back. Shandei shifted above her so that the quilt covered them both. Her fingers played on Iyone's scalp, carding through her hair, gentle as a feather. "I think we could," she said. "I think I'd like that."

CHAPTER 30

Hiraen opened his eyes as soon as Savonn sat down by the bed. His timing was so precise, one could not help but wonder if he had been awake all along. A slow, drowsy grin spread across his face. "Is that you, you mountebank?"

"I didn't want to come earlier," said Savonn, "in case you died and I had to forswear our friendship in a fit of pique."

He put his hand on Hiraen's to stop him getting up. It was hard to find a part of him that was not bandaged. Isemain's sword had all but unseamed his left arm, the worst of the wounds; the puncture in his chest was shallower than it looked. "You're leaving?" Hiraen asked.

"I promised I would."

For an actor, Savonn was not superstitious. Yet it felt perilous to talk about what awaited him in Bayarre—like tempting fate, or the Ceriyes, to intervene in characteristically bloody ways. Hiraen understood this without the need for words, and steered the conversation away. "They're making Iyone Governor. Just the thought of it will keep Oriane out of retirement for another decade."

He went pale, and had to pause for breath. "I thought she already *was* Governor," said Savonn, to cover the lapse.

"More or less," said Hiraen. "I've had my fill of the city. I'm going back to the Bitten Hill in the spring, even if they have to tie my stretcher to the horse."

"Half the city guard will desert to follow you."

Hiraen managed a wheezy laugh. "I'll keep the High Commander title for a while. I like the ring of it." He gestured to his arm, swaddled in cloth and linens. "They're not sure I'll ever draw a bow again."

This caught Savonn off-guard. He had girded himself for the worst, rehearsing the moment he would stand before Hiraen's bier in disguise or in chains; but he had not thought to imagine Hiraen without his bow. It had been part of him for as long as any of them could remember, much as the theatre was for Savonn. He tried to picture being a prisoner in his own body—never again to conceal himself in the safety of a mask, trapped in the onism of a single personality—and his mind flinched from the thought.

"Savonn," said Hiraen softly. Thinking of him first, as always.

Savonn brought himself back. "There is a great deal you can do without a bow. Hell, without an arm."

"Oh, yes," said Hiraen. His fingers twitched. "A few days ago, they didn't think I'd live, let alone sit up and complain about their foul medicines. So we're optimistic."

He hesitated, watching Savonn's face. "We've been short with each other a lot. That's all I've been able to think of, lying here. That if I died, that's what you'd remember, me snapping at you."

It took a while for Savonn to find his voice. He said, "That wouldn't be the case at all."

"No? I was worried. Next time I see you we should go for drinks and a play, blow up a thing or two for old time's sake."

They had been friends since the cradle. The rift between them had not been of their own making, and so, perhaps, was mendable. Savonn smiled. "That sounds brilliant."

The cosy silence lapped around them. Someone was dragging a pail and an armful of mops across the courtyard. Water splashed, and the sound of brushing and scrubbing came to them through the open window. The citadel was cheerful and bustling as it had never been. Henceforth, Savonn thought, people would not call it Ederen's citadel, but Iyone's. And maybe in a hundred years, a thousand, no one would even remember Kedris except as herald to the greatest commander the city had ever known.

Hiraen's eyelids were drooping again. "Sorry," he said. "They're giving me a lot of drugs, you know, to grow back all that blood. Yesterday I drew the line at eating a boar's heart."

Savonn had to laugh, and surprised himself with how much better he felt for it. "I need to borrow Emaris for a few weeks. I'd like his company, I think, where I'm going. I'll return him to you as soon as I can."

"He's his own man," said Hiraen. "And he'll probably insist on going with you anyway. That boy's more than either of us deserves." He tried without success to stifle a magnificent yawn. "Well, I won't say goodbye. Getting rid of you is like trying to peel a wet leaf off your shoe."

"Maybe just good night, then," said Savonn. He twitched the blanket into place, not troubling to hide his tenderness. "For now."

* * *

As the only man of Betronett present in Cassarah, Emaris found himself at Isemain's funeral that evening, attending as Hiraen's representative.

Saraian wakes were long, protracted affairs. The greater the deceased, the taller the pyre, and no one left until the fire had burned down to nothing. For the Marshal of Sarei, only a six-storey pyre would suffice. But there was a kind of eerie dignity to the proceedings, watching a foeman go to his gods beneath the city wall he had so recently flattened, and Emaris was not sorry to be there. He stood upwind of the smoke to watch the flames leap and dance, and for the first time in months, said a prayer of thanks.

It was past midnight when he got home. Shandei was still out, but Savonn was back, jingling a palmful of knucklebones on the hearth-rug. He was lost in thought, and his unguarded face was young and soft. Emaris said, "Are you all right?"

"Yes," said Savonn. Emaris waited for the inevitable change, for his expression to harden into something more familiar, but it did not. "I didn't hear you come in, is all."

Emaris pulled up a footstool and sat down next to him. The fire on the hearth was much closer than the Marshal's pyre had been, but he could manage. "How's Hiraen?"

"Better."

Savonn skimmed the knucklebones to Emaris, and they tossed them back and forth for a while. Without prompting, he added, "I said goodbye to a few people, in my way. Lady Aretel. Lord Lucien. They probably didn't notice, but"—he shrugged—"it seemed important. I even considered paying my respects to the late Governor, but cowardice won over."

Emaris threw the knucklebones at him, in case he dissolved into incorporeality once more. The fire snapped and crackled. "Where are you going? Bayarre?"

Savonn showed no surprise at the name. He leaned over to retrieve the stones, and when he came up again he had somehow manoeuvred his body between Emaris and the hearth, blocking his view of the fire. It was a magician's sleight of hand, so subtle one only noticed if one was looking for it. Emaris felt a sudden stab of bittersweet grief. If Savonn was going away, who would be left to notice such things about him?

"Bayarre," Savonn confirmed. "I—would like it if you came with me."

This was so unprecedented that Emaris drew up short. All day he had been inventing ways to go after Savonn without being noticed: which road they would take, and how he was going to find a horse or a boat with the city in such upheaval. "Why?"

"I don't know," said Savonn. "You witnessed the start of it. It's only right that you witness the end. Besides..."

The knucklebones rattled in his palm. He threw and caught them a few times, frowning. "I'm not sure how I will be received. That's why I don't want to be alone."

"Received by whom?"

The knucklebones whisked up and down. Savonn's expression remained blank. Emaris looked around for the urn, but it was gone. Likely it was with the Safins now, waiting to be presented to Marguerit. It had changed hands so easily. He wondered if Iyone had found it odd. Hiraen certainly had. *Did you see the Empath die?* he'd asked. And Emaris had said—

He had said no. Of course not. Which of them had?

"Savonn." He was breathless. "What have you done?"

In the firelight, Savonn's eyes were an unfamiliar shade of grey. "You tell me."

The rocking skiff. The boys staring down their arrow-shafts, holding the Empath's companions at bay. Shandei in the boat, and the man at the bottom of it—

"You went down with him," said Emaris slowly. "And you brought him back up."

The fire spat. Clack, rattle, clack went the knucklebones. "I wanted to tell you," said Savonn. "But I was afraid what you might think of me."

Emaris had always been sure what he thought of Savonn. He had come to a conclusion early on in their acquaintance, aged fifteen and twenty, and never changed it since—an enormous oversight when it came to someone as duplicitous as Savonn. Either everything Emaris had ever thought about him was wrong, or on some deeper level he was vindicated, having been right all along.

"Why on earth would you want me in Bayarre?" he asked. "If your—business—goes well, I can't imagine you'd want me underfoot."

The stones went up and down one last time, and ceased. "Do you suppose," said Savonn, "that I dislike your company? You may follow me wherever you please, as long as there is no imminent catastrophe. But after you have seen me to Bayarre and satisfied your grandmotherly instincts that all is well, I expect you will want to rejoin your patrol. They need you. And you need friends your own age."

"They're not," Emaris began, indignant. Then he remembered that Vion would be eighteen in the spring, and shut up.

"But," said Savonn, "when I have made a new home—alone, or otherwise—you will be welcome there any time you wish, for as long as you want. That is a promise."

Emaris let out a breath. Until now he had not admitted even to himself how afraid he was to be left behind for good, how much he had dreaded the inevitable parting. But Savonn's heart was a house with many rooms. Whatever fell out in Bayarre, Emaris would never lose him—not to the Empath, or anyone else.

They were no longer captain and squire. They were something else entirely, something brand new and brave.

"All right." He opened his palms, and Savonn threw him a shower of stones, warm from his own hands. "I'll come with you. You always knew I would."

EPILOGUE

The city of Bayarre stretched away before them: once half water, now all mud, a curious place for a curious encounter.

Savonn had read about it, like he read about everything else. The ancient Bayarrii had lived in houseboats on the delta where the Morivant fed into the sea, poling themselves about their daily business between shoals of fish and turtles, and their children learnt to swim before they could walk. But the capricious river had shifted course over the centuries, opening another mouth a dozen miles down the coast. The great distributaries shrank first to shallow canals, then silted drains, then waterlogged streets. And so—with admirable nonchalance—the Bayarrii had abandoned their rafts, built foundations under their houseboats, and taken to wading everywhere in high boots.

Savonn liked the story. Like all the best plays, it had a certain comedic pathos.

Made overland in leisurely stages, the journey from Cassarah had taken him and Emaris a week. They sloshed along drains-turned-footpaths in murky water up to their calves, avoiding the hawkers who importuned them with raw oysters and fried lilypads, until they found the place to which Shandei had directed them: a physician's house on a steep hill at the edge of town. They climbed to it slowly, following a narrow gutter that doubled as a stair. "Look," said Emaris.

He pointed past the physician's house, little more than a two-storey cabin with a tin roof. Savonn looked.

At first the sight boggled the eye. Far off, the streets and housetops gave way first to a thin crescent of golden sand, then a vast blue-grey plain, streaked with heaving brushstrokes of white. There was a low rumble on the threshold of hearing, like the snore of some great beast. The sharp breeze smelled of salt and rain. "The sea," said Emaris. He grinned in that sweet, open way he used to have as a boy, and had only recently relearned. "We spent a summer here when we were young. I've wanted to come back since."

It was nothing like seeing it in paintings. The call of the sea was different from the voice of the river: milder, gentler, the placid sigh of one who had reached his destination and had nowhere to rush off to. "Does it always sound like that?"

"I think so." Emaris looked out with the horizon reflected in his eyes, thoughtful and far-sighted. "I suppose you want to be alone for this part. I'll run down to the beach, see if I can find any conches."

Savonn wondered, sometimes, when Emaris had cultivated so much tact. "I may take a while," he said. "Don't go away."

He watched until Emaris's brilliant yellow head had receded out of sight down the hill. His palms were clammy.

The cabin was unlocked. The front door gave on a low-eaved sitting room, small but airy, with broad windows that let in the breeze. The physician was out. A boy of maybe fifteen was sitting on the floor among dozens of empty glass jars, writing out labels on bits of vellum. He lifted his head, squinted at Savonn, and uttered a question in Bayarric.

Savonn did not answer at once. Music was drifting from the upper room: the soft notes of a harpsichord, clear as a bell. The song halted, as if the musician had been distracted by a sudden thought. Then it picked up where it had left off, faster now. His presence had been noticed and acknowledged.

Goosebumps prickled down his arms. He pulled out a heavy pouch of silver and laid it on the floor beside the boy. The only other thing in his pack was a cedarwood box full of letters. "Shandei sent me."

The name produced instant comprehension. The boy emptied the pouch in his lap, counted the silver twice, and put it away. Then he waved Savonn to a rickety stair at the back of the room, and went back to his writing. The visit had been expected, the payment promised. A routine transaction completed. All was in order.

Savonn went to the stair and followed the music, climbing step by step up to the musician.

A cramped landing, and a wooden door that opened under his hand. A small room with a slanting roof: bed, nightstand, pewter ewer, basin. The harpsichord, under a window that looked out on the restive sea. And the musician himself, seated with his back to the door, his auburn head filigreed gold in the sun.

One could read Dervain's mind in the ebb and swell of his music, just as a geomancer predicted the earth's upheavals by its rumbling. His fingers danced on the keys. "Come to gloat, little bird? I am told my heart stopped. But of course you have survived."

The fire in his lungs. The bone-deep chill of the river. The last, all-important glimmer of consciousness, even as his own blood eddied around him in a clinging haze; and the kick to the sandy bottom of the cove that would send them careering back to the surface. If Savonn had mistimed it, they would both have drowned. It had taken an acrobat's skill, a drummer's rhythm, a snake-charmer's faith.

"I am notoriously hard to kill," said Savonn. He crossed the room to the harpsichord, placing himself within arm's reach, but came no closer. Touch was a road fraught with danger. "If you wanted to win, you might at least have taken a breath before you went under."

Dervain laughed. "I was six when they put me on the auction block. Seven when I went to the whipping-post for striking a priest who tried to touch me. Eight when they walled me up in a dark cave for a winter, with nothing to live on but a few rats and some dead girl. You think I am afraid of a little bit of water?"

He crashed both hands on the keys, and the cradle of music erupted into a brash crescendo. "So yes. You win. The war is over and you have denied me even my death. Boast away."

"Someone had to stop you," said Savonn. "Someone had to save you. You told me no one had ever escaped from the Sanctuary. Now you are the first."

The music faltered. The rigid sinews of Dervain's wrists stood out like anchor-cords. Savonn's knife had made a deep gash along the inside of his arm: the healing flesh was a ruddier brown than the rest of his skin, intersected by neat white stitches. Unlike Savonn, Dervain made no attempt to conceal his wounds. His was a different brand of pride.

"I killed you," said Savonn. "Witnesses from both sides saw you drown. Your remains have been presented to the Queen as a diplomatic gift. You can't go back even if you wanted to, and if you tried, no one would let you. Or Marguerit would have to admit that she'd been tricked like a fool."

He sat down, straddling the end of the bench. His spine tingled. They had not been this close since the tower cell. "There's something to be said for the freedom of a ghost. I highly recommend it."

"Cruel heart," said Dervain. He played a mocking chord in a minor key, then stopped and let his hands fall to his lap. His hair tumbled across his face like a mourning veil, shielding it from Savonn. "Death was all I had. First your father's, then my own. You knew that."

"I considered the fact," said Savonn. "But one will always have death as an option. I thought perhaps you ought to try living first."

Dervain lifted his head. "Living?"

It was as though the thought had never occurred to him. And why should it? He had been a slave-soldier all his life, reared on violence, consecrated to death. Even in Astorre, watching the stars on a grassy mountainside, he had not belonged to himself. Neither had Savonn. But Kedris was dead, and so was the Empath now.

"A life," said Savonn, "with me, *etruska*. Like we imagined before."

Dervain peered at him through his hair. His eyes lingered on Savonn's shoulder, the spot where he had stabbed him with his own knife. "I have hurt you."

The old echoes hissed in Savonn's ear anew. *He knows! He knows!* He was never going to avenge his father. In the dark of the Temple the gods had seen it, and yet had failed to strike him down. No doubt Kedris would have taken this as proof that they were false, powerless, but Kedris had never understood such things. The Ceriyes were a wild and hungry force, and in the river they had drunk their fill.

"I hurt you too," said Savonn. "But you died. We are done being enemies."

He tucked Dervain's tousled hair behind his ear, uncovering his face, his wide bright eyes, willing him to believe. "We are free," he said. "We can live as free men do, bound only to those our hearts choose. We can go far away, and make a home for two."

"A home?" Dervain seemed at a loss, and angry only with himself. "I offered you one, once. We were young fools."

"So we were," said Savonn. "But we are older now, and it is still possible."

Dervain closed his hands around Savonn's wrists. His grip was tremulous, beseeching. "I cannot see it. I cannot see it. All I see is the whip and the sword and the open grave." His voice shook, desperate. "What if I still choose death? What if the Father will not let me go? Will you release me?"

"No," said Savonn. "We had a pact, to go down together or not at all. I hold you to your word."

"You are ruined," said Dervain. "I am dead. What can there be for us?"

Savonn slipped his fingers around the base of Dervain's neck, over the smooth hot skin, the pulse beating fiercely under his palm. The years pressed in around them, heavy with the smells of their room in the consulate: woodsmoke and incense, cedar and jasmine, salt and sweat. "So much," he said, "if you will only look. Spring is beginning. The roses are budding, the mountains rolling back their mantles. In a few weeks the passes to Astorre will be clear. There will be plays and dancing, and bonfires under the stars…"

A tear spilled down Dervain's cheek, leaving a glistening trail in its wake. "Show me a sign."

Savonn leaned in. Gently, the way he would handle a pressed flower, he thumbed Dervain's lips apart and brought them to his own. A tentative invitation; and from there Dervain took over, as Savonn knew he would. He kissed the same way he did everything else: fey and whole-hearted, teeth scraping tongue, hands pulling hair, elbows jarring discordant noises from the harpsichord. He never believed in half measures.

"Thieving bird," said Dervain hoarsely, when they pulled apart. His lips were red, almost as red as his hair. "I should have known you would steal me too."

Soul thief! Thief soul! The Ceriyes no longer frightened Savonn. Neither did his father. He was the magpie demon, the shapeshifter of the fable: the most terrible thing in the wood, undone only by the minstrel's song. "You were mine first," he said. "I am only stealing you back. Can you see it now?"

Dervain's eyes crinkled at the corners, tear-bright under their lashes. Hope was difficult to escape once it had caught you. "I may. In time. Show me again."

His fingers were tangled in Savonn's curls, a delicious pressure. "As often as you want," said Savonn.

He drew Dervain close and demonstrated once more, with all the eloquence he could summon; and after that, laughing though their lungs were bursting, they came up for air together.

* * *

After some weeks, two men left Bayarre and started on the long road to Astorre, the russet head pressed close to the dark. The tall golden fellow with them was thoughtful and quiet, but not unhappy. He escorted them part of the way, then turned off towards Cassarah with a bag full of conches. It was the first time he had willingly parted ways from the man who had been his commander, but they did not trouble with farewells. The separation would be brief.

The city bustled with life and work, and his friends complained about his absence. Three days of feasting had just been declared in honour of the High Commander, who had emerged from his sickroom. The new Governor presided over the revelries, smiling and red-scarfed, accompanied everywhere by her sleek blonde captain of guards. Labourers toiled at the new houses near the piazza, and the Council bickered. There was much to be done.

The aerial gardens blossomed. The mountains doffed their caps of snow. Spring had begun.

THE END

ABOUT THE AUTHOR

Vale Aida lives in Singapore, with a stuffed whale and fewer cats than is optimal. She wrote most of this book from—among other places—a haunted psychology lab, the back of a boring lecture, an examining table (the curtain was drawn), and a thumbnail-sized window on the office computer. She likes coffee, podcasts, arch-nemeses, and not sweating to death in the sun.

Get the latest updates from Vale at http://valeaida.tumblr.com.

Printed in Great Britain
by Amazon